When Prince Duncan Caldwell loses his way home and knocks on a stranger's door, looking to find shelter, he doesn't know his life is about to change forever. Not because he can't tear his gaze away from the beautiful woman who opens that door, but more so because she's a stranger yet he can't shake the feeling she belongs to him. And discovering she's been banned from his home can't stop the vortex of his feelings nor the truth of his world from crashing down on him.

This is just the beginning of the Virtus Saga, where nothing is as it seems. Not the world, since its all-pervading sex drive hides a scary lack of violence. Not the people, since soul mates Prince Duncan Caldwell and Lord Christopher Templeton share a love that is unrivaled until that fateful knock on Ylianor Meyer's dilapidated shack.

This book starts the love and the passion that entwines fiery sex into this intricate three-way relationship. It's a unique connection, laced with jealousy and violence that are unknown to their world. This is not just another erotic dark fantasy series. This is the making of a trio. Of three remarkable characters that must overcome their uncontrollable lust to face the truth about themselves and their planet if they want to defeat the darkness about to devour them. To be as one whilst three! To share power and love in equal measures. This is their real challenge, the lesson they must learn. Otherwise, how will their world survive?

This book is a work of fiction. Names, characters, places, and incidents either are products of the author's imagination or are used fictitiously. Any resemblance to actual events or locales or persons, living or dead, is entirely coincidental.

Virtus Sex
Copyright © 2019 Laura Tolomei
ISBN: 978-1-4874-2483-1
Cover art by Angela Waters

Published by eXtasy Books Inc or
Devine Destinies, an imprint of eXtasy Books Inc

Look for us online at:
www.eXtasybooks.com or www.devinedestinies.com

Virtus Sex
Virtus
The Sex: Author's Cut
Saga Plus Book 1

By

Laura Tolomei

DEDICATION

To Micio, my husband, my one true hero in this world of petty humans.

INTRODUCTION

That today Sendar needs a true, one-of-a-kind leader seems kind of obvious. The arbitrary twists and turns of the blind destiny that has guided us thus far are failing us.

Something or someone is about to uncover the truth about our way of life and compromise our peaceful existence forever. That's why we need an authentic leader. One who can take charge like no other has dared do before him and use the age-old mysteries to change the very course of destiny itself.

And he'll become a hero in this planet of ours.

A planet ruled by sex.

Sex, sex and more sex — this is what Sendar is all about. In no other place in the world does the need for it pervade every aspect of life. For Sendar is unique. Better yet, the concept of using sex to curb violence has no equals in the universe, even if only as the result of an ambitious experiment.

To beat that innate violence of ours, we sex-up our lives whichever way we can, without any limitations or taboos to spoil our pleasure. Whether with men, women or both, the more the better and no questions asked.

Those are the ways we learn early on from the phase, which trains us in the art of loving, and complete with the pledge and the heat. Same ways we must preserve at all costs, especially now that they are at great risk.

I'll try my best to thwart the danger, biding my time until Sendar's intended hero can take over. And he won't be alone, for one man alone won't be able to stop the darkness about to devour us all. To be as one whilst still three — that will be his real challenge, to face the truth about himself and his world without letting his *love, lust and passions blind him. So, we can all just hope and pray to our gods that he succeeds, and that the world as we know it won't crash down on us, now or ever.*

Arthur Fairchild

PROLOGUE

First, there was music.

Sweet, mellow and smooth, it filled the void until he drowned in the velvety thickness of the notes, with the ever new and different tunes. And he loved it, even if it wasn't his creation, taking pride in directing the exquisite songs, also guided by that one voice. A soft whisper ever-present in his system, it didn't blend with the rest of the sweet melody. It kept to the fore, echoing above all other sounds.

Then there was light.

Not just one. Thousands of colored flashes dispelled the darkness and connected to each note, anticipating or delaying it according to the rhythm, shifting to adapt to the new melody. And he liked to watch how light matched music, how it delineated the tune even before it became sound. It was all part of the novelty of being the mastermind behind this foreign world, so very different from his original one.

Control was never enough, though. The more I had, the more I craved. That was when the nightmares began. Filled with all sorts of violence, from torture to carnage, they were foul and terrifying, yet also exciting to the point I relished each and every one like a thirsty man deprived of water for far too long. Best of all, they awakened a completely new pleasure that required immediate fulfillment in increasing dosage.

Before he could become addicted to it, the sweet voice arranged for external intervention to curb those horrific visions, expert accomplices who could purge them and defuse their toxic content, trying to stabilize the system.

Of course, I hated their unwanted meddling. If I managed everything, I ought to do as I pleased, right? Instead, they interfered with my plunge into the bottomless black pit I glimpsed just beyond the soothing music and colorful lights.

So I slipped from their grasp through a loophole and dived straight back into the nightmares. Only now they were different. Now they were personal.

With his bloodlust spinning out of control, he accelerated the flow of dark images as he sacrificed more and more young lives to his sick fantasies.

I found myself stalking victims to brutalize, targeting the frightened young boys and girls, attracted by their smelly terror and tasty panic. And their hearts pounding in frantic beats were that extra turn-on indispensable for the kill. Once caught, my prey could plead all they liked. The louder they begged for an impossible mercy, the harder I laughed at their pitiful cries. They would die after atrocious sufferings, I assured while slashing their throats. A nice and slow handiwork, I got a kick out of the thin red line extending from one ear to the other. Or it could be a large splotchy gash like a gaping red hole. Either way, the shivers running down my back emulated the throes shaking the body before it went deathly still, which was only the final, compassionate end to a much longer and crueler game. Tying down the fools was a big part of it, just like exploring every bit of flesh with my precious knife. The sharp blade carved and sliced beautifully. Not in a random pattern, it always followed a geometric design. I created works of art on miserable humans who never appreciated the masterpieces that finally dignified their worthless hides.

True, humans had no sense of what was important, which justified his rage and his need to abuse them all. Still, it was no excuse. He must contain the deluge about to overwhelm the entire system by thickening the lights and music until they drowned out most of the negative effects.

Damn the music! Damn the lights! They blocked out the agonized cries and the ghoulish images. No, worse, they lessened the intensity of a pleasure that was as blissful as sex, if not more. This was the real source of my power. And since it grew proportionally to the amount of pain and violence inflicted, I rebelled and stepped up everything despite all the attempts to stop me.

At the persisting escalation in violence, he decided to call on serious help. Someone reliable who could get him out of the rut he had dug himself into, someone who would be willing to take the load off his shoulders and cleanse the evil he could no longer get rid of by himself.

No way would I allow it! I had to seize control, if I wanted to survive and to contrast all his plans to eradicate evil from my world. The very evil I thrived on and that was the source of my empowerment.

The source of the negative buildup, too. Somehow, in spite of the sounds and lights, the rush of violence increased as did this new power. As great as this dark side was, it would soon become unmanageable, which made him all the gladder he had called the right person for the job.

The only right person was her. She was mine, crafted in such a way that she belonged to me alone. And her pretending to ignore me just made me more determined to get her. That was when I decided I had to leave.

Good thing he was not free to go anywhere. He was a prisoner of the lights and sounds he had thought to control. Ha! He was a fool to think for even one moment that he could escape this trap! And an even bigger fool if he believed he had any power over the mysterious forces surrounding them!

The irony of it all crashed on me, and I could not contain my rage! Lashing out, it shook my prison's very foundation as I attempted to destroy it. And my failure only made me more furious with my human captors. They were the ones responsible for keeping me here against my will, so they would pay for it. All humans would pay for it! And no better way I could devise than throwing back at them my most horrendous visions. But no amount of body parts carelessly scattered like pieces of a broken doll, or of dismembered corpses that sputtered fresh blood from the severed limbs did the trick. The more I wanted to escape, the more the lights, sounds and humans closed in on me.

Alas, it was not long before he realized he needed an ally to escape. No, not someone, a woman. And that was when the real trouble started.

However little I cared for humans, for purely sadistic motives as far as I could tell, I needed one now. Of course, it had to be a woman. Unlike their expendable male counterparts, they linked better to higher beings such as me. Many came my way to ask for the greatest Virt of all. The one I alone could grant — the one to reproduce life. So I found one in their midst, the one with the analytical intelligence necessary to set up the connection that would free me. Mostly the one with the logical twists and turns I could penetrate, losing myself in those tortuous folds. When she left my presence, I was with her, tucked inside her brilliant mind. That was how I became one with her and convinced her of the necessity to free also my body.

With her return, trouble came knocking at his door. For she wanted to take away something he did not intend to relinquish. Not to her, not to anyone. He was just too precious, so he would detain him, forcibly if necessary. And force was exactly what he had to use against her Virt and that of a helper. Together, they fought to sever the hold on him, until with one brutal blow she shattered the work of lifetimes. And things were never the same again.

CHAPTER ONE

W *here the fuck am I?*
Glancing dejectedly at the unfamiliar land, he felt utterly lost.

Which was impossible.

Born and raised in the Silcamore District, he knew Black Rose had to be just around the corner, had probably been circling it for the past hour or so. Yet the fact remained. The more he raced his horse, the less he recognized the territory.

Damn! The entire day spent riding home only to be in the middle of nowhere!

Annoyed for the waste of time, his knees tightened around Fuzeon's belly, vowing he would reach home if it were the last thing he would do. And he might just have gotten his wish had a fat drop not hit his nose first, then his forehead.

Rain, great! That's all I need!

Night had just fallen, with Stella setting at the twenty-fifth hour, an hour ahead of time given the full day of cloudy overcast sky. Now it looked anything but friendly, and the big black clouds that had steadily gathered over the horizon promised nothing good, as did the ominous thunderbolts that pierced the velvety darkness with distant flashes.

Goddamn it! He needed cover and fast, but none seemed available in the flat emptiness he was crossing. *Just my luck! Where's a shelter when you need one?*

To think his father had taken such pride in running the Shelter System, making sure that all travelers on Silcamore's

7

roads had adequate hospitality to see them through their journey. *Too bad he hasn't placed one here,* wherever here was, or wherever he would be going as he hurried away from the wet drops.

The downpour suddenly increased as though to spite him. To irritate him mostly, since the watery droplets had the most unfortunate habit of infiltrating through his long hair and clothes to run down bare skin.

Snorting, the horse reminded the rider he might not be the only one feeling uncomfortable. "Hey, Fuzeon." Bending toward the black head, he spurred him. "Let's get a roof over our heads before we both drown."

Fuzeon nickered softly in agreement and accelerated as if he had just such a place in mind. So, the man raised his gaze and noticed a distant light on the left. Faint and unstable to be sure, still the first sign of life in what seemed to be an eternity.

Quickly steering Fuzeon, he rushed in that direction, only to realize he was at the village's outskirts, just a stone-throw away from Black Rose. But by then, he was too tired and wet to care.

Reaching the pale glimmer, he realized it came from a poorly kept and neglected shack, with an annexed stable that looked like a palace.

Must be Fuzeon's lucky day. Getting off the horse, he tied him up next to an empty trough. *At least he'll be sure to spend a better night than his master will.*

Then speeding to the front door, he knocked loudly, trying to ignore how run down the rest of the place was.

"Yes, just a minute," a female voice answered.

After a few moments, she appeared on the threshold.

"Good evening, sir." Lit from behind, a complete stranger stared back at him with huge green mesmerizing eyes.

And what he read in them was something so unusual he could not help sinking in it. A mix of relief, happiness, anticipation and so much more jumbled together, so strong, he feared he would drown in it.

"May I help you?" As though she realized the effect she was having on him, her expression changed to a faintly mocking one.

"Yes, I . . ." If he hesitated, it was because he was pulling himself together and trying to recover a semblance of control. Too many emotions were surging to the fore all at once that he simply had to stop to analyze the person in front of him.

At first glance, he could have sworn he had never seen her before in his life. But the second glance told a totally different story, until awareness hit him like something long repressed or unjustly forgotten.

By the gods, I know her!

Which seemed as impossible as his getting lost in a territory he knew like the back of his hand.

Breath caught in his throat, he checked her over one more time. Young, tall, very slim with well-shaped muscles that testified to a life on horseback, dark hair and extremely beautiful — he could not shake the weird sensation of looking in a mirror, as if she were his reflection or a twin he had somehow lost without remembering where or how. Because something about her colors and general build was impressively like him.

Eighteen or nineteen at the most, her thick silky hair had the same raven black hue and texture as his, even if hers was longer also compared to his below-the-shoulder cut. Her perfect oval face had stolen some definite features from him, like the straight nose, exquisitely designed soft lips and the clear-cut almond shape of the dazzling green eyes. If this was the only discordant note, for his eyes were as black as cinders, it only strengthened the feeling he knew her at some intimate level he could not quite define at the moment. No, not a casual acquaintance at all — the more he examined her, the more she felt over and beyond familiar as if she belonged to him, which again was impossible because no member of his family lived in the village.

Maybe she has worked at Black Rose. But hard as he thought of the many women employed at his home over the course of his twenty-one years of age, he found no trace of a name to associate to this startling creature.

"Hem . . ." The woman cleared her throat. "May I help you?"

"I'm sorry, Milady." Snapping out of his odd musings, he shifted on his feet. "But with the storm and all, I seem to have lost my way to—"

"Black Rose?" There was a note of incredulity in her voice he found a bit taunting.

"Well, I guess you know where I live." Then again, everyone in the village knew of Black Rose.

"Also who you are, for that matter." The hint of a smile curved her lips before she made a show of bowing. "Welcome to my humble home, Prince Duncan Caldwell."

"All right." No surprise here, either. He was the local celebrity after all. "Since you seem to know all about me, may I enquire on your name, Miss . . ."

"Ylianor." Angling her head, she leveled her gaze with his. "Just Ylianor."

"Who's there?" The angry man's voice broke the strange magic that had trapped him, rooted him to the ground it seemed, to the point he had also ignored the rain beating down on his back.

"I'm sorry." With a start, she jumped away from the door looking every bit as bewitched as he was. "It's raining harder, and I've kept you outside." She gestured behind her. "Please, come in." Then turning around, she raised her voice, "Coming, Father." Focusing back on him, an apologetic smile split her lovely face. "If you'll excuse me . . ." Without waiting for a reply, she went to a nearby table, picked up a small candle and disappeared up a flight of stairs.

Hailed by loud thunder, he entered the house, as poor and desolate on the inside as it was on the outside. Sparse candles lit the table and the few chairs scattered around a cold fireplace next to an empty kitchen. Nothing more to see, he waited patiently for her to return, which she did shortly after.

"Here." She handed him a towel. "At least you can get dry."

"Thanks." He smiled gratefully, shifting the long hair to rub the back of his neck.

"Would you like to stay the night?" Slightly embarrassed, her cheeks colored of an adorable red shade. "I mean, with the rain and all, maybe it would be better." She seemed to pull herself together. "There's a free bed upstairs, and I could fix you something to eat."

Judging from the little furniture he had seen, he guessed the small shack would be unable to provide for too many sleeping arrangements. "Where will you sleep?"

"Oh, I won't be doing much sleeping tonight." Retrieving his towel, she folded it on the back of a chair. "My father is dying, so I'll keep to his bedside."

"I'm sorry." He really was, even if nothing she had said so far had shed any light on who she really was, or on what her connection to him might be. "Can I be of assistance?"

"No, thank you." She did not sound sad, just exhausted. "He's been ill for a long time, but tonight I feel it's his last one in this dimension."

"I see." Not sure he did, he tried to be convincing.

Averting her gaze, she glanced out the window. "If you'd like, I'll take care of Fuzeon." For a moment, she seemed lost as though fascinated by what she was fixing so intently. "I'm sure this thunderstorm has frightened him enough already.

My father always keeps a few bales of hay stashed away for just such occasions."

"You seem to know an awful lot about me." Surprised, he cocked his head. "And about my horse."

"Not to worry, Prince." She patted his shoulder gently, as though he were a child in need of reassurance. "I'm the stable keeper's daughter, so not only do I know your family quite well, but also your horses."

"You are John Meyer's daughter?" *That explains the familiar air!*

But not why he did not remember her.

At her nod, he knew things were not adding up at all. "Until he became ill, John stayed in Black Rose." That had happened a year or so ago. "He had a place above the stables that was for him and his family —"

"I didn't live there," she was quick to grasp where he was going.

Too quick.

"I lived here, in the village." Then she pursed her lips, evidently unwilling to keep talking about it.

Which only perked up his curiosity. "Never even came to visit him while he was working?"

John Meyer had been Black Rose's stable-keeper forever, the man both he and his father had blindly entrusted with the precious charge of their four-legged friends. Like Prince Charles loved to tell his son, John had no equals, and it had become more evident since the man had fallen ill and left his service without Duncan being able to find an adequate replacement anywhere.

"No, I never did." Averting her focus, she stared away from him. "About Fuzeon, would you like me to —"

"Yes, please, if you could look after him, I'd be most grateful." Following her gaze, he noticed that the window next to the door gave a clear view of the horse inside the stable. "We come from a long journey, and maybe I taxed him more than I should have."

Nodding in understanding, she grabbed a candle and went outside. He spied her from the window as she entered the stable to reach Fuzeon, his dark frame already moving to welcome her. Then resting his muzzle on her shoulders, he allowed her to caress his back. So he grew more perplexed.

Fuzeon was a very special horse that did not trust people, often including his own friends. Fuzeon privileged him alone after he had managed to overcome the horse's diffident nature. And considering the fact he had accepted neither his mother nor his sister, the animal's behavior seemed even more puzzling.

On returning, she placed the candle near the table and pulled out a chair. "You can sit if you'd like." Her voice trailed to the kitchen, "While I fix dinner."

Accepting her offer, he plopped down, feeling every tired bone in his body. On the opposite side, she gathered a few plates then retraced her steps, bringing a vegetable soup, some bread and a small piece of cheese.

"Here you go." She set everything in front of him. "I know it's not much." A trace of regret veiling her lovely eyes, she went around the table to sit in front of him. "But with Father's illness, I haven't had time to look after anything else."

"Aren't you going to eat?" Not that it was enough for two, practically not for one either.

She glanced at the little food as though it were her dinner *und* breakfast. "I ate already."

It sounded like a lie, pure and simple. And judging from her extremely thin frame, he was about to decline her offer when a noise distracted him.

"Hey, slut, where's my food?" The voice upstairs shouted, "Are you going to let me starve, you bitch?"

No, he could not believe his ears, nor could he recognize

his friend since childhood in the spiteful vulgarity of this enraged tone. His John Meyer had been a quiet and patient man, not very talkative, much preferring the company of his beloved horses, always hard at work with a passion few others possessed.

"Please forgive my father." As though reading his mind, she leaned forward. "He's very sick. The disease has consumed his mind as well as his body. Now he doesn't know what he's saying half the times." She got up from her chair. "If you'll excuse me, I'll bring him dinner."

"Is there anything I can do?" Rising himself, he felt embarrassed and concerned for her.

"No, thank you." But she seemed to have things under control. "No one can do anything for him anymore." In the kitchen, she grabbed a tray and headed upstairs.

Falling back down, he tasted the first spoonful of soup, wondering where she found the strength to put up with this strenuous situation. True, she seemed resourceful and organized. Yet also alone, as alone as if she did not have a living relative besides the one who was dying now. Not one person in the whole world who gave a damn about her—

"Are you done, stupid cow?" John's overbearing voice crashed in his thoughts. "Get out of here! I don't want to see your ugly face again. Fuck off and leave me alone." There was a slight pause, as though perhaps she was trying to make him see reason.

Only he could not catch her soft voice.

"I said get out! Get out of my house and stay out!" John's breath appeared to be unusually strong for a dying man. "Leave filthy bitch. Do you hear me?"

Next thing, she came down two steps at a time, face pale and drawn.

"Are you all right?" He immediately got out of the chair and strode to meet her halfway.

"Yes, I'm fine." Another lie, though he lacked the heart to challenge it. "Don't worry. I know it's hard to believe he's dying, but it will happen tonight, so . . ." She shrugged as if to indicate she would tolerate the nasty behavior to make his passing easier.

"Maybe I could talk to him." He tried to ignore the fact she had read his mind again, for the second time. "We used to be friends when he worked at Black Rose, and he's taught me all I know and appreciate about horses—"

"No, please." She raised a hand in frustration. "His mind is so far gone that he hardly recognizes anyone anymore. Or if he did, he'd just treat you as badly as he's been treating me lately." She peeked at the stairs behind her shoulders, her long hair falling on her breasts. "It's best if you remember him in his better days, handling his adored animals, rather than this bitter shell that has nothing left of the man he used to be. Besides, his energy's slipping away fast, and it might be too much of a strain for him."

"Maybe you're right." Understanding her point, he let it go. "But what will happen to you when he does pass away? Will you stay here?"

"I . . ." At the hesitation, her brilliant green eyes clouded. "I might."

"Is something wrong?" Not fooled, he breached the distance between them. "Whatever it is, I might be able to help you."

Then he was on her, and all he wanted to do was pull her in his arms, stroke her head and reassure her everything would be all right. And the way she swayed, as though expecting him to do just that, made his need more pressing. But at the last moment, she drew back.

"You haven't finished your dinner." Averting her gaze, she gestured at the table. "Maybe you don't like it . . ." Dejectedly, she looked to the kitchen, clearly thinking about what to give him in alternative when it seemed obvious none was available.

And he could not stand it.

"No, it's fine." So he returned to sit at the table and grabbed his spoon. "In fact, it's delicious." With a couple more spoonful, he finished the soup. "But you sit here and tell me what's wrong." After moving the empty dish aside, he took the bread and cheese. "And stop lying." Raising his gaze, he made a point of narrowing it on her as she reluctantly settled on the chair opposite his. "Remember I'm in charge of this district, and the village council leader refers to me for any big decisions." At her violent blush, he knew she would have tried to lie again like he had guessed. "Is that clear?"

"Aye, sir." The flush deepened into a purplish hue. "If you really must know, this used to be my grandparents' house. Now the village council needs to reassign it to a bigger family." She wrung her hands nervously, clearly uneasy and unwilling to share her load. "Out of respect for Father, they won't claim it until he's alive, but then I'll have to find other accommodations."

"In the village?" Something told him she wanted to be as far away from the place as possible.

"I'm not sure I want to stay." But the way she said it sounded more like it was not her choice, rather someone else's.

"What about your job?" Breaking the first piece of bread, he nibbled it together with the cheese.

"Nothing I can't leave behind." She smirked in indifference. "I work part-time at the bakery, and that's something I could do anywhere else."

"Have you ever worked at Black Rose?" He searched her face, still working on why he could not remember her at all. Because something told him, it had to be more than the fact that she was the daughter of Black Rose's stable keeper.

"Why do you ask?" A curious expression crossed her lovely eyes, an urgency he could not quite understand. "Do you remember that I did?"

"No." *Can't remember you at all.* And he was becoming truly sorry for it. "Just wondering." With another bite, he finished the bread and cheese.

It was her turn to regard him coolly. "You have no memory of me, right?" And it was evident she expected he would not.

"To be honest, I don't." He sighed. "And telling me you're John's daughter doesn't help, 'cause I can't seem to place you anywhere in my life or remember the first thing about you." Clearing the space on the table, he stretched an arm toward her. "I didn't know your name. I still don't know how we met or what we used to do together . . ." Which could not have been anything related to sex, given their age. "But you feel so awfully familiar, like I've known you all my life." He clasped her hand. "Like I grew up with you or something equally close."

"You . . . hem . . ." Taking a deep breath, she squeezed his hand. "You probably saw me around the stables."

"Yeah . . ." *No, it's something more. Something you don't want to tell me.* "Probably." Letting go of her hand, he reclined on his seat. "So what are you going to do? Where are you going to live?"

"I don't know." She folded her arms, a sign he interpreted as a refusal to talk about it. "I'll worry about it tomorrow," she added noncommittally. "Now, if you don't mind, I'll take you to your room." Rising, she picked up the empty dish and went to the kitchen. "So I can check on my father for the rest of the night."

"Of course." He rose, ready to go. "I'm so tired nothing could keep me awake tonight."

"I hope so." After leaving everything in the sink, she clutched a couple of candles and blew out a few others. "Here." Having handed him the lit candle, she walked to the staircase, and he tagged along.

"Your room is right over there." She directed the candle-light toward a door at the far end of the landing. "I'll be here if you need anything." She pointed at the door behind her. "So good night—"

"No, wait." Clutching her arm, he detained her. "Are you sure . . ." Then he dragged her forward, so close her warm body suddenly pressed against his. "Really sure you don't need anything?" So close, he could have easily kissed her.

"I . . ." And it was having a definite effect on her, too, her body trembling in sheer hunger. And her empty stomach had nothing to do with it. "I . . ." A flash crossed her eyes, giving him hope that maybe she would allow him to help her, really help her. But then she pulled herself together. "Yes, I'm sure." And from her inflexible tone, he understood there was nothing he could do.

"All right." So he let her go. "Good night. I'll see you in the morning." Holding out his candle, he entered his bed-room and closed the door.

Chapter Two

"Y our time here is over!" Lady Sophia Caldwell glared at her. "Do you understand?" Mean and spiteful, the woman had spelled out the words probably wanting the nine-year-old girl to catch them all. "My mate can't protect you anymore."

Small wonder. Prince Charles Caldwell had just died, and her heart had already shattered in so many pieces she knew she would never be able to retrieve them all. While the awful woman just could not wait before taking her revenge on a child she had hated from the moment she had been born. No, not even for her mate's body to grow cold, rushing through the motions of banning little Ylianor from Black Rose before her only remaining protector returned from wherever his mother had sent him, and in such hurry, too.

"Nor can anyone else anymore." As though reading her mind, the jealous lady swung her head to a side, where her daughter, Elizabeth, had been standing, watching the show with a smug smile stamped on her lips and lights flashing in open dislike.

As if it were her fault Lizzy, as her younger brother called her, did not receive enough love. Not from her mother, too taken by her son. Not from her father or from her brother, either, both too taken by more attractive people. And plain, downright ugly, Elizabeth did not fit the bill in the least, while Ylianor totally did. And Elizabeth could not stand it.

"So pack your things and get out!" Gaze blinded by fury, the malicious snarl twisting her lips made Sophia look uglier than ever. "And don't come back! Ever!" Pointing a menacing finger, she advanced, so Ylianor jumped back, literally shaking in fear. "If I ever catch you around Black Rose, I will personally whip your ass

19

and throw you out myself."

Ten years had since passed, yet Ylianor still shivered at the memory of the devastating pain she had worked so hard to forget. But Duncan Caldwell knocking at her door after a ten-year absence from her life had brought it all back in a flash.

Wearily, she sat next to her father's bed, glad that he had dozed off and seemed at peace after so many days of suffering and bad temper. She caressed his brow lovingly, checking on his lights. Like she had noticed earlier, they were fading fast, dimming one after another, which was what had made her reasonably sure he would not last the night.

If she had not said as much to Duncan, it was because he would have thought she was crazy or a witch, like most people believed. One look at his aura and she had realized he knew nothing of the power he must have inherited from his father. Or so it felt because she had seen the odd current coursing through him. Like a wave of no color, or rather of all colors blended together, it had been one man's distinctive trait. Now that man was long dead, and his son was as unaware of it all as when they had been kids, and he had chased her on every one of Black Rose's hills. Then that other one had come, and things had never been the same again. Then Prince Charles had died, and things had gone from bad to irretrievably worse. So unbelievably horrible, Duncan seemed to have lost all memory about her.

Saddened by the mere thought, she closed her eyes to repress the tears welling at the back of her throat. No, she did not want to remember that terrible day she had gone looking for him in Black Rose, in open violation of his mother's order, only to find she had become a total stranger to him.

To think they could have easily passed as brother and sister. Not that they were. Not at all, since they shared no single drop of blood. They came from different parents, however much she had believed Prince Charles Caldwell to be her father during her childhood. Growing up, she had realized he could have never been, not since he never pledged to her mother, Mary Jane Elspeth. And everyone knew that no pledge meant no children.

Still, it had not stopped people from blabbing their mouths off about sorcery, witchcraft or other things they knew nothing about, just because she and Duncan resembled one another like twins. And perhaps also Prince Charles holding on to her like she was his own flesh and blood, his favorite daughter to all effects and purposes, had not helped either. Nor had it placated Sophia Caldwell's insane jealousy for her and for her mother. So gossip had raged, and not just after her birth.

After Sophia had thrown her out of Black Rose, people in the village could seem to talk of nothing else. *Here comes the witch,* they would whisper behind her shoulders, loud enough so she could hear.

But in all conscience, she was proud to be one.

For without a doubt, she was one.

There could be no other explanation to what she could do that others could not. Like head talking to the man whom she had wrongly called Father or seeing the lights and flashes that surrounded people's bodies. This second skill in particular was proving invaluable now that she had mastered it, for it revealed a person's true feelings like no hollow words ever could. Mostly, it had helped her detect the burning desire to possess her underneath all those allegations of witchcraft tossed in her face by men too scared or too insecure to claim her sexually. Or the truth in Duncan's contention that he did not remember her.

Which hurt.

Like crazy.

As much today as it had on that distant day she had gone

looking for him.

Because they had grown up together in Black Rose, the place she still considered home and where she had been the happiest, Sophia Caldwell notwithstanding. And Duncan was still *her* prince, the one person she had always admired and loved with all her heart and mind ever since she had been old enough to crawl and to become a privileged, almost inseparable, companion of his boyhood adventures. Only now he had become the most handsome man she had ever laid eyes on, which made everything more difficult. More exciting, too, since she had not been able to suppress a naughty pounding in between her legs that had gone wild when he had pinned her to his very tall, very masculine body.

Boy! Had his lights flashed like crazy in heated excitement, while she was melting all over the place, had been melting all through the evening.

Just having his liquid black eyes on her had felt like she was sitting on a burning pile of cinders, heating her from the tip of her toes all the way to her hair. His chiseled features were absolute perfection, with his square jaw and strong chin, the straight nose and those full lips that promised delights. His large chest and shoulders that tapered to a slim waist and miles long muscular legs had seemed almost too big for her poor surroundings, filling the cramped space beyond its capacity. His long silky hair—oh, how she had longed to rake a hand through the thick strands so like hers, in both color and texture. And she had lost count of the times she had wanted to bury her head on his broad chest and let him take care of everything.

Yeah, it would have been real easy to let it all go—the load she had been carrying forever.

Now she understood why most girls around the village could talk of nothing else, dreaming about him as though he were the only man worth a damn of the entire human species. She had heard more than one wishing for his attentions, especially if they went to work at Black Rose. Strangely, though, and completely unlike his father, Duncan was no easy target. He preferred women of his own standing, something she would do well to remember should it ever be necessary.

John Meyer shifted position, and she focused back on him. No, no use dwelling on it or harboring unhealthy delusions. It hurt simply to feel the pangs of hunger of her empty stomach without worsening the situation by brooding about the past or about improbable fantasies. Better to concentrate on the future, whatever that might turn out to be, possibly away from the village, away from the Caldwells that had already affected her life so deeply and not always so pleasantly.

Sophia Caldwell did not want her around anyway. From Anne, she had learned that the odious woman had put pressure on the council to get rid of her. And with John Meyer gone, who was to stop her?

Not her mother for sure, since she had lost Mary Jane at a very early age. Besides Anne, there was no one in this world who cared whether she lived or died, so it seemed like the perfect opportunity to seek her fortune somewhere where people would not know who she was.

Her father moaned. Her gaze ran to the window. Dawn was not far away, and John's lights trembled like flames prey of the strongest wind ever. Most of them already snuffed out, only a few remained. So she grabbed his hand and squeezed it. A little extra energy could not hurt, even if she did not have the healing power that might have prolonged his life. Still, it might ease his passage into the other dimension, and the gods only knew how badly John Meyer needed it.

That he was a broken man inside, she had no trouble perceiving from his lights, which flashed every day in unrequited love. That he loved her, his daughter, was indisputable. That this love could never make up for what his pledge mate, Mary Jane, had been unable to give him was equally undeniable. And there lay the source of all John's pain.

For Mary Jane had loved Prince Charles above everyone else. And Prince Charles reciprocating in a way he would never with his pledge mate, Sophia, had only worsened matters. This was something she knew for a fact, having felt it straight from his mind and from his lights. Which had not been very often, given how broken up his heart had been about her premature and quite sudden death.

The gnawing cramps at her stomach reminded her time was passing fast. So she ignored them once more, peering at her father's face instead. After the mix-up about Prince Charles and her real father, she had come to appreciate his introverted ways and his love for animals, which she totally shared. Mostly, she could not forget she owed him for shielding her once Prince Charles's death and Duncan's abandonment had caused darkness to fall like a heavy curtain on her crushed heart.

When dawn finally broke, her father opened his eyes and trained his gaze on her. "I'm sorry," he managed to whisper. "About everything . . ." A raspy breath caught off his air for a moment. "Please forgive me."

Then he was gone forever.

CHAPTER THREE

"Duncan, you're twenty-one. It's time you start thinking about pledging." Sophia Caldwell looked at him annoyed. "We need heirs to pass on the family name."

"Can't Lizzy do it for the both of us?" Duncan provoked, knowing exactly what the answer would be.

"Your sister Elizabeth is not . . ." His mother seemed to be in search of a suitable word. "Qualified."

"Why not?" Now this was something he really could not understand. "Since those who pledge choose one family name, Lizzy's mate can take ours, so you won't have to worry about it." Something his mother had never quite explained.

"You forget you're the official heir, not Elizabeth." Nor would she this time, either.

"Even so, she can still have a Caldwell offspring." If he insisted, it was because it made no sense.

"It still wouldn't be . . ." His mother's jaw set in that characteristic way that told him she was being stubborn on purpose. "Proper."

"To have a Caldwell heir from your son is proper, but not one from your daughter?" No, there had to be something else because this logic totally escaped him.

His mother shook her head in frustration. "Duncan, you're giving me a headache." Then she held her head as if to emphasize her point. "Anyway, I don't understand why it should bother you so much. With your looks, I'm sure you won't have any trouble finding a woman to mate."

Ha! If only I found the right one! He sighed inwardly, thinking of the many he had already seen and tried.

"*If you need a suitable candidate, why don't you go to Harbor Town to visit the Turners?*" She waved what looked like a letter in the air. "*You know what a good friend of your father Walter Turner was, and he has written me a very nice letter inquiring after our family and after you.*" She studied him intently. "*You know he has a daughter, Isabella, who is about your age, so you could — *"

"*Mom, I don't need for you to fix me up with women,*" he scoffed. "*I'm quite capable of doing it by myself. Why else do you think I've been traveling so much around?*"

"*Not to Harbor Town,*" she was quick to remind him. "*Which is much closer to home and where you have a lot of friends, like the Turners and the Macys.*"

"*All right, if you insist, I'll go to Harbor Town.*" If he agreed so readily, it was only because he knew she would torment him until he did. "*But don't expect me to return with a pledge mate by my side.*"

"*If she's nice and suitable, why not?*" His mother glared at him, irritated beyond words.

He had to think fast. "*'Cause I'm too young to pledge.*"

"*Nonsense!*" Straightening her back, Sophia gave him her stern and very severe look. "*Your father pledged at the same age.*"

"*So what?*" He shrugged. "*A pledge is a commitment, and I should at least hope I like the person I'm committing to, or how else do you suppose we'd get the precious heirs you crave so much?*"

"*That's what the heat is for, dear son.*" Her eyes flashed in victory, as though she had trapped him right where she wanted him.

"*The heat?*" Yes, he had heard talks about it, though never bothered to inquire. "*What is it?*"

"*It's what makes every pledge work.*" Her face took a dreamy expression. "*Even the most difficult ones.*" Then her tone became matter-of-fact, "*Sort of like the phase, only with your pledge mate.*"

However much this new twist added to the obligations of a pledge, it was hardly enough to convince him to jump into it with *just any woman. None of the many he had known inspired any thoughts of a permanent union, most too boring or insignificant. In bed, they were not bad . . . the first time. Repeating the experience was bound to be as predictable as their conversations, which justified his growing lack of enthusiasm despite his heartfelt belief she existed somewhere – not just the perfect woman for him, the one made just for him.*

Waking up from the dream, which was no dream at all but the conversation he had with his mother before leaving for Harbor Town, he stretched.

Funny how this trip was turning out so interesting in the end, not the waste of time he had thought upon spending just one hour in Isabella's bed. All thanks to Ylianor and her mysterious connection to him, something he intended to figure out at all costs. Too bad, he would have to wait until he returned to Black Rose, for she seemed deliberately evasive. The one thing he had understood quite clearly about her was that she was not a talker. Shy and introvert like her father – that seemed to be Ylianor Meyer's nature or the surface of it anyway. Underneath, he had glimpsed a world she desperately tried to conceal from everyone, an intimate sphere he itched to uncover, if he could only find a way to detain her long enough.

Yawning, he glanced outside. From the light filtering through the window, he guessed it was around the fourteenth or fifteenth hour, four or five hours away from lunch judging from his stomach's grumbling. Definitely hungry, he rose from the bed and dressed quickly, determined to get something to eat, even if he had to get it himself.

Stopping on the first landing in front of John's room, he heard no noise, just felt a sense of peace that had not been there the night before. Maybe she had been right, and her father had died. But he did not dare open the door to enquire.

Instead, he climbed down the stairs, reaching the empty ground floor. So he was about to exit the house all together when he caught sight of her, cuddling Fuzeon in the stable. Fascinated, he neared the window and watched her as she fed him in between hugs and caresses that Fuzeon reciprocated in a rare show of affection. The woman sure had a way with horses, another trait she shared with her father, which might just be the key he needed to solve her problem and his.

When he saw her heading for the house, he moved away from the window, getting to the door just as she opened it.

"Good morning, Prince." A bright smile split her lovely face. "Did you sleep well?"

He returned her infectious smile. "Like a baby." By the gods, seen under Stella's bright rays, she looked more beautiful than he had initially assessed. "What about your father?"

"He . . . he . . ." Her lower lip trembled as though she was trying to keep the tears at bay. "He passed away this morning."

"I'm sorry." Impulsively, he pulled her into his arms and hugged her tight, her smaller frame disappearing inside his, her curves fitting nicely against his.

Maybe too nicely.

"I truly am." Drawing back, he tilted up her face. "Is there anything I can do?"

"Thank you, but I think you did enough already." Like an animal in need of protection, she buried her face on his chest, and he pressed her head gently, wanting to give her all the warmth and comfort he could. "I'll wait until you leave before calling the council leader." Instinctively, she shifted to snuggle closer.

"Before I leave, I want to see you eat something." He did not intend to let her go hungry a moment longer. "I was just about to go get something—"

"I have exactly what you need." Dangling a package, she giggled mischievously. "Generously offered by the baker at the end of my shift."

"Then it'll be a real feast." Reluctant to let her go, he tightened his grip around her shoulders, before a tug in his crotch made him realize he was far more inclined to take her to a bed and let his body do all the talking.

Which was not his usual reaction.

Not when it came to servants.

A matter of aristocratic taste, as his phase mate liked to tease. But not his fault if he found people below his class unexciting. He liked his women to be on the same level, in body *and* mind. So what was so different about her?

For one thing, she looked too much like him to relegate her to a mere servant position. Had that not been enough, the nagging sense of familiarity added its own brand of uniqueness to this woman. But what most got him was the firm belief she belonged to him in a way no other person in the world ever would. And that really blew his mind away, not to mention his cock.

"So . . . hem . . . maybe, I should set the table . . ." Not that she moved any, merely shifted to slip further inside his arms.

All right, so she wanted him, too. "Yeah, maybe you should." But if he did decide to go for her, it would be on his terms, not hers. "I think it's time I got back home anyway." So his arms fell, and she was free to go.

None too happy about it, she went about setting the table and bringing a dish with flat wheat cakes, scones and honey muffins. "At least you won't have any problems finding your way to Black Rose now." Picking a scone, she munched it while pulling out the chairs for both of them.

"None at all, I'm sure." Wondering how she could look so

beautiful after a sleepless night, the loss of a father and a half-day's work, he sat down, choosing a wheat cake. "But if I were you, I'd be more concerned about myself." If he devoured it in two bites, it was all his growling stomach's fault. "What are you going to do now?"

"Me?" She shrugged as though uncaring about her future. "I'll probably find a decent job and start afresh."

"When do you have to leave the house?" No, he would not let her off the hook so easily.

"Soon, I bet." Swallowing the last bite of her scone, she grabbed a honey muffin. "But I'll survive." Leveling her gaze to his, she put up a brave face. "Don't worry."

He wished he could.

"I looked in on Fuzeon." Slowly, she nibbled the muffin. "He's fine and ready for action."

"You like horses, don't you?" He was now working on a honey muffin himself.

"I love them!" Her green eyes sparkled, and her face lit up with the enthusiasm of a little girl playing with her first doll. "I love all animals, but horses are my favorite, and Father taught me to take care of them. It's just too bad I never had a horse of my own."

"Did you ever ride Fuzeon?" Finishing off his muffin, he eyed the plate. A scone and a wheat cake remained, none of which he took because he wanted her to have the final choice.

"Please, have some more." As though understanding his intention, she pushed the plate forward. "I don't think I'll be able to eat another bite after this." She held out the muffin to show him it was only half eaten. "As for Fuzeon, yes, I did ride him." As she took another bite, she gave him the sensation she was already full. "He and I are good friends, especially since he helped me during a very difficult time."

"I'm surprised." Unable to endure his belly's cramps, he

picked up the remaining scone. "Fuzeon doesn't usually allow people to touch him, much less ride on him." He tried to keep his tone normal, not wanting to give off how impressed he was. "You must really be a close friend of his."

A sweet smile curved her lips. "I am."

Leaving him to wonder about what the *difficult situation* had been or how a horse could offer so much help.

The important thing was that he had enough elements to decide about her. So, having swallowed also the last of the wheat cakes, he rose from the table. "I think I'd better go. You have things to do and —"

"Sure." She jumped off her chair. "I'll get Fuzeon for you." Then whirling around, she hurried to the stables, with him following close behind.

As soon as she emerged with the horse at her heels, he clutched the bridles she handed him. "Thank you for the hospitality and condolences for your father's death." Then without even realizing it, he bent and pressed his mouth on her soft lips, the tip of his tongue tracing the edges without pressuring to enter.

She froze, but acting as if nothing had happened, he straightened, mounted on Fuzeon and left.

CHAPTER FOUR

While riding through the countryside, an ancestor of the Caldwells had fallen in love with a ruined property poised on the hills overlooking the sea. Only a few fallen down brick stones remained of what had once been a flourishing estate built atop the sea itself, but what made all the difference was the solitary black rose that defied the salty air and impetuous wind. Bravely standing against the forces of nature, the rose seemed to be gazing at its reflection in the water, and the sight was so beautiful that his faraway Caldwell relative decided he would spend the rest of his life there.

With his father's fascinating tale echoing in his head, Duncan raised his gaze to admire Black Rose's magnificence upon nearing it. To him who loved the place probably more than his ancestor ever had, Black Rose had always looked like a beautiful woman. As if sprawled seductively on a bed, she stared across the distance to the sea. Something he spent hours doing while standing out on his balcony, lost in the crashing waves hurling against the high cliffs.

The journey back had not taken long. As he had guessed all along, his home was right around the corner from her shack so that, soon after he had mounted Fuzeon, he had smelled the fresh sea air brought by the gusty wind rushing at his face.

Approaching the stables, he wondered who would care for Fuzeon this time. Maybe David had finally found a replacement, but if not, he had the perfect candidate under hand.

"A woman for this job?" Sitting in front of the large desk in Duncan's office, David could not hide his disagreement.

"Need I remind you how many men we've already tried without any success?" Most had lasted only a handful of days, complaining the job required too much effort. The truth, as David had told him countless times already, lay in their inability to handle animals, treating them as things rather than living beings. As a result, his faithful valet had taken over this task, too. *As if he didn't have enough to do already on top of his other duties!*

"Yes, but a woman . . ." David's hazel eyes clouded. "Are you sure, Prince?"

A handsome man of twenty-five, David Smith was slightly shorter than he was, with fine features, partially hidden by a mass of brownish hair. Employed directly by Charles Caldwell, Duncan trusted his judgment and often turned to him for guidance as well as useful advice, always finding an honest answer and a sensible heart.

"Sir, you cannot think to put a woman in a position that requires a man's strength." Shifting nervously on his chair, David glanced around the office as though in search of someone to support his opinion.

"Actually, she's perfectly capable of handling horses." Annoyed the man should object so much, he regarded him from behind his desk. "She received her training from the best of them." And since the Meyers had served the Caldwells for so long, they were family in a way . . . well, in a distant sort of way perhaps.

It might even explain the sense of familiarity, though not why he had been unable to think of nothing else except the dark-haired village beauty with the smoky green eyes.

"Impossible, sir," David scoffed, getting irritated himself. "The best of them just died this morning—"

"I know." He got up from the chair. "I was there." Then he spun to look out the window. "And no, it's not impossible." He swung back to face David again. "The woman I have in mind is John Meyer's daughter."

"Ylianor?" David's voice sounded even more worried. "Sir, you don't know what you're saying."

"Why not?" Why was David being so difficult? "She's perfect for the job. And now that her father died, she's alone in this world and practically unemployed."

"But . . ." Visibly distressed, David averted his gaze. "Your mother will never allow it."

"My mother?" Unsure of what he had heard, he took a step forward. "What does she have to do with it?"

"Everything." David's eyes flashed. "Since she banned Ylianor from Black Rose when she was just nine years old."

"Banned?" The news shocked him. "What are you talking about?"

"Well, neither one of us was here when it happened, 'cause it was right after your father died." David swallowed hard. "But you must surely remember Ylianor and that she was gone when we returned."

"I . . ." Frustrated, he tried once more to find an image to associate to the bewitching vixen he had just met, failing as miserably as he had the other times. "I don't." He searched David's face, wanting him to understand his predicament. "I can't remember the first thing about her, not her face or her name, not even the things we did together." He frowned in frustration. "But when I saw her yesterday, she seemed awfully familiar, like I grew up with her or something."

"I see." Given the strangeness of it all, he was grateful he did not detect any trace of judgment in David's even tone. "Please, sit down." The valet gestured toward the chair. "And I'll try to fill you in."

Duncan returned to his desk. Lunchtime, the nineteenth

hour, had long passed, but Stella's warm light filtered through the large bay window at his shoulders.

"About Ylianor, her mother was Mary Jane Elspeth who used to work as a house cleaner." David changed position to settle more comfortably. "Does that ring a bell?"

It fucking does! Suddenly feeling icy inside, he reclined on his seat. "It does."

"Then you remember that your father had a special bond with her," David continued. "So special, your mother became very angry about it."

"Downright jealous," he sniggered, recalling some of his mother's most colorful scenes.

"Something like that, yes." David shrugged inconsequentially. His discretion so absolute, he often downplayed things on purpose. "But maybe it was because Prince Charles seemed quite attached to her."

Actually, he had been madly in love with the woman, if Duncan remembered correctly. A passion so strong, nothing could stop it.

David cleared his throat. "Whatever the case, your mother did not have a particular liking for Mary Jane."

Could not stand her, to be sure, and she said as much in more than one occasion. Still, he appreciated David's diplomacy.

"Though she couldn't do much about it." David's lips twisted in a wry smile. "Especially after Mary Jane pledged to John Meyer and became pregnant. But things didn't get really bad until Ylianor was born—"

"And she looked too much like me for Mother to stand it." Even without definite recollections, it was the only logical conclusion.

"Yeah, that aggravated her most of all," David confirmed.

Aggravation was an understatement. As if hit by a flash, his mother's high-pitched, tone screamed in his mind something about *that servant slut and her evil daughter*.

"But to be fair, everyone back then kind of talked about it." David took a deep breath. "Everybody wondering if Prince Charles could be the girl's father." He snorted, "As if everyone didn't know that there could be no children without a pledge."

At least I won't be running the risk of an incest in case I do decide to bed her. That was a comforting thought.

"Still, people love to run their mouths off, and this sort of thing was just perfect to bring out all kinds of wild allegations." David pursed lips told Duncan he had not approved of any of it. "Like sorcery and witchcraft, which were totally out of place, for whatever Mary Jane was, she was a decent, honest woman who just happened to love the wrong man."

"You liked her, David, didn't you?" He himself had only a few vague memories of the woman. David, on the other hand, was older than him, so he probably knew her much better.

"I did," the man admitted candidly. "But not her daughter, I must confess. Not because of her as a person," he was quick to add. "Because of all the negative things she stirred up, and that haven't settled down yet."

"But it wasn't her fault," his sense of justice had to intervene.

"I know, but she was still at the center of it, just like she still is. Has been since her mother died and she was just three or four years old at the time." His valet paused briefly, as though debating whether to continue. "Which is why I was relieved when your mother forbade her from coming to Black Rose."

"She could've thrown her out sooner, right after Mary Jane died." Not that he forgave his mother for taking her revenge on an innocent girl. "Instead of waiting until she was nine."

"Your father wouldn't let her." David seemed to have his

facts in order. "Mary Jane's sudden and tragic death devastated him so much that he clung to the little girl, like she was a true sister of yours, sir." The hazel gaze had an almost apologetic look to it. "In fact, he insisted on raising her with you. The two of you are only three years apart after all, so he saw to it that you did everything together. From studying to playing, you spent a great deal of time together." He sloped sideway across the desk. "So you see, sir, your sense of familiarity is totally justified."

"I bet my mother didn't like that new twist of things." He chuckled.

"Let's say she resented the little girl a tad bit more." Which was a euphemism for *she hated her guts.* "Already, she was none too happy about how Prince Charles treated Ylianor, which in her mind was better than how he treated Elizabeth."

And Mom was probably right, if there was any truth to what David was telling.

"But what really got her off her horses was how attached you were getting to her." David drew back. "You two were quite close when you were younger. She adored you, and you were very protective of her, at least until . . ." His voice trailed off in embarrassed silence.

"So he knows her, too." Well, that was something he had not expected.

"He does." David nodded. "But he might not remember," he warned. "Your mother kicked her out right after your father died, so he did not have too many chances to see her."

"Then he might remember her like I do," he joked. "Which is to say—not at all."

Going over the story with David, he had retrieved fragments of it, like his mind was full of holes. Not a smooth sequence of events, rather a series of milestones without apparent connections between them. No matter how hard he tried, he could retrieve no visual trace of little Ylianor, as if something had wiped her out from his mental pictures, leaving the rest of the images untouched.

"I'm sure your mother has no trouble remembering," David retorted. "Or barring her door against a girl she's always considered an enemy."

"She's grown a beautiful woman." Talking to himself, his voice took on a dreamy tone. "And she must've changed now—"

"Not in people's minds," David was quick to interrupt him. "They haven't forgotten the rumors surrounding her birth, or the fact she looks more like you with each passing day. Many are afraid of her, claiming she's a witch worse than her mother ever was, and that Lady Caldwell was right to throw her out of Black Rose. They don't trust her, and her beauty hasn't made matters any easier. She's too beautiful for her own good, they tell me. Which is why many believe she should leave the village, if not the Silcamore District all together. And your mother is one of them, 'cause I know for a fact she's put pressure on the council to reassign the place where she's lived since leaving Black Rose, a house that belonged to Mary Jane's parents, if I'm not mistaken, though they died shortly after Ylianor arrived."

"So who looked after her?" Extremely interested, he bent forward.

"I believe Anne, our cook, and her parents." Hardly surprising David would know so much about what went on. He collected information like most people would collect bedmates. "The Elspeths and the Peacocks were neighbors, so it seemed natural they'd take care of the little girl."

"Well, she isn't a little girl anymore," he pointed out once more. "But the way you're talking about her, I'm guessing you haven't seen her lately." He locked gazes with the hazel one. "Right?"

"No, she doesn't get around much." David shook his head. "She's always been a quiet type, not very talkative. Like her father, she seems more comfortable around animals. So she has few friends, just Anne I think."

"And everything she's suffered at Black Rose surely hasn't helped her esteem of humans." He felt confident David would agree to this because they were on the same wavelength when it came to assessing people. "So don't you think we owe her? That it's time we make it up to her?"

"Sir, bringing her back will only stir things best left asleep." David's sensible tone could not hide his heartfelt concern. "So I wouldn't start something if I didn't know where it led."

"I don't intend to go anywhere." Deliberately misunderstanding David's advice, he made up his mind. "I'm only offering a job to someone in need. A person highly qualified for the position, I might add."

"The fact she has a history with your family should deter you from involving her any further," the even tone pressed his point.

That's exactly what makes her all the more intriguing, my dear David. "Enough." He held up a hand to stop further objections. "My mother's inappropriate behavior was almost ten years ago, so I'll try to make her see reason." He groaned inwardly, already anticipating it might be an impossible task. "If she doesn't, I'll simply remind her who is in charge now." Back pressed against the chair, he focused on David's face. "Please bring Ylianor here as soon as John's funeral is over, conveying my job proposal and ..." He paused to think over what would convince her to accept his offer. "These days Harbor Town is hosting the annual fair, isn't it?"

"Yes, the best place to get fine horses around here." The hazel eyes lit up in excitement.

"Exactly." Angling his head, he fixed the ceiling. "And

since I need to repay for last night's hospitality, you'll go there tomorrow and get her a horse."

"A horse?" David's eyebrows flew upward. "Isn't it a bit exaggerated as a gift?"

"Not nearly enough." Just thinking about his night at her shack made his heart heavy. "The woman skipped her dinner to feed me. I think she's more than entitled to a fair repayment." Spinning his head toward the window, he glanced at several horses grazing in one of the backfields. "Besides, we have several young stallions we need to trade back. What they offer in return will fit her needs. You'll deliver her the horse, along with my work offer. The moment she accepts, inform the village leader she'll be living in Black Rose from now on." That settled her. "Is that clear?"

"Crystal." Probably working out the organizational details, David got up, whirled around and headed toward the door but stopped midway. "Excuse me, sir." Slowly turning and retracing his steps, he came to stand in front of Duncan's desk again. "What should I do in case she refuses your offer?"

"Refuse?" That it was a definite possibility had crossed his mind, however fast he had suppressed it. "Why should she?"

"You said it yourself the Caldwells haven't treated her fairly," David argued reasonably.

"True, but from everything you told me, Black Rose has been the place where she's been happiest." It was enough to think of her relationship with his father and with himself to know he was right. "She won't pass up the offer that easily. I'm sure because it's simply too tempting."

"I understand." After turning to leave, David reached the door then hesitated as if struck by a new thought. Leaning against it, he narrowed his focus on an invisible point in midair. "Does this decision come from your head or your heart?" Without waiting for an answer, he stepped out of the room and closed the door.

CHAPTER FIVE

David glanced at the poorly kept shack before knocking.
"Just a moment." The female voice could only be hers,
since he had waited until the funeral pyre had burned out
John Meyer's body.

Hidden among the many who had gone to pay their respects to a much-loved member of the community, he had
watched her, standing tall and aloof, seemingly uncaring
about the blaze lighting up the village square. She just had
not been there, apparently as far away as though the ordeal
had not concern her in the least. Gaze trained on the fire, it
had looked like she had been staring at something no one
else could see.

"David Smith?" Standing on the threshold, she was evidently surprised to see him on her doorstep. "Is it really
you?"

Annoyed she had recognized him so fast, he played it cool
and detached, as though he had no idea who she was. "Are
you Ylianor Meyer?"

The question was redundant.

One look at her and it was like being with his adored
master. While he studied her hair, her face and her body, only one thought kept running through his head. *Amazing her
resemblance to the prince!* What made it more remarkable, if
not downright damning, was a certain Caldwell air she
seemed to possess innately, which reminded him of Duncan
in the assured pose and the way she held her head.

"Oh, David." She stepped forward, after having done

some checking of her own. "You know I am."

"Then I have a gift for you from Prince Caldwell." Unwilling to get any friendlier than necessary, he kept his distance. "He wishes to thank you for the hospitality." He gestured at a beautiful gray mare behind him.

"Oh . . ." Moving toward her, she looked overwhelmed to the point of being speechless.

Spinning around to observe the woman, he wondered if she would convince the mare to accept her. Her owner at the horse fair in Harbor Town had warned him she was not an easy one to tame. Since many had tried and failed, what better way to test Ylianor's skills if she was to become Black Rose's stable keeper?

Perhaps, he would get lucky, and she would flunk, thereby saving him a lot of headaches. For there was no way around it—the more he looked at her, the more she smelled like trouble. For sure, Lady Caldwell would have a fit, and what if the prince fell in love with her, like his father had with Mary Jane?

Watching her circling the horse, he realized two things. The first was that she was so much more beautiful than he had expected, too gorgeous for someone in her position. The second was that she was sure to alter Black Rose's peaceful balance.

And to think he was part of it. Had been part of it ever since Prince Charles in person had chosen him as young Duncan's companion. Then growing up, he had taken on more responsibilities until he now ran Black Rose behind the scenes. But if he loved his job, he loved his master more. The real deal for him was the closeness he shared with Duncan that went beyond mere duty. That he craved the prince's attention in a more intimate way had become apparent to him only recently. That Duncan would never agree to it had also become quite clear.

Unlike most everybody else, the striking dark-haired man was just not interested in sex with someone he did not consider at his same level. And he totally approved of Prince Caldwell's rigid selection in bed, however open and unconventional he was about everything else. The world was broken up in classes after all, so only logical masters belonged with masters, servants with servants. Clear-cut and precise, there was no doubt in his mind that he had to conform to this natural order of things.

Just his bad luck he was born servant to a man so far above him, so stunning in his looks, so very desirable at every possible level that sometimes he drowned in his unrequited lust.

Shaking his head clear of the dangerous thoughts, he focused on her once more as she held out her hand in front of the wet muzzle.

"Hello, Starlet," she cooed softly. "You are a beauty. You know that?"

The horse shook her head.

"Why Starlet?" Curious, he walked toward her.

"That's her name," she assured as though the mare herself had revealed it to her.

Starlet shook her head again. Then approaching the outstretched hand of the motionless woman, she stopped to smell the raised palm. Probably sensing an acceptance of sorts, she reached over with the other hand and patted her neck.

"Starlet, you are a beautiful fine horse." Her small hand became lost in the mare's backside.

"She is." He had to admit he was proud of his choice. "And she's your new care."

"Your prince is very generous." Without looking at him, she spoke the words as though talking to herself.

"Hem . . . actually . . ." He cleared his throat. "He was

hoping this gift would make you accept a job he has in mind for you."

"A job?" Still cuddling the mare, she did not bother facing him. "What kind of job?"

Annoyed that she continued to ignore him, he went round the horse to stand in front of her. "He would like you to take charge of the stables in Black Rose."

"He wants me to fill my father's position?" Her startling green eyes flashed half-amused, half-worried.

"Precisely." And his heart sank.

Because in that one flash, he saw how strongly she still felt about Duncan Caldwell, in spite of her ten-year estrangement. Something he remembered noticing when she was just a little girl following the prince around with an adoring stare, a lovesick puppy always tagging alongside him wherever he went.

"So what do you say?" Whatever the case, it was not his position to question his master's decision, however rash he thought it was. He had a job to do, and he would do it as commanded.

At first, it looked like she had not heard. Without giving him any attention, she kept stroking the horse that responded by nuzzling her forehead.

Then she raised her gaze, training her sparkling green eyes squarely on his face. "Does he know his mother banished me from Black Rose?"

"At first, he didn't remember." That Duncan apparently had no recollection of his childhood's playmate and friend had seemed odd to him, yet stranger things had been known to happen. So he had not worried about it, just taken the prince's words at face value, like he always did. "But then I supplied the missing pieces."

"And . . ." She hesitated as though afraid of his answer.

"He doesn't care." He heaved. The confrontation would

be inevitable, and he doubted the prince was ready for it. "He's the master now, so he decides who comes and goes in the estate."

"I don't think it's a good idea." Again, she seemed to talk to no one in particular.

"Neither do I." The opportunity to speak his mind was simply too irresistible to drop.

"You think so, too?" As she searched his face intently, all the gossip he had heard about her came rushing to the fore, and he had no doubt her frank approach was partly to blame for the mistrust she aroused. Which combined to her striking resemblance to Duncan, more than justified those who called her a witch.

"Yes, partly because of the past." Averting his gaze, he tried to quell a strange sense of excitement that had no reason of being. "Mostly because of the future. I cannot ignore the fact people consider you a troublemaker, not to mention those rumors about your birth, even if I personally don't believe any of it."

"I know what you mean." She focused back on Starlet. "But it's the best offer I've had all day."

"It could be dangerous," he snapped.

"Indeed, it could." A hint of mischief lit her eyes. "On the other hand, what's life without some risk?"

"Life is nice just as it is," he spat. "With its orderly structure and its class distinctions. If you take that away, all that remains is—"

"Chaos," she finished as though she could read his thoughts. Then she shrugged, almost indifferent to this fate. "Perhaps, but it's probably a lot more fun than any boring order."

"Does this mean you accept?" Irritated, he shifted uncomfortably.

"I suppose it does." A light flush spread on her face.

"Funny, I had every intention of refusing, but . . ." She frowned perplexed.

"You still can." Taking a step forward, he breached their distance.

"What choice do I have?" She lifted a shoulder carelessly. "I could remain where I'm unwanted or go to a place I still consider home. True, no welcoming committee there either, but at least I have an ally . . ." Shyly, she lifted her gaze. "Or maybe two." Her intriguing eyes blazed, begging him to understand.

"Look, Ylianor . . ." What really got him on edge was how defenseless she appeared to be, like a lost little girl in need of protection. Already, he had failed her once since he had allowed her memory to vanish from Black Rose, like Lady Caldwell demanded. Now realizing it might have been a mistake, he wondered whether he could make up for the lost time, if maybe she could turn out to be something more than he had originally assessed. Maybe even a way to have what he so desperately craved in the flesh yet could not have. "I'm simply following orders." He deliberately hardened his voice to avoid giving her any false hopes. "As you said, no welcoming committee is waiting for you except for the prince, but I honestly don't know if it'll be enough."

"It'll have to do." She tossed back her head in defiance, her splendid mass of hair falling all the way to her ass. "But thank you for helping me make up my mind."

"Glad to be of service." He bowed in mocking deference. "I just hope we won't regret it."

"So do I." She said it like a whisper that he almost did not catch.

"All right." Ready to leave, he went to get his horse. "I'll see you later this evening."

She nodded. "I'll pack up my things and come straight over."

"By the way . . ." Reaching his horse, he whirled around. "I'm sorry about your father. He was a good man, and we all miss him at Black Rose." Then he mounted and left her alone.

CHAPTER SIX

Princess . . .

Prince Charles's throaty whisper boomed in her head as he caught sight of her poised on the windowsill of his room. I'm so glad you came to see me.

Sure he was. Since he had fallen ill, Sophia Caldwell had locked him in his bedroom and kept everyone out. Not little Ylianor, though. She climbed through the window every day to visit him, sitting by his bed and holding his hand tightly. Most of the times, she did not even dare breathe, lest she disturbed him, for she could tell how weak he really was. That funny way his lights had of shutting down was something she had only seen in an old horse. And then the horse had died, so she presumed Prince Charles would, too. But she refused to think it would happen any time soon.

So am I, Father. *Jumping down, she neared his bed.*

He winced. You know I'm not your **father.** *Yes, she knew the term disturbed him.* John is your father.

I know, but . . . *Ill at ease, she shifted her feet, staring at them as though they were the most fascinating things in the world.* It just seems so right . . .

Truth was — her nine-year-old self lacked the proper word to express how deeply she felt about him.

His eyes flashed in disagreement, but he did not repeat what he had told her a thousand times already — about how wrong it was for her to think of him as her father.

And you know I'm right. *She stomped her feet to prove her point.* If he's really my father, why can't I talk to him like I can to you? Without opening my mouth, I mean.

Ah, Princess, it doesn't work like that. *He chuckled softly.*

Then tell me how it works, Father. *But this she had not shared seeing how exhausted he was, more than any of the previous times before.*

Suddenly, a noise at the door had her scurrying away, after placing a soft kiss on his cheek.

Gotta run now. *Whatever happened, she dreaded Sophia catching her inside the room. It would mean the end of her stolen times with Prince Charles, and she did not have the heart to stand it.* Someone's coming, so I'll see you tomorrow —

No, wait. *Already balanced on the windowsill, one leg dangled outside, while the other was still inside, gaze locking on his burning eyes.* Don't ever forget that I love you, sweet princess.

No, Father, please don't go! *She rushed back, cold fear gripping her stomach as all his lights went off all together, all at once.*

Just promise. *After this final painful breath, his eyes closed, and the room went completely dark.*

I promise, Father. Holding on bravely, she tried to stifle the *pain threatening to swallow her whole. But how could she now that her world had gone eerily silent and empty?*

Upon riding away from the village, it seemed hardly a coincidence that she relived Prince Charles's dying moment. Then again, she did not believe in coincidences for everything always happened for a purpose. And having just burned her father's body in the town's square seemed enough of a purpose.

She knew she had looked distant and cold through it all. Deeply lost in herself was how she had felt, unable to handle the many, too many, lights flashing around her. As if the giant blaze had not been enough! But shutting off everyone's lights sparking brighter than the dancing flames was an impossible task. So she had withdrawn further into herself, the place she knew best, and stared at the void that had seemed her future.

Then David and Starlet had changed everything. Up until their arrival, hard reasoning had almost convinced her to leave the village, if not the district all together. Yet here she was, returning home, rushing through the front gate and curving around the hills to reach the top. So what had changed?

And no, she did not want to think of the unexpected kiss that had spun her senses to a place they had no business going.

As Black Rose came into view, she plunged straight into memory lane. Right around the second bend, she had played hide and seek with Duncan. A little further up, Prince Charles had liked to walk with his little princess. And up there was where she had confronted him . . . nah, she preferred to suppress that reminiscence. Too much love filled this beloved place to spoil it with that one rotten incident she would rather forget.

Accelerating to the stables, she glanced at the graceful house, standing proud on top of the cliff.

Oh, boy, had she missed it!

More, since she was completely alone in the deserted and dark yard, the welcoming committee evidently too busy or too tired to bother with her arrival.

Dismounting and taking Starlet inside her new home, she checked around and again, it was like stepping back in time. Just as she recalled, the place was big and comfortable, hardly changed despite the years, looking also reasonably clean and well kept under the light of a few torches hanging on the starch white walls. Not enough, though, to hide an eerie sense of abandonment and loss that hit her like a punch in the stomach the moment she was fully inside. Almost doubling over from the pain, she had to stop and catch her breath. What was that all about?

Pushing out air slowly, she checked cautiously around.

Nothing was out of place as far as she could tell. Nothing that justified this terrible and acute sense of loss, devastation and suffering that clung on tenaciously like a child's inconsolable despair. It felt like something really bad had happened here. Something she had no definite memory of, but instinctively remembered at a very physical level.

Unsettled, she took the first steps forward, and the horrible sensation quelled all together as if by magic.

No, no magic. That she knew for a fact. The horses had stopped it, using their energy to block out whatever negative buildup had thrown her off balance. Gratefully, she clasped the first horse that came her way, burying her head against his powerful neck.

Fuzeon! She need not use words with him. He understood perfectly, just like all the other horses whose tails were shaking in pleasure and recognition.

Lady Rose. Untangling from Fuzeon, she embraced the beautiful white mare, generously patting her shiny mantel.

And hello to you, too. Spinning around to a brown horse, she recognized him as being David's ride on coming to her place earlier. "Though I'm afraid I didn't catch your name."

"He's Oscar," David's voice rang out from behind her.

"Pleased to meet you, Oscar." She did not bother turning around. "I'm sorry we didn't have much time to get properly acquainted today." Taking a step back, she broadened her gaze to include all the horses with a single sweep. "This is Starlet, your new mate." She tugged her mare's reins to bring her forth.

"Prince Duncan would like to talk to you." David could not hide his impatience. "What took you so long anyway? It's the twenty-eighth hour, and we thought you weren't coming anymore."

"I've had a little convincing to do." She smiled, taking the gray mare to the back of the stables. She had proved more difficult to tame, her trust issues working hard against Ylianor's attempts to gain her confidence.

"I said the prince is waiting." Annoyed by now, he huffed.

"First, I'll settle Starlet." Unruffled by his reprimand, she continued with her business. "Since the prince has waited so long already, I'm sure a few more minutes won't make any difference." Finding an empty stall at the back end, she took the horse, stroked her reassuringly, provided her with food and water, then turned to him. "All right, let's go."

"About time," he snapped truly irritated as he whirled around and went out of the stables.

Pitch dark outside, except for a few candles burning in the windows on the first floor, she followed him to a side entrance, which she remembered gave access to Black Rose's ample kitchen.

After he had opened the door and disappeared inside, she quickened her pace and stepped through the threshold of the familiar place, warmth and the tantalizing smell of food rushing at her.

Well, not only.

"My dear pet, you made it finally!" A stocky, plump woman threw her arms around Ylianor and smothered her in a generous squeeze. "I couldn't believe my ears when I heard you'd be coming back."

"Aunt Anne, I couldn't believe it, either." *Still can't as a matter of fact.*

Not really her aunt, still she loved her as one, if not more. Anne Peacock, the Caldwell's cook ever since she could remember, had been a close friend of her mother and had looked after her ever since Mary Jane had died. Also when thrown out of Black Rose, Anne had never abandoned her, not even after Ylianor's grandparents had died. As if it were the most natural thing in the world, Anne's family had stepped in to take care of her.

"The important thing is that you're here." Taking a step back, Anne kept her at arm's length. "Now let me look at you." A quick penetrating glance seemed to be enough for the woman. "Pet, I done told you a thousand times you're way too thin," she scoffed. "Gotta put some meat on those skinny little bones of yours." Then her expression saddened all together. "Oh, I'm sorry for your father's death." She shook her head. "He was a good man."

"Yes, he was." She nodded gravely. "I burned his body this morning and many people came to pay their respects."

"I wish I could've been there." Anne hugged her again. "But with all the work to do here—"

"Ladies, if you please." David was close to exasperation. "The prince is still waiting." His hazel eyes flashed in frustration. "Remember?"

"Right, dear, you mustn't keep him waiting." After one last caress on her cheek, Anne drew back. "There'll be plenty of time to catch up." Gently, she pushed her forward. "Go now."

If David did not repeat, "About time," it was only because he had already left the kitchen, headed down the hallway that connected it to the main building.

Close at his heels, she passed in front of the main entrance then curved to the left until he stopped at a door on his right. As she tried to remember what that room had been for, he knocked.

"Come in," a voice called out from within.

Opening the door, he stuck his head around the threshold. "She's here, sir." He made way for her to enter in an office furnished in a man's taste. Blue carpet on the floor, a large desk faced two leather armchairs, its back on to a grand three-sided bay window. On the right, the fireplace shed a warm light that enhanced the candles' dimmer glow. A library full of books and papers covered the opposite wall.

In front of it, a couple of leather couches and a low table in between completed the room.

Once inside, David closed the door, and she was alone with the handsome prince.

CHAPTER SEVEN

"Welcome to Black Rose." Sitting behind the desk, Duncan regarded her trying to ignore his stomach caving in and his heart skipping a beat or two.

More, if he had to count.

Which he did not, since he had waited the whole damn day long for her to show up, refusing to believe she might not or that he might never see her again.

"I'm glad you made it." He rose to greet her properly. "Please, take a seat." Gesturing at the armchair in front of his desk, he checked her over to determine the truth about her origins. Disappointed that her face revealed nothing different from the previous night, but surprised that the feeling of familiarity seemed stronger than ever.

"To be honest, I'm not sure I want to stay." Plopping down, she fixed him in a challenging way.

I thought so. He sat down again. "Why not?" If she wanted to play hard to get, he was more than ready for her.

"Some people might not take my return too kindly." However plausible her explanation, he suspected she had an ulterior motive.

"Are you planning some kind of revenge?" He kept his tone light on purpose, "Perhaps a curse or some other witchcraft?" Duncan teased.

"If I did, would that bother you?" Instead of being embarrassed like he expected, she dared him back.

"It might." He grinned amused. "Or it might not, depending on what kind of revenge we're talking about." He searched her face. "But I find it hard to believe a person so caring of animals and of a bad-mannered dying father could harbor such thoughts."

"I beg to differ, Prince." Evidently at ease, she relaxed on her chair. "You don't know me at all." She spelled out the words, as though he were a child who had trouble understanding.

"I think I do, given our past." Excited at the turn in the conversation, he straightened.

"Of which you remember nothing." She threw back her head in defiance, black hair flying around.

"So what?" He would not allow such an insignificant detail to give her the upper hand. "David helped me piece your story together."

"If you have no memory of me . . ." She sounded hurt and disappointed that he did not.

Nothing he could do about it. The gods knew how hard he had tried to retrieve something, anything at all, from his usually good memory, without any success.

"Why did you want me back here?" Her incredibly green eyes flashed.

"To take John Meyer's place." He kept it simple. "From what I can see, you're the most qualified, and I'm in sore need of someone to take proper care of Fuzeon."

"Liar." She said it as smoothly as she would have said, *Thank you for this opportunity.*

"You're probably right." So the girl had brains *and* insight. He liked that. "I may have some . . . ulterior motive in mind."

"And I can't wait to hear it." An ironic smile curved her lips.

You'd just love to know, wouldn't you? And since he was sure she was thinking along the same horizontal positions he was, he would be damned if he gave her the satisfaction. "When I find out, you'll be the first one to know." He chuckled getting a real kick out of it all. "Now enough playing and let's talk about serious stuff." Stretching out across the desk, he leveled his gaze to hers. "Have you had dinner?"

She shook her head. "Not real hungry right now."

"Listen, Princess, I . . ." If his voice trailed off abruptly, it was because she had become so pale he was afraid she would faint. "What's wrong?"

"Why did you call me like that?" Seemingly out of breath, her voice came out raspy.

"Like what?" He noticed how cloudy her brilliant green gaze had become.

"Princess," she whispered hoarsely.

"I don't know." He shrugged in puzzlement. "It just came to me." He settled more comfortably. "Why do you ask?"

"Your father, Prince Charles . . ." She took a deep breath. "He used to call me like that when I was little."

In the momentary silence, broken only by the sound of wood crackling in the fireplace, he felt his father's presence as if she had conjured him from the dead. The impression lasted the space of a moment, but it felt so real that he had to sweep the room just to be sure they were still alone.

"Maybe it was an old memory," he joked.

"Can't be." She shook her head. "He only called me Princess in private, never in front of his family or worse, his son."

"Then it could be a promotion." He smiled broadly at the pun.

"Already?" She giggled. "I haven't even started yet."

"Life's full of surprises, isn't it?" His smile deepened. "But before I make it official, you do well to remember that I need a healthy stable keeper. So I won't have you skipping meals, as you did the other night."

She blushed violently. "I didn't—"

"And the first rule about stable keepers is they never lie," he cut her off abruptly. "I know that was your dinner, if not the only food you'd have eaten all day," he added more gently. "So go to Anne, and she'll fix you something to eat."

"Yes, sir." She moved as if to rise. "Is there anything else?"

"Like you probably know, your quarters are above the stables." He frowned to get his priorities straight. "Keep your strength and look after the horses. That's all."

"All right." Getting up, she was about to head for the door when she hesitated. "Thank you for Starlet. I really appreciated the gift, though you shouldn't have."

"You shared everything you had with me." His heart melted at the thought. "So it was the least I could do to thank you."

"I'd have done the same for anyone, but thank you just the same." She stepped away from his desk. "She's a beauty."

"I haven't had the chance to see her yet." Something he was sure he would rectify soon. "But I trust your judgment and David's. If I have some spare time, I'd like to see her tomorrow."

"I'd be happy if you did." She bowed slightly. "Good night then."

"Sleep tight." Watching her leave, he felt suddenly alone.

He should have asked her to warm his bed, rather than sending her to a cold and empty room. And since it was too late to call her back, he jerked off then spent the rest of the night in one erotic dream after another about her.

CHAPTER EIGHT

"Good morning, pet." Anne's beefy arms flew around her smaller frame as soon as she entered the kitchen. "Boy, you sure woke early. It's just nine o'clock and dawn just broke." Having smothered her sufficiently, she let her go to glance out the window. "How did you sleep?"

Sleep? What's sleep? Fitful spells of unconsciousness fragmented by frequent visions of scorching sex with Duncan—that had been her very hot, very agitated night.

"I hope well." Not giving her any chance to reply, Anne continued as though she had. "So how are you this morning? Take a seat." She pulled out a chair from under the table and patted the seat. "And some warm breakfast."

"I'm fine." It was almost impossible to interrupt her flood of words, but Ylianor tried anyway. "And good morning to you, Anne."

"How can you be fine?" The cook looked at her with that skeptical air that always told her she would never be able to fool the woman. "You hardly touched what I left you yesterday for dinner."

"I was too tired to eat," she lied shamelessly.

"Is that why you look like you didn't sleep a wink last night?" The woman's penetrating gaze scanned her up and down.

"I'm fine, really." She hurried to sit down before the cook had the chance to check her over one more time.

"If you say so." Not believing her at all, Anne grabbed a plate and piled it high with eggs, wheat cakes, rolls and potatoes all in one. "Here you go." She handed her the huge platter. "Eat up."

"Anne, I can't possibly eat all this food." She had not eaten that much during the whole time of her father's illness.

"Just try, honey, at least to make up for everything you didn't eat last night." Anne squeezed her shoulder. "You're all skin and bones, and that's what skipping meals can do to you." So like Duncan, she knew it, too. "You're too thin for my taste and for this new job of yours. And a little food never hurt anybody anyway." She did not quit watching until Ylianor nibbled the first piece of what came under her fingers. "So how did you really sleep?"

About to repeat her earlier assurances, she opened her mouth—

"Not so good, eh?" Anne beat her to the answer. "I can tell from your face. It must be hard to be back, considering all the painful memories you left behind."

Surprised at how Anne had summed up with a few simple words the anguish tormenting her, she nodded. "I'm still wondering why he called me here." Bravely, she tried her mouth on a plump buttery roll. "And whether he told..." She swallowed the lump in her throat along with the piece of bread. "You know who that I'm back." To keep a measure of balance, she finished the excellent roll.

"You mean if he has told his mother?" Of course, Anne had no trouble understanding. "No, I don't believe he has, or we'd have heard the screams." Her broad smile broke the tension that had been building in Ylianor. "He's probably keeping the surprise in store for today. As to why he wants you here..." Anne shrugged. "Who knows? It's true we need a stable keeper and have been looking for one since your father fell ill." Grabbing a few dirty pots and pans, Anne went to the sink. "No one so far seems good enough for Prince Caldwell. He's so particular about his horses, about how they're treated and that Fuzeon makes it an im-possible task for anyone just trying to be friendly with him." She began washing everything under a jet of running water. "Come to think of it, Duncan is particular about his women, too. His mother is tormenting him about pledging, but he just won't give her the satisfaction," she snickered.

"What do you think is the problem?" Suddenly very curi-ous, she leaned forward.

"The same as the stable keeper, I suppose." Angling her head above her shoulder, Anne managed to catch her gaze. "He hasn't found the right one yet." She focused back on the sink. "The gods know he tried more than his share, but none seem good enough for our prince. I think he's just too choosy about everything, from horses to people. That's why he's got few friends, no mate and no stable keeper."

"Come on, Anne." She laughed. "Aren't you being a bit hard on poor Duncan?"

"Don't get me wrong." After turning off the water, Anne dried her hands. "He knows a lot of people, but most of them hardly qualify as friends." She moved to the stove to check on a boiling pot then poured hot water inside a cup. "As for women, they're always after him, one way or anoth-er. But that's different from having a mate, don't you think?" She returned to the table bringing the scalding cup and set-ting it in front of Ylianor. "Here, drink." She pushed it for-ward. "Some tea will do you good."

"Thanks." She sipped the brew. "What about his sister, Elizabeth? Has she pledged?"

"Of course not!" Anne's tone strongly suggested that poor Elizabeth did not stand a chance. "Who'd want an ugly crea-ture like her for a mate?"

"Anne, aren't you exaggerating?" Digging up a warm wheat cake from under a stack of pancakes, she began munching it. "Just a bit, perhaps?"

"I wish I were, pet." Sighing loudly, Anne's tone became gentler, "I'm only telling the truth as I see it in the face of all the unpledged man who have come by Black Rose." She shook her head resigned. "But I hope things will change. She deserves to be happy 'cause she hasn't been much so far." Seeing Ylianor licking off the extra honey from her fingers, Anne fetched a couple of napkins. "Now she's become Lady Sophia's favorite victim, and that woman is so terrible she hardly gives her space to breathe, while her brother spends way too much time away from Black Rose to give her the attention she craves."

"I'm sorry." She truly was. Cleaning up her fingers, she realized how lonely it must feel to Elizabeth Caldwell. "To think she used to adore Duncan." Gulping down the last of the tea, she watched Anne's reaction, knowing full well the woman would not resist spilling her guts about the Caldwell family history.

Of which she was an expert.

"Oh, she still does." Anne swallowed the bait along with the entire hook. "She worships the ground he walks on. That's how crazy she is about him, and I've heard her say more than once she thinks he's the most beautiful and most perfect man in the world. Which we all know he is." There was a definite note of pride in Anne's admired tone.

"Seems to me like she felt much the same for Prince Charles." She could not help drawing the comparison.

"Aye, she did, didn't she?" Anne's eyebrows rose as though she had never thought about it. "Yet neither one has given her a fraction of what she feels for them."

This saddened her and Anne, too, judging from the grim expression on her face.

"Good morning, Missus Peacock." Opening the hallway door, a blondish woman a bit on the plump side entered. "Is breakfast ready?"

"Yes, Sarah, have a seat." Anne set another chair at the table. "This here is Ylianor Meyer, the new stable keeper." She gestured as a way of an introduction. "Ylianor, meet Sarah Jennings, our chambermaid."

"So you're the one?" Sarah's blue eyes widened with interest. "I didn't think it possible the prince would give this man's job to a woman."

"Shut your mouth and sit down." Taking a step forward, Anne nearly pushed Sarah into the chair. "She's perfectly qualified, better than any man for that matter, and I don't recall too many experts filling that position lately."

"That's because the prince is never satisfied," Sarah spat. "No one's good enough for him or for that black beast of his."

"Ylianor will be for the both of them." Self-assured, Anne circled her shoulders in a protective and very touching gesture. "Don't worry." Letting her go, she prepared another steaming cup of herb tea and handed it to Sarah, together with a plate filled with all sorts of sweet cakes. "Here, take your breakfast."

"Thanks, Missus Peacock." After setting everything on the table, Sarah's gaze swung her way. "Does Lady Caldwell know you're here?" Her round buxom ass dropping on the chair, she immediately got down to the eating business, attacking her food with a hungry growl.

"Hmm . . ." Which made her slightly nauseous, to the point she pushed away her own plate. "I don't know."

"I don't think it's any of your business, Missy!" Anne scolded, refilling Ylianor's cup with fresh infusion.

"Just wondering." Burying her nose in her plate, Sarah wolfed down two honey cakes in rapid succession. "Don't get ruffled."

"People around here mind everybody's business except their own." The cook's mumbles trailed away as she returned the kettle to the fire. "Sarah here, for instance, makes the prince's affairs her own."

"That's not true!" Sarah flared. "I simply look after his chamber."

"And his bed in particular," Anne sniggered. "To the point she gives us detailed accounts on how he spends his nights and with whom." Chortling, she turned to her. "I swear, sometimes I think she spies on him."

"I certainly do not!" Sarah cried. "I'm just curious. That's all."

"Too bad the prince never notices her." Before going back to the table, Anne fetched more napkins for Sarah. "As we were saying before, he's too choosy about people, especially the ones below his level who delude themselves he'll ever invite them inside his bed."

"Missus Peacock, if you please . . ." Sarah's face became crimson. "I never said —"

"Save it." Waving a dismissive hand in the air, Anne made her close her mouth. "If your mouth never did, the rest of you did plenty of talking. One would have to be blind, deaf or stupid to ignore all your wasted attempts to get his attention."

"Well, he is so handsome I wouldn't mind if he asked for some playtime." Sarah smiled mischievously. "Don't you agree, Ylianor?"

"Me?" *I've never seen anybody more gorgeous than him in all my life.* "He's attractive, true, but unavailable."

"Yeah, isn't that a shame?" Sarah nodded in agreement. "Most of my friends don't have any trouble having a little fun on the side with their masters, who aren't half as good-looking as our prince." She heaved perplexed before plunging back on her food. "Anyway, don't take Missus Peacock seriously. She likes to think the worst of people, but she cooks so wonderfully we always forgive her in the end." At that, Sarah got up and embraced Anne, kissing her softly on the cheek.

Anne returned the kiss. "My child, I say those things because I hate to see people get hurt."

"But few listen, right, Anne?" Ylianor giggled. Then her gaze ran to the window, and she noticed the hour had grown late. "I had better go to my horses." Rising, she hugged Anne. "Thanks for the delicious breakfast, and—"

"Has everything been set in the breakfast room?" Rushing inside, a middle-aged woman looked first at Anne, then at Sarah. "Lady Caldwell is about to come down any minute now, and she likes her herb tea hot." Spinning to Ylianor, she scrutinized her. "And who might you be?"

"She's Ylianor Meyer, the new stable keeper." Again, the cook took care of introductions. "This is Alicia Merryweather, our housekeeper."

"Ah, the stable keeper." Alicia showed her contempt with a simple headshake. "Yes, well . . ." Moving away, she focused once more on her concern. "Is the tea ready?"

"Here it is." Anne handed her a tray containing several full dishes.

"It was about time." Evidently having learned at David's same school, Alicia grabbed the tray, as though she had wasted enough time already, and hurried toward the door.

"Pleased to meet you, Missus Merryweather." *And good riddance.* She could not resist the snappy retort, watching the woman disappear from the kitchen.

Then, before the cook had the chance to tell her all about the housekeeper, Ylianor squeezed her plump hand. "See you later, Anne."

"Yes, pet, I'll call you when it's lunchtime." And from Anne's set expression, she had no doubt the woman would drag her to the kitchen no matter what.

CHAPTER NINE

Coming out of his bedroom and going downstairs, Duncan saw Ylianor crossing the space between the kitchen and the stables. So he stopped on the landing to stare at her from one of the upper windows.

The little witch looked intriguing even by daylight, which made him remember the agitated night filled with erotic dreams about her. His gaze unwavering, he even went as far as devising a seduction strategy before realizing he needed something very hot and very strong to wash away her erotic distraction. So he hurried to reach the breakfast room.

"Good morning, Mother." On entering, Lady Caldwell caught his eyes first. "Good morning, Lizzy." Then his sister, Elizabeth. "Did you sleep well?"

Lady Caldwell did not just ignore him. She did not even bother raising her gaze.

"Fine, I guess." His sister eyed him coldly.

"Is something wrong, Mother?" He braced himself for the inevitable argument. "If so, please tell me." Deceptively disguising his feelings, he worked to keep calm while sitting in front of her at the breakfast table. "Perhaps I can do something about it."

"Don't you think you've done enough already?" Sophia Caldwell nearly choked on her flat wheat cake. "You're the reason something is wrong, and now you want to do something about it?" She tossed the uneaten piece in her plate. "Ha! That's a laugh! Congratulations, son, you've outdone yourself this time."

No, he did not let her get to him. "Are we talking about—"

"Yes, we're talking about your outright disregard of my orders," Sophia spat venomously. "How dare you bring back that hateful creature into our home?" Yelling at the top of her lungs, her eyes bulged as though they would fall off her sockets at any moment.

"Mother, please lower your voice if you want to talk to me." With the pressure growing, he sat up straighter. "I'll explain my reasons and—"

"I don't care about your reasons!" To have Sophia listening instead of shouting was an impossible task, considering how agitated she really was. "She should have never set foot back here."

"Fine." Throwing his chair aside, he glared at her. "But need I remind you who makes decisions around here now?"

"I banished that creature when you were a mere child." Lady Caldwell's eyes flashed. "So I had every right to."

Wrenching an empty mug from the table, he counted mentally to restrain what would have been a snappy comeback. "Then it's about time things changed around here," he retorted at last, reaching for the steamy teapot and filling his cup with scorching brew.

"You cannot do this to me!" His mother just would not let it go. "That slut has no business staying here." Her insistence had become a shout. "She's got to leave immediately!"

"All right, Mother, it's obvious you're too angry to talk." Without even tasting the infusion, he left it on the table, ready to bolt out of the room. "Be sure to call me in the rare chance you calm down."

"Mother, let him talk." Turning, Elizabeth looked at him apologetically. "Duncan, you know how Mother is. She's upset because that . . . woman really hurt her a lot, and there's no need to remind her of all that pain."

"Lizzy, tell Mother that people grow and change." He moved closer to Sophia. "I don't think that girl caused any pain," he added in a gentler tone. "If anybody harmed you, it was probably the girl's mother, but she's long dead."

"That woman was an evil bitch, and her daughter is even worse." Hardly mollified by his attempts, Lady Caldwell snapped, "Two witches who trapped your father, both of them. They work dark magic on men, and I remember you weren't immune either." Her gaze now pleading, she lowered her voice, "Don't you understand, Duncan? I'm trying to protect you."

"I'm a big boy now, Mother." He caressed her cheek. "I can take care of myself. I know there are many dangers out there. But you and Father taught me well, so please have a little faith in my judgment." He deepened his touch. "Father did, otherwise he'd have never left me in charge."

"Not in an official capacity, yet." Her eyes narrowed to the point they became thin menacing cracks. "We still have to read his will."

"Which we will in a very short time from now." Nervously, he raked a hand through his hair. "I've already arranged for the lawyer to—"

"Reading it won't make up for your lack of experience with women," Sophia quipped.

"I already told you I haven't been doing nothing else lately if not working on my *experience with women*." His patience about to reach its limit, he pulled away from her.

"Then why haven't you chosen one, yet?" At this point, it was kind of obvious his mother wanted to pick a fight no matter what. "What are you waiting for?"

"I told you already." Exasperated, he walked to the door. "I haven't found the right one yet."

"Well, try to find her soon," Lady Caldwell snarled in a threatening tone he did not like at all. "Once we read your father's will, I expect you to carry out your responsibilities and stop harboring unsavory creatures in our midst."

"Ylianor stays!" He made it sound final. "As for my duties, don't worry. I'll fulfill them." With an angry scowl, he threw the door open and left the room, more upset than he cared to admit, heading for the stables.

CHAPTER TEN

"Get me Fuzeon," he snapped when Ylianor came out of the stables.

She glanced at him first, then at the sky, nose twitching in midair as though she could smell the rain coming.

So the weather was terrible! What else was new?

Heavy clouds steadily piling up on the horizon and chilly air blowing in from the sea were not going to stop him. He needed a ride to clear his head and fast.

"Immediately, Prince." After checking on the approaching darkness that threatened to cover Stella's few remaining rays and unleash a violent storm, one last peek at him and she whirled around and fetched the horse.

About to leave after mounting on Fuzeon, he changed his mind at the last moment. "Come along. I'd like to see your mare in action."

It came out as an order, rather than an invitation. Seemingly unaware of the difference, she quickly brought out a silvery grey horse and mounted on her back.

"I called her Starlet," she mumbled shyly, in such a low tone it sounded more like a whisper.

Looking at her for the first time since he had reached the stables, he noticed she was wearing an old pair of trousers, which probably had belonged to John Meyer, judging from the worn fabric and loose fit.

Not loose enough to hide the shape of her firm buttocks.

"That's a curious name for a horse." He spurred Fuzeon forward, toward Black Rose's front gate. "Does it have a special meaning?"

"Well, it's for my mother." Her smile was a bit crooked, but enchanting. "People who knew her told me she shone like a star, so it's a way to remember her."

Great! That's all I fucking need. A goddamn reminder of Mary Jane and of my mother's pig-headed attitude!

In no mood for conversation, he trained his gaze straight in front of him and totally ignored her and the magnificent countryside around Black Rose. Wrapped up in his anger, oblivious of the weather, the hills, the valleys, the lake and the river, he pushed his horse onward.

Time flew.

Morning became evening.

Yet he did not break once.

Finally, he reached the dark cover that had been a distant mass at the beginning of his stroll. The clouds were so black they turned day into night. The only light now came from faraway flashes. And he felt revitalized by the air's crackling energy coursing through his blood, charging his senses to the point he craved the explosive release only a storm, or something very physical, could provide.

Yes, a tempest was exactly what he needed to get rid of the negative effects from the ugly scene in the breakfast room. Without thinking twice about it, he propelled Fuzeon to go faster, despite the horse's increasing nervousness. The wind taking a turn for the worse made it impossible to maintain a steady pace, but he could care less. Tightening his knees around his horse's belly, he forced Fuzeon to keep riding, until thunder broke overhead and he had to veer off course because Starlet whined terrified, rising on her hind legs.

"What's happening?" Coming out of his trance, he became suddenly aware of nature's temper.

"I think a storm is about to drown us." Showing admirable self-control, she managed to quiet down her mare enough to convince her to get on all fours again.

"We should find cover." He glanced around the semi-darkness trying to remember where a shelter might be.

"I know just the place." Confident of her knowledge, she pointed toward a clump of trees a short distance away. "There's a shelter right there."

"Are you sure?" Peering ahead, he could not see a damn thing. Too dark and too many flashes lessened visibility in the thick forest he had been crossing.

"Positive." She smiled sweetly, looking gorgeous in the howling wind, hair flying around, straight shoulders and blazing green eyes.

Then he caught the familiar sight of Lake Lilly and knew she was right. His father himself had set up a shelter exactly where she had indicated.

"Yeah, I see it, too," he yelled to overcome the wind and the background noise. How the fuck she could have known was beyond him. "Go ahead. I'll follow."

His priority now was to reach it before nature hit them with the full force of its fury. With a firm grip, he steered Fuzeon in his intended direction and not one moment too soon. A flood of water crashed from above, the thick, fat drops whipping his back while he hurried behind her. When he finally saw it, he sighed with relief, truly grateful for the Shelter System that offered travelers and their horses a safe haven.

One last acceleration and he arrived at the stable where she had already settled a very scared Starlet.

"We can stay here until the worst is over." Handing her the bridles, he waited for her to place Fuzeon next to her mare and in front of a full trough, before heading to the front door.

The layers of dust inside the log cabin testified to its in-frequent use. Still, it lacked none of the usual supplies, like a pile of dry wood next to the fireplace, which he lit up in no time at all. Then sitting back on his heels, he let the blazing flames reach all the way to his bones, where the wetness had penetrated and stuck.

"Just what we need with these drenched clothes." Amused, she shook her head, water dripping all over the ground as she neared the fire.

Raising his gaze, he could not help admiring her figure, wet cloth clinging to her body like a second skin and hiding nothing of her curves. "Maybe we should take them off." He grinned mischievously.

"Yes, we should, so they can dry off." Her lips curved in a smile. "But what are we going to wear in the meantime?"

How about nothing at all? "If we look hard enough, we might find some blankets." Getting up, he made a show of checking around the place. "I believe shelters are equipped also for this."

In the bedroom, after a brief search, he found a couple of blankets and some towels.

"Where would you like to change, Princess?" Slightly mocking, he handed her one of each.

"In front of the fire, Prince." She bowed in an equally playful mood. "So at least I won't freeze to death."

"Very well, I'll take the bedroom then." Returning to the room, he did not close the door, and she was either too wet or too cold to care.

With growing excitement, his gaze traveled down her naked back with the enticing round ass wriggling free from its soaked confinement. Stripped naked, she rubbed her skin dry then wrapped the blanket around it.

Having enjoyed the last of the show, he tossed aside his own wet clothes and rubbed the towel on his skin until it was reasonably dry. Then he wrapped a blanket around his waist and returned to the fireplace. "Feeling better?"

CHAPTER ELEVEN

Her breath caught in her throat as she whirled around to answer.

Like the first time she had seen him, he gave the impression of being too big for the available space. His magnificent body more attractive than ever with the long black strands dripping tiny streaks of water on a bare chest that displayed an impressive set of muscles before narrowing to the waist, wrapped by the blanket. And the heat he gave off was simply unbearable, with the need to touch him driving her crazy.

"Much." Abruptly, she turned to face the fire, so she would not have to look at him.

Dropping down on a comfortable carpet, she pretended to stare at the leaping flames. His sitting right next to her did not help matters any, not with his powerful muscles flexing from the tension of his scorching desire.

Sure, she had no trouble picking it up from his wildly sparking lights whose hue had suddenly become very red. Ironic as it seemed, this was the second-time fate had trapped her in a secluded cabin, alone with a man all women would have done anything to drag to their beds. Ha, if only Sarah Jennings were in her place, there would have been no trace of a blanket anywhere on her body!

Shaking her head amused, she worked hard to suppress a giggle.

"Is there something funny you'd like to share?" Angling his head on a side, the black eyes caught her gaze.

And held hers mesmerized.

"This whole situation is kind of funny." Exercising a tight control on herself, she commanded her heartbeat to slow down, her lungs to breathe normally and her stomach to unclench. "Here I am with a person I thought I'd never see again in my life, forced to spend another night together." The hint of a smile curved her lips. "I guess, when you're back in a girl's life, you make sure she notices it, even if she'd rather forget," she joked.

He regarded her coolly then called her bluff. "My dear, you're not a prisoner," he snarled softly. "You're free to leave whenever you want."

"Sure, if I don't drown first!" Heating up, she had the urge to toss away her blanket.

"I meant when the weather calms down." He chuckled. "But I'd be surprised if you did. It must've taken a lot of guts to return to Black Rose—"

"I'd call it stupidity." *Especially now that I want you so bad, I'm burning in my own skin. Literally.*

"Perhaps . . ." His tantalizing black eyes flashed in disaccord. "Whatever it was, it mustn't have been easy to return to Black Rose after how my family treated you, especially considering nothing ties you to the place."

"Nothing except the past." Ruefully, she let out a deep breath, her thoughts running to Prince Charles and his soothing love.

"Aren't I a part of that past?" He searched her face for a moment. "Judging from what David told me, you used to like me." He smiled mischievously. "And people tell me I'm quite likable, now more than ever."

"You don't need to play games with me, Prince Caldwell," she spat annoyed. "You've always had my complete attention then and now, even if I'm not sure I want you back in my life."

"Why not?" She could tell he was really trying to understand. "Was it better without me?" Suddenly, the black eyes clouded. "Or do you perceive me as a threat?"

Gaze still locked on him, she only wanted to drown in him, forgetting about stupid questions, too dizzy by now from hunger and cold. His nearness was enflaming her senses to a spasm, the acute awareness of his body pressing at her side making her legs weak with the aching need to feel his arms around her and his warm lips claiming hers—

With a start, she pulled away her gaze from temptation. "Yes, I do." She pursed her lips. "It's probably got something to do with our childhood."

"Since I can't remember . . ." He smirked regretfully. "Maybe you ought to fill me in."

"I'm sure you don't need my share of bad memories." Her lips curved in bitter awareness. "It's better if you stick to the pleasant ones in which I don't appear."

His head bent on his knees, as if he were trying hard to resist some impulse or simply to take his mind off whatever was gnawing at him. She had noticed, of course, could not help noticing it, his erratic aura speaking louder than any word.

"I'm sorry." Raising his head, he looked at her remorseful. "I don't know you, or what your life has been like. I shouldn't have asked."

"No, forgive me." Her heart went out to him. "I shouldn't have snapped like that. I'm grateful that you gave me the opportunity to do something with my life. Really. I'd have wandered aimlessly in search of . . ." She shrugged indifferent to how she would have turned out. "Something," she added eventually, before a stray thought hit her. "And it's not as bad as it seems." She giggled uncontrollably. "We've been friends before, so I don't see why we can't be again." She spun to him, but her confidence vanished upon realizing how much she wanted to touch him.

Yeah, sure! As if I could ever be friends with someone who turns my stomach upside down simply by looking at him!

Her heart raced. Her thighs tingled. And an insistent thud between her legs was having a devastating effect on the simple task of holding a normal conversation.

"I'm not sure I can think of you as a friend," was his cold reply.

Of course not. How could I have been such a fool? To think even for one moment that he —

"Damn!" Wrenching her shoulders, he cursed again. "I might regret this for the rest of my life, but the gods know I want more, much more from you."

Attacking her mouth, his tongue requested an entry she readily gave. Sweeping the warm cavity with forceful strokes, he made her head spin and her body burn for more.

He had no trouble delivering it. Deepening his claim, his tongue reached her throat. So she opened wider to let him have it all.

It belonged to him anyway — body, mind and spirit his for the taking. Like her mouth, ravaged by his tongue's fiercer onslaughts that cut off her breath. Like her body trembling to have its share of attention.

Pushing her down on the carpet, he flattened her to the ground under his weight. Tossing the blanket aside, he went for her hard nipple, drawing it fully inside his mouth and quaffing it avidly. She did not mind his teeth grazing it at times. Loved it in fact, for it added a tiny bit of pain she found strangely exciting.

Pressing his head, she urged him to swallow her whole, unwilling to let him go ever again. Still, he had no trouble switching to the other tight bud begging for a lavish pampering of its own.

Overwhelmed by the new sensations, she arched her back craving his full lips on every bit of flesh, which was a practical impossibility that did not stop her from crushing him against her.

His long strands tickling, she tried feeding him parts of

herself, the ones that most throbbed in hungry anticipation. Without success, he did not allow her, brushing her hands away and making it clear who was in charge. And he went where he most pleased — the drenched cunt pounding furiously between her legs. One lick and she thought she would die from the explosive pleasure she perceived just a few laps away on that exceedingly bare cunt of hers.

Partly her natural lack of body hair in her most intimate parts. Partly her shaving it off since the time it had started growing, to the point its slightest presence had become a bother.

Whatever the reason, his tongue had no annoying obstacles to hamper its succulent glides on the whole of her slit. So the fire inside her intensified, together with the dull hammering she could not endure a second longer. And his tongue circling it one more time did not help any.

On the verge of something incredible, she stretched luxuriously, tensing her muscles and dripping honeydew all the way down to her asshole. Oh, she wanted more and more as she raked his thick hair frantically, not really knowing what to ask but thrashing for it all the same.

He had no trouble understanding her needs and zeroing on the very center of the pounding driving her insane. Out of her mind now that he sucked it. And she could not take it anymore. It was simply too much.

She froze all together. Body taut in expectation, her swollen clit drowned in his forceful rubs until her mind went blank. Because wave after exquisite wave burst in rapid successions, the tide shattering her very core with its repeated coils.

Unable to withstand it, she opened her mouth wide to let out the scream that had been building nearly as long as her orgasm had, its loudness rising and falling with the vehemence of the throes melting her body into liquid fire.

Clearly startled, he lifted his head, which was the last thing she wanted him to do. Swinging her pelvis up and forward, she begged him to continue, using a seductive hip rotation with consequent ass shaking to convince him.

Amused, he watched her futile attempts for a second, before grasping her hips and immobilizing her. "I don't suppose you had a phase, did you?"

It was not really a question. It was a statement as though he knew the answer already.

"No, I didn't." There was no way she could catch his gaze given her position, but she tried anyway. "How did you know?"

"Wasn't hard to figure out." He shrugged as though it did not make any difference to him. "And I'm also guessing you haven't had any sex with men *or* women until now."

"Right again." Palpitating as loud as a drum, her heart skipped several beats just because she finally succeeded in locking her gaze on the lust-filled black eyes.

He sprawled on top of her. "Then this might hurt a bit."

His warning reached her ear before his kiss took her breath away.

He tasted different now, a bitter stinging yet familiar flavor that he shared as his tongue possessed her mouth again. And knowing it belonged to her only aroused her more, to the point she dared push her tongue for some tentative exploration of her own.

Lost in their combined tastes, she curved upward to brush her clit against him. The aching thud was back, engorging the knot faster with each rocking gyration. Legs spread out. She increased her spinning until something very hard and very huge nailed her to the carpet.

Literally.

Shoving again, he broke through whatever barrier had separated them up to a second before, and the searing pain paralyzed her despite his warning.

He froze. "Do you want me to pull out?" Concerned, his black eyes were pools of tenderness.

"No, don't." Who cared about pain when the reward was the shattering bliss that had already been hers? No matter what, she wanted him worse than before. So she clasped his neck and brought him down on her. "Just kiss me harder."

"I'll do my best." He grinned as his lips swung down in one hearty intake of her wet cavity.

Could anything be sweeter?

True, his cock penetrating to the hilt was not all that exciting. With its sliding up and down, it enlarged her painfully, digging through her delicate flesh until it was raw from the friction. And when he had screwed his entire long thick length inside, he upped the tempo to a wilder beat that scorched her poor flesh to bits.

Still, she did not complain, had no reason to, not at all. She simply could not allow herself to dwell on the pain. Only on his tongue sinking to her stomach and gagging her at times, which unleashed uncontrollable shivers like fiery sparks creasing her skin.

This seemed to heighten his pleasure. As he sped up the blows to her slit, she realized he had gotten bigger and stiffer. With a loud gasp, he shuddered, slamming into her with double the impact power as before.

Then finally, he was still.

CHAPTER TWELVE

"Good morning, Prince," Ylianor chirped cheerfully the moment he opened his eyes.

"Good morning." Yawning and stretching, he watched her elegant moves around the shelter, her slender body going back and forth from the kitchen. Beautiful and so very tempting also now that he had tasted what she had to offer. So very erotic and passionate, all he craved was to pin her to the mattress and start everything over again.

Goddamn it! He could not believe how much he liked her! And last night's sex had been mind-blowing to say the least, so very right yet so very wrong at so many different levels he had no wish to dwell on any single one of them.

"It's the eleventh hour, and I'm starving. Luckily, I found some tea and gingerbread, so I fixed breakfast." She flashed a mischievous smile. "After last night, I think we need to replenish our energy."

Now that she mentioned it, he was hungry. And having skipped breakfast, lunch *and* dinner might have something to do with it. Feeling lazy, his gaze traveled out the window where the overcast weather promised nothing good. Well, at least it had stopped raining, and he had the chance to leave before he did any more damage.

Then he wondered how the horses were doing.

"Fuzeon and Starlet are fine." Somehow catching his thought, she glanced at him reassuringly. "I went to check on them five minutes ago. They spent the night safe and dry."

"That's good news." Another quick stretch, then he got out of bed and got dressed, his clothes fully dried by now.

After a brief stopover in the bathroom, he sat at the table just as she brought the tea and the gingerbread, filling his cup first.

"Careful, it's hot." She slid seductively on the chair next to his. Then nibbling on a piece of bread, she glanced at the gray sky outside, a look of concern clouding her beautiful eyes.

He followed her gaze. "Yeah, we should leave right after breakfast."

"Do you have the power to read minds?" If it was a tease, she did not laugh. "I was just thinking that." Nor did she sound at all surprised.

"Actually, I thought you did." Clutching his cup, he took a sip of scalding brew. "I was thinking of the horses when you mentioned them."

"Perhaps we're just in tune with each other's thoughts." She smiled.

"Yeah, perhaps." The idea made him uneasy.

"By the way, I couldn't help noticing you still have that scar on your left shoulder." And this comment of hers did not help any, nor did the flush spreading on her cheeks, as though she was embarrassed she had watched him while he slept.

"The scar?" Instinctively, he fingered it from above the shirt.

More than a scar, it was a pronounced mark engraved on his flesh by who knows what childhood mishap. Only thing, this one had never faded like it should have given how long he had it, leaving instead a definite and quite visible blemish on his skin, to the point his phase mate had often joked about it.

"You remember it?" He could not help wondering why

she had stored such an insignificant detail about him for all this time.

"It's so unique, and you've had it forever it seems that it's impossible to forget." She drank down her tea. "So of course, I remember it very clearly, like most everything else about you," she teased.

Do you now?

No, if he went down this path, he knew it would be the end of him. There was just so much more he wanted to ask her that he would never be able to leave the shelter. Questions like, *Did you like your first time? Did I hurt you a lot? Did you like it anyway? Would you want to do it again soon? How about right here, right now?*

Damn! The only thing really on his mind was how fucking bad he wanted her, would have taken her again and again if he did not leave this place. And he had to do it fast, before his cock got out of control and bloomed into full erection what was just stirring now. Her seductive body was simply too close and too tempting. To ignore its erotic pull would have taken a greater willpower than he felt endowed with at the moment. And remembering the thrill of finding her cunt nice and shaven, his task was even harder. A real novelty, for sure it had been the first time he had ever had sex with a woman so bare the mere sight had almost made him spill it all before even claiming it.

"Come on." Since it was a losing battle, he rose and pretended to check around. "Let's clean up and go." His priority was the fireplace. Not just because it was dirty, mostly because he could avoid looking at her.

"Sure." After clearing the table, she began stripping the bed. "There's blood on the sheets and on the blankets." Sensually, she cocked her head over her shoulder to catch his gaze. "What should I do?"

"Let's take them to Black Rose." For the life of him, he could not stop sinking into her brilliant green eyes. "I'll have them cleaned and brought back here." But he could not allow her to read his raw craving.

With an effort, he focused back on the fireplace and on his task of gathering the cinders in a bag.

"All right." After folding them neatly, she neared him. "If you're almost done there, I'll get the horses."

At his nod of agreement, she left.

One last look around, and he followed her out. Mounting on Fuzeon, he set off as though his life depended on it. With Lake Lilly behind him, he rushed forward on the false urgency he had business in Black Rose that needed his immediate attention. All he wanted was to stop thinking about the intriguing witch at his side.

Why did she feel so different from anyone else? And why had the sense that she belonged to him increased right after the sex?

A servant's daughter to all effects and purposes, yet no woman had ever attracted him quite this way. While he had been attacking her lips, he had told himself she resembled him too much to pass up the opportunity to fuck with someone who could have been a twin. Sheer curiosity had been his primary motivation, or so he had played it while his cock ravaged the tightest pussy he had ever screwed.

But it had all been a lie, pure and simple.

Because he could not get over her incredible reactions. The trusting way she had opened to him, even if it had been her first time. How she had tensed her muscles before her explosive release, or how her tantalizing body had flexed in its blind search for more pleasure.

And that scream of hers had told him just how effective he had been in delivering what she must have long denied herself. Probably too introvert and shy to seek it out, he felt a rush of adrenaline just thinking he had been her first one.

But that was not what had blown his mind about her.

No, what really got to him was the way she allowed him to take charge of her completely. Surrendering at such a level, he could have done anything he wished with her, like he did with only one other person in all the world. And up 'till the day before, he had thought he would never find someone at quite that height.

Now she was riding quietly by his side, asking nothing of him nor playing silly games with his intelligence like a few of his latest bedmates had after a passionate night.

He shook his head to clear it. Perhaps this was all beside the point. His life simply did not need more complications than it already had, not now anyway. If only he could stop picturing her naked body with its high breasts and long legs, not to mention that intoxicating clean-shaven pussy that had bared everything to his lustful gaze. Which was nothing if compared to that magnificent ass of hers and to what he would do to it first chance he got. And simply thinking about it stiffened his cock.

"I think we ought to split up now." Sometime when he had not noticed, she had maneuvered Starlet next to Fuzeon. "I can take the turnpike and go to the village, while you continue to Black Rose." She gestured at the junction dividing the path between the two. "So they won't see us returning together."

Not having planned it through, he focused on the road ahead of him. "Yes, I guess you're right."

Spurring Starlet forward, she overcame Fuzeon and disappeared down the left turn while he continued straight, past Black Rose's wide-open front gate.

A worried David rushed out of the house as soon as he approached the stables. "Where have you been since yesterday?" He grabbed Fuzeon's bridles. "I was about to come look for you."

"I went riding, and the storm caught up with me." He slid

down the horse's back. "So I spent the night in Lake Lilly's shelter."

"Alone?" From David's expression, it was clear he did not think so.

"Of course." Annoyed, he waved a dismissive hand in the air. "Who else should've been with me?"

"Ylianor has been missing since last night, too." Deferential yet persistent, David held his point.

"She had a few errands to run in the village." So he improvised. "If the storm caught her, she must've spent the night over. Don't worry. She'll be back soon."

"I thought I saw you leave together . . ." David's voice trailed off as though he realized it was none of his business.

"We did because I wanted to see the mare." No, it was kind of evident that David did not want to let it go. "But at the turnpike our paths separated." Before taking the first steps toward the house, he glanced inside the stables.

And his heart stopped at the sight of a splendid black stallion.

"Is the angel here?" Heart pounding in anticipation, he tried to locate the blue-gray eyes ready to spark and light the beautiful face at the sight of him.

Unsuccessfully, alas.

"Yes, Lord Templeton arrived early this morning." David's lips pursed in that characteristic way he had whenever he talked about the angel. "He's with your mother and sister in the breakfast room."

"Then he's in sore need of rescuing." Chuckling to himself, Duncan hurried away, heart now in his throat and stomach churning in anticipation.

CHAPTER THIRTEEN

"I'm so glad you're here," Lady Caldwell repeated to a bored Chris for the tenth time.

"So am I, Lady Caldwell." He worked hard at keeping his irritation down to a minimum.

Lucky for him, a glance at a large mirror in the wall shifted his mood. Nineteen years old, blond and clear-eyed, angelic face with regular features, fair skin, tall, lean and graceful frame—without a doubt, Christopher Templeton was one of the most attractive men around.

Reluctantly returning his gaze from his reflection, he fixed Sophia Caldwell again. "But I wish you knew where Duncan is."

"That bad boy left yesterday with a storm coming." Lady Caldwell did not sound worried, however annoyed her tone. "The gods only know if and where he found shelter."

"I wonder why he'd be so reckless." It just did not sound like Duncan at all. Not to him who knew the dark-haired prince better than he knew himself.

"Because Mother made him angry." Plain, kind of ugly, Elizabeth had to throw in her two bits' worth.

"Elizabeth, hush!" Which to Lady Caldwell seemed like an affront. "You shouldn't burden our guest with our family quarrels."

"But, Mother, Chris is Duncan's phase mate . . ." Her bovine eyes strayed toward him. "A close friend almost like a brother . . ." With that hunger of hers stamped all over them.

Which exasperated him for he could not believe the girl

would be so stupid to keep harboring hopes about him despite his blatant disregard of her.

Then again, she was Duncan's sister, which was the only reason he had always restrained his biting manners, not to mention his better judgment to send her where she really belonged.

"So who better than him to make your son come to his senses?" Elizabeth smiled smugly as though proud of her reasoning.

"Why?" Suddenly interested, he brightened. "What happened?"

"Well . . ." Sophia Caldwell's hesitation lasted a fraction of a second. "My son had the bad taste of employing a woman as a stable keeper and of course, we aren't very happy about it."

"Mother, if Chris is to help Duncan, he must know the truth." Spinning to him, she obviously relished the attention he had no choice but give her. "You see, this woman is the daughter of a servant that had bewitched my father and had the nerve to manipulate him." She frowned as though suddenly remembering something. "I think you may have known her, too. The daughter I mean. She used to play with Duncan when they were still children."

Ylianor Meyer! "Vaguely." *How could I forget?*

"Anyway . . ." Elizabeth seemed happy of his answer. "When Father died, Mother banished this hateful creature from the house." Same happiness she must have felt when her mother had thrown out Ylianor from Black Rose, no doubt.

Still, she had all his sympathy. At least on this, he, Sophia Caldwell and Elizabeth were on the same side.

"I had to!" Sophia spat. "To have to put up with her detestable presence after Charles died would've been intolerable."

"So it happened after your mate died in . . ." He creased his forehead in an effort to remember dates.

"About ten years ago," Elizabeth supplied.

"And you've had no contact with her in all this time, right?" He kind of figured they did not. Only wanted to be sure.

"None whatsoever!" Sophia scoffed as if the mere idea was offensive to her.

"Not even Duncan?" Again, just double-checking.

"If he has, he made no mention of it." Elizabeth shrugged. "But I really don't think so."

"Then how did he find her?" *And more importantly, how did he manage to remember her?*

"We . . ." Elizabeth faltered and looked at her mother. "We don't know."

"I'm not interested in how he found her," Lady Caldwell snapped. "I don't want that witch here, so he's got to get rid of her. Period."

"Unfortunately, he offered her the position her father once held as stable keeper." Elizabeth shook her head sadly.

"Really?" He clearly remembered Ylianor's father had worked at Black Rose. "So why did David get my horse now?" Something was definitely not adding up, and he did not like it one bit.

"She's probably as lazy as that bitch of her mother was." No, Lady Caldwell really could not stand either one. "Hiding somewhere to avoid working, I bet."

"And that's the least of it." Elizabeth heaved. "Now that she's back, people will start spreading their malicious lies about her and father—"

"My mate is *not* that creature's father!" Sophia Caldwell practically shouted.

"Mother, calm down!" Elizabeth glanced at him apologetically. "Please, forgive her. It's still a touchy subject for her, and she tends to get very upset about it."

"Of course, I understand." How could he not?

He would have personally wiped the girl out of the face of every known land.

"Naturally, we know she's no blood relation of ours." Elizabeth's tone was firm, probably to dispel any residual doubts. "It's ridiculous even to think it, but people can be very cruel sometimes, especially if they can talk bad about someone."

"As if people didn't know that no pledge, no children." Sophia snickered. "And that despicable servant had the baby after pledging to John Meyer, our stable keeper," she explained in a gentler tone. "While Charles never pledged to her."

"John Meyer is Ylianor's father." Elizabeth set the record straight once and for all. "Or rather was." At the brief pause, her expression became sad. "He died two days ago."

"And this made Duncan want to replace him with his daughter?" He frowned skeptically for the sense of it all continued to escape him.

"Hem . . ." Confused, Elizabeth was out of ready answers. "I don't think —"

"John's death has nothing to do with it," Lady Caldwell was quick to put her daughter's doubts to rest. "That ill-mannered creature, just like her mother, is a witch who used her black arts to seduce and enslave my Duncan into bringing her back here. That's exactly how her mother worked her way into my poor mate's heart."

"Come now, Mother." Elizabeth threw back her shoulders as though getting ready for a fight. "I know how deeply they hurt you, both of them, but maybe you're exaggerating just a bit."

Not according to him.

"Can you really see Duncan fall prey to witchcraft?" With a totally adoring stare, Elizabeth could not tear her gaze away from him. "Maybe you can find out why he insists on keeping her on the premises."

"If I ever get to see him." He shrugged deeply frustrated by now with Duncan's disappearance.

"He'll be back. Don't worry." Elizabeth smiled confidently. "By the way, are you going to stay long?"

Not if I'm stuck with you. "I'm afraid not." He tried to sound as disappointed as possible. "Arthur Fairchild, the Leader of the High Council, has summoned us with a certain urgency, so we should leave as soon as possible."

"Then you're not planning to stay?" Elizabeth worked hard at hiding her dismay.

Without any success as far as he was concerned.

"Not at all." And seeing her face, he was all the gladder he would not. "I'm just here to pick up Duncan and go to the Hall."

"So when exactly will you be leaving?" Elizabeth could not seem to accept the idea.

He cleared his throat. "Well . . ." Such organizational details were usually up to Duncan. "I'm not really sure—"

"We're not leaving immediately, Lizzy," Prince Caldwell cut in as he entered the room, obviously catching the last part of the conversation. "Don't worry." Then he turned to him, flashing a most attractive smile. "Welcome to Black Rose, Angel."

"There you are, naughty Duncan." Whirling in his direction, Chris returned the smile with all the gladness he could muster. "So you wanted to try out a storm for a change?" He searched his face in amusement.

But what he read sank his heart all the way down to his feet.

"I guess I underestimated the weather." Somehow knowing he had caught the lie, Duncan averted his gaze. "And the storm caught up with me around Lake Lilly." His gaze now focused first on his mother, then on his sister. "Luckily, Father had provided a shelter just there, so I didn't get too wet."

"And that's where you spent the night?" Hardly fooled, Lady Caldwell gave him a skeptical look.

"Yes, Mother, nothing to worry about." The black eyes flashed in his direction. "Care to discuss travel plans in my office?"

Thought you'd never ask. "That's what I'm here for." Grinning broadly, he moved to reach Duncan, halting at the door to address Elizabeth and Sophia, "If you'll excuse me, ladies, I'll see you later."

Falling in step with the striking prince, he left the breakfast room, heading down the hallway. Stopping in front of his office, Duncan opened the door, making way for him to enter. He was about to close the door when Chris spun around and pinned him to that same door. Avid mouth attacking the very tempting full lips, his hand pressed on Duncan's stirring erection. Sweeping the hot space to get the full taste of him, his tongue worked at the same rhythm of his palm sensually sliding up and down what was swelling to a beastly size. And he thought he would melt before he had the chance to pull away.

Which he managed to do eventually, nibbling upward from the prince's mouth to his ear. "Hello, lover." He paused the hoarse whisper to deepen his touch on the now gigantic shaft. "Missed me?"

Chapter Fourteen

"This boy must be the demon's child," James Templeton told his pledge mate. "You must send him away for a while."

"He's just a child." Claire Templeton pressed eight-year-old Chris to her skirt. "He doesn't know what he's doing."

"You're wrong, Claire." His father checked him over, the third and last of three Templeton sons. "I can read it in his eyes." For sure, the one he loved less, too taken by Steve, the eldest, and then Bran, to notice him except if he did something wrong. "He knows all too well he shouldn't be doing those things, yet he continues to do them." His father's gaze burned him to the spot. "It's as if he wants to defy me every way he can."

Yes, 'cause I'm different from everybody else, and there's nothing you can do about it! Not that he dared say it to his father's face.

"How could that be?" Anguished, his mother squeezed his shoulders. "He's just a child."

"That's no excuse." Stern and inflexible, the last thing his father wanted was to be reasonable. "Let's send him over to Charles. Maybe he can help him, and his son can only be a good influence on this wicked boy."

"Charles Caldwell?" Her shocked tone scared him.

Was his father planning to get rid of him forever?

"But Black Rose is very far from here." Aghast, she clung to him as though James was about to tear him away from her. "Why punish me by sending my child so far away?"

"Dear Claire, can't you see he's taken a dangerous path?" His tone softer, James tried blandishing her.

A trick he did not fall for, no matter how young he was.

"If we send him to the Caldwell's, he'll have the company of a boy slightly older than him who, according to his father and to Arthur, could straighten him up and perhaps make something of him." He pursed his lips. "Don't you want him to have a better future? If we send him there, it's only for his good."

Liar! You just don't want me around.

But sending him away would prove useless. The way he was would never change, no matter how far he went.

"How can you be sure?" Evidently, she did not believe him, either. "You took him to the Hall and look where that's gotten him."

"He was just a toddler back then," James scoffed annoyed. "And one summer isn't enough anyway."

So regardless of his mother's protests, the desolate conclusion was that his father shipped him off to a place he did not know nor cared about knowing. Rejected, hurt, furious and exiled from his home, Fair Haven, he traveled northbound the long miles to Black Rose until he stared at the hills surrounding it. Cursing the Caldwells every step of the way, he vowed to wreak havoc on the blasted family and on anyone even remotely connected to it. He had the power to do it, after all, and he would not have thought twice about using it, had destiny not caught up with him at that last bend.

Twisting around the many hills leading up to the estate, he first heard a boy's happy shout, "Ready or not, here I come." Another curve and he glimpsed the back of him, raven black long hair to the shoulders lit by Stella's rays.

"It's no use running, Ylianor," the boy yelled at a little girl. "I'll catch you."

A scrawny dark-haired little thing, she stood atop the hill closest to him, looking down at him as though he were an invading army come to steal the most precious thing around. And she played it like someone had appointed her to stop him, an official defender of the place.

Of the boy, mostly, or so was his impression.

Worst of all, and so very surprising, she might just have the power to pull it off, the same kind of power he alone had thought to possess in the entire world.

Which infuriated him.

For how did a girl dare have something so unique?

And now she was flaring up, ready to strike at him!

Ha! Whatever her skills, she was no match for him! And he would show her, giving her a lesson she would never forget, not even if she lived to be a hundred. Mind made up, he was about to hit her with his potent brand of energy when something distracted him.

It was the boy, now looking at him from over his shoulder, with piercing black eyes staring directly at his core.

And his heart froze.

Transfixed and unmoving, he was unable to think, breathe or do much of anything besides recognizing the dark-haired boy. Not that he had ever laid eyes on him before in his life. If anything, the boy was a virtual stranger. So why did he have the sense of having known him since a time he could have no memory of? And why did the other boy appear to know him, too?

He read it so clearly in the inquisitive black gaze he could have no doubts about it. So compelling, too, he could not bother with insignificantly trivial things wanting to hurt him.

One dismissive fiery discharge and she was history, while he hurried to dismount and run the rest of the way to reach the intriguing boy.

"Hi, I'm Chris." Nearing him, the urge to touch him was overwhelming. "What's your name?" So he clasped his hand.

"I'm Duncan." Squeezing him hard, the boy searched his face as if looking for a sign that he evidently found. "Want to play?"

"Sure, but not with girls." He made a yak face to indicate how thoroughly they disgusted him.

"What girls?" Duncan grinned.

The innocent question made him feel like he and Duncan were alone in the world.

"I thought I saw one . . ." Unsure, he glanced around.

"Who? Ylianor?" Now smiling broadly, Duncan waved a hand aimlessly in the air. "Oh, don't mind her."

And looking at the incredibly handsome face framed by the long hair, he knew he had just met his one true love, the one and only person he would ever allow access to the whole of him. So he surrendered his heart, body and spirit right there on the spot. Then the phase sealed his destiny forever, and there could be no turning back.

The phase! What glorious time! He had simply loved every minute of the uncontrollable sexual urge for explosive releases that, once unleashed, quenched usually after a couple years of experiencing pure, unabated carnal pleasures with a special mate. If many considered it a rite of passage into adulthood, not everyone had it. Now why some would while others would not, he had no idea. He was just glad he got his and with the most gorgeous and intoxicating man of all, the tempest of the senses blowing his mind and body away.

Literally!

Then again, with a phase mate like Prince Duncan Caldwell, he had kind of expected it from the second he had laid eyes on the stunning boy playing in Black Rose. His only regret was that he had to wait until Duncan's adolescent years, which was the official time the phase started for boys and girls learning about sex with a friend of the same gender and age. So what if Duncan was two years his senior?

It made no difference to him. Not at the beginning, since he had decided that Prince Duncan Caldwell belonged to him. Not now that it was supposedly over and that he had known sex with so many different men, since Duncan remained the unparalleled paragon against which he rated anyone coming near his cock or ass. Not ever, since his ardent and aroused response to Duncan defied rationality and conventions even before sex complicated matters.

Impossible to define with mere words, he had known from the start he could never be *just friends* with Duncan Caldwell. For one thing, he loved the man too fucking much.

Had fallen in love with him from the moment his eyes had crossed the black liquid ones, to be precise. For another, sexual intimacy was a must that only added and renewed his connection to the prince. Simply being in the same room with him built up an erotic tension that hit him like a blow to the stomach. And it would not stop, until he had exhausted all the infinite sexual possibilities with the man he adored above and beyond his very life. So how to explain a link far deeper than skin level that went beyond any phase, beyond sex itself, no matter how much energy he devoted to it?

Safe to say, Duncan remained his deepest passion to date, even if it had not been smooth sailing all the way. But that was a thing of the past.

At least until she had to spoil everything by coming back.

CHAPTER FIFTEEN

When the phase began for Duncan, he could not but have it with Chris, even if a couple of years younger than him, powerless against the blond angel's overwhelming erotic attraction that literally consumed his throbbing desire like a fire.

That it had been something unusual, he had known it right from the start. The fever Chris unleashed so effortlessly with his mere presence had marked the difference even before any cock-wrenching phase. And it had made his uncontrollable lust last far beyond any reasonable expectation, until he had managed to end it. For it could not go on forever, regardless of how painfully his heart and cock ached for the loss of the fiery touch that alone seemed to quell his demanding sexual requirements.

Not that it had been an easy task.

Far from it.

His justification had been the need to have sex with women, something the phase did not give men any chance of doing. Naturally, Chris had not understood. For him, women were just a nuisance he barely tolerated. Which would not have bothered him, had only Chris left him room to explore a fascinatingly different world. But since it had set off Chris in a jealous rage, he had to kick him out of Black Rose.

Literally.

Not all Chris's fault, though. Seeing him inevitably led to hot sex, as though he just could not keep his hands off the tempting and extremely seductive body that always succeeded to plunge him right back into old patterns he had vowed to break. Impossible to trust his senses, he had enforced a physical distance from his phase mate, avoiding not only sex with Chris, but Chris all together.

That had left the angel no choice in the matter. Heartbroken, scorned and angry, the ravishing and intolerably captivating creature had gone to hide at the Hall, the seat of the High Council and of its leader, Arthur Fairchild. While he had sampled a great many variety of women from near and far. And things had worked just fine, at least until that blasted reunion at Belleview. Or rather, seeing Chris again during Carl Strepton's awful pledge reception had proved once and for all how bitter his freedom tasted.

No way around it. He missed the blond angel like crazy. Like a hole in his heart. Like the air from his lungs. It had taken only one glance to know he had been deceiving himself for the past two years. Because the fiery energy was all he craved, for that alone gave purpose to his life.

So the truth had crashed down on him, along with every wasted attempt to avoid thinking about him or pretending the world was the same without him. Tossing and turning during sleepless nights, his heartache had been all too real and painfully raw to mistake the feeling for anything else. Beyond the sex and games they had played when kids, he loved Chris as he would no one else in all his life, and there was no running away from this awareness. No amount of denials or women would ever change it. Because there was no one even remotely comparable to the blond angel's spark of vibrant life and torrid emotions that spoke to his heart with a secret code he had no trouble understanding.

As for the women, for a while he had deluded himself he just had not found the right one yet. Bottom line, though— women did not excite him as much as Chris had. At times, they even became annoying and boring, often with strings attached that prevented him from replicating the carefree sex and easy-going relationship he had with Chris. But how to breach what had become an unbearably cold distance and confess his love to his dazzling angel without incurring in rejection or worse?

CHAPTER SIXTEEN

W hen Arthur Fairchild, Leader of the High Council, had sent him an invitation to one of Rhapsen Hall's renowned parties, he thought he could have asked for no better occasion. And since it was the first time Arthur asked him to attend one, he rushed to the Hall with heart pounding in his throat and stomach clenched in anticipation every step of the way, relaxing only when the famous red roofs came into view.

"Welcome, my dear prince." Standing in front of the Hall's entrance, Lord Fairchild opened his arms. "I trust you had a pleasant journey."

"I did." He fell into them.

Arthur was not just Leader of the High Council, the highest commanding position of all. He had also been a close friend of his father, to the point he had ridden out to Black Rose when he had been born.

"And I thank you for the invitation." Pulling away, he took a step back.

"It was my pleasure and duty." Probably catching his puzzled look, he had been quick to add. "Go change, if you must, then reach us in the attic where everyone is." He gestured to a woman at his side. "Lillian will show you to your quarters and direct you to the attic."

He was about to follow the servant when Arthur clasped his arm tightly.

"Did I mention that you look impressively like your father?" The leader's eyes blazed in appreciation as he studied his face. "He was a great man, and you should be proud to resemble him so closely."

"I am, Leader." Touched more than he cared to admit, he lowered his gaze. "And there's not a day that goes by that I don't miss him."

"As do I." Arthur's voice was so soft he was not sure he heard correctly. "All right, now go." Slapping his shoulder, Arthur pushed him forward. "And I'll see you in the attic."

At Lillian's heels, he was exceedingly glad he had someone showing him around the diabolic place. Too complicated for his taste, this Hall appeared to be a labyrinth someone had deliberately built to befuddle people trying to get around it. Lucky for him, it was his first time there and from all the twists and turns he had to suffer through, he hoped it would be his last.

Which would not be the case, alas.

His father's death had left him the responsibility of filling the Caldwell's permanent council seat for the Silcamore District. A duty no heir could refuse, and one that he would fulfill as soon as he read Prince Charles's will. But since it was still a while away, he had no obligations yet to learn his way around the Hall and its devious maze.

Unlike him, Lillian had no trouble finding her way around the complex structure, and after what seemed like unending turnarounds, she finally stopped in front of a door on the second floor.

"Here you are, sir." Throwing it open, she gestured inside a big and spacious room, lit and warmed by a cozy fire. "I'll let you unpack and check on you later—"

"No, wait." Tossing his sac on the floor, something told him he had no time to waste. "Just take me to the attic now." Wherever that was, he knew he would never find it by himself.

"As you wish, sir." Spinning around, she went in the opposite direction, and he braced himself for another half an hour of aimless twisting in vain.

But the moment he saw men of all ages milling around a staircase, he knew he had reached his destination. So he dismissed the girl and climbed up two steps at a time. Heart now drumming in his ears, he went past the many who streamed up and down the stairs, some carrying food or drinks, most talking with amused smirks on their faces. If he recognized anybody at all, he hardly noticed, prey as he was to a nagging feeling someone waited for him inside the crowded attic.

Which was impossible, for he had told no one he would be there.

Heart about to explode from his chest, he was stepping through the threshold when a young man stopped him.

"Duncan, I had no idea you'd be coming." Eyes ablaze in interest, the young man approached him and raised his voice to overcome the loud background chatter, "How have you been?"

"Fine, I guess and . . ." The words died in his throat.

There he was. The most beautiful and impossibly gorgeous man of all was coming right at him from across the room, the blue-gray eyes that had tormented his dreams staring straight at him.

In a rush of uncontrollable excitement, his mouth went dry as he melted in liquid fire, the rest of the world fading into nothingness. Unable to tear his gaze away, time returned him to his childhood, at the exact moment he had first laid eyes on his stunning angel. So the flood of long denied emotions was simply too powerful and shattered whatever slight form of control he had achieved in the years without Chris at his side.

By the gods, how could he have been so foolish to think it could ever be over between him and the fiery angel? To believe, even for one second, his heart could have forgotten the one man who had exalted his senses like no one else before or since?

"Hello, lover." Halting in front of him, the blue-gray gaze ate him up literally. "Missed me?"

"I can't even begin to tell you how much." Out of breath, he could not avoid the painful lurch of his cock.

If anything, Chris had grown more splendid and desirable than ever. And his shaft's sudden erection was proof he hungered only to touch him and make love until he was too exhausted to think straight.

"I knew you would." Gaze dropping to his groin, Chris's smug smile of satisfaction was clear indication he had not missed the swift reaction. "Come." Clasping his hand, he pulled him out of the attic. "Let's go somewhere more private." Hurrying to the stairs, he hesitated to search his face. "How about your room?"

"If you can find it," he joked. "For I certainly can't."

"Oh, I've got a pretty good guess of where Arthur has placed you." Spinning around, he flew downward. "On the second floor, right?"

"Right." Close at his heels, he did not stop to wonder how the angel knew.

He just followed blindly, not surprised to notice many wistful glances in Chris's direction.

Small wonder!

His blond angel inevitably attracted attention, with some even attempting to detain him in spite of his evident lack of interest. Not that he allowed them. Without even bothering to be polite, he continued his hasty flight through the bewildering intricacy whose sole purpose was to confound his orientation.

But as long as Chris led him, who gave a damn about where he was? Or where he was going for that matter?

His destination was bliss.

Of that, he had no doubts.

So he followed as in a daze, until he reached his room and slammed the world outside.

CHAPTER SEVENTEEN

The first round did not last longer than a blowjob. The pressure was simply too strong to hope for any real fun and game. It was enough to swallow the long thick gland standing straight up in the air, while nailing Chris's throat to the mattress with his own gigantic erection for things to get too hot, too soon. One sharp intake and Chris spilled his guts, just as he was doing all the way to his angel's stomach.

The second round was fiercer. Pulling Chris to his feet, he flattened him to the nearest wall, his fingers already probing the tender ass ring that opened completely at his rimming. That someone had fucked Chris recently, very recently, was obvious from the enlargement sucking his fingers to the hilt. And goddamn it! It spun his excitement to the stars.

His cock as rigid as before the explosive climax, he shoved into the scorching hole and the sensation of melting inside liquid fire almost made him come again. It was something so unique no one else felt quite like Chris in or out of bed. Like he was pure fire all over, ready to flare up and shatter the world itself at any moment. And he just could not get over how much he had missed him and the sensation of riding on a scalding pyre of leaping flames.

Adjusting his position, Chris flung out his butt further, and he penetrated to his guts with one swift thrust. Then wanting to take complete charge, he wrapped his palm around his angel's swollen stick twitching in anticipation from the master's touch. And that blew his mind away.

Not because he would be commanding Chris's pleasure.

Because somehow, he had the feeling he, Duncan Caldwell, alone in the universe, had the power to control the burning blaze twisting his hips to screw his monster all the way to his throat.

Which seemed absurd, but so very arousing at so many levels that he could not hold it together anymore. Ramming and jerking faster, he sped up the tempo for both, spelling inevitable jets of whitish juice all over the ass and the floor.

"Oh, lover, I'd almost forgotten how good it feels with you." Slumping against the wall, Chris tightened his asshole as though to prevent his shaft from falling out.

"Liar." He challenged. "As if I didn't know this is all you thought about."

"Maybe it's not such a great idea to have sex with someone who knows me so well." Spinning around, Chris grinned and wrenched his newly stirring erection, stroking it forcefully. "Or has such a great big juicy piece."

"As if you didn't get your fill already." That his angel loved cocks was no mystery. "I bet all you do around here is spread your ass and have someone stuff it to your ears." Clamping Chris's shoulders, he threw him to the ground in front of the bed. "Just tell me." Lowering, he snapped back the blond head, digging it onto the mattress. "How much of a slut have you become?" Duncan whispered in his ear.

"Enough to please as demanding a master as you are," Chris immediately upped the stakes.

"Then prove it." Calling his bluff, he aimed for his wide-open mouth then slammed hard and deep.

On his knees, back and head arched on the bed, the angel was helpless to do anything except swallow the stiff rod to the throat. The gagging and spurting did not ease the force or the swing of his repeated blows. Wanting Chris to devour it all, he did not slow down or show any mercy. Did not give him time to breathe, either, relishing each sharp intake that squeezed and lapped every side of him.

Drowning by now, he loved every exquisite moment of it. All to Chris's credit, since all the extra experience had perfected his art of sucking to unparalleled skill.

"Stop, Angel." Holding the blond head still, he removed his pulsating beast from the heated cavity. "I can't come in your mouth again." Sliding him up on the bed, he flailed out the long elegant legs, ass dangling beyond the edge of the mattress. "When I haven't gotten enough of this." Widening the firm buttocks, he flung into the constricted entrance, stretching it to fit his huge size.

"It's all yours." Breathing hoarsely, Chris rotated to impale the taut equipment to the balls. "It never belonged to anyone else." From the regret in his tone, he knew he meant it.

So what if his angel had been giving it around to just about anybody who had asked for it?

"Damn right it is." His and his alone, marked and sealed by a phase that allowed men and women to be the first sexual partners of a friend of the same age and gender. It was the reason phases became privileged relationships, often valued far above pledges themselves. "I've been the first to claim it, so it's mine." Grabbing Chris's hips, he tugged him down, so fiercely that his shaft hit with double the impact. "No matter how many will possess it now or in the future, you'll always remember how I cracked it the first time around."

"As long as you keep ramming it as hard as right now . . ." Bending backward, Chris managed to get more cock up his ass. "I'll never need anybody else."

"Shut up." One thing he had always known about his angel was that one lover would never be enough, not even one as skilled as he was. There was just something about Christopher Templeton that called for greater amounts of sex and varieties than anybody else, even if most everybody spent endless days and nights in sexual activities alone. "I kind of prefer you as a slut."

"You really don't want this to last much longer, do you?" Barely hanging on, this comment sent Chris reeling toward the edge.

"Oh, no, you don't." Blocking his near burst, he rolled back on his knees, carrying Chris to an upright position, practically having him seat on his erection. "There'll be no coming for you until I say so." Swinging upward, he made his angel feel just how powerfully he could blow his behind from this position, too. "Or until I crack your ass for real." He grinned. "Whichever comes first."

"Then hurry, lover." Accelerating, Chris wrapped his neck, muscles already quivering in anticipation of the coming release. "'Cause I can't take it much longer."

The last was a husky whisper that liquefied his insides.

"You'll have to." Easier said than done, he had the same urge to let it go.

Still, he did not comply.

Flipping Chris on the floor, he crushed the lithe body to the ground. Legs cradled to his chest, his beefy piece had no obstacles to split the ass as it pumped to advance to the guts.

The hammering turned frantic. His potent blows forced Chris to dance to his frenzied tune. An intense rhythm that was sure to crack his ass, like he had promised. Not that the angel seemed to mind. He returned every thrust with a swing back that gobbled up the thick rod to its very root. Not content, he splayed those legs and sprawled on top of him, his body crushing the slimmer one under his weight.

The new position allowed for greater leeway, so he plunged headfirst into the accommodating flesh that drew him deeper with every pounding. And Chris's rear responded beautifully, rising up whenever he pushed down, coming together in the delicious slamming that also rubbed the blond angel's throbbing cock against his belly.

"Fuck, lover." Another shove and Chris was about to unload everything on his chest. "I really can't resist one second longer."

"Not yet." Pulling out of the snug confinement, he rolled him on all fours. A quick adjustment and he impaled him again, turgid gland so slick it slipped so far up he hoped it would never come out again.

The beat resumed, faster than before. More cock wrenching, too, for he clutched Chris's vibrating shaft. The sheer pressure of the come about to explode from its tip was jerking it uncontrollably on its own, which told him his game was about to end whether he wanted to or not.

So he took pity on his seductive phase mate.

"All right, Angel." Stretching forward, his lips caught Chris's ear. "Come for me now."

The words hardly out of his mouth, Chris gasped and clenched around his bursting equipment. No, no way he could have held it given the potency of Chris's orgasm that shattered him inside and out.

But the night was still young, and his senses so very hungry for his blond magnificent lover that quitting was the farthest thing from his mind. And if Chris's ass was as large and as sore as if gangbanged an entire nightlong, it was just a sign of how badly he had missed him for the past two years.

CHAPTER EIGHTEEN

"By the gods, I did miss you so fucking much." As dawn broke, Chris's chin dug on his chest, lying as he was on the bed belly down. "I was so mad at you I wished I never saw you again in my life." He caressed his face lovingly. "But, boy, am I glad no god cared to listen, or I'd have missed this glorious night with all its incredible sex." His gaze sparkled mischievously as though already reliving it.

"I'm sorry I hurt you." Catching Chris's hand, he squeezed it tightly. "But I needed the space to know women, and you just wouldn't give it to me."

"Is that why you kicked me out of Black Rose?" Chris grinned, though the hint of a pained expression crossed his arresting blue-gray eyes.

"No." Pulling him up, he nuzzled his neck. "That was because you were too distracting, and I couldn't resist having sex with you every time you were around."

"I knew it was all your fault!" With a triumphant gleam, Chris straightened.

"No, it was all yours." Tackling the man down took him no effort. "You and your goddamn insisting I had sex with you even if I made it clear I just wanted to be friends—"

"Ha! As if you and I could ever be *just friends*!" Chris spat. "Do you honestly think you can ever ignore me?" He grabbed his now limp piece. "That your cock won't stiffen the moment it sees me?"

The blasted angel knew it did better than anybody else. Now more than ever, since his equipment was already turning to stone in spite of an entire night's worth of sex.

"All right, I was wrong." Halting the angel's erotic up and down slides, he locked gazes with the blue-gray one. "Totally and completely." He just had to taste Chris's thin lips before everything that pressed on his chest burst out with the explosive force he felt brewing beneath the surface. "Because I love you, Christopher Templeton, and it has nothing to do with our fantastic sex." At the second kiss, he pushed his tongue inside to sweep the warm cavity opening up immediately. Then he drew away for he had just skimmed the surface of the deep emotions setting him on fire. "I love you with everything I've got—body, mind and spirit." He spelled out the words clearly, so Chris would have no room for misunderstanding. "There's no way I can ever live without you, which is why I was twice as wrong in sending you away. Only I didn't understand it at the time, because I was too busy trying to deny it." He shook his head, long hair flying around. "But it was no use. You're all I think about, Angel, the one thought before I close my eyes and the first when I open them again." Crushing the lithe body to him, his lips reached Chris's ear. "And this power you have over me leaves no room for anybody else, no matter how hard I convinced myself I'd find the right woman if I didn't see you."

"So it's my fault you didn't find her?" Chris snuggled inside his embrace, trying to hide a smug smirk.

"Yeah, it absolutely is." Lowering his gaze, he loved the play of fire lighting the fair skin from behind. "Because I kept looking for you in every woman I met. And I met quite a few."

"I know." Disentangling, Chris stretched back to level their gazes, the blue-gray eyes blazing maliciously. "People at the Hall do nothing but have sex and gossip all day long, so they kept me up to date about your conquests. I hated it whenever a new woman got in the picture, but I'd rejoice when it didn't work out."

"You bastard!" Playfully, he faked a punch at Chris's arm. "So it really was you."

"Of course it was." Laughing, the blond angel caught his fist and kissed it. "The last thing I wanted was for our phase to turn into a pledge, like it happened to so many around here." Clasping his arm, Chris dragged himself closer. "Like with Trent, who's a real jerk but didn't deserve that his phase mate pledged a couple of weeks after their phase was over. And it crushed him."

"Maybe his mom made him do it." He chuckled. "I know how hard mine tries to get me to pledge, and she hasn't stopped since."

"Your mom won't stop until you do." Chris joined in the amusement. "She's like most who think that a good phase should result in a hasty pledge."

"Didn't your mom push you in that direction, too?" Although he had seen Claire Templeton only twice in his life, he was pretty sure she would have wanted the same thing for her son.

Particularly since he was her favorite.

"My mom?" Chris smirked. "Haven't seen her since you kicked me out of Black Rose."

"You mean to tell me you haven't been back home since then?" That was a surprise.

"Nope, I carefully avoided the place." *Because I was too broken up inside.*

If Chris did not actually say it in so many words, he had no problem picking it up from his troubled expression.

"Just stuck to the Hall the whole time," the stunning blond man added huskily.

"What about your father? How did you avoid him?" Settling back on his heels, he regarded his angel. "As I recall, he's the vice-leader, so I guess he spends most of his time here, too."

"Oh, the Hall is such a big place there's no risk of running into each other." A naughty smile twisted the thin lips. "Particularly if you keep different hours."

"As different as day and night?" He was getting a clear picture of just how Chris had spent the two years of separation.

"Exactly." Rewarding his intuition with a huge smile that split his agonizingly beautiful face, Chris slid on his knees to get closer. "Being part of the Arthur boys as they call us, I stick pretty much to the night hours and seldom get around in the day. My father instead keeps busy during the daytime."

"Arthur boys?" Duncan frowned not sure he understood. "What's—"

"Nothing you need to worry about, lover." Quick to intercept him, Chris pressed his palm on his open lips. "Just a bunch of us having wild sex and parties every goddamn night we can."

He said it all at once as though he wanted to get it off his chest.

"What you need concern yourself about is that I love you, Duncan Caldwell." There was no disguising the depth of the emotion exploding from every word and shining from his eyes. "Love you like I've never loved anybody in my whole life, like I'll never love anybody in my whole life. You are the only person that matters to me, the only one I'd die for in a heartbeat were you only to ask. For you, and you alone, I'd do anything, and even if you broke my heart, I'm ready to start everything over with you. To surrender everything I've got as long as you claim it."

The intensity of the words took his breath away.

"I told you all this before." His gaze trained steadily on him. "But you didn't believe me then. I hope tonight I've proven just how much you mean to me once and for all."

"As if I ever needed proof, Angel." Taking advantage of their nearness, he attacked Chris's lips in a hard, sweeping kiss aimed at getting his tongue down his stomach. "But like I said, I needed the space."

"Didn't help you much," Chris retorted. "Not in the way of finding any suitable woman."

He scoffed, "Just because I haven't found the right one yet, doesn't mean she isn't out there somewhere."

"After having tried so many, how do you know for sure?" Chris challenged on purpose. "How do you know she even exists?"

"I just do." Wanting to drive his point across, he landed the angel on the bed, sprawling on top to keep him down. "Just gotta find her."

"If you do, she'll turn out to be some stupid willy-nilly who'll be so much in awe of your good looks that all she'll be able to do is spreading her legs during the heat," the angel spat venomously. "A boring nobody who won't believe her luck she has such a handsome man wanting to pledge to—"

"You don't like women much, do you?" He could not help the irony lacing his tone.

"As a matter of fact, I don't." That sounded final. "You, more than anyone, should know I'm not interested in them, since we've talked about it so many times during the phase."

"That was kids' talk." He dismissed the whole thing with a careless wave of the hand. "Now we're older and hopefully, we've changed enough to—"

"Not me!" Chris almost jumped away from his grasp. "Ever since I can remember I've liked only men. And after you threw me out, I wanted to fuck as many as I could. That's why I came straight here, and I worked my way from the top down to the lowliest servant, including everything in between." The blue-gray eyes flared in triumph. "I've had sex with just about anything that moves with a cock."

"Including the leader himself?" Knowing his angel, he assumed he had.

"He was the first one I got my hands on." Evidently proud of himself, Chris did not hide it. "Or rather my mouth," he was quick to set the record straight. "After blowing him good and proper the moment I got here, I went straight to the very top of the Hall." His eyes glittered triumphantly at his achievement. "It's amazing what skillful cock sucking can get you these days."

"Well I'm impressed." He truly was. "And knowing your competitive nature, I'm also guessing you're the first of the Arthur boys." Dots were connecting fast in his mind.

"Of course, how could I not?" Definitely modesty was not one of his angel's strong suits. "Every night we all meet in the attic, and Arthur makes up all sorts of contests like, *How many cocks can you blow*, or, *How many cocks can your ass take*. The more the better, but you have to take the most to win first prize, the chance to sleep with the leader. And even if competition is fierce, I always end up sleeping with him 'cause no one is at my level. So now, I practically spend every night with Arthur, even if I always have to prove myself worthy of the honor." He beamed one of his special smiles. "Just think, even if I have a room all my own, I never use it 'cause I always stay with him."

"And his pledge mate doesn't mind?" True, pledges were mostly a matter of convenience. Still, to be so out of touch with one's mate seemed kind of strange.

"She doesn't even live here." Chris shrugged indifferently. "Just proves pledges don't have to get in the way of satisfying sex." He shifted position. "And that's what Arthur wants me to have day in and day out."

"I guess the heat doesn't work for them, either." Not that

he would know anything about it. Just what he heard from his mother.

"I guess not, though I don't believe too much in this heat thing." Chris frowned in puzzlement. "Most of the pledges I know here at the Hall can't seem to stand one another. So how can anything overcome that?"

"Whatever it is, it must work, and the sooner you pledge, the sooner you'll find out." The last one was a provocation, of course.

"I'm never going to pledge," Chris hissed vehemently. "Not with a woman anyway." His expression relaxed as his gaze leveled to Duncan's. "I'd do it with you, though."

"Not a possibility, I'm afraid, however flattering your offer." And he felt a small twinge of regret at the realization. "But I'm sure there are plenty of women here at the Hall who'd give their right arm to have you—"

"Something more, actually." Superciliously, Chris looked like he had taken due notice and turned down each and every one. "But they're all as boring as their conversation, as unappealing as their treacherous curves, as revoltingly yielding as—"

"So you just need to find the one who defies you." Seemed like the logical solution.

"I . . ." Something undefinable flashed in the blue-gray eyes as though maybe he had found her already. "I don't think she exists." Quickly suppressed, it was gone before he could analyze it. "Plus, I'd rather stick to men. And as a third born, I don't think my family will want me to pledge as hard as they want Steve or Bran to."

It made sense that Chris's older brothers would have far greater pressure to fulfill what was a family obligation.

"Which is just as well, 'cause I really detest women." Chris sounded adamant.

"Good thing at yesterday's party there were so many of

them." He chortled.

"Not a coincidence, lover, since I was in charge of the organization," Chris snickered. "I had sex with at least two thirds of them, which is the reason I invited them."

"So you invited me?" Something did not add up, for he clearly remembered Arthur's seal on the envelope he had received.

"No, I . . ." A wave like pain made Chris's lower lip tremble. "I would have never invited you. I was too afraid you'd simply ignore it, and I couldn't have stood another rejection." Getting a hold of himself, his expression relaxed. "Arthur himself must have sent you the invitation without telling me."

"He probably figured you'd keep busy with all the one third you hadn't fucked yet," he joked.

"True, I could've fucked them all." Nestling closer, Chris fixed his face. "But the saddest thing is that I don't give a damn about any of them. Not even of Arthur who practically adores me and can't wait to split my ass every chance he gets." He sighed. "Truth is—the more men fuck me, the more I wanted you and the more I felt empty inside." A defiant light brightening his blue-gray eyes, he raised his gaze. "So you see things haven't changed for me, not one bit. And even if I'm older now, I don't feel any different about you than I did at the height of our phase." Pulling back a little, he raked nimble fingers through Duncan's long hair. "You are and remain all my heart craves despite all my attempts to erase you from it." Chris's lips curled in a snarl. "Hardly surprising it never worked, if you consider I loved you from the first moment I laid eyes on you. And as if it wasn't enough, now I love you a whole lot more than I ever did."

"And I love you." Having the angel so sweet and yielding beneath him, his cock began to stir to life. "I just don't understand why we're so into each other years after our phase ended. I mean, other people's phases seem nothing like ours, particularly after it's over — "

"In case you haven't noticed, we're different — always have been, always will be." The angel seemed to have no doubts about it. "And our feelings are so unique they'll never just disappear, no matter how hard we try." Arching up his hips, the tantalizing creature signaled that the conversation was having a definite effect on him as well, given the stone-like bulge digging in his stomach. "You belong to me, lover. That's all there is to it and the sooner you accept it, the better off we'll be."

"What if I found my special woman and pledged?" Duncan goaded for the fun of it.

"You can do whatever you like." But Chris did not fall for it. "Just don't shut me out again." The blue-gray eyes clouded. "That's all I ask of you. That you spare me another agony."

"Just for the record, I suffered, too." He did not want to dwell on how bad it had been. "So I don't intend to go through it again. Believe me."

"Then don't." Rocking his hips, it was clear Chris was ready to move on.

At least as far as sex went, for he was driving him crazy again.

"We can have our fun like old times." Immediately responding to his arousal, Chris accelerated his swinging. "Which won't prevent you from doing whatever else you need to do, including fucking as many women as you like." And imprisoned him inside an impossibly seductive trap. "I know that's what I'm planning to do."

"Women will be delighted to know you changed your mind." Jamming a knee between Chris's legs, he spread them wide, then aimed for the center hole and impaled the not-so-narrow asshole with one decisive thrust. The cramped space welcomed him without any hesitation, wrapping the fleshy walls around his demanding equipment pumping to possess everything, guts included.

"I meant men," the blond angel snapped, raising his hips to facilitate the penetration.

"What if I asked you to share one with me?" Sinking to the hilt, he was about to lose it.

Again!

"I'm so not interested." That it was a tease was kind of evident from the lightness of the tone. "But if you fuck me like this with her watching, I just might consent."

"Slutty vain and heartless angel." The mere image turned him on so much he had to work hard not to spill it all. "You just can't wait to have one who'll eat her heart out from just staring at your magnificent cock." He groaned picturing the scene. "'Cause you aren't going to let her touch it, much less play with it, right?"

"That's the idea." And it appealed so much to Chris that he was barely holding on.

"Then I'll find you plenty of them." Unbelievable how fiercely Chris's fire was now consuming him with the need to burst.

Adjusting his aim, he hammered what remained of a once tight ass until it sucked him up completely. Gone apparently the barriers that separated them, he had the sense of falling straight into Chris's essence, which blew his mind and body apart, shattered by the rapid jets flooding that scorching behind.

And Chris's come swamping his chest and belly was a sure sign their phase was evolving to a different level, with increasing challenges that promised a brand-new world of possibilities.

CHAPTER NINETEEN

"So, did you miss me, lover?" *And why did you have to god-damn fuck her?*

Duncan stank of her all over. From his mouth to his cock, her stench had seeped to every one of his pores, and he could not stand it.

It enraged him, to be precise, particularly when he realized she had been a virgin. For nothing could hide that metallic taste of blood on his lover's cock that must have spent the night embedded in her, cooped up in that shelter on Lake Lilly he had told his mother about.

Which further infuriated him.

How dare she?

Even before the phase, Duncan Caldwell had been his chosen one, and that pesky little nuisance had been the only real threat in the competition for Duncan's love, if not the only one foolish enough to challenge him openly. Not that she stood a chance against him. He would just have to see to it she did not now, either, or he would have to teach her another lesson Templeton style. After all, he had taken care of that bothersome pest once already.

He would this time, too.

She could count on it.

Only this time, he would have no pity!

"More than I can say." Pressing Chris's face to his hips, Duncan gagged him good and proper.

Thank the gods he could use his fury to fuel up the very fiery blowjob he was delivering. On his knees in front of

Duncan, he had not allowed his lover to budge since shutting the office door behind him. Stuffed to his ears, he swallowed the giant beast without caring if he quaffed to death. That magnificent piece of firm, hard meat was worth it, particularly now that someone was trying to steal it away from him and from right under his very nose.

Ha! Over his dead body!

"This delectable mouth of yours, especially." With one swift thrust, Duncan gagged him, ramming a veritable monster all the way to his stomach.

No escape possible, not since the prince clamped his head and blocked it, pushing his hips forward and fucking his mouth as though it were his ass. Delightful if he did not have to gurgle so much or breathe whenever Duncan slammed so deep inside he could do nothing except suffocate. But since the cock was becoming only more monstrous, he dared not pull back or stop any of it.

"Which is incomparable to anything else." Yanking his blond hair, Prince Caldwell tossed his head as far back as it could go, then cramped it with a fierce swing that had him reeling back.

Spurting, he kept his balance somehow, fighting the fat crown with an apt tongue trying to prevent more dangerous lurches. Not that he could. Duncan was a master in domination, had only become more skilled at it since hooking up with him again. And that was something he adored about the prince, which usually made him surrender time after time to the man he recognized as his superior.

But this time, he was way too pissed off to play games.

Managing to wriggle free from Duncan's iron hold, he raised his gaze. "Which didn't stop you from sticking it somewhere it didn't belong for sure."

"Tsk, tsk, I don't recall giving you permission to speak." Amused, Duncan stuck his rigid shaft right where it had been. "First, I want to come—"

"'Cause she wasn't good enough for that either?" Somehow dodging the bulging tip wanting to shut him up, he challenged Duncan openly.

"No, because this is your job." Undeterred, Duncan clamped his neck tighter. "To suck me and choke on her taste." Then he got the gigantic erection all the way inside, ravaging the wet cavity fiercer than before.

Goddamn you, lover! This time, he had no choice except open wide and let him claim the entire space available. His tongue powerless to halt the vigorous attack to his throat, he could only submit and harden his intakes to speed up his lover's orgasm, which was building faster than he expected.

Hitting the tip of his tongue right around the fat crown did the trick. It was his lover's secret spot. The one he prided himself on knowing best than anybody. It was the same one that, if rubbed in the right way, would make Prince Caldwell explode like he was doing at the moment, drowning his mouth in a deluge of sperm.

"Much better." Holding on to him, the man smirked in satisfaction.

"I can't believe you'd go with such a poor lay that your cock was in dire need of release," he spat, trying to get free.

"Hate to admit it, but you're right." Still gripping him, Duncan refused to let him go. "Isabella Turner was a disappointingly boring ass, in and out of bed."

"I wasn't talking about her," he scoffed through clenched teeth. "But about the other one."

"The other one?" Black eyes clearly making fun of him, Duncan chortled. "Oh, you mean *the other one.*" For undoubtedly, he was getting a kick out of it all. "That other one was more than good." From the husky aroused tone, he meant it for sure. "She was great."

"Was she now?" Chris snapped. "Then why couldn't you

wait to stick your cock in me—"

"Jealous, Angel?" Grinning broadly, Duncan pushed him to the ground, flipped him on his belly and pulled down his pants.

All in one gesture alone, it seemed.

"Of a boring virgin who nobody bothered to fuck until she was too old for a decent phase?" He did not care how cruel he sounded. Plus, he remembered her well enough to suppose she had not gone through the phase. "Never!"

"You know that not everyone has a phase." And Duncan's regretful tone was not helping any. "So not her fault she didn't." Nor was that scrumptious piece of hard meat sliding on the crack between his ass cheeks and getting stiffer by the second. "But very good about the virgin part. How did you figure that out?"

"In case you haven't noticed, you have her blood all over your cock." Not exactly the truth, still it was a close approximation.

"Oh, I did notice." If it was a lie, Duncan worked hard not to make it sound like one. "Only she was so exciting I didn't want to wash away her taste."

Before he could retort, his buttocks were spread wide and his ass impaled. So forcefully that, had he not had all the years of training, he would have jumped from the pain. Instead, he relaxed all together, taking one deep breath after another until the initial burning faded.

By then, Duncan's long gland had reached his guts and was now aiming for his throat.

"Trust me, lover." He tried to keep focused, however good the steady back pumping. "It wasn't that hot."

"Only because you already hate her guts." Pulling out and getting up, Duncan raised his rear. "And you don't even know her."

"But I do." Face squashed to the ground, he could barely

move. "That Ylianor Meyer has always smelled like trouble to me from the first day."

"You even remember her name?" Duncan bent to peer at him. "I'm damn impressed. You never remember anybody's name, not even if your life depended on it. Not even if you've sucked his cock for hours—"

"I didn't remember her name," he lied, cursing himself for the slip.

Of course, Duncan would notice. The gorgeous man knew him better than anybody else after all.

"I don't waste my time on people I don't give a damn about." His mind spun frantically to come up with a good excuse. "If it wasn't for your mother's chatter—"

"You're lying," Duncan whispered hoarsely in his ear. Then straightening, he bent his knees and shoved from above.

Ouch!

Again, he said nothing. The new position allowed for greater impact, something the prince took immediate advantage of, while Chris had to hang on for dear life. And fuck if he did not love it!

This rough treatment from the man who was the absolute best in sex was fast pushing him over the edge of a shattering climax.

"David told me you knew her when we were kids." Then again, nothing like Duncan's words to quell the hot wave coiling around the tip of his erection.

"David told you?" That nosy twerp always did stick his nose where it did not belong, minding everyone's business except his own. "Why did he have to tell you? Don't you remember her?"

"Funny thing is I don't, not at all." Still pounding his behind, Duncan stepped up the tempo until his balls almost followed the cock inside. "My memory has blanks when it comes to her, and I can't find any trace of her anywhere."

No wonder. "But I bet she must've taken great pains to re-mind you."

"Actually, she didn't." Sliding to the root, fat heavy balls slapped his thighs. "David told me all about her after I met her."

"And you still fucked her?" Part of him could not get over the fact Duncan had actually done it.

"What can I say?" Inflicting merciless hits, Duncan seemed bent on cracking his butt sooner rather than later. "She's as irresistible as your ass."

"Fuck you, lover!" Damn if his competitive nature did not flare up all together at the detestable comparison. "And her!"

"Too late, Angel." Laughing outright, Duncan freed his ass ring. "I already did." Then hauling him to his feet, he dragged him to the large desk and sprawled him on it. "And she was fantastic."

"Then why aren't you screwing her now?" Back flattened to the wooden surface, legs splayed, butt up in the air, he seethed in pure rage.

"'Cause I wanted to tell you all about it first." That Dun-can was goading him on purpose seemed kind of evident.

That Chris was falling for it harder than he should have was equally clear.

"About how much fun I had ripping her apart." And it appeared he wanted to do the same to him, if the powerful slam inside the already sore butt was any indication.

"Including her ass?" Well, if the prince wanted to play, he would go along with it, particularly since the relentless beat was pounding his backside to a pulp.

"Didn't get around to that yet." Which meant he would soon enough.

And he could have just kicked himself for giving his lover one more excuse to fuck her again.

"But I'm sure it'll be worth my time." Without fail, Duncan did not let the opportunity to rub it in escape him. "Just imagine a virgin ass."

This last was a throaty whisper the dastardly man breathed in his ears while crushing him under his weight.

"How long has it been since you had one?" He licked the earlobe before biting it.

And Chris began losing it.

For real.

Because it was impossible to ignore the scorching surge of pleasure shooting from his ass up, or Duncan's huge equipment now firmly embedded and crushed between his fleshy walls. Which only made him want more—more cock, more length, more thickness. His ass had to explode from it all. Literally.

Then Duncan wrapped a cool, very cool palm around his taut gland. And this was really the end.

Ever since childhood, he could never stand people touching him. Probably a matter of his extreme heat that always boiled him like a fever, which made other people's warmth unbearable. But it never happened with Duncan. He, alone in all the world, had a cool touch that Chris craved like crazy. The sharp contrast between their body temperatures always heightened his arousal, to the point that a mere touch from Duncan would turn him on to immediate stone-like hardness.

Now it was no different, and the dark energy mixing with his fiery brand spun his senses into a vortex of sensations. Ass fucked and cock jerked, he gave in to the tide bursting from the tip of his erection in uncontrollable fat drops that stained the side of the desk. And Duncan trying to hold on was simply ridiculous at this point, and Chris's maximum satisfaction was hearing his gasp and feeling the hot load releasing all inside his ass.

CHAPTER TWENTY

"Goddamn you, lover." Gone the fierce and bitter anger, he relaxed all together, pinned to the desk by Duncan's weight collapsing on him. "You didn't have to go into so much detail."

"Why not?" Tilting his face to a side, the dark-haired man trapped his lips and ravaged them in a hard kiss that made him want to start everything over.

Tongue sticking through, he swept the warm cavity at leisure, drinking of his taste until he moaned from the sheer hunger of wanting his prince all over again.

Which was not going to happen soon for his dastardly lover drew back.

"I knew it would make for fantastic sex." Straightening, Duncan closed his fly. "And for the perfect way to steam you off." Going toward the fireplace, he fell on the couch.

Hardly surprising the man would know precisely what ticked him off and how to cool him down. "It's just too bad you can't use it for your mother and sister." Pulling up his pants, he reached his phase mate and sat next to him. "And they're a lot more enraged than I am." Well, maybe he was exaggerating it a bit. "In case you haven't noticed, Ylianor is your mother's only topic now." Catching the liquid black gaze, he held it. "She's obsessed by her and asked me to do something to avoid your entrapment, same as your father's with Ylianor's mother. But I'm too late." By the gods, he wanted to drown inside the stunning black pools caressing his face. "So what's the idea of bringing her back here and fucking with her, too?"

"She just lost her father, her job and her home, so I wanted to help her." Evidently in need of physical contact, Duncan pulled him against his very masculine frame, digging the blond head in his chest. "Especially since she offered me shelter and food when I lost my way back from Isabella."

"How could you possibly get lost so close to Black Rose?" This really did not make sense! "When you can ride from here to Harbor Town blindfold?"

"I don't know." The prince shrugged. "I just did until I stumbled into the village. By then, it was raining so hard I couldn't keep going, so I knocked on her door. And when she opened it, I had no idea who she was."

"And now that you do, why did you bring her here anyway?" *Why didn't you leave her to rot in that goddamn hole where you were never supposed to find her?*

"I told you." The black eyes flashed annoyed. "I felt sorry for her."

"Enough to screw her, apparently." No, he would not let it rest.

"Enough to know she's different, very different from any other woman I know," Duncan retorted. "And not just because she looks like me."

"She still does?" *As if things aren't bad enough already.* "I thought it was a childhood resemblance, and that she'd outgrow it."

"She didn't, and it's quite striking." Duncan paused as though lost in some kind of memory. "But that's not the strangest thing when it comes to her." Absentmindedly, a hand raked a hand through his short blond hair. "Call me crazy, but when she opened that door all I could think about was that she belonged to me." He angled his head to lock their gazes. "I didn't know the first thing about her, but deep down I knew she was mine like no other person will ever be." He sighed. "Not even you, Angel."

Ouch!

That fucking hurt!

Worse than when he had slammed in his ass.

"Is that why you already care for her?" So he bit back with all the venom he could muster.

Duncan huffed, "I don't —"

"Save it, lover." He regarded him coldly. "Whatever you say, she remains a servant, and you never bothered with the likes of them." Maybe appealing to his lover's aristocratic taste might bring some sense into him. "No, there must be something else entirely at work, like that witchcraft your mother seems to be fixated on, something that has nothing to do with her level or her appearance. 'Cause I know for a fact you wouldn't have looked at her twice if you didn't think she was worth something beyond a heated fuck." Raising his head, his lips traveled to Duncan's ear. "Maybe all that talk about her being your father's child —"

"Which is impossible, and you know it." Duncan pushed him back.

"So all right, your father never pledged to that servant he fancied so much, which means Ylianor isn't his daughter." *But she's a witch all the same. Trust me.*

Nothing he could share, alas, not if he hoped to keep a measure of sanity.

Instead, he went through an elaborate show of yawning and stretching in the most exaggerated manner possible to fake how bored he had grown with this turn of the conversation. "Whatever it is, I'm sure you'll soon get over her." Yes, at the moment, downplaying it seemed his best option. "You know how bored you get of women." Making it sound as if it were an inconsequential thing did not change the fact she remained his only real competitor. Not because she was a woman, a category certainly not worth his worries or jealousies, but because she had returned to challenge his place. "So when are we leaving for the Hall?" He snuggled closer to Duncan. "Arthur is anxious to see us."

"Is it for another one of his parties?" A smirk crossed his beautiful face.

"No. I think it's something serious this time." At least judging from his grave tone urging him to fetch Duncan. "Although he wouldn't tell me much."

"It must be important then, if you couldn't get him to talk." Duncan chuckled amused.

"In spite of everything you heard, I don't hold any special power over our leader." His lips twisted in a bitter snarl.

"Come now." A finger under his chin, Duncan lifted his head. "People can't talk about anything else but you and him, and about how he practically eats out of your hand."

"Oh, I wouldn't give those rumors any credit." Uncomfortable, he lowered his gaze. "You know how people at the Hall are. All they do all day long is have sex and run their mouths off with just about any juicy piece of information that comes their way." What really made him uneasy were the deep feelings he had for Arthur that he had never shared with anyone. Not even with Duncan, who was more than a lover. Who was his best friend, as close as a brother could ever be, if not closer. "And I'm at the top of their list because I'm the vice-leader's son and part of the Arthur boys." He pushed out a heavy breath of air. "The women can't stand me 'cause I've never fucked a single one of them." Nor would he ever. He had kind of vowed it to himself. "And the boys are certainly livid 'cause he favors me all the time, to the point I practically live in his room, even if he assigned me quarters of my own for the sake of convenience." Shifting position, he straightened. "It's just that Arthur wants to have sex with me all the time. But he's never explicit about it, so I have to work my ass off to deserve it. Literally." He had told Duncan exactly how the evenings in the attic turned out, so he did not linger. "And if I pass his test, which I always do, he takes me to his room, and I end up staying there the entire night. And at times, he does say he loves me, but—"

"You don't want to believe him." As though reading his mind, Duncan's tone was very gentle and understanding, "'Cause it would mean acknowledging your feelings for him."

"I . . ." He wrung his hands nervously. "At first, I thought he said it 'Cause I'm so great at sex," he joked trying to lighten his mood. "Then I wasn't sure if they could qualify as . . ." Frustrated, he shook his head to clear it. "I mean, if I think about it, it feels like I'm betraying you just by admitting I feel something for him—"

"Listen, Angel." Cradling his head, Duncan kissed his forehead lovingly. "The real betrayal would be denying who you really are and the unique way you live your feelings. For it is unlike anyone I've ever known, so passionate and fiery that they define you like nothing else ever can." Full lips descended to press on his half-open mouth. "So how could I feel betrayed or jealous of who you are? It's the reason I love you so much. And this love of ours is so strong and powerful, nothing and nobody will ever come between us, no matter how much we may feel for them."

"Yeah, you're right." All of a sudden, all his silly fears disappeared, and he had no more uncertainties. "And Arthur, he means a whole lot to me. And not just for the things he's done for me, most of which I give for granted. Like taking me in without any hesitation when I knocked on his door right after you had thrown me out of Black Rose." And, boy, did that memory still hurt like crazy.

"I don't see how he could've refused hospitality to the vice-leader's son." The full lips curved in an ironic smile.

"Oh, he did much more than just open his door." Returning the infectious smile, he beamed at the prince. "He kept my father off my back, which was no small achievement, and gave me room to do just about whatever I wanted, like organizing those parties at the Hall." But this was just skimming the surface. "What I really never thanked him for is all those nights I couldn't sleep 'cause I couldn't stop thinking or crying about you. And he'd just hold me real tight until I fell asleep again, exhausted by how badly I missed you, how much I wanted you back."

"Must be the reason he invited me to that party at the Hall." Duncan stroked his head in a loving caress he found oddly erotic.

"Yeah, and that's another thing I have to thank him for." He heaved. "I guess I do love him in my own way, even if I never told him." He lifted a shoulder helplessly. "Didn't see the reason to until now, but maybe I will when we get to the Hall." He raised his gaze expectantly. "So when are we leaving?"

"In a few days' time." Shifting position, Duncan reclined against one side of the couch.

"Why not now?" Chris pushed, wanting to get him as far away from the witch as possible.

"'Cause I have to meet with the lawyer who will have to read my father's will." Which was a duty no son or daughter could refrain from once the father passed away.

"Hey, aren't you supposed to do the reading at the end of summer?" He checked out the window to make sure he was still at the beginning of spring.

"Yeah, but there are a few details he wants to discuss beforehand." Duncan's gaze also averted to stare out the window. "So he'll be coming over in the next few days."

"Then I'll have to endure your sister's company far longer than I anticipated." He hung his head in mock despair.

"Hey, don't I count for anything, Angel?" Tugging him up by the shoulders, Duncan's lips closed on his for a furious kiss that left him breathless and cock-tight. "Will it be so bad?"

"I'll survive, I guess." Raising his gaze, he flashed a smile. "But will she? I feel sorry for her." He stretched out, belly down, chin pressing on Duncan's broad chest. "It's almost pathetic the way she throws herself at me as if I could ever be interested." His lips twisted bitterly.

"I'm sure she'll make some guy very happy one day." From the sound of it, Prince Caldwell seemed quite certain of it. "Once she finds the right one, she'll pledge, and things will be just fine."

"Hey, you're right." Raising himself on his elbows, he leveled his gaze with Duncan. "She'd be just perfect in case my father ever insisted I pledge."

"You wouldn't dare!" In mocking shock, Duncan glared at him.

"Why not?" So he upped the stakes. "Just imagine. If I pledge to her, we'd both get what we want. Only it wouldn't necessarily be the same thing." There was no need to add more since he was now fondling Duncan's stirring erection to make it clear what he wanted, had always wanted as a matter of fact.

"I wouldn't let you." Shifting long muscular legs upward, his phase mate signaled he was more than ready for whatever he had in mind. "Call me romantic, but I still believe love or at least physical attraction should be part of a pledge."

"Oh, lover, you're so outdated." Taking full advantage of the offer, he stripped off Duncan's pants and settled between his legs. "Pledges have nothing to do with love. They're merely a commitment to have children." Reaching over, his tongue traced Duncan's lips before pushing through to taste his full, inebriating flavor. The kiss deepened as the prince opened up and allowed him to brush his wet cavity with re-peated strokes of a hungry tongue. And the play on the cock was heating up everything real fast. "But don't worry. As I said, I'm not interested, so I'm not going to pop the question any time soon." Sliding downward, he stopped at the groin, breathing stifling air over what had now a marble consistency. "Too hungry for something else entirely."

It was simply delicious to taste Duncan again and not with any anger. This time, he could take it nice and slow, and savor his adored prince's huge monster sticking in his face and demanding immediate pampering.

So he obeyed, like he always did whenever Duncan requested, his tongue running down each side to lap it vigorously. He loved every bump and crevice on it, all of which he knew by heart, and lingered on the few the prince would most appreciate. From tip to balls, he did not disdain brushing the perineum all the way to the tight entry at its end.

That was when he realized Duncan wanted him inside. The way the ring enlarged to fit the tongue and the fingers rimming its edges was clear indication. And the fact Duncan had not allowed any other man to take him since the end of the phase was a further come on to his already stiff piece.

Sliding his tongue up and down, he drenched both cock and ass to Duncan's satisfaction. Keeping his own unruly equipment in check was the real problem. His shaft throbbed painfully from the urge to plunge into the narrow space that would swallow it. And the butt yielding at his every finger penetration seemed equally anxious.

So he straightened, nudged the tip of his erection and shoved.

Just breaking through the tiny opening was blissful. Stretching it to fit his beastly size was even more delightful, feeling the flesh giving in at every thrust until it gobbled up the entire stuffing to the root. And the balls, too, had he only insisted a tad bit more.

Not this time, unfortunately. Still, he had the whole of

Duncan at his disposal. Well, except his mouth, something he immediately rectified by claiming the full lips. Inside the warm cavity, he moved his tongue at the same tempo as his cock, both ravaging the scorching flesh holding them prisoner. Melted inside Duncan, he hoped he would never have to emerge again. Alas, the mix of his cool energy wrapped around his fiery essence was simply too good and too powerful to keep it together.

His head swimming, he increased the blows to the rear and to the mouth, every impact fiercer than the one before, every impact trying to reach Duncan's core and explode inside it. Already the cramped fleshy walls were driving his sperm to the tip of the erection faster than he could control it. Then Duncan sucked his tongue to his throat, and it was the beginning of the end. Then the prince's sticky jets hit his belly, and he lost it for good.

Gasping inside Duncan's mouth, he shoved twice and burst.

"Fuck, lover, you're going to be the death of me." Still stuck inside Duncan, he threw back his shoulders.

"Me?" Eyes glittering from pleasure, Duncan reached up for a quick kiss. "You and that fire of yours are going to consume me to death."

His stomach growled in approval, which reminded him he had skipped breakfast in his haste to reach Black Rose. "Speaking of consuming, I'm so hungry now I hope your cook has fixed lunch for a hundred of us." Scrambling to his feet, he closed his fly. "And I can't wait to eat it all."

"I think I'll skip lunch." After wearing his pants, Prince Caldwell sat back down. "I'm not very hungry."

"Aren't you now?" No, he did not fall for it. "Suit yourself, lover." So he pretended indifference because pressing his point would get him nowhere. "I know you just want to punish me by leaving me at your sister's mercy, but your plan's destined to fail." Chuckling, he bent to rake his hand through Duncan's thick, luxurious hair. "I won't let anything spoil our time together." Lowering further down, he nipped the tempting ear. "By the way, have I told you lately how much I love you?"

"Not in so many words, Angel." A wide smile curved the full lips. "If memory serves me right."

"Mmm . . ." He loved hearing this low and throaty Angel, which sounded more like Demon and promised nothing of the goodness usually associated with angels. "I could begin right now with the first of a long list —"

"I'm sure you could." Duncan laughed. "But lunch won't wait that long."

"Time's forever my enemy," he joked. Then tearing himself away, he went to the door and left.

CHAPTER TWENTY-ONE

T*en-year old Duncan was chasing seven-year old Ylianor down the slope of Black Rose's highest hill, and she could not believe she could be so happy. So ecstatic to have her adored prince all to herself for a change, just the two of them alone, and no one around to interfere in their game or spoil her illusion he was all her own. Only thing, it was hot, maybe too much given that it was just the beginning of summer, and a cold one at that. But she did not honestly notice it.*

At least not until it was too late.

By then, everything had kind of hushed up, and an odd quietness had deafened her senses. Nature itself had gone deadly still, and an eerie silence had fallen on the land.

Frightened, she stopped and turned in time to catch sight of a black ominous figure rushing around the bend. And the fact the little boy coming her way looked like an angel only scared her out of her wits. An alarmed shiver ran down her back. No, the deceptive façade did not fool her one bit. Somehow, she knew it was a disguise, and the real essence of what was coiling around the hills of her beloved Black Rose was anything but good.

For he was no angel.

He was a black-hearted demon.

And he was so angry he cast a threatening shadow that almost snuffed out Stella herself.

Dismayed, she spun around to seek her prince's help. He would protect her! She was so sure of it she took her first step toward him. But one glance at his handsome face and her foot faltered, her blood turned cold.

Impossible as it seemed, he was completely oblivious of the ap-

proaching danger, running after her as though nothing was wrong. So it was up to her to save him from the blond imposter. How dare he anyway? How dare he come here under false pretenses, thinking he could pass off as an angel when in fact he was nothing short of an evil demon?

She would show that horrifying fiend exactly what he deserved!

And send it crawling back into the dark pit it had wormed out of, no question about it.

Full of hate, rage, fear and something else she could not quite understand, she gathered her energy, folded it into a ball and threw it at him with all the force she could muster.

He did not even cringe.

He merely blocked it with a fiery wall that burned her anger, along with the rest of her spirit, and would have incinerated her on the spot had not something more compelling enticed his attention.

So she whirled around.

And her heart stopped.

Literally.

For there was Duncan, and he was totally under the fake angel's spell.

Time stood still while the two boys stared at one another bewitched. What went through their minds, she could only guess from her fertile imagination, which was enough to shatter her inside. Like a punch in the stomach, this awareness broke her into so many pieces she could never hope to put them all back together. In the space of that one look, it was like they recognized one another. No, worse, like they belonged to one another, destined to be together somehow, as if there was a prior connection between them forged in some unknown and very distant lifetime.

Then Duncan smiled at the little boy riding up the hill, and a million lights exploded everywhere. So bright and fiery, they blinded her and forced her to close her eyes. Never, ever, had she seen anything like this. Like the world was set ablaze all together and all at once but by a single person alone. And that one person seemed to have enough fire inside him to light a hundred more worlds like this.

Confused, little Ylianor opened her eyes and blinked once then twice, hoping the fastidious brightness would go away just as suddenly as it had appeared. When that did not work, she squinted and could recognize a sort of pattern to it. Leaping flames – that was what sprung out of the young boy rushing to Duncan's side. They burned all around him like a halo that shimmered at every turn. Amazing, strange yet beautiful, she stood transfixed, narrowing her gaze to catch the infinite nuances glittering at every frantic wave. And when she finally managed to peer through the thick blinding curtain, she could not believe her eyes.

The black demon had disappeared.

In its place, there was a shiny angel, a real one this time.

It was like the prince's smile had magically turned the black vortex into pure light. Incredulous, she rubbed her eyes, afraid the luminescence played tricks. But on focusing again, the angel remained with no trace of the demon anywhere.

So things changed, and they were never the same again.

"About time you got back, Missy," David scoffed as soon as she reached Black Rose's stables. "Isn't it customary to tell someone where you go?" His lights kind of erratic, it took no effort to know he was making a show of his mastery. "We've been worried about you." This, however, was no act.

"I'm sorry, but I told the prince I needed to pick up a few things from the village." Getting off the mare, she avoided intercepting his gaze. "Didn't he inform you?"

"He might have, had he been here, instead of going missing last night . . ." He eyed her suspiciously as if expecting she would betray herself. "Just like you."

That he was afraid she and Duncan had spent the night together was obvious, and it explained the need for a show, his instinct probably alert to anything he would consider a threat to his beloved master. And now he was fishing for any incongruences in her reactions that would confirm his suspicions.

"Really? How strange." Not at all threatened, she ignored him on purpose. "I guess he got caught in the storm . . ." She returned his look, telling him she would not fall for his bait. "Just like I was."

Defeated, he glanced away, so she turned her attention to the stables and noticed a new black horse next to Fuzeon. "We have guests?"

"Yes." He nodded slowly. "Lord Christopher Templeton is here on a visit." Everything in the agitated flashes of his aura told her David had no great liking for Christopher Templeton.

None at all.

Which was not surprising, considering they could not stand one another when they were all younger, both competing over Duncan as though he were the only thing that would give meaning to their lives. Something he probably had the power to do, considering how fiercely she had fought for just the same thing.

"Really?" If this made her look stupid, it gave her time to come up with some meaningless gibberish like, "How nice . . ."

Yeah, sure!

Whom was she fooling?

Her blood had become ice at the mere mention of the name. "Well, I should be getting back to work. I've wasted enough time already."

"Would you like some breakfast first?" Dropping his act once and for all, his voice softened.

"No, thank you." *Who can eat after such news?* Not to mention with a stomach as heavy as stone. "I've eaten at the village." Hoping it did not sound like the lie it was, she took Starlet inside the stables.

So he was back!

And what impeccable timing, too.

Not twelve hours since Duncan had made love to her, and

here he was, claiming what he thought was his.

Well, guess what Lord Christopher Templeton?

I'm back, and I'm gonna get the prince this time!

Well, at least in her dreams. In the real world, it was highly doubtful she might actually succeed. He had beaten her once before, chased her away from Black Rose, so nothing prevented him from doing it again.

True, he thought he had gotten rid of her, yet here she was. Also true, now she was no sniveling child anymore. She had grown and become fully aware of her power. But would that be enough?

The one thing she most remembered about Chris was his mighty power, something she had learned to treat with a great deal of respect since that resounding beating of ten years before. Something inextricably linked to his wondrous lights, too, which irritated her all the more. That his should have been the first aura she ever saw seemed unfair, the one that had made her realize all people had lights of their own. Only she had never perceived them until he had come along and turned them all on for her. Still and in spite of everything, his remained the most fascinating aura of all, and she had often laid awake at nights picturing it in her mind. And the way it reacted was the most amazing thing of all.

For Chris became pure light whenever around Duncan, shining brighter than Stella herself. Around anyone else, he had a dimmer hue, as though everybody else turned him off no matter what. It was uncanny and mesmerized the prince to the point he completely forgot about her.

Both of them had.

Which still burned her, particularly remembering how Chris had dismissed her threat as an inconsequential child's prank and flown to Duncan's side.

Betrayed and hurt, she had not realized at the time that it was the beginning of the end. Not just of her prince, of Charles Caldwell and of Black Rose, too. In the blink of an eye, her entire world had vanished forever. And now, what she had managed to salvage through much pain and tears, her heart's integrity, was again at risk. All the prince's fault, him and his crashing back into her life, undoing with a single touch what had taken her agonizing years to put behind her. And knowing he loved Chris the passionate way he did, only entangled the existing ties between them, which seemed as undeniable as those linking him to Chris. But such was Duncan Caldwell's appeal, she was ready to accept whatever offer he was willing to make, even if it meant getting her old rival in the bargain.

For she had just discovered, and with no surprise, she still loved him as deeply as she had in the past, and that no attempt at erasing him from her heart would ever succeed.

CHAPTER TWENTY-TWO

"Hello, Princess." She had looked so inviting from his office window the mere sight had lured him out.

She raised her gaze as he approached. "Hello, stranger." She was just too beautiful for words, especially when she beamed the most radiant of smiles.

He could not help returning her infectious happiness with a smile of his own, heart racing from the odd tension his blond angel had immediately noticed. "I was wondering whether you made it back."

"Of course, I did, Prince." She stopped to catch her breath.

As though she could not handle the surge of emotions he glimpsed crossing her face.

"It's not a great distance from the village to Black Rose . . ." She smirked naughtily. "Except when you get lost."

"Hey, it might turn out to be the best misfortune of my life," he joked, getting very close.

So close, he could have easily kissed her.

"Not if it makes you skip lunch." Her nose twitched.

And he could not help wondering whether she smelled Chris on him, despite the pungent sea air carried by the soft breeze.

"Don't feel too hungry." He glanced around the deserted place. "At least not for food." Then he trained his gaze on her.

"Hungry for something else?" And she immediately understood him, her green eyes alight and tempting, clearly

145

wanting him to make his move.

"For a green-eyed princess." He could not wait to get his hands on her. "Do you happen to know where I can find one?"

"Hem . . . let me think." She made a show of frowning in mock concentration. "Perhaps you should look inside the stables . . ." Her voice trailed off as she walked to the cooler interior.

The second he stepped inside, he was all over her, his mouth and hands unable to get enough while picking her up and carrying her to the upstairs quarters.

Flinging her on the bed, he stripped her. Her scent seeping to his cock, he went for her breasts first, the hard nipples imploring for his wet kiss. He complied readily, teasing them with a hard tongue tip until they were about to burst, which of course made sucking them such a delight. And he would have never quit, had not his now stone-like shaft demanded something more substantial.

So he hurried downward, nipping her flat stomach with playful bites, loving the way she arched to get more. Oh, she was just begging for a come, her muscles taut from ache and lust, her cunt swimming from the extreme moistness dripping to her thighs. And since this was too good to pass up, he silenced his undisciplined erection and delved into her sweetness, longing to fill his senses with her taste.

Spreading her legs wide, he dipped inside her clean-shaven slit. Not one bothersome hair hindered his extreme pleasure of gliding on her silky flesh, with fingers and tongue drowning in her dense honeydew. But at her jolt of pain, he realized her flesh was still raw from the other night's banging. So he immediately eased the pressure and focused on the swollen clit throbbing in impatience. A few licks and she relaxed again, before tensing all together from the climax building inside of her. He brushed the pounding knot harder, drowning it with avid laps and sucking it up until she froze.

Not a setback at all.

Just her body getting ready to convulse in rhythmic throes, which it did as though prey to consecutive waves and in perfect synch with the scream bursting out of her.

This time, he anticipated it, relishing the feel of power and total control over her, which swelled his already marble equipment into a beast whose sole aim was to possess her completely. And even if her pussy was off limits, she still had one very interesting hole that had to be his.

For like he had told Chris, a virgin ass was incomparable to anything else, and hers had looked mighty tempting from the beginning. And just recalling this particular exchange with the blond angel tightened his cock to a spasm.

"Turn around," he ordered as soon as her contractions abated. "I want you to lie on your stomach."

When she did not comply, he raised his gaze. And, boy, was she tense! Not from excitement, from the question hovering in her heart stopping green eyes.

"I can't take you like this." His tone gentler, he caressed her cheek. "You're still sore from last night, and it could be too painful. So I'll try something different today."

"Will it hurt?" Ylianor's voice trembled slightly.

"Well . . ." Recalling his first time with Chris, he could not but be truthful. "Initially, it might." Then again, his ass was still dancing now from his angel's latest beat, and he knew no other feeling was quite as satisfying. "It's not that bad, really. Just don't let the first sensations spoil it for you, and the reward will be incredible." His hand traveled on her body to ease her tension, soon lost in her skin's silky texture and in her intoxicating curves.

She could not seem to relax.

So he bent to whisper in her ear, "Do you trust me?"

"Do I have a choice?" A bit defiant, she stared back at him with an unspoken challenge he put down to her inexperience and to the novelty of it all.

"You always have a choice, Princess." Stroking her breasts, he toyed with the raised tips to increase her desire. "But when your master orders—"

"Since when are you my master?" Perplexed, her arresting green eyes flew wide-open.

"Since always," he breathed huskily. "You belong to me, and that's what I felt when I laid my eyes on you. I had no idea who you were, yet I knew you were mine." His tongue played in her ear. "Which makes you my slave." He spelled out the word, so there would be no misunderstanding.

Not because he truly believed she could be his slave. Because this game was turning out to be more arousing than he had anticipated.

"Now, are you ready to submit to your rightful master and owner?" At these last words, his cock tugged so hard he feared it would go ahead and take her without consulting him.

Straightening, he did not touch her anymore. It was part of his act—to make her feel cold and empty was sure to hasten her acceptance. So he waited, reading the conflicting emotions crossing her beautiful face, until she simply nodded.

"Not good enough." No, not even close. "You're not getting off the hook that easily. I want a verbal answer. Do you recognize me as your master? As the man who will always command over you, take you and use you if and when I please, 'cause you'll be nothing more than a slave to me?"

"I . . ." She shifted, probably wanting to get away.

Clamping her hips, he did not allow her to budge. Her answer was too important at this stage of the game.

"Yes, yes." Out of breath and out of excuses, she went all

limp. "I do."

"You do what?" Inflexible, he did not allow her to avert her gaze.

"I accept you as my master," she blurted as though in a hurry to get it over. "And I'll be your slave."

"Then turn around." However much he wanted to flip her around himself, his game required she did it herself. "And I'll show you what pleasure is."

She obeyed at last.

"By the gods . . ." He had to catch his breath. "What a magnificent ass!" And he knew just who would appreciate it the most. "One that begs to be possessed." Amused, he watched her wriggle it as if to show her appreciation at the comment. "And if you keep shaking it like that, I'll just take it and not give a damn about you."

She stopped moving all together.

So he admired the firm consistency, the round shape and the perfect size. So perfect, he knew the high buttocks would not lose their enticement no matter what position she took.

"Get on your hands and knees." His voice thick with lust, he made it sound more like an order than he originally intended. "And bend your back." Still, he wanted to test his theory.

And his cock's yelp of craving was proof enough he had been right.

Definitely, his blond angel would just love to play with an ass like hers, if only it were not so . . . feminine.

Blocking off his thoughts of Chris, he clenched both ass cheeks and spread them. The crack between them was a further turn on. So straight and narrow, it led to the tight ring in a seductive slide he had noticed only in Chris. Then wetting his finger, he rimmed the tiny edges, and it pulsated. Out of fear or pleasure it was hard to tell.

For sure, he had to seduce it into submission, and nothing

worked better than his tantalizing circles, or than his tongue urging the tight hole to surrender with drenched laps. At her first moan, he dipped two fingers, which she sucked to the hilt. So he increased the pressure to three, then four until her swaying confirmed what her pliant flesh had already told him.

She was ready.

All he had to do was nudge his stiff monster to her rear hole and break through its virgin confinement. One forceful thrust and the fathead cracked her ass, flinging wide open what had been exceedingly small just a second before.

"No, wait." Tensing all together, she tried to scuttle away. "It hurts."

"Like it was burning?" Whatever it was, he immobilized her so she could not get away from him.

"I think . . ." In obvious distress, she lifted her back to level it with her ass.

"Relax, Princess, and breathe." Gently, he pressed his palm on her back. "But lower your back 'cause I didn't give you permission to raise it." He made it sound harsh on purpose because he was still in charge. "Now tell me what you feel exactly."

"It's more of a burning sensation." Even if the position was sure to hurt her more, she complied, pushing up her ass higher in the air.

Which only made it more fabulous.

"All right, it'll soon pass." The tip of his erection still stuck inside, he forced himself to bide his time. "Just breathe slowly and deeply."

"I wish I could," she snapped ironically.

"Here." Grinning, he bent her way. "I'll help you." Slipping a hand between her legs, he zeroed in on her cunt, stroking her dripping pussy while brushing the tender clit forcefully.

Just a few rubs, and she could not keep still. But in throwing back her butt, his greedy cock managed to sink inside her cramped space and penetrate deeper at every swaying. To think he was not moving at all. She was doing all the work and beautifully, too, until nothing remained out except the balls.

Fuck! Was she tight! So tight, she would soon explode from her voraciousness to gobble up what was too big for her untrained rear ring. To him trying to accelerate such explosion, it was pure bliss, and the urge to stretch and enlarge her even more took precedence over any other concern. Because he would not rest until he had split her apart.

Literally.

So he pumped, slow at first to give her time to get used to it, faster when she began responding enthusiastically. With every shove, her ass gave in that tad bit more to drive him crazy, coiling around his thick long length and refusing to let it go. So he claimed it all, sliding to her guts and out once she truly opened up to him.

Stuffed to the hilt, squeezed to perfection, he was about to lose it. *Hurry, Princess.* To help her, he had never ceased his sensual play on her cunt and clit, rewarded by her matching his thrusts, which in turn heated up everything, including the friction of their skins rubbing against one another. *I don't think I can resist much longer, but I'd hate to leave you behind.*

As if reading his mind, she stepped up the tempo. Feeling her about to climax, he intensified his beat until the scream pierced the air. Caught in the waves wrecking her body, he let it all go, pleasure shooting through his every fiber, at least until something wrenched him away from it all.

From his own body, it seemed, because everything was flashing and blinding him now, to the point he could not see straight. It was more of a haze through which he perceived people not in their usual corporeal form. No, the ones he was seeing now had innumerable lights shining all around them, like a glimmering halo that reflected back to him in a confusing blur.

Hallucination or plain illusion?

Hard to make out what it was exactly. Yet, once he adapted to the shocking brightness, he realized the sparks that reverberated through each aura were in fact a shift in the person's mood, which was surprising to say the least.

Dumbfounded yet fascinated, he guessed that she was the one who had brought him there, trapping him somewhere inside her. How the fuck she had managed it, he had no idea. He only knew she had total control over him and his perceptions, which kind of enraged and disturbed him, had the feeling that he somehow belonged there not calmed him down.

Or perhaps her scream was doing the trick, still perceivable and strong enough to shatter the barriers of reality itself.

Whatever it was, he could not stay there. But when he tried pulling back, to return to a shred of reality, he could not. She did not release him, not until the acute sound faded. Then, just as suddenly as she had captured him, she tossed him back whence he had come.

Exhausted as if something had drained all his energy, he rolled away from the woman, unable to do anything except plunge into a dark, dreamless sleep that took him away once and for all.

CHAPTER TWENTY-THREE

"I have to go." In the stable keeper's room, Duncan bolted out of the bed, making her feel cold all of a sudden.

"Mmm . . ." Opening her eyes, she watched him getting dressed in a hurry. Turning her head to the small window at the side of the bed, one look at Stella's setting rays, and she knew it was late. "Sure."

Dazed, she watched him wear his pants and tie his shoes, obviously still reeling from the experience and the bottomless void that had swallowed him, like it had her.

But she could hardly contain her excitement.

Wanted to shout it out, in fact, if only he were not running away as fast as he was.

So he had the gift! Like his father before him, he had the power, and more potent if she was any judge of it. Or maybe awakening it with sex gave it a force she would have never suspected. Either way, he was ready for the next level— mind sharing.

Like she had with Prince Charles alone, she could not wait to explore the powerful connection his penetration of her body and mind had unwittingly unleashed, already savoring his deep throaty voice exploding inside her head and the silent exchange of the most intimate thoughts and sensations.

Stretching luxuriously, she tried to summon enough energy to get up from the bed. Maybe skipping lunch had not been such a clever move after all, and the terrible ache in the pit of her stomach agreed with her wholeheartedly. But who cared now that she had the prince right where she wanted him?

With the last of her strength, she managed to get dressed and reach the kitchen.

"There you are, pet." A concerned expression crossing her face, Anne came up to her. "I was worried you were going to skip dinner, too." Holding her at arm's length, she checked Ylianor through and through. "It's not good for you."

"I wasn't hungry at lunch." She tried wriggling free from her scrutinizing gaze.

"But you do hard work out there." Not allowing her to go anywhere, Anne tightened her grip. "And you must eat to keep up your strength."

"That's why I'm here and can't wait to get started on your great dinner." She looked around the empty kitchen with the central table full of food. "But where is everybody?"

"Oh, now that *the great* Lord Templeton is here, they're all running around like crazy." Resigned to let her go, Anne dropped her arm to a side. "Never liked the boy anyway. And never will." Going to the stove, she stirred a large boiling pot. "He's not a good influence on our prince, if you know what I mean."

I sure do! "I just remember him as a little boy."

"A hateful and spiteful one at that. And that's the kind of man he's going to become." Anne seemed to have no doubts about it. "It's just a shame he only has eyes for our prince, while poor Lady Elizabeth pines after him in vain." An ironic smile curved her lips. "I heard her say it with my own ears." She nodded vigorously as if to stress the truth of her statement. "And it's plain to see how she wears her heart out on a sleeve simply to attract his attention, and he barely looks at her twice. Still, she keeps hoping one day he'll ask her to pledge." A hearty laugh broke out loud. "Ha, that'll be the day!" Opening the oven, she checked on something that smelled oh so mouthwatering and seemed to be perfectly broiled. "And she's a fool if she hasn't figured it out already, not to mention plain blind to set her heart on someone as gorgeous as Lord Templeton." Closing the oven, she shook her head philosophically. "I mean the man looks like a god!"

Yeah, she already suspected it.

"Plus he's never been interested in her," Anne scoffed. "And just between you and me, I don't think he's interested in women at all."

Well, if his behavior as a child was any indication, she could agree with this, too.

"At least not like our prince is." Anne angled her head behind a shoulder to catch Ylianor's gaze. "Even if he doesn't like them too thin."

"The prince?" Her face grew hot. "What does he have to do with anything?"

Anne's voice lowered a notch, "He's the master, isn't he?"

"He definitely is." *And don't I know it.*

"So he pretty much gets to decide things around here, including how his women should look." After wiping her hands-on a nearby towel, Anne pulled out a chair from the table. "Come on, pet. Sit down."

"Is everything ready for the masters' dinner?" Missus Merryweather bursting in the kitchen nearly made her jump out of the chair she had just occupied. "They also have an illustrious guest like Lord Templeton, and you know how Lady Caldwell gets—"

"Yes, relax, Alicia," Anne cut her off hastily. "They have plenty to eat, and it's all delicious."

Just as Anne finished talking, people streamed in, randomly sitting around the large table. From David to the butler, from the kitchen helpers to the house cleaners—everyone was there.

"All right, people." When everyone had settled in, Anne placed a large full tray of vegetables in the center of the table. "Let's eat." Then she brought more filled dishes.

"Has anybody seen the prince since lunchtime?" Taking an empty plate, David filled it with vegetables and cheese.

"Why?" Perplexed, a cute servant tried catching his gaze. "What happened to him?"

"Don't you know?" Sarah looked at her as if she were living in a different world. "No one's seen him since he returned this morning. Don't you all think he's been acting strange of late?" She glanced at the faces around the table in between bites. "First, he disappears for an entire night. Then today, he skips lunch and vanishes the whole afternoon, without anyone being able to find him."

She stared at her plate, pretending to concentrate on her food.

"Yes, it's not like him to disappear like that," David added. "Do you know anything about it, Ylianor?"

"Me?" She blinked as if unsure he was really asking her. "No, I don't. I worked all day at the stables then fell asleep in the afternoon."

"That's because you didn't eat anything, pet." Anne's worried scowl said more than her words did.

"The funny thing is even his phase mate didn't know where he was." A smug smirk twisted Sarah's lips.

"Lord Templeton looked for him everywhere." The butler nodded gravely. "Then he had to take a walk alone with Lady Elizabeth."

"It's plain to see he can't stand the sight of her." Many snickered with knowing grins, but only Sarah felt it her duty to comment.

"Like he can't stand most women," Anne retorted wryly.

"Don't I know it?" A wistful expression crossing her eyes, Sarah heaved. "Too bad he's so good-looking I'd have a go at him if he consented."

"He probably won't," Reginald, the butler, snapped. "So stop talking about it as if it were going to happen anytime soon."

A bell rang at the back of the kitchen.

"Hey, the master is alive and back in action." Sarah beamed, glancing toward the bell. "For sure, he took a bath."

"Yes, so I had better go." David rose from the table and hurried away.

"I wish he were calling me." Sarah sighed wishfully.

"It's not your call, Missy." Alicia Merryweather's malicious gaze fixed on the girl. "Sometimes, I think you're impossible."

"I just want what most other households have," Sarah spat. "A master who has fun with his servants. Is that too much to ask?" She searched around the table for consensus, before stopping on her. "Don't you agree, Ylianor?"

"I wouldn't know about that . . ." Uncomfortable, she shifted in her seat. "Especially since I don't know him that well."

"The problem is that he never seems available." Then having finished her meal, Sarah got to her feet.

"There are others available." The butler cleared his throat. "If you just quit thinking of him alone."

Sarah looked at him for a moment as if evaluating him. "I may do it eventually." Then she scrambled away before Reginald could add anything further.

CHAPTER TWENTY-FOUR

"Prince, where have you been all afternoon?" On entering, David examined him with a concerned look. "It's the twenty-ninth hour, and we looked for you everywhere since lunchtime."

"We?" Standing in front of the fire wrapped in a towel, anger barely held in check, he spun around to face David.

"Lord Templeton, your sister, Reginald and I." David advanced, still checking him over. "We combed the house without finding you. Lady Elizabeth wanted to take a walk on the cliffs, but Lord Templeton insisted you go along." He suppressed a snicker. "In the end, they had to go by themselves."

"I'm sorry." He, too, had to refrain from cracking up at the image of Chris and Lizzy out on a romantic stroll over the cliffs. "I fell asleep under a tree outside and woke up just a few minutes ago." *And goddamn her and her fucking tricks!*

"Outside?" Skeptical, David eyed him coldly.

"Yes, I was taking a walk, then felt tired and . . ." *Why am I justifying myself to David?* "Anyway, since I have a few minutes before dinner, I want to know about the latest news."

"Well . . ." David's forehead creased as though in concentration. "There are some bad news from Harbor Town," he began at last. "Jeff Macy's father fell from his horses, and there are rumors he might not be able to walk again."

"But I was just there." If it seemed like a stupid objection, he still recalled how fit and trim Jeff's father had looked to him upon seeing him when he had gone to Isabella Turner.

Same trip that marked his encounter with the blasted woman that was running through his blood like a fever or something.

"It happened right after you left." David seemed to have his facts in order. "Now Jeff and his brother, Robin, are calling all the doctors they can think of to help their father recover." His lips pressed together in that characteristic way of his when a situation seemed hopeless to him. "But so far, nothing has worked."

"I'm truly sorry for them." He was, honestly. And he would have been even more, had he not been fixated with one thought alone. "What about other news closer to home?"

"You mean with us?" David took a step forward.

No, I mean with her. "Yeah." He was so furious with her he did not even want to mention her. In any case, he often used David to keep track of things, so nothing strange in his request.

"The usual, I guess." The man frowned as though making a mental list of things. "Sarah still pines after you—"

"Will the girl ever learn?" He was so not interested in her and had told her in a variety of ways.

"I think she'll never lose hope, even if Reginald is trying to divert her attention on himself." David's lips curved in the hint of a smile. "She rather prefers younger types—"

"How to blame her?" He turned to face the fire again.

David followed him. "Tonight, she even went as far as considering Lord Templeton as a possible—"

"That'll be the day," he quipped sarcastically.

"That's what we all told her." David grinned in response.

"What about Ylianor?" Oh, fuck! Why couldn't he stop thinking of her?

"Well . . ." As if knowing where he had been heading all along, David made a strategic pause. "She hasn't been around much, so it's difficult to say." He cleared his throat. "For the time being, only Anne seems to be happy she's back." He pursed his lips. "But then that's understandable, since she and her parents took care of Ylianor after Mary Jane died." He shrugged. "As for the others, they have barely seen her. The men seem interested, judging from some looks I caught around the dinner table tonight. After all, you cannot help noticing her."

"And you, David?" Sensing his nervousness at the turn of the conversation, he searched his face. "How do you feel about her?"

"All right, Prince." David took a deep breath. "But first tell me what you plan to do with her."

"Technically, I asked first." He beamed, breaching their distance. "Come on, David." Slapping him on his back, he raised an eyebrow. "We've never had any secrets between us, so why start now?"

"I like her . . ." David sighed. "A lot." Then he raised his gaze. "She has an air about her . . ." He creased his forehead as though to find the right words. "It's odd actually. She doesn't really look like you physically, but some details inevitably remind me of you, like her hair, the way she smiles or even how she moves. And the likeness is so uncanny it's disheartening. Yet she also scares me."

Welcome to the club. "Why?"

"She seems to have some kind of . . ." From David's hesitation, he guessed it had to be something distinctive and unusual. "Power."

Don't I know it! "What sort of power?" *And why can't I stop thinking about what she just pulled on me?*

"I don't know." David shrugged, evidently at a loss. "Someone might call it witchcraft, but I can't honestly say that's what it is."

I can! "I also think she has power." *But I'll wait to give it a definite name until I know exactly what it is.* "Which only complicates matters and makes it impossible to plan anything."

"Which didn't prevent you from having sex with her." There was no challenge in David's tone or in his intentions. "Right, Prince?"

"No, it didn't." *But is it her or is it her magic that got me so bewitched?* "I guess it just proves she may be a witch after all," he joked, even if the laugh was on him.

"Whatever it is, don't forget her mother had the same hold on your father." For David, instead, it was no laughing matter. "At least that's what many say. And if it's true your father was under a spell from Mary Jane, then Ylianor might cast one on you, too."

"Now, David, let's be reasonable." It sounded too preposterous.

Sure, he was downright mad at the woman for what she had pulled on him earlier. Still, it was no excuse to throw rationality to the wind and start believing all sorts of crazy things.

"Have you heard of other families with a tradition of witches hunting them down?" Just picturing it made it look funny.

David shook his head.

"So why should they bother only the Caldwells, and only the men at that? Not just one, but two of them?" He caught the doubt now clouding David's hazel eyes. "What's so special about us to attract them above anyone else?"

Of course, he did not expect any answer. How could he?

He himself still did not know what had hit him. All he knew was that he could not shake the nagging feeling he had somehow stumbled on what he had sought ever since the end of his phase, which was enough to piss him off like crazy. Worst of all, he had so loved the sex that he would have called her to his room just to stick his cock in her ass again. If that was his excuse, what was hers?

Certainly not a taste for gossip since the rest of the house-hold knew nothing of this new twist. Maybe she just liked him a lot, or maybe she just wanted to get even with his family. Either way, it was useless to waste his time like this. He first had to understand what was going on, and that seemed to be his only option at the moment.

And the gods help him if she was the woman he had been searching for, the one made especially for him.

"Never mind, David." He waved a dismissive hand in the air. "Thanks, it'll be all for now."

"Very well, sir." Nodding, David went to the door and left him alone with his doubts.

CHAPTER TWENTY-FIVE

"Look who's here." Chris's sarcastic tone could not disguise his relief the second he entered the dining room and caught sight of him. "What happened today?"

One glance at his blond angel and he knew just how bored he had been the entire afternoon long.

"Yes, brother, we looked everywhere for you." She threw herself in his arms. "But couldn't find you anywhere."

"I'm sorry, Lizzy." He returned her embrace. "I fell asleep outside and woke up only an hour ago." His eyes searched for his stunningly beautiful angel, looking mighty fuckable in a tight-fitting dark orange suit that exalted his blond complexion and blue-gray eyes. "I guess last night was more tiring than I realized."

Yeah, lover, too much fucking around can get to you eventually, the blue-gray eyes seemed to taunt him. *Didn't you know?*

I'm just finding out, Angel. Moving closer to Chris, he grinned as if he could actually share thoughts with him. "I trust you had a pleasant time even without my company."

"You bastard!" Chris muttered under his breath, so only he could hear.

"We sure did!" His sister beamed. "Chris and I went for a walk on the cliffs." Her smug face said it all. "It was beautiful out there, wasn't it, Chris? The sea was in tempest and the air was so crisp I couldn't get enough of it."

"I could," Chris snarled, again low enough only he caught it.

"Glad you didn't throw Lizzy off the cliff," he whispered

back.

"Come on, boys." His mother gestured toward the table. "Duncan, it's good to have you back, but now it's time to eat."

"Tomorrow we could go for a ride, if the weather holds up." Sitting next to Mother, his sister fixed him first, before switching her focus on the angel. "What do you think, Chris?"

"I don't know." The arresting blue-gray eyes locked on him. "Planning on disappearing again, or will you allow us the privilege of your company from now on?"

"I can be all yours tomorrow." He grinned widely. "Except if the lawyer comes."

"Tomorrow?" Lizzy cried dismayed.

"Actually, I don't know when he'll be here," he was quick to calm her down.

"What's he coming for?" Sophia eyed him intently. "We aren't reading the will until the end of summer."

"I'm not sure." He moved aside to let Missus Merryweather set a steamy bowl of soup in front of him. "He just wrote me a brief note asking to see me because he had to straighten up some last-minute details about the will."

"Last minute details?" Lady Caldwell scoffed. "Your father's been dead ten years, and only now he remembers about these details?"

"Maybe because only now we're getting ready to read the will," he argued sensibly. "So he'll be here in the coming days. But even if he shows up tomorrow, I'm sure he won't mind waiting should we be out."

"Then it's settled." Lizzy giggled happily, taking her first spoonful of the vegetable soup. "We can meet around the twelfth hour and take it from there. Praline needs the exercise. I haven't taken her out for a while."

"It's not good to keep the horses so cooped up in the stables." It really was not healthy for them. "I'll ask Ylianor to keep them trained."

"I don't want that . . . creature near my horse." Sophia's hostile tone was infuriatingly cold, "Lady Rose is just fine without her."

"So is Praline," his sister pitched in after exchanging a glance with Sophia.

"Mother, why do you have to be so difficult?" *And why the fuck did I bring the witch's name up?*

He was in no better terms with her than during his talk with David, yet like a fever in his blood, he could not stop thinking about her. Or bringing up her name without solicitation, where it was not even wanted. "It would be good for the horses."

"I don't care." More stubborn than her usual, his mother set her chin in that characteristic way of hers that told him she did not intend to listen to him anymore. "I don't want her near Lady Rose or any of the other horses! And that's final."

"All right, forget it." With an angry scowl, he dropped the subject and turned to Chris. "Angel, why don't you tell us about the latest news from the Hall?"

"Oh, there's so many I wouldn't know where to start." Taking his cue, Chris frowned as though seemingly adding up his facts.

In reality, he was thinking about the subject that would be less damaging. Duncan was sure of it. For the Hall was not just where Chris had decided to live since the end of their phase. It was also the seat of the High Council, which ruled over the twelve districts of his homeland and comprised two representatives from each.

"But I'm afraid they're all from last season." Having finished his soup, the angel went for the platter of vegetables at the center of the table. "You know the council meets only from late spring to the end of summer." Taking a generous ration, he filled up his plate. "So most people won't get to the Hall until at least a month from now." He began eating, soon stopping as though taken by a sudden thought. "Speaking of which, Prince, your father's seat has been vacant for the past ten years, so when are you going to fill it?"

"Right after he reads the will," Sophia was quick to set the record straight. "He was too young before for such an important duty." She smiled at him with pride.

Which did nothing to soothe his fury at her pigheadedness.

"But now you're twenty-one." Absolutely unruffled by his reaction, she continued as smoothly as if everything was fine. "And it's time you take your rightful place in the High Council."

I don't want it! Not exactly the truth, still he would have said it just to spite her.

"What about you, Chris?" Eyes flashing in barely suppressed curiosity, Lizzy eyed his angel intently. "When are you going to take a seat in the High Council?"

"I . . ." Chris's cheeks flared in the most adorable blush he could remember. "I don't think I'll ever be in the High Council." He averted his gaze from her adoring stare.

Well, how to blame him?

"Why not?" Of course, his sister insisted.

"Because my father would rather have Steve, my oldest brother, instead of me." From the tone, he could not tell whether Chris was glad of it or not. "Even if Steve's not cut out for the Hall."

So maybe Chris was a bit disappointed.

"What do you mean, Lord Templeton?" His mother was filling her plate for the second time.

While he discovered he had not recovered his appetite at all, still stuck at the soup as though he was finding it hard to swallow it down.

"Just that the Hall is a place of . . ." Creasing his lovely forehead, Chris seemed to be thinking of some appropriate word that would not offend his mother. "Intrigue and too much gossip." He seemed happy with his choice. "Many people don't know how to handle that kind of pressure, so they get really agitated. I'm talking mostly about the temporary members." Swinging his head, he fixed Duncan alone. "Or temps as we call them." Then he broadened his gaze to Lizzy and Sophia. "Unlike the permanent members, the temps change every three years, so they're really not used to the Hall's way of doing things." He sniggered, "And when they finally get the hang of it, they've gotta leave."

"There are still twenty-four members, right?" Sophia was gobbling up her cheese and vegetables like she had not eaten for days.

"Yep." Clearing up his dish, Chris laid down his fork. "Twelve permanent and twelve temporary ones, two from each of our districts to ensure a fair and adequate representation of all the people and problems of our homeland." This textbook definition had a distinct Arthur-style ring to it.

"Must be exciting just being there." His sister's dreamy tone indicated she would have loved nothing else.

"Depends on how you define exciting." While the angel's tart tone indicated he never hoped to see her at the Hall.

"I don't know if it's a place you'd like, Lizzy." Taking pity on Chris, he tried to dissuade her bright idea.

"I wouldn't know about that." As stubborn as Mother, his sister raised a defiant gaze. "But I'll have the chance to see for myself when I'll come visit you, right, brother?"

"Aren't you running a bit?" He chuckled. "I haven't been but twice to the Hall and you're already fishing for an invitation?"

"Just reminding you that I'm not going to disappear from your life once you become a permanent council member."

Gathering the last of her green beans, she devoured them.

"I never thought you would." His tone softer, he sent her a loving look. "But there's still plenty of time before that comes about, so quit thinking about it."

"Yes, Elizabeth, it's a bit premature." At least his mother was on his side for a change. Then she flashed a smile at Chris. "Lord Templeton, would you like an after-dinner drink?"

"Oh, yes, please, something stiff to pick me up." Blue-gray eyes blazing at him, Chris nudged him from under the table. "It's been . . ." He eyed Lizzy significantly. "A very rough day."

"Of course, Angel." After that mere touch, he burned from the need to be alone with him. "I can surely fix you something to your taste in my office and also find something suitable for Mother and—"

"No, thank you, dear." Lady Caldwell raised a hand to stop him. "I'm quite exhausted and want to retire." Pushing her chair back, she got up to leave the table. "I hope you'll excuse me, Lord Templeton . . ."

"Of course, Lady Caldwell." Chris got up as well.

"Have a good night, and I'll see you tomorrow." On heading toward the door, she halted to kiss Duncan lightly on the cheek. "Good night, son, I'll see you tomorrow." She was about to stride away when she whirled around. "Oh, Elizabeth, would you mind joining me upstairs? I need to talk to you."

"Yes, Mother." With a disappointed look, Lizzy rose. "I'm coming." Head lowered, she dutifully followed her, sending one last glance at both him and Chris, her gaze fixing mostly on the latter. "I guess I'll see you tomorrow, and don't forget our date." Then she stepped out, the trace of her sad expression lingering even after she was gone.

CHAPTER TWENTY-SIX

"She's a real torment!" Chris spat as he entered the office. "And I'm not going to forgive you that easily for what you did today."

"What did I do?" Pretending to be all innocent, he closed the office door.

"Don't play games with me, lover." Cornering him next to the fireplace, Chris's breath tickled his ear. "You know damn well what you did and leaving me alone with your sister was one of the most despicable things you ever did . . ." He hesitated. "Besides breaking up with me, I mean. Had I found you when we got back from those fucking cliffs, I'd have personally strangled you."

"I'm touched," he taunted sarcastic. "But weren't you interested in asking her a certain question?"

"Are you kidding?" The angel drew back, dropping on the leather couch in front of the fireplace. "She's way too boring and plain. Frankly, if she holds no attraction for regular men, imagine what a turn off she can be for me." Sitting up straighter, his blue-gray eyes flashed. "But enough talking of her. Where were you screwing around?"

"Can't you guess?" Going to a cabinet, he fetched two glasses and a bottle of distilled cider. Then sitting next to Chris, he poured the amber-colored liquid and handed him a full glass.

"I don't need guessing." His phase mate's nasty snarl twisted his thin lips. "I know you were with her." Of course, he would know. "She must really be something different if she hasn't bored you yet. She's . . . what?" He creased his forehead. "The third woman you've fucked twice in a row." He twirled the glass around his palms. "Certainly the only one you've run to after being with me." He turned to search for Duncan's gaze, which had fixed on the leaping flames. "Should I start worrying?"

"Worrying about what?" Shifting his gaze, he locked it on Chris's clouded one. "Even if I wanted, I couldn't do anything with her." And that was a real shame.

"Except consume her to death," Chris snapped annoyed.

"You don't seem to mind the treatment." So he pushed back.

"Are you comparing me to her?" Chris's eyebrow shot up in obvious disbelief. "In case you haven't noticed, we're different."

"How different?" Duncan challenged on purpose.

For as strange as it sounded, there was some sort of common element linking the two together, even if he had no idea what it was.

"Are you joking or being serious?" On top of him, Chris pinned him to the couch.

"A little of both." Twisting around, he slipped from under Chris's hold, lying next to him. "I'm sorry, Angel. I can't give you any straight answers now." *Not with that damn trick of hers of stealing my mind that has tormented me ever since I woke up in her damn bed.* "I'm quite confused about it myself."

"What's there to be confused?" The blue-gray eyes sparked in anger. "She's just a fuck, while we share a connection." Chris's gaze traveling over his face was clearly looking for reassurance. "Or have you forgotten?"

"Relax, Angel." He cupped his worried face. "This has nothing to do with you and of course, I haven't forgotten about us." The tip of his tongue traced the tempting lips, briefly darting into the warm cavity. "I feel our connection every time I see and touch you." One hand slipped down his angel's back. "But the funny thing is I feel one with her, too."

"The same kind?" It was kind of evident Chris was holding his breath in anxious wait of his answer.

"Of course not." Still, a bond did exist, however hard it was for him to discern exactly what it was. "It's different, but just like yours, I can't ignore it."

"Are you sure it isn't witchcraft as your mother suggests?" Chris insisted.

His heart went out to his blond angel, for the ground was falling away from under his feet.

"I know for sure, 'cause witchcraft doesn't exist." No, not even if he was already thinking of her as a witch did he seriously believe she was one. It simply was not rational. Endowed with great power, yes, he had no trouble accepting that. He was also pretty sure she ran the risk of misusing it because untrained in it. But he would never stoop so low as believing in such superstitions.

And looking at his angel, he had the feeling he did not, either, however much he insisted on such explanations.

"It's just a woman's allure, which is far more intoxicating than I gave her credit for at the beginning." Pushing Chris down on the couch, he flattened him. "Then again, I also underestimated a very particular man's allure, and look where that's gotten me." Taking full possession of the thin lips, his tongue swept the wet cavity and filled his senses with his lover's pungent taste. "Fuck her, Angel." His breath came short after he managed to pull away. "All I wonder now is how to take you upstairs and fuck you until I'm too exhausted to think about anything."

"Thought you'd never ask." A wide grin spreading on the beautiful face, a mischievous twinkle lit up his intriguing eyes. "Come on." Scrambling to his feet, the angel stretched out a hand to help him rise.

So Duncan clasped it firmly then led the way to the dark

hall, flying up the stairs to the safety of his bedroom.

CHAPTER TWENTY-SEVEN

It must be early morning. Too early if the pale light filtering through thick gray clouds was any indication. Already awake, he rolled on a side, glancing around his semi-circular room at the tower's upper level.

He just loved all of it—the low steps dividing the room into two sections, the large fireplace next to the door with the comfortable couches in front of it, the wide table and chairs at the end opposite the fireplace, the huge bed nestled between two giant glass doors, and the intense-blue carpet lining the floor. Big yet cozy, the room usually had a soothing effect on him.

Not today, alas.

And even staring out of the glass door was no help. The side he was on faced Black Rose's green valleys. Behind him, the other one led to a balcony overlooking the cliffs, straight above the sea. Only today, the sound of the waves crashing against the high steep bluffs agitated him more.

Annoyed, he turned around in the spacious bed, his gaze falling on the angel sleeping on his belly. Blond hair ruffled, body relaxed for once, he resisted the urge to touch him, knowing full well the predictable ending was he to wake the seductive creature. Which did not seem like such a bad idea, since he had woken up with the same fixed thought he had when he had fallen asleep—Ylianor Meyer.

He cursed under his breath. Chris and the other night's amazing sex had brought no relief, and now he had to do something.

Leaving the warm bed, he descended the couple of steps that separated the night from the dayside, the early morning air cool on his naked skin. After a quick stop in the bathroom, he sat at the table and grabbed the nearest piece of paper. A moment's concentration, then he scribbled, *Come to my room at the thirty-sixth hour. I need to talk to you. D.*

Folding the slip of paper, he had to locate his pants, lost in the tangle of clothes strewn on the floor. Too hungry and excited, he and Chris had just tossed them aside, and now his pants lay in a confused heap near one of the couches. Picking them up, he placed the note in a pocket. After dropping them back on the floor, he raised his gaze and caught the brilliant blue-gray eyes trained on him.

"Good morning, lover." Not quite fully awake if his sleepy tone was any indication, Chris yawned and stretched luxuriously, still lying on his belly.

"Good morning, Angel." Returning to bed, he rolled Chris on a side, not surprised to see the hard cock, jutting up proudly. "Someone certainly woke up with an appetite." Clasping its firm length, he began a slow jerking. "Dreaming of anybody in particular?" That folded the skin over the bulging head, then down to the balls in a rhythmical slide.

Which of course perked up his own cock to immediate attention.

"Maybe . . ." Chris grinned playfully. "But if you give me a moment, I'll try to come up with a name."

Reluctantly letting go of the scrumptious piece of firm meat, he watched him going to the bathroom. Just a few seconds absence, then he came back with an erection that seemed bigger than when he had left.

"Now, where were we?" Laughing like a little boy, the angel fell back into the bed.

"Right here, I believe." Gripping the swollen shaft, he gulped it in one intake alone, rewarded by a loud gasp and by his own stick turned into slab of stone all together.

Clamping his neck, Chris pushed his head further down until he swallowed the balls, too. Practically gagged on them, for his angel's piece was so far down his throat, it was going for his stomach.

Not that he complained.

It was always like that between them. Rough and hard, which was exactly how they both liked it best.

Only thing, having the stiff cock so deep in his mouth had just spun his craving to a whole new level. So he had to grab his marble-like rod and jerk it forcefully to give himself a measure of relief. Then again, the best way to achieve it was cracking that scrumptious ass, regardless of how sore it must still be from the other night's fierce possession.

Sucking the angel to the hilt, he could not stop thinking about that tight behind of his. The scorching way it stretched then squeezed him to milk all the juice out always drove him crazy. Literally. And lapping the taut gland from top to bottom, his only thought was to impale it again and make it sorer than all the previous night's ruthless ramming.

That did it!

He just could not take it anymore!

Getting free of Chris's hold, he straightened, flipped him on his belly and shoved his huge shaft through the pliable ring. From the fat crown to the balls, he reached the guts with a single thrust.

Well, almost.

Safe to say, he plunged into liquid fire, already losing it as that fabulous rear sucked him to the root. Kind of evident the angel wanted it as badly as he did, so Duncan wasted no time, except what strictly needed to ensure that friction did not interfere with their pleasure. Once slicked up the channel from the first slower pumping, he increased the beat to a frenzied tempo. He truly wanted to get to the throat going through the guts, and the fiercer his blows, the more chances he had of success. And with Chris swinging upward at each of his downward slams, he might get his wish sooner than he anticipated.

Or would have, had that sensual angel of his not crumbled under pressure.

He knew the signs all too well to have any doubts. Chris was about to explode from his own pleasure. But he was right along, the tip of his erection already throbbing impatiently from the need to burst.

At the first contraction, the cramped space clenched all at once around his cock. And since each consecutive wave was like a jerk off, he had no way to resist the infectious tide enfolding him, too, and letting it all go straight into his angel's capacious butt.

CHAPTER TWENTY-EIGHT

"Wow! What a great way to wake up!" Shifting away from under his weight, the angel trapped him, kissing him fiercely. "How can I ever dream of anyone else?" Chris scoffed, in between gulps of air and tongue slides to his throat. "Lover, you are the only one who constantly sets me on fire, and that's what keeps me alive and coming back for more." Eyes fixed on Duncan's face, he pressed his point, "As for all the others, Arthur included, I just use them whenever you're not available. I know it's hard to believe seeing how much sex I have with others—"

"And how you love to give your ass around to just about any cock wanting to take it," he teased.

"Only because you're not around all thirty-six hours of my day to take it for yourself," Chris retorted.

"While Arthur and his boys are." He chuckled.

"They're better than nothing." Chris smirked.

"I think you don't give Arthur enough credit." In spite of what he had admitted about Arthur, his angel continued to have the tendency to downplay the deep effect the leader had on him. "He's the most powerful man of our lands after all."

And damn Ylianor and her show of power for making him realize things were not always what they appeared to be!

"Powerful?" Chris shrugged. "Arthur never struck me as having much power."

"But he must have it." There was no way around it. "Or

177

he wouldn't be Leader of the High Council."

"You really think the High Council is a place of power?" The angel's forehead creased. "Seeing all the petty jealousies, the aimless gossip and the obsessive sex, I find it hard to believe. Most of the times, those people sitting there don't seem fit to represent their districts, imagine how they could wield any sort of power." Mocking to the point of being offensive, Chris shook his head with such determination that he wondered whether he knew more than he was telling. "No, nothing ever gave me the impression that most of them were anything but bored, spoiled oafs out to have a good time, rather than rule, or whatever it is they're supposed to be doing."

"Could be . . ." Unconvinced, he glanced out the glass door with the sea view and realized it was later than he thought.

And they had a date to keep.

"Come on." Freeing himself from Chris's entanglement, he got to his feet. "We're late, and if we don't get ready, my sister will come looking for us here."

"Mmm . . . can't wait." That seductive angel of his stretched in such an erotic way he knew he was just looking for an excuse to delay the inevitable meeting. "It's a pity she hasn't gone through the phase."

"She'll make up for it with a grand pledge." Or so he hoped as he went through the jumble of clothes on the floor to find his own.

"Only if she's very, very . . ." A sarcastic snarl twisted Chris's thin lips. "No, make that extremely lucky." Finally leaving the bed, he retrieved his pants.

And just in time, since a knock had them both scrambling to finish dressing.

"Yes?" Opening the door, he faced a very anxious butler. "Good morning, Reginald." Angling his head behind his shoulders, he caught the blue-gray eyes. *Told you she'd send someone.*

From the smirk crossing Chris's beautiful face, he had no doubt his angel had understood, even if it had been just a thought.

"Good morning, Prince." Reginald bowed deferentially.

Well, the man always did have impeccable manners. It was the motive his father had named him butler, and he never saw a reason to doubt this choice.

"What can I do for you?" Confronting him, he played it like he had no idea what he was doing there.

"Lady Elizabeth says she's ready and will meet you in ten minutes at the front door." Reginald's impassible tone lessened his sister's urgency for sure.

"Can we make it a half hour?" Taking a step forward, Chris looked at Duncan. "We still have to eat breakfast." The enchantingly apologetic smile was for Reginald.

"Yes, please tell her we'll make it in a half hour." Resisting the urge to wrap his arm around Chris and crush the lithe body to him, he forced himself to keep his gaze trained on Reginald. "Is there something else?"

"Yes, sir." The butler nodded. "The lawyer has just sent this note." He handed him a piece of paper.

"Thank you, and I'll see you later." Shutting the door, he skimmed the note quickly.

His blond angel still at his side, he circled his waist and dragged him closer. "He's coming tomorrow after lunchtime."

"Excellent!" Chris threw his arms around him. "So we can leave right after." Then nuzzled his neck before biting it. "Now let's hurry. I'm so hungry I could eat a horse."

Just a figure of speech, of course. The mere idea of eating animals was disgusting, if not downright unconceivable since his people never ate meat. Ever.

"And you, my beautiful lover, better eat something, too."

Suddenly serious, Chris cupped his face between heated palms. "You've barely eaten since yesterday. Skipping lunch and probably breakfast, and those few spoonsful of soup you managed to swallow during dinner aren't certainly enough to keep up your strength." So Chris had noticed. "Maybe you've forgotten I'm not particularly keen on skinny lovers."

"I don't think I run the risk, not yet anyway." He grinned. "But I promise I'll try and eat more."

"You better." A ferocious kiss took his breath away. "This ass of mine needs a whole lot of cock to keep it satisfied, so you better not fail me, especially when we'll be on the road."

"I won't. Don't worry." Clutching both buttocks, he squeezed them tight. "I'll ram it so hard and so often you won't be able to ride."

"I sincerely hope so," Chris breathed huskily.

One last tantalizing kiss, then Chris stepped out and he followed him to the breakfast room.

CHAPTER TWENTY-NINE

"Good morning, pet." Anne's scowl promised nothing good. "I hope you came to get some breakfast, 'cause it's way past the time you should've been here." She glanced around the empty kitchen. "In case you didn't know, breakfast is around nine—"

"I know, Anne, sorry." It was almost the thirteenth hour, after all, too late for breakfast yet too early for lunch. "And I don't need breakfast, anyway. I just needed—"

"You need food, so sit down." With a tone that did not admit any objections, Anne pulled out a chair from under the table. "Lucky for you, I always overcook, so there are plenty of leftovers all the time." Going to the stove, she filled up a dish in no time at all. "Here."

At the sight of the giant platter, her stomach yelped dismayed. "Anne, I can't possibly eat all this."

"Just start, honey." Her tone gentler, Anne sat next to her. "That's all I ask."

"Oh, all right." Resigned, she grabbed the fork Anne handed her and eyed her favorite cheese half-hidden under the beans and the eggplants. "A few bites won't hurt." After carefully freeing the cheese, she brought it to her lips.

"More than a few bites, I hope." Shaking her head, Anne regarded her critically. "You really have to put on more meat on those bones—"

"Anne, quick." Entering like she had the most pressing business in the world, Alicia Merryweather rushed to the table. "Lady Elizabeth asked me to fix a few sandwiches to

181

bring along during her ride with her brother and Lord Templeton."

"Sure, no problem." Rising, Anne returned to the stove and got immediately busy.

"They'll also be needing their horses." This was for her, since Alicia narrowed her gaze on Ylianor.

"Right now?" The half-eaten bite of cheese still in her mouth, she wondered whether she should get up and run out like Missus Merryweather seemed to expect her to do.

"It would be preferable," Alicia snapped. "Instead of sitting here for a late breakfast."

Kind of obvious the woman could not stand her, and she had no need of lights to confirm it.

"Hush, Alicia." Quick to jump in her defense, Anne glared at the housekeeper. "I know for a fact that neither the prince nor his phase mate have been anywhere near the breakfast room, so it's obvious they are nowhere near ready to go."

"Lady Elizabeth just sent Reginald up to the prince's room to inquire about him." Tart and malicious, Missus Merryweather did not intend to let her off the hook. "So I believe it's just a matter of minutes before they come looking for their horses."

"All right, then I'm going." *Couldn't possibly finish all this food anyway.* "Thanks, Anne, it was delicious." Glad for the excuse, she scrambled to the door. "The cheese especially."

CHAPTER THIRTY

Walking to the stables, she could not help noticing how dismal the day really was, with thick clouds looming at the horizon and heavy grey skies pressing everything into a deathly stillness. If anything, it looked worse than when she had gone out with the prince, which in the end had not turned out so bad. *Maybe they'll be as lucky.* She giggled, hurrying to the stables.

Even if the place was fairly clean, she wanted everything to be spotless for their arrival and began from Starlet's stall, working her way through each one until she came to Fuzeon's.

"The stables seem empty." On hearing the woman's voice ringing out, she immediately recognized Elizabeth, her high-pitched tone unforgettable no matter how many years had passed.

"Duncan, didn't you tell me you hired a new stable keeper?" This male voice she did not recognize immediately. But guessing from the frenzied shivers running down her back, it must belong to Christopher Templeton. "I'm anxious to know him."

And guessing just from the anger she detected in his tone, he must be as pissed off as he sounded.

"It's a she, not a he." Elizabeth obviously could not wait to set him straight.

They were definitely coming her way. And she had no wish to confront them, one in particular.

"You hired a woman?" She recognized the demon's biting

inflexion. "Now that's what I call a smart move. Is she better qualified?" Openly taunting, it was like he was daring her to show her face. "Please enlighten me. We're having problems with stable keepers at Fair Haven, so perhaps I could tell my father to try a woman for a change. I'm sure he'll think it's a splendid idea."

Fuck you, Christopher Templeton! I'm not afraid of you and of your smoldering energy!

She had to think it to give herself that extra courage she needed to face the dastardly demon. Knowing him, he would not go away until he had put her down as he had when they were just kids. Only this time, she was ready for him.

"Oh, hush, Chris." From Elizabeth's elated notes, Ylianor supposed she was very happy. "Don't spoil this perfect day, not when I'm about to get on Praline again."

Heck of a day to go riding. Then again, knowing Elizabeth, she would have braved the worst storm just to be with Chris.

Gathering Fuzeon, Praline and the newly arrived black horse, she approached the entrance and spied their advances toward the stables from a crack in the wood.

By the gods, could that really be Lord Christopher Templeton?

She remembered the beautiful boy riding to Black Rose in his false angel disguise. She did not expect the striking man striding down the small slope that connected the main building to the stables. No, not even Anne's admired words had prepared her for such a shocking sight. Because he was a god, like Anne had said, a veritable one that was out of anybody's reach but the handsome prince walking by his side. And poor Elizabeth simply disappeared between the two gorgeous men.

Particularly now that one of them was charging up, his lights flashing red like crazy. Similar to the leaping flames she remembered from her childhood, his pattern had not changed at all nor had Elizabeth's, in spite of the ten years that had passed since she had last seen them.

Well, like it or not, she was back to stay, so the sooner they got used to it, the better.

She stepped outside, and the first thing that caught her eye was the sudden switch in Chris's aura. A change so brusque, it was as if his heart had dropped to his stomach upon seeing her, like he had not expected her to be a replica of the prince, rather a fat ugly woman who had conquered his lover's favors only thanks to her power. Too bad for him, her resemblance to Duncan was as uncanny as her connection to him, which fueled Chris's rage to a point of no return. Same point she remembered he had reached on his arrival at Black Rose, the first time he had ever set foot in her native home.

No, worse!

In his rush to charge up, she felt him yanking Elizabeth's fury and blending it with his to make it stronger. And from the fast way this combined energy was building up, he would show no mercy this time.

Which meant she was in deep shit.

And that she had to find help, if she did not want to go up in smoke.

As Chris was about to throw his flaming ball of fire, she seized the closest and most abundant source of energy available and combined it with hers, becoming twice as powerful as the demon in the space of seconds.

It was just unfortunate that the energy she literally stole belonged to Duncan, the appropriation so violent and invasive she felt his shock and outrage. But, in spite of his stupefied and deceived look, he chose not to stop the power flowing between them, even if she would direct it against his lover.

Which threw off Chris completely.

He could not believe it! Just could not get why his precious prince would actively support her against him. And that sense of betrayal sagged the avalanche he was about to throw at her like a balloon that had lost air too fast, too soon.

In the general uncertainty and odd stillness that followed, she handed Praline's reins to Elizabeth, the black horse to Chris and Fuzeon to Duncan. On touching his hand, she felt a jolt as though his numbness wore off all together. Even more surprised than before, his black eyes lingered on her face while he fumbled in his pocket, taking out a slip of paper that he gave her. She took it before mentally clapping to release time, watching them ride off, bewildered and utterly confused.

CHAPTER THIRTY-ONE

"What was that all about?" David came charging from the house just as the prince disappeared behind the bend, an angry black cloud hanging over him. "What sort of evil witchcraft have you worked on them?"

Pocketing the prince's note, Ylianor spun around. "What are you talking about?"

"I saw everything from the kitchen." His lights were definitely off, dangerously close to a bursting point. "What have you done?"

"Nothing." She honestly did not know nor cared to explain. Not to him anyway. "I assure you." Not when the man needed something more effective than words to calm down. "They came to get their horses, and I complied. That's it."

"You're lying." More upset, he was on her before she even realized it.

"What if I am?" Ylianor challenged. "What are you going to do about it?"

There was only one thing to do, and she knew it. So she pushed him to it. The moment his indignation turned into uncontrollable lust he ripped off her clothes and squeezed the naked flesh in frenzy.

She surrendered immediately. She had too much negative buildup herself to oppose him in any way.

He carried her upstairs, threw her on the bed, removed the last of her clothes and sprawled on her. Hard cock digging in her belly, he forced her mouth open and plunged a hungry tongue to her throat. His hand continued to stroke her side and buttock, his rough touch more arousing than she would have thought.

That was when she realized how wet she really was, how much she wanted him to take her. Arching, she spread her legs wide, and he sank in her pussy. Wrapping her legs around his waist, she trapped him inside her cunt, relishing his forceful shoves, which grew fiercer because of the constricted position.

And while she melted under his erratic beat, she noticed the black cloud of rage evaporating with every slam that enlarged her slit to his convenience. And he was definitely large and thick enough to stretch it far beyond what she had initially imagined.

When his breath became shorter, she knew she had to hurry if she did not want him to leave her behind. Even if she was still kind of new at this game, the prince had already made her discover a few things about her body that came in handy just for the occasion. Like tensing the muscles of her legs, swinging her hips to screw him deep inside her, balls included, and bending backward so her clit rubbed against his belly, which made her climax at the same moment he did.

"I'm sorry, Ylianor." Still quivering from the potency of his orgasm, he rolled off her. "I don't know what came over me."

"You were angry." She raked her hand through his thick short brown hair. "And I helped you feel more . . ." *Positive? Free?* "Relaxed." That seemed like the best choice of word.

"Then you're really a witch." He looked at her, a hint of suspicion clouding his hazel eyes.

"Come on, David." She giggled. "It takes no witchcraft to seduce a man, or all women would be witches."

"This never happened to me before." His gaze traveled

188

over her naked body for the first time. "You really are very beautiful."

His soft tone and light touch unleashed a storm of shivers that creased her skin, going wild in the strange mix of irritation and pleasure.

"You know, I can't explain it, but you feel so much like . . ." Embarrassed, he averted his gaze.

"Like him?" Not hard to guess. "Do you think we look alike?"

"Not exactly." He narrowed his focus on her as though he wanted to study her. "There's something about you . . ." He paused, probably trying to get it first right in his head. "An air about you that makes me think of him."

"You love him, don't you?" She searched his face to confirm what his lights had already revealed. "And before you ask, this is no more witchcraft than what I said before." Affectionately, she caressed his handsome face. "It's just that you have it written all over you, I can't help picking it up."

"He's all I've got." Turning on his back, hands behind his head, he stared at the ceiling. "I've dedicated my life to him, but he's too much in love with . . ." He hesitated, obviously unsure if she knew about it.

"I know he loves Christopher Templeton." So she came to his rescue.

"He told you?" Looking surprised, he raised an eyebrow.

"He doesn't have to, David." Curling on a side, she leaned her head against his chest. "I've known it from the start, even before he did." While Chris, he had known from the beginning that Duncan was his, marking and sealing him like only a demon could. "And this is no witchcraft, either." Laughing, she pressed a hand to his mouth.

He kissed her palm before lifting it. "For a while, I deluded myself it was just the phase, but now — "

"No, David, the phase has little to do with their feelings."

And who better than she knew it?

She had seen their connection and the deep entanglement of emotions and feelings it carried along, and how it had burst out that faraway summer day on the hills of Black Rose.

"Then I really don't stand a chance," he breathed heavily.

"Come on, David." His disappointment touched her deeper than she cared to admit. "I'm sure there are plenty of people out there who'd be delighted to have you, men and women alike."

"No one is like him." Well, she could certainly agree to that.

Duncan Caldwell was one of a kind. And if she had thought so when just a silly little girl running after her prince, what she had glimpsed the other day, in this very room, had made her realize his immense potential.

"Which is why I could never love anyone else." Then his lips curved in a tentative smile. "But there are a few I like out there, so I guess that's a start, right?" Playfully, he tapped her nose.

"It's a great start." She smiled at him encouragingly. "But just so you know, you can love more than one person at a time."

"I could never." From his resigned tone, she gathered he might have given this some considerable thought. "It's simply impossible for me. As for Prince Caldwell, you said it yourself. He has loved Christopher Templeton since childhood, and no one else has even come close to his heart in all this time."

I will. "Oh, I wouldn't be so sure." She grinned confidently. "Life can be full of surprises."

"What about you?" Shifting on a side, he pinned her to the mattress, weighing on her. "Have you found your special one?"

I have, only he doesn't know it yet. "I haven't been looking, nor have I come in contact with too many people . . ." She left it vague on purpose. What was the use of remembering how alone she had really been?

"That's because many are afraid of you." His hazel eyes flashed with worry, as though he had caught her unspoken question. "You're too different for their simple taste."

"Does that include you, David?" A provocative smile curved her lips.

"I could get used to you." Then brushing his lips against hers, he stroked her breasts.

With a sigh of pleasure, she arched her back to give him more flesh to caress, knowing he would be gentler this time. The fury forgotten, his slow brushes won her over, making her desire spin when he bent to flick his tongue on the hard nipples begging for attention. He sucked avidly, taking each taut bud in his mouth and lapping it leisurely.

Thrashing under him, she pushed her hips against his swollen cock, swaying to make him feel the intensity of her cunt's aching need.

He did not fall for it, his tongue busy tracing her sensual curves. But when his fingers slipped between her legs and glided on her dripping juice, he had no further qualms.

Oh, she did love how he took her, nice and slow, penetrating an inch at a time as though he wanted to savor it all. And she did want the whole of him, opening up to his demanding shaft and to his long, forceful shoves that were so unlike the earlier frenzy. Still, he pumped her good and proper, sliding in and out of her slit with a tempo he accelerated the moment she increased her hip rotation to brush her clit against his crotch.

Lost in his erotic dance, the pressure and the friction became unbearable when he stepped up his tempo to a hammering, and intense heat waves drowned her in rapid, consecutive contractions that made her spin out of control.

And for the second time, she did not scream. Not one sound, not even a moan escaped her lips. Not because she did not like it. Because, unlike Duncan, he seemed unable to go beyond the physical plane, his raw spirit feeling as cold and impenetrable as ice. Which gave her the impression there was more than one secret he wanted to protect from the world.

Well, he could keep them. She was not after anybody's secrets, just her power often revealed more than she wanted to know.

When he came, she was still convulsing in her own throes, clenching his stone-like beast so hard he obviously could not resist.

"Feeling better?" He beamed at her while tracing the contours of her face.

"I'm great!" She returned his infectious smile. "What about you?"

A loud crash ruptured the sky. Then a veritable deluge hit the land, every dense cloud flooding whatever came under it. Thunder and lightning spiced up the storm with bright flashes and low rumbles.

"Are all the horses inside?" Scrambling to his feet, he quickly dressed.

"Yes." Jumping out of the bed, she wore the pieces of clothes he had scattered around the room and on the stairs. "But I'll go check on them."

"I'll help you before I return to the house." He handed her the shirt he had tossed aside before flinging her on the bed. "The gods only know how damaging these thunderstorms can be."

Racing downstairs behind him, she stopped in the back to look on Starlet. David, instead, reached the entrance in time to take the riders wet horses before they ran to the safety of the house.

"I'll take care of them." Clutching the three pair of bridles off David's hands, she tugged the horses forward. "You better go check if they need anything."

He hesitated, unwilling it seemed to leave her there alone. "Aren't you coming for lunch?"

"I'm not hungry, thank you." Why was everybody always overly concerned about her eating habits? "I'll see you later."

"Anne isn't going to like it," he sniggered.

"Just tell her I'm too busy to eat." She squeezed his shoulder reassuringly. "Don't worry." She placed a gentle kiss on his cheek. "I'll be fine."

But he turned his head and trapped her mouth in a fierce exchange. As though he had not gotten enough of her, he slid his tongue deep inside her mouth, sweeping her wet cavity with possessive strokes of flaming desire that started a dull throb in her cunt. Then, before she had the chance to recover, he pulled away and was gone.

CHAPTER THIRTY-TWO

"Yes?" At the knock, Elizabeth went to stand behind the closed door.

Not that she wanted to see anyone.

Not after the disastrous day out, the hurried return and the forced indoor staying. All the storm's fault for having continued beyond the morning's initial thick downpour and spoiled the rest of the day, not just the aborted ride. And what had been that thing that happened at the stables? That thing that had yanked her insides and ripped them right out as if they had not belonged to her anymore?

Whatever it had been, she could not shake the feeling Ylianor had done something to her. Maybe the witchcraft Mother had been howling about was not a fabrication after all. Maybe Ylianor was really a witch and had cast some sort of spell over them all.

That would certainly explain why the air in Black Rose was so thick she had avoided both Duncan and Chris.

Which to her was unimaginable!

To stay away from Lord Christopher Templeton that is. Every time he came to Black Rose, she would have liked to stay by his side the whole daylong. Every time he came to Black Rose, he was forever engaged with Duncan, and she could do nothing except wish things could be different. As if they ever could be.

She had seen eight-year-old Chris riding into Black Rose, had seen how he had looked at Duncan, had known she stood no chance. Still, she hoped. She just could not help it.

"Lady Elizabeth." A second knock, this time more forceful, made her jump.

"Yes, yes." Hurriedly throwing open the door, she found herself face to face with Sarah. "What is it?"

"It's your mom, Milady." The servant shifted her feet nervously. "She'd like to see you."

"Thank you, Sarah." *Exactly what I need, my mother breathing down my neck.* "Tell her I'll be right there." Then she closed the door.

A quick check in the large mirror on her wall and she headed to her mother's room.

"My dear, what happened to you today?" Lady Caldwell patted the seat next to her on the couch she was occupying. "The servants told me you remained in your room the whole day."

"It's raining, Mother." She glanced at the storm still in full progress out the window as she sat next to her. "Haven't you noticed?"

"Of course, I have." Not that it made any difference to her.

She knew it well enough. When her mother was preoccupied with something, it became a sort of obsession that engaged all her thoughts and her attention.

"But that's hardly an excuse to stay locked up in your room." Another thing about her mother—she had the best spy network of all of Black Rose! "But let's start at the beginning. Didn't you go out riding this morning?"

"We did, but the rain caught us after only half an hour." Which in retrospect was not such a terrible thing.

Something had been definitely off between Duncan and Chris right after that . . . incident at the stables.

"I've never seen so much water in all my life." Sighing wearily, she glanced outside again. "And it hasn't stopped since."

"No, it hasn't, and it isn't natural." Her mother pursed her lips as though she did not like it at all. "Like most of the things that have been happening since Duncan brought that wretched creature back where she doesn't belong."

She groaned inwardly. Now why was she so not surprised that the main topic would be Ylianor?

"You mean about the storm?" Unsure whether her mother would blame Ylianor for that, too, she stared at Sophia perplexed.

"The storm is just nature's way of telling us things aren't right." Lady Caldwell shrugged. "And since she comes from a long line of witches, I wouldn't put it past her to have provoked it. I mean, after the way she weaseled her way back here and with Duncan catering to her every whim as if he didn't have a mind of his own, nothing would surprise me," she spat, positively livid with jealousy and hatred.

"Come on, Mother." Aghast at what she was glimpsing of her real nature, she refused to think Sophia Caldwell could really harbor those feelings.

Sure, she herself had no great love for Ylianor, either. In fact, she had been happy her mother had kicked out of Black Rose what she considered a rival. She remembered how envious she had been of the beautiful little girl when just a child, how jealous she had been of her father and brother's complete bewitchment with her. While she, Elizabeth, had been kind of plain and had never quite caught half of the attention Ylianor had. Nor had she ever looked like Duncan, for that matter. As unlike him as a complete stranger, it was just a cruel joke on destiny's part that a complete stranger was so like him. Still, she knew she would never reach the abysses she saw her mother sinking in every day more.

"Do you really believe my brother to be under a spell?" No, somehow her mother's logic was faulty, and she was finding it increasingly hard to believe her.

"I know he is," Sophia scoffed, looking annoyed Elizabeth dared doubt her. "I remember these symptoms all too well, having gone through them with your father."

"It started like this?" Suddenly curious, she leaned closer.

"Well, not quite, but I knew the girl was trouble the moment I set eyes on her." From the assured way her mother said it, she wondered whether the girl had carried a mark or something that Sophia had recognized at first glance.

"But how could Father fall for that woman?" This still escaped her.

"They are not ordinary women." Sophia sighed deeply. "They are witches who manipulate men."

This sounded farfetched. True, she had little experience with men, yet it seemed improbable one could command them like horses. Still, and on the rare chance such women did exist, she would have loved to learn their secrets in the hope they might work on Chris, too.

"Do you think it works on any man . . ." She cleared her throat. "Or only on specific ones?"

"What exactly do you want to know?" Somehow, her mother knew where she was going.

"Nothing, Mother." Steadily fixing the floor, she shifted her feet nervously. "Just wondering aloud."

"Always thinking about Lord Templeton, aren't you?" Sophia reached out to stroke her cheek. "I told you, it's too early. You have to be patient with him. Eventually, he'll outgrow his phase and be free to notice you."

"You keep saying this, but I don't believe it anymore," she scoffed angrily, choking on a burst of the morning's rage and shock at finding her rival turned into a beautiful woman, with that old envy clogging her up again. But what had really hurt had been catching Chris staring at Ylianor with something so intense she could not quite define. *Was it hate? Desire? Lust? Amazement? All of these and more.* A downright

197

appreciation laced with a sensual craving that had crushed all of her hopes, because the arresting blue-gray eyes had never looked at her in quite the same way.

And it had made her furious!

At least until something or someone had ripped off that incandescent mass of flaming rage, and she was still wondering how anything or anyone could have pulled such a stunt.

"Just give it time, honey." All nice and sweet, her mother brushed back a loose strand of hair from Elizabeth's face. "You'll see."

"But why are he and Duncan so tight?" If she had to be honest, she envied their relationship — so easygoing, so close, so sensual, so unlike any other she had ever seen. "Sometimes they look to me like they're closer than brothers or best friends." And she could not help feeling bitter at the unfairness of the situation. "And I just don't understand it."

"That's because you haven't had a phase," her tone gentle for a change. "You see, whatever else you do in life, your phase mate will always remain special, a friend above all other friends. He or she becomes an important part of your life, whatever direction you choose to take afterward." Sophia shifted position. "That's why phases are often more important than pledges themselves, 'cause that bond is such a unique one."

"Then why didn't I have a phase?" Elizabeth sniveled resentfully.

"No one knows, dear," her mother cooed softly. "It's just the way of life that some people have it, and some don't." She bit her lower lip as though lost in meditation. "For sure, people never, ever forget their phase. I can still remember mine, the joy, the anticipation and wonder of exploring new horizons with my special girlfriend." Caressing Elizabeth's long hair, she paused, probably to relive her experience. "I had hoped you'd live it, too, but . . ." She hesitated. "I'm sorry you didn't."

A knock and Sophia turned to the door. "Yes, who is it?"

"It's Alicia Merryweather, Lady Caldwell," the woman raised her voice, "I wanted to inform you dinner's ready."

"Come in, please." Her mother stared at the door, smiling the moment Alicia entered and came to stand in front of her. "Thank you." Lady Caldwell reclined on the seat, which to Elizabeth looked like she did not want to get up any time soon. "We'll be down in a moment. How are things with the staff?"

"There seems to be a certain strain among the servants these days." Missus Merryweather cleared her throat. "I'm not sure I like what is happening."

"Is it that wretched creature's fault?" Quick to lay blame, Sophia snarled malevolent.

Of course, Alicia knew perfectly who that wretched creature was, as did everyone else in Black Rose.

"Frankly, Milady, I'm not sure." Alicia shook her head. "I haven't seen much of her around."

"Isn't she always hanging around *my* house?" Astonished, Lady Caldwell's eyes widened. "Around *my son*, to be more specific, to cast her wicked spells on him?"

"She spends most of her time secluded in the stables," Alicia was quick to set the record straight. "She hardly even joins us during meals, has skipped lots of those actually."

"Does she talk a lot?" Somehow, Elizabeth expected she did not.

The proud and self-assured woman she had seen at the stables did not strike her as much of a talker.

"Hardly said two words in a row since she's been here." Alicia confirmed her impression. "She only answers when spoken to, otherwise she eats in silence and leaves as soon as she's done. Only the cook has some sort of hold over her, but that's understandable. It seems Anne and her family raised the girl after her mother died."

"Still, I'm sure life was better before she came," Lady Caldwell's mellifluous tone sounded insistent.

"Well . . ." Alicia seemed like she was trying to remember how exactly it had been. "She does put a lot of strain on the men, particularly on David."

"My son's personal valet?" Shocked, Sophia's eyebrows flew up in the air.

"Yes." Missus Merryweather nodded. "His eyes never leave her."

"Not a good sign." A malicious gleam crossed her gaze. "But if my son wants her here, I guess we can't do anything about it."

Now that was strange coming from Sophia, an unexpected change of heart Elizabeth could not quite understand.

"At least not until he leaves with Lord Templeton," Lady Caldwell sniggered in a cold tone that sent an icy shiver down Elizabeth's back. "And if something were to happen to her before he returns, he could never blame us." Her gaze swung on the housekeeper. "Could he, Alicia?"

Wondering if she had heard correctly, she jumped in alarmed, "Mother, what are you talking about?"

"I guess not, Milady," Missus Merryweather's voice, instead, was as calm and as even as though she understood perfectly and agreed with Sophia.

Which stopped Elizabeth's heartbeat.

"Working with horses can be very dangerous, especially for a woman." As silky and as treacherous as a snake, her mother licked her lips in satisfaction and probably in anticipation. "Accidents can happen any time, and she skips her meals too often to keep up her strength . . ." Even if she did not finish, the scenario she painted was unmistakable.

No, she must be having hearing hallucinations.

"Mother—"

"Hush, Elizabeth." Sophia's bright eyes burned with repressed glee. "Missus Merryweather and I are just talking. That's all." She spun back to Alicia. "When my son leaves, we'll have plenty of time to get to know this . . . young lady better, aren't we?"

"We most certainly will." A sinister snarl twisted the housekeeper's lips. "I'm sure we'll find more than one opportunity, Lady Caldwell."

"Good!" Her obsession sated for once, Sophia nodded vigorously. "Thank you, Alicia. That'll be all." She waved a hand to dismiss the servant. "We'll be down soon."

"Yes, Milady." Bowing, the buxom woman retreated to the door and left.

While astonished and bewildered, she wondered if her mother would really dare hurt Ylianor. *And if so, what am I going to do about it?*

CHAPTER THIRTY-THREE

"Thank you for coming." After jumping up the moment she had knocked on his door at the thirty-sixth hour, he searched inside the arresting green eyes while standing on the threshold. "Please, come in." Stepping aside to let her through, he gestured toward the couch, all the while wondering why he would have rather taken her to his bed in spite of his priorities.

Now why did the damn woman have such a spell over him? Did the anger he had nursed the whole daylong have something to do with it?

Not a clue.

All he knew was that he was a fool!

That he would have kicked himself for being unable to tear his gaze off her sensual body, wrapped in a faded and worn blue dress that exalted her every tempting curve.

Which stirred his cock painfully, already twitching from the craving to have her, urging him to forget about anything and just claim her as his own.

For such she was, despite everything that had happened at the stables. Also despite his angel's furious rage that had hung like an ominous cloud over Black Rose, worse than the storm beating on the roof and glass doors or the sea crashing angry waves on the cliffs.

But this was all beside the point.

First, he needed to understand, not just what happened, how she managed to get to him so fast, so deep.

"Would you care for a drink?" Opening a small cabinet

hanging on the wall, he reached for a bottle and a couple of glasses, offering her one.

"No, thank you." She held up her hand. "Not if we have to talk —"

"Damn right we do!" Duncan spat, sounding angrier than he wished. "What in the gods' name happened yesterday and today?" Tossing glasses and bottle on the table, he went to the fireplace and sat next to her.

"You have the gift." Her green eyes fixed him intently.

"Gift?" *What the fuck is she talking about?* "What gift?"

"It's a special ability, a talent to do something ordinary people can't." Leaning against the arm stand, she continued to stare him in the face. "You and I both have it. Call it power if you prefer, it's a way to manipulate energy —"

"If it's anything like what you did at the stables, I'd call it more like *stealing energy*." Ironic to the point of being offensive, he charged the words to make her feel how despicable she had been.

"Hem . . ." She cleared her throat. "That's another way of seeing it, but it isn't —"

"Listen, Princess. I don't give a damn about what it is really." His tone harsh on purpose, he wanted to drive into her the concept she had been wrong. "Whatever you did these past days has opened a rift between me and the one person I love more than anything else in the world." No, he definitely could not tolerate this sort of behavior. "And that's unforgivable, no matter how reasonable your explanations may be."

"I didn't mean to, honest." Nervously, she twisted her hands. "It's just that . . ." Swallowing hard, her eyes became so huge her face practically disappeared. "Things are more complicated . . . and I don't know where to start."

Trapped!

She felt trapped like a wild animal cornered in a no-win

situation. And that heart of hers beating so loud he could have sworn he heard it was proof enough to him.

So his tone became gentler, "Then let's start with this power you claim we both have." His heart reaching out to her, he would have held her tight and cooed soft nonsense in her ear just to calm her down, had not the need to understand been more pressing. "Is it just limited to us?"

"No, Chris has it, too." Somehow picking up his intention, she regained a measure of control over herself.

And her heart was suddenly not pounding as hard as before.

"My angel?" *Now why am I not surprised?*

"Yes, he has the greatest one I know," she confirmed with a note of healthy respect. "The most powerful for sure, one I've learned not to mess with." Probably on her own skin, seeing how it cringed with visible shivers. "And like me, he has been aware of it ever since he was a child." And she sounded damn proud of it. "Now he has trained it, so wields it in the most destructive way possible. Especially when it comes to you, since you are his only true love."

"How can you tell?" Fascinated, he leaned forward.

"Because I can see it." Her green eyes flashed. "I can see how deeply connected you two are. Passionate lovers, best friends, phase mates and kindred spirits—you share a bond stronger than love, sex or time, which is practically impossible to break."

"Is it that obvious?" Amazed she could read something so private, he sat up straighter.

"Just to me." Her tone tried to reassure him she was not a threat. "'Cause I can see beyond mere appearances. Beyond your flesh and blood, I see the aura that surrounds you, the flashing lights that define your energy form or your immaterial body. And their pattern is unique to every person and shifts according to your mood, which is why I know what you feel—"

"Is that how you know I love the angel?" *And how can you be so sure of something that has taken me years to acknowledge?*

"Partly." The hint of a smile curved her lips, and he had the weird sensation she had read his thought. "Mostly because I was there when it happened during that summer day. Do you remember it?"

"Not with you in it. Everything else . . ." *Can I ever forget it?*

As the images filled his head, he could not shake the sneaky suspicion she was somehow sending them.

Which was absurd.

His stomach churning in anticipation when Chris had come round at the bend was a memory all his own, as was the shiny blond head a sight forever impressed in his mind. Or was it?

"So, where were you?" Because damn it, he could not see her anywhere!

"I was, standing next to you, waiting to continue our game." She pursed her lips. "As soon as I saw him, I knew he wanted you for himself, and it made me furious. You were mine, the handsome prince who belonged to me alone, so I couldn't allow him to take you away."

Then it hit him hard—the unbearable weight of a pain so deep it suffocated his spirit. And it all came from her and from her shattered heart. "Because you were already in love with me—"

"Still am." She blushed violently. "I've loved you since I was a little girl, and you chased me around Black Rose, before he ever came to claim you." Which had broken her heart.

And no, he did not need her to say it out loud. Not with the heaviness weighing on his chest and with the sad look clouding her amazing green eyes.

"Seeing you again, I knew the feeling hadn't changed one

bit, which is also when I realized you might have the gift." She pushed out a heavy breath of air. "And I was so sure of it I'd have used whatever means to make you aware of it, including sex." She shook her head in frustration. "But please don't judge me too harshly. Another part of me is literally terrified of the consequences and insisted I have nothing to do with you." Hanging her head, she averted her gaze as though fearing his rejection. "And maybe I can still leave and avoid more damage, if only you didn't make me feel alive again, for the first time in years."

Well, it was goddamn flattering. He could not deny it, however complicated it would all turn out to be, inevitably altering the balance of things he had worked so hard to achieve.

"Like I haven't felt since Father . . ." Her face turned crimson. "Hem . . ." She looked at him guiltily from under her very long, very thick eyelashes. "I meant your father." Then she raised her gaze. "He had the gift, you know?"

No, of course he did not. "Really?" And the way she said it promised nothing good.

Nothing he would like for sure, however torn he was between curiosity and irritation.

"Is that why he called you Princess?" Still, the former got the better of him.

"Yes, absolutely." A wave of buried memories resurfacing all together seemed to overwhelm her, as though she had denied them for too long. "We were close." As though she had convinced herself she had forgotten them. "So close, he would be in my head all the time, and I was in his. I was part of him just as he was part of me, to the point we could share every thought, every feeling without uttering a single word." It was obvious everything was coming back in a rush. "He made me feel the safest, most loved and most wanted child in the world, and it was simply . . . wonderful." The warmth of the memory made her body glow. "No, make that incredible, because his love flowed like energy waves, rather than mere sounds." Shaking her head, her long hair fluttering around her shoulders, she seemed to be coming out of a trance. "That's why I thought he was my father." She glanced apologetically. "Our connection was too intimate for me to believe otherwise."

My father! He was my father for gods' sake! Not yours!

Now, why was he so angry all of a sudden?

Did not make much sense. Prince Charles had always kept an emotional distance from both his children, so for sure he could not have possibly been so close to a little girl who was a stranger to all effects and purposes. A servant's daughter no less!

No, this was probably her imagination working overtime, something he put down to her loneliness and ten-year estrangement from his family.

"Of course, now I know better," she was quick to point out as though reading his mind. "It would have been impossible for him to be my father, and there's no blood relation between us." Averting her gaze, she stared at the flames flickering in the fireplace. "Still, the bond was there, though I can't explain why, and neither could Prince Charles. Naturally, it all ended with his death."

And her sadness, pain and regret punched him like a blow to the stomach that nearly had him double over from a sense of loss so devastating, there were no words apt to describe it. "It must've been particularly painful for you."

"It was horrible . . ." Her bottom lip trembled, and for a moment he was afraid she would start crying.

Which fortunately for him, she did not.

"I was in the room with him when it happened." Instead, she regained a measure of control. "I know it must sound crazy, but I actually perceived death take him away from me, and I was powerless to stop it. I remember thinking that had I only a fraction of Chris's power, I could've buried it under a shower of fire and saved him." A bitter snarl twisted her lips. "Stupid, I know, but I was desperate and furious it dared take him away from me."

"So where did you steal the energy to help you deal that time?" Duncan teased, partly because he was beginning to understand her mechanism. Mostly because he could not bear the intensity of her pain and wanted to soothe her in his own limited way.

"From the horses." She giggled at the pun. "Having no language, they communicate much the same way I used to with your father. They share emotions with energy waves that anyone receptive enough can pick up. In that particular occasion, Fuzeon came to my rescue, offering his support and strength."

"That's why you have a privileged relationship with him." Dots were definitely connecting in his head.

"Oh, not to worry." An amused twinkle lighting her eyes, she brushed his arm. "Fuzeon loves you above anyone else, even if he keeps an open space for me in case I should need it. Actually, it's funny." She frowned as if realizing something for the first time. "Now that I think of it, at the time I didn't know the first thing about energy. But Fuzeon did, so he taught me how I could use it when I needed extra support, which of course, doesn't excuse what I did today. And even if you might not believe me, I only reacted in self-defense."

"All right." He folded his arms over his chest. "All right, I'm listening."

"I don't want to shift blames." She shrugged as though it really did not matter to her. "But you have to realize how jealous Chris is of you."

He had already, though he would be damned before he admitted it to her.

"Not of your body," she was quick to add. "Of your energy mostly, and of any sex that could unleash your gift, connecting you to me."

Unbidden, the memory of what had so disturbed him after he had flooded her ass rushed to the fore. "So what I saw . . ." Furrowing his brow, he attempted to define exactly his sensations. "No, felt after we had sex was your way of opening a channel between us?"

"It was the start of it." She licked her lips, probably satisfied with her work. "And I'm sure Chris perceived it right away, which is why he was so jealous today he'd have burned me alive." She shuddered as though reliving the moment. "And that little trick of wrenching your sister's rage and combining it to his made him only more powerful and threatening."

"Come on, Princess." This really sounded exaggerated. "How could he possibly —"

"'Cause he's all fire," she spat. "And that's what fuels his power and makes it so much more dangerous than mine ever will be. And he proved it all too soon the first time he stepped in Black Rose." Whatever his angel had done, she had not liked it one bit. "I was just a kid then." At least judging from her expression. "I didn't know the first thing about energy, but I was so jealous of Chris I attacked him with my every power the moment I saw him come toward you."

"How did he react?" If he knew anything of his angel, he would have struck back without a second thought.

"Oh, he couldn't care less about my pitiful efforts." A bitter smile crossed her lips. "He moved energy like a kid moving a pebble and buried me under a fiery mass without even glancing at me. It was like I was inconsequential, so he dismissed me like an annoying insect. No, I never stood a chance against him, especially when he proved he could make me become invisible to your eyes."

"You really think he's the reason I don't remember you?" No, he refused to believe it.

"I can't tell for sure." While she did, no question about it. "But he probably made sure you wouldn't remember me."

"So today was a sort of belated revenge on my angel?" *If not on me all together?*

"I was only defending myself from an opponent I already knew I couldn't beat." She shifted position. "That's why I seized your energy like Chris did with your sister's, even if I was wrong in doing it. I . . ." She glanced at him nervously. "I wasn't thinking clearly. I acted on pure instinct alone, reaching out like I used to do with your father." At her pause, an image of Prince Charles flashed in his mind. "And you were there, a convenient energy source that I had no qualms in stealing, as you cleverly put it."

"You made me feel violated." Just remembering it turned his blood to ice. "And deceived like an intruder had taken a piece of me away."

"I know, and I'm sorry." Her inquisitive gaze searched his face. "But you could've easily stopped me."

How does she manage to know me so goddamn well?

"Yeah, I know." Turning to stare at the fire, he could not deny his responsibility any longer. "After the initial shock, I could've easily pulled back, but you were so scared I didn't want to abandon you."

"So you stood by me . . ." A malicious gleam sparked her green eyes. "In spite of Chris."

And in spite of his angel, all he wanted to do was kiss her senseless, then fuck her until the night was through, instead of acknowledging he had betrayed his adored angel.

Which he had to do, for Chris's hurt gaze had been tormenting him since dinnertime. "And I'll never forgive myself for it."

"I wouldn't be so hard," she retorted. "You chose to support the weaker side."

"Funny, I can't see you as the weaker side." He looked at her skeptically. "Not after today. Wheeling and dealing your way into my father's heart, then between me and my lover—"

"You insisted I return here." Defiant now, he read the challenge in her blazing eyes. "After you came looking for me at the village—"

"I was lost, remember?" Duncan huffed.

"No, you weren't," she snapped. "I'm sure everything happens for a reason—"

"Do you really believe that?" Taken aback, he could not tear his gaze off her mesmerizing green eyes.

"Oh, yes." A warm smile spread on her beautiful face. "Nothing happens by chance. Believe me." Changing position, she settled closer to him. "Life's not a series of random events, rather a complicated pattern, a master plan where things occur for a specific reason, though we may not see it." It was kind of evident she was trying to convince him. "And people often miss it all together, too busy concentrating on inconsequential details of day-to-day routine to notice the greater picture underlying it all."

"While you can see it?" Duncan snarled sarcastic.

"I see beyond the obvious." Spoken without any pride, her tone left no doubt she was telling a truth. "That's why I know you didn't lose your way by accident."

No, he did not believe her.

Still and just for the fun of it, he would play along. "So what's the greater picture here?"

"Even if you might not be aware of it." From her words, not to mention her cold look, it was clear he had not fooled her one bit. "You need to reconnect our severed link. The one Chris has broken that summer day."

"Why?" In spite of himself, he wanted to humor her, unwilling to close the door on someone that was turning out to be more intriguing than he had expected.

"Well, I'm not sure exactly." She shrugged, uncertainty darkening her green eyes. "All I can tell you is that, when I saw you standing on my doorsteps, a part of me knew I could get back the special relationship I had shared with your father." A blaze in her eyes seemed to dispel the earlier doubt. "Actually, you were the only one who could fill his shoes."

"Because I'm my father's son?" Pressing her to a corner, he raised his voice, "Or because you loved me?" Merciless, he continued attacking her. "And used the sex to tie me, hands and feet?"

"No, you got it all wrong." Her hand flew to his chest, pushing him back. "I think we were on the verge of opening our own channel when we were kids, before Chris came I mean."

"You seem to pile an awful lot of negative responsibilities on my angel," he hissed, tired of her attitude. "You make him sound like an irresponsible—"

"An irresponsible evil demon, which is exactly what he is." Unafraid, she threw back her shoulders as though getting ready for a fight. "Who'd destroy whatever stood in the way of your love."

One thing he had to hand her—Chris could become an unpredictable menace. He had glimpsed it at times, the dark side that lurked behind the shiny angel. If provoked, he dared not imagine the consequences, especially now that she had made him aware of just how much power the striking creature could wield.

"No, you don't have to wonder what he's capable of doing." Picking up his thought as easily as if he had uttered it out loud, she squeezed his hand. "Because you can control him. In fact, you're the only one who can." At her second squeeze, he resisted the impulse to kiss her. "I know because

I saw it when he came here the first time. He was destructively angry. So evil, I can still feel the earth caving in around him." A shiver ran down her arm. "The contrast between his angelic face and the blackness inside made it even more striking and scary. But when he saw you, everything changed." Her eyes widened as though she still could not believe it. "All of a sudden, he became the brightest star I've ever seen, with a light so intense it blinded me. I was amazed. Not just for this transformation. For the lights themselves, 'cause I had never seen lights on anybody before Chris came along."

"He was the first, uh?" Now this was interesting.

"He was." Much like her reluctant admission. "This made me discover just how different I was from everyone else, and how similar I was to him."

And he wondered why he felt suddenly trapped in a power struggle that would have seemed unreal just a few days before, so far removed was it from the material reality he had taken for granted all his life.

"He had always known he was different." She seemed certain of it. "And that day he proved it beyond any doubt, turning from black to white the second he caught sight of you."

"He changed from black to white when he saw me?" Duncan repeated, just to be sure he understood correctly.

"Yes, you made it happen for reasons I can't understand myself." She frowned in puzzlement. "Anyway, it seems evident you alone can reach him in his darkest corners and make him different."

Which probably explained why he always felt in control of his angel, why that burning pyre that always melted his senses had never seemed a threat to him. Sensations and half-forgotten wonderings fell into place as he recognized the truth of what she was saying.

"So how does all this fit into the energy flow, the lights and all?" And maybe she had been right about that master plan theory of hers, however farfetched it had seemed before.

"I think it's all-connected somehow." From her brief hesitation, he guessed it would be hard for her to fit the pieces in the right places, regardless of how much more she seemed to know compared to him.

Also with the images you've been sending me since you got here? Glad to have figured out this much, he did not bother saying it.

I can send you thoughts and feelings, too, my prince, if only you allow me.

By the gods! Her sweet voice booming in his head was really the last thing he expected!

But it's the first thing we can do, you and I. She seemed to be mocking him on purpose, her brilliant green eyes dancing in glee.

Then it's true! Shocked, he trained his gaze on her to make sure she did not move her lips. *You can read my mind!*

I most definitely can, and so can you. As she shared the flickering lights, he drowned in a magical mist of sparkling hazes, each with distinct colors, which he now understood was her way of seeing the world. *I told you before.* She smirked, evidently thrilled out of her skin. *You have the same gift as your father. We can communicate without talking.*

How true, because she was inside him! Not just a voice in his head, she had taken up the whole of him, her essence seeping to his guts. No, to his cock to be precise, which awakened a hunger he found hard to keep at bay.

And the images of their times in bed were not helping any, nor did the dull throbbing between her legs, which he now perceived as though it were his own.

Voracious! She was literally starving for a piece of him! And he of her, sinking as he was in her lust . . . or was it his?

As boundaries began to fade, he became so aroused his shaft went slab of marble before he realized it had. And all without touching her, the fever gripping his senses seemingly building on its own.

Well, not if he could help it.

Insinuating a hand beneath her old blue dress, he traveled up a smooth leg, already relishing the feel of her drenched cunt, when a knock stopped further advances.

I think that's my angel. Hardly surprised, he got up to reach the door. *Can he read minds, too?*

Not that he believed it for a moment.

I hope not. She was not as certain. *You probably just summoned him unconsciously.*

Throwing open the door, he fixed the troubled blue-gray eyes staring back at him.

"Lover." Standing on the threshold, Chris's voice was almost shaking, "I need to talk to you."

"All right." With a curt nod, he stepped aside to let him through, his cock twitching in taut anticipation of the consequences.

Which came sooner than he expected. The moment Chris set foot in his room, his gaze narrowed on her, the arresting blue-gray eyes turning icy cold. "Am I interrupting something?"

CHAPTER THIRTY-FOUR

"Not at all, Angel." After shutting the door, Prince Caldwell dragged Chris to the couch. "We were just about to get started, but three's more fun than two."

According to who?

If she burned to ask the question, she dared not speak. She dared not move, either. Her body immobilized in the effort of surviving what could turn out to be the worst confrontation of her life. For Christopher Templeton was as charged as when he had come down to the stables, if not more. Furious to the point he need just look at her to incinerate her on the spot. And the prince was no match, his power too new and too raw to be of any use, should the situation precipitate.

Then again, Duncan Caldwell had other weapons at his disposal, and his strategy of attacking the demon's thin lips was probably the best way to defuse his threat. Hard and fierce, she was right there with him when he stuck his tongue inside to overcome Chris's surprise, while demanding his complete surrender.

And the taste of the mouthwatering man exploded inside her, doubling the craving that had been steadily growing since she had become aware of Duncan's extreme arousal. Then his fondling of Chris's groin made her realize he was turning everything into an exciting new game, one that even an enraged demon found impossible to resist. If his lights shifting from anger to lust were not indication enough, she could tell from his cock stirring into a firm erection under

Duncan's skillful pampering.

"You weren't kidding, lover." Chris grinned, drawing back. "You really want to do it now." The blue-gray eyes flashed in feverish anticipation. "But what about her?"

Of course, the bastard did not even look at her.

"She's my slave." Nor did Duncan, who had eyes for Chris alone. "So she's at our complete service." Thick and raspy, his voice carried over to her, even though he had lowered it to a husky whisper in the demon's ear. "Come on. We've shared women before, so it'll be no different this time." Then he opened Chris's fly, gripped the stiff erection and slid it seductively.

Chris gasped, and she knew his cock's needs now outweighed any objections he might have. The kissing was also keeping him under Duncan's erotic spell, which to her was only good news.

If he was too busy kissing and making out, he would have no time to kill her, right?

After jerking the swollen piece of meat, Duncan bent and swallowed it whole, pulling her into his awareness with a sharp tug she could not oppose.

Entangled in his steamy web, Chris's pungent taste filled her senses, her tongue, or rather Duncan's, lapping the huge shaft from the tender foreskin to the balls. Then the sharp intake nearly gagged her as though her mouth were actually full, when in fact it was all part of his perception.

Your turn now, Princess. Picking her up, he carried her in front of his lover and forced her down on her knees. *Let me see how good you are at sucking.* To emphasize his order, he pressed her face over the gigantic monster. *Now swallow.*

Since he clamped her neck, she had no way out of it. Opening wide, she did her best to gobble the proud stick to the root, failing miserably. She barely managed to accommodate the fat crown, and already the rest of it pushed to get to her throat, choking her in the process.

Immediately, the pressure on her neck eased, and she panted for air.

When she managed to focus again, not one, but two veritable beasts waved in front of her nose, demanding her oral attention.

By the gods, what was she to do?

It certainly was not like she had swallowed cocks all her life. And he knew it!

That's what makes it more exciting, Princess! Again, he pushed her head on Chris's bulging tip and held it down.

With her master taking charge, she had no choice except to suffocate on the thick length repeatedly slamming to her throat.

In other words, *Ouch!*

"Not so hard, Angel." Pulling her back, he allowed her to gulp down some much-needed air. "Not if we want to keep playing with her."

"I'm not sure I do." Merciless, the demon continued to swing his hips forward and centering her throat every time. "She isn't particularly good —"

"She will be." Slowing down Chris's beat, he steadied those frenetic shoves. "Trust me." *And you've got to do better than that.* This was for her. "'Cause I want you to come all over her face, Angel."

Unconvinced, Chris spun to him. "I don't know —"

"Shut up and kiss me." Plunging into a passionate exchange, he blocked all of the demon's protests.

He doesn't think I'm good enough, eh?

Ha, she would show him, if it was the last thing she did in her life.

And since he liked it rough, she would blow him even if she had no breath left, preventing the spurting and coughing to get in the way of her intakes. If she was supposed to choke on him, she would just have to prove her worth. And having him come all over her face was exactly the prize she needed to double her efforts in sliding her lips to his thick root. What she lacked in skills, she tried compensating with a voraciousness that she hoped would satisfy Lord Templeton's very sophisticated taste.

Use your tongue to avoid choking. His twinge of sympathy spurred her to do more.

Dipping on the tip of Chris's erection, she submitted to its insistent plunges, relishing the feel of his soft skin, of the engorged blood vessels that broke the surface into bumps and crevices. His hitting her palate and her attempts to trap it between her cheeks were also incredibly exciting, drenching her cunt and accelerating the pounding in her clit. And when her master stepped up the tempo, her total loss of control spun her senses wild.

Not that Christopher Templeton cared a fig for her sensations. He kept pushing, so deep down it seemed like he had decided to reach her stomach, rather than stop at her throat. Which turned his rigid equipment into a smoldering mass of flaming meat that was about to explode.

And all thanks to her!

Well, almost.

Duncan and his fiery kiss were probably the best turn on of all, only he had now freed the demon's mouth and bobbed her head frantically over the entire length of Chris.

Too taken by the frenzied rhythm, she barely heard his hoarse order, "Go ahead and choke her, Angel," before the first jets reached her throat. Then yanking her hair, Duncan tossed back her head, and all the rest of Chris's seemingly inexhaustible juice sprayed her face and neck.

"Great come, Angel." Letting her head go, he grinned in satisfaction. "And now for some serious fun."

"But first, you deserve some sucking of your own, lover." Grabbing her head, Chris pressed it on Duncan's untouched cock. "If she's your slave, she's sorely neglected her master." Forcing her down, he went for total suffocation. "And we can't have that, can we?"

No, not him for sure, but would she live to tell?

Far harsher than Duncan, Chris wanted to see her squirm and gag from her inability to get his impossibly large and long length all the way down. If it was inconceivable, she would be damned if she gave the conceited demon any satisfaction, not even if it would make him more beautiful than ever.

Point of fact—she could not decide which of the two men was more gorgeous, however different their looks. The striking contrast between the dark prince and the shiny demon made it all the more impressive and titillating. Or maybe their diverse styles of doing things made it so irresistible, particularly now that she had his cock stuck to her throat.

The amazing thing was his continuous sharing of his sensations, like the jolts of pleasure she caused him every time she managed to wrap the whole of him inside her wet cavity, or the twitches whenever her tongue succeeded to curl around him and draw him further inside. And she would have continued to lavish attention on him, in spite of the odious demon's interference, had he not pulled back at one point.

"I said I want serious fun." Lifting her up, he carried her to the bed. Shedding her dress along the way, his tongue ravaged her mouth. *And you'll have to work your ass off for that to happen.* Squeezing her buttocks possessively was just another way of demanding her complete submission.

I will, Master. She had vowed to be his slave anyway, and she realized there could be no turning back. Besides, for a kiss as hungry and as passionate as his, she would have agreed to just about anything.

Reaching the bed, he placed her on all fours. *Now throw out your ass.*

Immediately, Master. Too hot to be thinking straight, her body was a tight ball of fire wanting only to burst.

"It's all yours, Angel." Wet fingers enlarged her narrow ring all of a sudden, shocking her with the intensity of her craving.

She wanted something bigger there, much bigger and fiercer, too, than mere fingers, something to stuff her good and proper.

"And hurry." Having evidently picked up her desire, he increased the backpressure to four fingers, twisting them inside the cramped space to get it ready. "It's hungry for you."

That was no lie for sure!

"By the gods!" Chris pushed out a heavy breath of air. "She's got a magnificent ass," he blurted with a reluctant admiration that propelled her lust to the very stars. "It's too bad it probably isn't virgin anymore."

Something about his disappointed note told her they had talked about her ass, which she was not sure was such a good thing.

"Not anymore, I'm afraid." Sliding in and out, his fingers were pure torture. "But I only did it once, so it's still worth the ride."

Then she felt the demon behind her, his body giving off such intense sparks of heat it was impossible for anyone to miss them. As he adjusted his position, Duncan slipped beneath her and went for the tense swell between her legs. One lick and she jumped. And she would have hit the ceiling, had Chris not held her down.

"Oh, it's just too good to be true." His cock slid down her cleft. "And you say she's ready for me, lover?"

She wondered why the sarcastic note. Then a ferocious blow flung her asshole wide open all together, all at once. And she knew she better avoid stupid questions.

Ouch! Curling on herself, she tried to escape the enormous monster wanting to impale her guts.

Breathe, Princess, he was quick to come to her aid. *Relax and concentrate on what I'm doing.*

Yeah, easy for him to say! Regardless of her sharing, he did not have the searing pain in his butt, worsened now by Chris's smug presumption he could get to her throat from the back way. And in one single shove no less!

Still, she clenched her teeth, lest the fiendish creature got more pleasure out of hurting her, which for the record he already was. Because he was punishing her, she knew it now. Not just because she had dared return. Not even because she had sex with his prince. What really burned him was the fact she had awakened his prince's power. That was unforgivable! It pissed him off, to the point he would have blown her ass to bits, had Duncan not intervened.

"Remember she's practically a virgin." Pushing on Chris's hips, the game master blocked his furious swings. "If you take it more gently, it'll still be fun, only it'll last longer."

"I think it's a waste of our time to let her worthless performance last any longer than it should." Still, the pressure on her backside eased.

Not that he stopped. He merely took it more slowly. Then again, what was the use?

Already embedded to the hilt, he had no more space to stuff, unless he tried getting his balls through. Which knowing him, he would have no qualms in attempting.

She did not dwell on it. Like Duncan had suggested, she focused on his sensual play in her cunt. His stroking of her velvety flesh was simply divine. His zeroing on her throbbing clit was pure ecstasy. His penetration of her dripping slit was sheer bliss. Slipping away from Chris's merciless impacts, she melted in her master's erotic enchantment, particularly when he had her live his side of the game. So her mouth filled with her taste, and her fingers became sticky from tracing her slippery slit, the honeydew trickling also in his wet cavity and down her thighs.

Kind of obvious he loved it, this seductive exploration of her moist folds, with the extra bit about sucking her swollen knot that was driving her beyond the initial pain, almost to a point of no return.

"Someone's having too much fun now." As though he had guessed how close she was to a climax, Chris shoved her head on his phase mate's upright cock. "And this mouth is way too idle for my taste."

How he could possibly know her timing was a matter of speculation. Safe to say, with the stone-like piece stuck up her mouth, things definitely turned scorching.

For one thing, the prince's shock of pleasure reverberated through her, and she was about to come. Everything was on fire — from her full mouth fighting against an exceedingly greedy beast, to her wide-open rear smoking from friction as it rubbed faster against the demon's erection, to her cunt ravaged by his steady brushing. It was all too maddening to last. Feverish, she pressed her aching clit to get a measure of relief, before thrusting back her butt to meet Chris's shoves.

Then the demon accelerated.

Her ass and mouth squeezed the giant shafts possessing her all, and heat grew to a point she could not contain it any longer.

Spitting out the beefy equipment, her head fell on the mattress in the throes of the violent and repeated contractions. Ripped apart, literally, she swelled under the waves that coiled from her toes to her hair without respite, relieved only partly by the scream that inevitably followed.

"What . . ." Sounding surprised, Chris stopped all together. "What's that?"

"Don't worry." Coming up from beneath her, Duncan shifted, his cock now at the entrance of her enflamed pussy. "Just keep pumping." Then he slammed inside.

With the second stick sinking into her, she raised her back and clenched around the two erections filling both holes at the same time. Incredible to say—they moved as one, hammering her front and back in a hurried rhythm that might have lasted longer had her master's tongue not claimed her mouth. So she climaxed again, screaming her pleasure in his head alone. And evidently, it was too much for them.

With a loud groan, they both burst simultaneously, screwing both their pieces to the root. As she milked them dry, she knew she had to act fast. It was her chance after all, for their barriers were down on account of their orgasms, while their powers were at their strongest.

Tugging both men into her mind, she drowned them in her essence, flooding them with her blinding lights and the hazy perception of her auras. Then she took things one-step further, blending them into herself until they were as one. Not three separate beings anymore, she wrapped them all into a single unity that did not feel strange at all. No, this tight-knit form belonged to them, and it had for the longest time.

Or so it felt, until the demon decided to end it. With a sharp pull, his fierce resistance and sheer hatred dissolved the mass of energy she had neatly curled in a ball after mere seconds. Still enough for her to catch, not without some satisfaction, his shivers of disconcert and unease, before she collapsed on Duncan exhausted.

CHAPTER THIRTY-FIVE

"Fuck, lover!" Spent and bewildered, Chris fell on a side, gazing at Duncan cradling the woman to his chest. "That was ..." *Goddamn fantastic, in spite of the witch and her meddling to awaken your power.* Which should have been up to him, not to that nosy pest he had sent packing years before.

"Goddamn fantastic!" His phase mate seemed to pluck the sensation right off his head. "I had imagined it would be incredible, but I never dreamed it could be this good." Turning, the black eyes trapped his. "Or that you'd like it so much."

Sure, Duncan had brought women in their bed before. Him and his damn attraction for that despicable gender, though the gods alone knew what he found in it, had inevitably led to a different kind of sex. Nothing exciting as far as he was concerned. Nothing worth repeating either. Alas, nothing comparable to this one and to her impressive display of eros and power, both of which had pissed him off to the point all he wanted was to start everything over again. No woman ever had him quite by the balls as she had. Few men, too, if he had to be honest, or rather just one — Prince Duncan Caldwell. And he simply could not stand it!

"Is that why you wanted to play game master?" Chuckling, he locked his gaze on Duncan's. "To make me come all over her, not once but twice?" Just another thing he could not forgive her, one more he had to add to her already extensive list of grievances.

"It was the best part of it all." Duncan grinned proudly.

"Even if you were kind of rough with her." Stroking her back absent-mindedly, he focused on the shivers creasing her skin.

Of course, she did not stir.

"Don't waste your time," he sniggered. "She's asleep." He had known it from the moment he had seen her collapse on Duncan. "She can't handle the amount of energy needed for these games."

"How could she?" If this was another small victory of his, the tender way Duncan placed her under the covers made him want to strangle her with his bare hands. "She certainly doesn't have enough of an experience as far as sex goes."

Luckily, the prince motioning him to go to the fireplace prevented any of his usually rash acts. So he obliged immediately, glad to plop on the floor's thick carpet and get away from her.

"So you're serious about her?" Not far enough to stop thinking about her, alas.

"What do you mean by serious?" Fetching distilled cider and two glasses, Duncan settled next to him. "The kid has a long way to go." After filling both glasses, he handed one to him. "She's just great in bed, and you can't deny it." Challenging Chris to prove him wrong, his black eyes flashed. "The way you went for that splendid ass of hers is something I've never seen you do."

Fuck! Why did she have such magnificent behind?

Not just its shape. The way it had sucked his cock to the hilt had been unexpected to say the least. Screwed to his balls, he felt that fabulously cramped space still wrapped around his cock, squeezing him dry with her every throwback. Then her hips' rotation had added an erotic allure that had been irresistible. So the question remained. Why was her ass so fuckable and cock wrenching he could not wait to possess it again?

"For now, we can just use her to spice up our games."

And from Duncan's tone, there was little doubt he could not wait either.

But there was so much more to her that he had to set the record straight even against his better judgment. "Come on," he puffed impatiently. "The girl has too much power to be just a sex toy." However hard he tried, he could not suppress the note of admiration, because he had noticed it from the start, fascinated in spite of himself by the intoxicating mix he had sensed in her.

No one knew it better than him, since he had dabbled with it ever since he could remember. Then catching the hint of a protest in Duncan's heartbreaking black eyes, he was quick to add, "And don't tell me you don't know what power is 'cause I can tell she awakened yours somehow."

"Yes, she did." Picking up his dare, Duncan threw back his shoulders. "And since you're so interested, she used sex."

Now why was he not surprised? And why did it make him twice as furious with the goddamn witch?

"Now she talks to me directly in my head . . . no . . ." Duncan frowned, and Chris waited, knowing he was grappling with unfamiliar matters. "It's not just talk. She and I can also share images, feelings, sensations, everything with the bat of an eye." From the amazement in his voice and in his expression, it was evident he was still digesting it all. "It's like she's inside my head, like she's a part of me, which only makes me more certain *she belongs to me*." However hard he tried, he could not suppress a possessive note. "And it made for quite a different erotic game tonight since I ordered her what to do and how to move without having to say it out loud."

He had guessed as much. It was what had warned him things with his lover were very different now.

"Then I shared every sensation that was happening to

me." After taking a sip of cider, Duncan placed the glass on the floor next to him. "As she did with hers."

I hope you got a kick out of her pain, then. Too cruel to say, he regarded his phase mate coldly, wondering how this would affect things. "Well, that's power for you."

"I guess so." Duncan nodded. "And you knew all about it, didn't you?" If the question seemed natural enough, there was no disguising the veiled accusation. "Or why else would you get ready to attack her at the stables?"

"Me?" *Fuck, yeah!*

He had wanted to destroy her at the stables. Incinerate her on the spot, had he only been free to do it. Up in smoke—that was the only fate she deserved. She and her messing around in things she had no business in, which she should have left alone. And what was the idea of looking like him?

Sure, the similarity had been there ever since he had first seen her. But instead of turning into a fat, ugly woman whose only hold on Duncan was through her magical art, she had become strikingly beautiful. To the point his cock had tightened at the sight of her, though he would never, ever, admit it to anyone, least of all himself.

Women never, ever had that effect on him!

If she had, it had been a mere accident, or the fact that time had accentuated her disconcerting resemblance to his stunning lover. Her build, her colors and that familiar air he had learned to associate and love in the prince alone—all belonged to her, too. Worst of all, he could not deny her connection to Duncan, not again, not even to himself. There, in plain view, he had seen it despite his rage, just as he had perceived it more than ten years before.

But unlike that distant day, what had really grabbed his attention this time had been her incredible power!

No wonder she had awakened Duncan. Besides him, she

was the only one who could have done it. For never before or since meeting her, had he found someone as aware of it as she was. And like him, she had learned to wield it, standing proud and tall in front of those stables, ready to strike back at him instead of cowering away like she had when a simple wave of his hand had taken care of her for the years that had followed.

Not that hers was any match to his! Then or now, she did not have what it took to bring him down. Which was the reason she had seized his lover's abundant supply, forcing him to stand down. And Duncan surrendering it to her had been too much for him.

"What about you?" Chris snapped. "What's the idea of letting her manipulate you in such shameless way and getting away with it, too? Of letting her have your power? Power she would have used against *me*?" The betrayal still hurt if he just thought about it. "Who have loved you since —"

"The moment you cut me off from her, back when we were just kids." Tossing back his head, his magnificent black hair flew all around.

"Is this one of her lies?" Narrowing his gaze on the black one, he fumed. "Don't tell me you believe her!"

"Knowing what you were about to do today, why shouldn't I?" On the attack, Duncan leaned toward him.

"Because you don't know the first thing about power or its consequences," he spat. "While she does and stole your energy —"

"Don't give me another fucking lecture on power," the prince snarled. "I've heard enough for one day." He swallowed a generous sip with one draw. "And to be frank, you never bothered talking about it, not once in the ten years we've known each other, so I don't see why you should start now." He scoffed, "Unless you're scared she might have uncovered more of your dirty little secrets than—"

"Ha!" Glaring at Duncan, he raised his voice, "She's no match for me, never has been, so there's really nothing she can uncover—"

"Yeah, she told me as much." Suddenly standing down, Duncan averted his gaze to the fire. "And I'm sorry I betrayed you today." He reached out to touch his arm. "Like you said, I don't know the first thing about it, just felt how scared she was of you I couldn't—"

"I understand." Suddenly ashamed of his jealous reaction, he hung his head. "And you're right. I should've talked about power and energy sooner, especially since you seem to have it in abundance, judging from your reaction today." A bitter smile twisted his lips. "The only difference with me and her is that we've both known about it from the start, which made her all the more dangerous to me." He stretched luxuriously, his long arms thrown up in the air before falling down to wrap around his knees. "At first, I wasn't sure she and I were . . . alike in our difference. As a child, I knew I wasn't like the others 'cause I could do things that no one else could." Thinking back on those early times, he relived his first intoxicating surge of power that had coursed through his blood and drowned every other sense. "And if I didn't tell you, it's only because I thought you would never have loved me without those powers." Raising a hand, he stopped Duncan's denial. "Lover, the moment I saw you, I knew you were special. And how could someone like you ever fall for someone like me if I didn't have some special trait of my own?"

Folding his arms around him, Duncan crushed him to his broad chest. "I never—"

"You have to remember I was merely eight years old at the time." Snuggling deeper inside the embrace, he inhaled him all the way down to the lungs.

"I wasn't even aware of it until today." Tightening his hold, Duncan deposited a soft kiss on his forehead. "So I can assure I love you, have always loved you because of who you are, never because of what you can or cannot do however powerful it turns out to be."

"It still doesn't change the fact you seem to attract it." Shifting slightly, he managed to raise his gaze. "Or she would have never been at your side from early on."

Oh, he had been so furious upon discovering the only other person with power at the side of the man he had decided would be his forever. So he had lashed out and driven her as far away from his lover as possible.

Not far enough, apparently, for the cursed woman had returned and now lay claim to what had never belonged to her.

"Maybe you're right." Duncan frowned as though taken by a new thought. "And maybe it's no coincidence, either." He tousled the blond hair in a reassuring gesture. "Since she believes that our meeting again is no accident."

"She's probably right." Chris shrugged. "You obviously needed her to awaken your power."

Yanking back his head, Duncan cupped his face. "To be honest, I couldn't care less about having power if the price is to have someone or something come between you and me." His lips brushed Chris's mouth. "Just one word from you and I'll get rid of her again."

Uh, how he longed to say that one word! It was burning on the tip of his tongue, and it would have burst out on its own, had he still been a child.

Which he was not.

Which made it all the more frustrating he had to keep her around. Not for his sake, naturally. For Duncan's and for his need to grow.

She had already changed him anyway, so what would be

the point? Yes, because power changed people, so it would be extremely selfish to deny Duncan his chance to explore his incredible potential.

"You know what really gets me about her?" Raising his head, he could not avoid kissing the prince again. "She reminds me of you. Maybe it's the long dark hair or the shape of the eyes . . ." His voice trailed off as he recalled the painful air of familiarity that had hit him at the stables. "I can't quite put my finger on it, but there's something that connects her to you."

"Funny you should mention it, Angel." Disentangling from him and sitting back on his heels, Duncan regarded him intently. "David said the same thing."

Well, well, so he had noticed her. And if Chris knew anything of David Smith, he was willing to bet Duncan's valet would fall for her as hard as he had already fallen for his master. With the extra bonus of having sex with her, something Prince Caldwell would never do with David, not even if he were the last person left standing in the world.

"Then I guess it's more obvious than I thought." Distending his legs, he leaned against the couch.

"Is that why she deserves punishment?" Taking another sip of cider, Duncan made a show as though it did not really matter to him.

"Among other things." He chuckled. "And don't make me list all the others, or we'll never get a decent night's sleep." *Just be sure she'll pay for them all!*

"You have nothing to fear, Angel." Reaching out, Duncan squeezed his hands. "I love you. And no woman, no man either, will ever fill your place in my heart, which is yours alone, nor will I allow anyone to come between us."

"Like she did today?" An ugly smile twisted his lips.

"What happened today was the angry reaction of two hotheads." Duncan pursed his lips as though he did not approve of it.

"That's easy for you to say." Straightening, Chris confronted him. "You're not caught up in the middle, left wondering whether I'll lose you again. I lost you once before for two whole years." And it still fucking hurt like it had the first time! "I'm not about to lose you again, not if I can help it." Reading the objection blazing in the black eyes, he was quick to scramble to his knees to whisper in his lover's ear, "And before you say I'm too exaggerated, my gut instinct tells me she might become a permanent addition in your life."

Duncan raked Chris's hair. "All right."

The fact that he did not deny his gut instinct was definitely *not* a good sign. So maybe he should have spoken that word when he had the chance.

"We could use her knowledge to help us learn more." Reasoning out loud, the black eyes fixed an invisible point in midair. "For she seems to know a lot about it."

"I've learned enough already, thank you." No way would he allow her to have even the tiniest piece of his adored prince.

Not if he could help it any!

"Have you really?" The prince eyed him skeptically. "I'm sure a little extra training won't do you any harm, considering how powerful you are and how easily you lose control . . ." At the slight hesitation, he knew he would not like what was to follow. "Like you almost did today."

"I wasn't losing it!" Chris hissed angrily, raising his gaze defiant. "If she hadn't—"

"Provoked you, I know," Duncan cut in sarcastically. "Is that also why you had to grab Lizzy's energy?"

"So what if I have?" For once, Elizabeth had come in handy. "What do you know of power that makes you such an expert all of a sudden?" Chris snorted annoyed. "Until yesterday, you didn't even know what it was—"

"But I know you." Again, Duncan seemed to be one-step ahead. "And that's all I need to know."

"Fuck you, lover." His anger cooling as fast as it had heated up, he shook his head resigned. "And me for having handed you the key to understanding me like no other." Not that he would have wanted it any other way. "All right, so maybe she might be useful—"

"In more ways than one." A mischievous twinkle brightened the black eyes. "And I have quite a few in mind already, none of which she's in a position to refuse."

"So you weren't kidding when you said she's your slave?" That had certainly been an unexpected and very exciting twist.

"Absolutely not." Prince Caldwell grinned smugly. "In bed, she'll do whatever I tell her. She swore to it, and I'll hold her to that vow."

"So she's already that much in love, uh?" He knew it! Had known it since before he had managed to get rid of her. "I just hope you won't be disappointed."

"Disappointed how?" A flash of curiosity crossed Duncan's face.

"Not because I don't trust women, but they have the bad habit of pretending to agree to your conditions, then changing the rules without even informing you." No, he really did not like women. "In the end, they drain all your energy and give nothing in return."

"I don't see why you worry about this when all we want from her is sex and eventually, training." Filling his glass again, he swallowed a generous dose of the amber liquid.

"Not to burst your balloons, but she seems a resourceful girl." After emptying his glass, he swirled it between his palms. "One who could easily leave Black Rose to find a job elsewhere, or who knows . . ." He shrugged nonchalantly.

"Even pledge."

"Nah." Duncan waved a hand aimlessly in the air. "Who'd take her?"

"David would in a heartbeat." He was sure of it.

"David?" Wide-eyed, Duncan looked and sounded astonished. "Why do you think he'd be interested?"

"He seemed embarrassed today when we got back under the rain." Remembering David's expression, he knew he was on the right track. "I bet he was fucking your girlfriend."

"She's not *my girlfriend*." Quick to set the record straight, the prince grasped the bottle and refilled both their glasses, setting it back on the floor. "And she's free to have sex with whomever she likes." He drank down a sip. "But I don't think she'll ever pledge to him."

"Why not?" Made sense to him. "It's exactly what her mother did. Tied to your father's bed, she pledged to the stable keeper for appearance's sakes. And in case you haven't noticed, family patterns have the bad habit of repeating themselves."

"That was different." Duncan huffed.

"Are you sure, lover?" Chris provoked.

Stretching, Duncan yawned loudly. "No." His tone sounded remorseful. "And right now, I'm too tired to care." Rising, he gathered the glasses and the bottle. "Come on." Leaving everything on the table, he gestured at Chris. "Let's catch some sleep while we still have a few hours left." He smiled regretfully. "The lawyer's coming later today, and that's something I can't miss."

Getting up and going to the bed, he glanced at the sleeping form under the covers. "What about her?"

"The bed's big enough for the three of us." Totally unconcerned, his phase mate crawled inside, right next to her.

Fuck! That's all I needed. "Never thought I'd see the day I'd be sleeping with a woman."

"Hey, there's a first time for everything." Chuckling, Duncan patted the place beside him. "So shut up and get in here." Sliding to her side, the prince made room for him.

So he had no other choice except slipping under the covers, his ass pressing against Duncan's crotch, while a woman slept at his lover's side.

Chapter Thirty-six

"Prince Duncan will be down shortly." At the valet's words, Mark Hamill sighed in relief.

Seated in the Caldwell's lounge between Lady Sophia and Elizabeth, the lawyer hoped the prince would not be long. Sophia Caldwell was nice enough, but like many women, she tended to be a bit overbearing when it came to such crucial matters as testaments. And Prince Charles's was extremely important to her, just as it would have been to any pledge mate.

Perhaps more if she came to learn of its finer details.

Maybe it was the reason Prince Charles had chosen him to carry out this delicate affair, trusting on his capacity to bend the rules in more ways than one.

"I hope my son will be ready." Sophia sighed loudly. "He's not been himself lately."

"Don't worry, Mother." Elizabeth's eyes flashed. "I'm sure he's just tired. That's all."

Glancing outside uneasy and uncomfortable, he prayed again for the prince's speedy arrival. The sound of soft rain, mixed with the angry sea waves, lulled his senses as he stared at the overwhelming grayness, blending sky and sea like they had no distinguishable boundary between them.

"Do you think he's ready?" Lady Caldwell pressed her point.

He cleared his throat. "I'm sure he's adequately prepared for it."

The lie slipped out smoothly for he knew in his heart the news he was about to deliver would be no easy matter to handle. Still, the reading of a will represented a symbolic rite of passage for noblemen, the formal gateway into adulthood and responsibility. *So what better way to test its effectiveness?*

"Yes, I know." Leaning so far forward that she practically

landed on his lap, Sophia Caldwell glared at him. "But did my mate —"

"Good morning," a cheerful male voice stopped Sophia's next objection.

"Good morning," another voice pitched in, as two handsome men entered the room.

"Good morning, Prince." Jumping up and going toward the dark-haired man who was the spit image of Prince Charles, he smiled in relief.

"Good to see you again." Extending his arm, Duncan clasped him in a firm handshake. Then he moved to his sister. "Good morning, Lizzy." And kissed her on the cheek.

"Good morning, brother." As though she had not seen him for ages, she threw her arms around his neck and hung on far longer than he would have expected.

Finally, the prince managed to disentangle himself and went to Lady Caldwell's side. "Good morning, Mother." He pecked her cheek lightly.

"Good morning, son." She clasped his neck. "I hope you're feeling better than you did yesterday. Your foul mood was unbearable."

"Yes, absolutely." The prince grinned broadly, and Mark could not help noticing what a gorgeous man he was.

No wonder he should feel so attracted to him, even now that he had long outgrown his phase. He still preferred men to women after all, and the prince's handsome face, his natural elegance and style affected him more than he cared to admit.

"Today I'm feeling great." And Mark had no doubt he was speaking the truth, not after catching the knowing glance he exchanged with his friend.

"I'm glad you made him see reason, Chris." Elizabeth teased.

"I can be very persuasive if I want to." The blond man, a

stranger to him, intercepted another mischievous glance from the prince who was moving toward Mark.

"Sorry I'm late." His enchanting apologetic smile was enough for Mark to forgive him of everything. "We had some rough weather lately . . ."

"I know." He nodded in understanding. "It wasn't easy to come all the way here, even if Harbor Town is just a few miles away."

"Can I introduce you to my phase mate?" Prince Caldwell gestured at the gorgeous blond man.

Yes, of course, the intimacy he had glimpsed before made perfect sense now. Not just because of the tight bond a phase inevitably established between two men. Because they were still lovers.

"Christopher Templeton." The prince gestured for the striking blond man to reach them. "Angel, this is the lawyer I was telling you about, Mark Hamill."

"Ah, the son of our vice-leader, I presume." Extending his hand, he looked at him more closely.

"The one and only." Amused, Chris shook the out-stretched hand in a firm grasp while his eyes blatantly appraised him.

"It's a pleasure, sir." Ill at ease, the lawyer was quick to take his hand back, the young man too sensually disturbing for his taste. "Hem . . ." The words were not yet out of his mouth that his gaze had already swung back to the prince. "I'm sorry to be abrupt, Prince, but the business at hand can take a bit longer than I told you, so . . ."

"Sure, Mark, if you follow me . . ." The dark-haired man strode to the door. "I think we'll be more comfortable in my office."

"Yes, thank you." Already at his heels, Mark trailed after him.

Halting on the threshold, Duncan Caldwell's gaze swept

the room. "I'll see you later." If he had addressed everyone, it was kind of obvious he meant it for Christopher Templeton, considering how his black eyes narrowed on him alone.

"I'm sorry if I came at a bad time." Now seated in front of the prince's large desk, he studied his attractive features, wondering how to breach what was a difficult subject at best.

"Oh, no." The prince played with a red cardboard slip lying on his desk, richly engraved by an emblem he thought he recognized as belonging to the lady in charge of the Blandry District.

Could it be the invitation to her renowned Game of Masters and Slaves?

Shaking the wondering out of his head, he focused back on the issue at hand. "We've had some . . . rough times lately, but nothing serious. Besides, I'm to leave for the Hall tomorrow."

"Alone?" Mark asked to buy more time.

"Only with my phase mate, Lord Templeton." And his gaze seemed lost in midair, as if he were already imagining the trip.

"Then I'm glad I caught you today." He shifted on the chair. "We have to decide on a definite date in which to read your father's will."

"I should be back in a couple of months, so we could arrange it then." Leaning across the desk, Prince Caldwell peered at him. "But don't tell me you came all the way over here just to set a date we could've easily arranged through a messenger."

"Hem . . ." He cleared his throat. "It's true, Prince, but . . ." He blinked, not really knowing how to continue.

"Is there a problem with my father's will?" The black eyes flashed in concern.

"I wouldn't call it exactly . . . *a problem*," he was quick to reassure. "There's an unexpected addition to the usual provisions of a will, which I'm afraid you might not approve of."

"What do you mean?" The prince sat up straight.

"Your father decided to include a new clause, which is . . ." He took a deep breath. "Questionable at best." The words felt as heavy as stone particularly knowing how hard they would hit the prince. "I did not approve of it but had no choice in the matter."

"Is this clause legal?" From his concentrated expression, he guessed the prince was already analyzing the situation, however little the elements at his disposal.

"There are no precedents." And the gods only knew how hard he had looked for at least one. "But as far as I could re-search, I can't honestly say it's illegal."

He was a bit disconcerted, for his heartfelt loyalty to Prince Charles clashed with what he knew would place the family in a very difficult spot. He had strenuously argued against it with the deceased prince, begging him to consider his family's reactions and the negative consequences. To no avail, alas. More than that, Charles had asked him to support the clause, especially against his son's certain disapproval. So in the end, the lawyer in him had promised.

Now torn between loyalty and traditions, he stared at him not knowing how to argue Charles's point successfully.

"You know, I suspected my father would give us a head-ache." Prince Caldwell reclined on his chair with a resigned look. "Even after his death." He smiled encouragingly, as if reading his doubts. "But whatever it is, we'll handle it, right, Mark?"

The question seemed rhetorical, so the lawyer simply nodded in agreement.

"Good." Seemingly satisfied as if he had won a victory of sorts, the prince continued to fix him intently. "Now what unusual provision did my father include?"

"In the will, Charles Caldwell formally adopts a certain Ylianor Meyer, a stranger to the family as I understand, making her his legal daughter and legitimate heir." The pause was in order so that the prince could start digesting the news. "And she'll have the formal right to carry the Caldwell name."

There!

He had said it finally!

The black eyes were wide in consternation. "He adopts her?"

"Yes, Prince." That was exactly what he had feared. "An unusual procedure, I'm aware, but—"

"Did he think she was his daughter?" Instead of focusing on the legal implications, the prince seemed to be following a track all his own.

"Well, I never understood it myself." Fact was—it had totally baffled him. "Your father had no grounds for claiming she was, no blood relation he assured more than once. Still, he insisted she felt like his own, so he needed to provide for her along with the rest of his children." This was enough to shock any son, he realized, considering how totally dumbfounded he had been on first learning about it. "He used those exact words to my surprise and amazement, not to mention objections." Shifting his gaze, he paused to let the memory of the animated discussion seep in, before focusing on the prince again. "With this adoption, your father also bequeaths a house in Harbor Town to the exclusive use of the Lady Ylianor."

"And it's legal you say?" It was clear Duncan Caldwell was trying to grapple with the news and not let them crush him.

"Even if no one, to my knowledge, has used adoptions before . . ." For what purpose could they possibly serve, given how pledges defined family ties so accurately? "There are no bans or laws against it." If for the sake of honesty alone, he had to speak the truth, no matter how inconvenient it would be to the prince. "So yes, it's perfectly legal." *Unfortunately for you, prince.* "The good news is that only me, and now you, know of this clause."

"What's good about it?" If Duncan growled it was probably due to the strain strangling him.

"Well . . ." He cleared his throat. "True, I promised Charles Caldwell I'd uphold it even to your face, but just seeing your first reaction, I feel I was right all along in advising him against it." He heaved. "Since we're the only ones to know, I could discreetly remove it from the will without anyone ever finding out."

"Alter the will?" Duncan's voice was icy cold. "You mean cheat?"

"Well, not exactly." He shifted nervously in his seat. "Technically, your father was not feeling well the last few days of his life, when he drew the will." Glancing at the prince, he noticed his scornful expression had not changed. "We could easily infer his faculties failed him when he asked for this provision."

"In your legal opinion, could my father understand what he was doing?" The prince stared hard, as though wondering if he dared betray his father's wishes with such outright defiance.

Or perhaps what was really getting to him was the awareness that, whoever this woman was, Prince Charles had loved her until the end. And that was something that galled him far beyond any legal issues.

"Well . . ." He played around with the implications of the question, before his memory reminded him of just how fit Prince Charles's mind had been in spite of his imminent death. "I don't suppose you'd accept a lie."

"This is just between you and me, right?" A wry smile

curved the prince's full lips. "So why lie?" Mark had to admit his logic was faultless. "I want to know where I stand, fair and square, which is why I need to know what my father's true wishes were."

"Fair enough, Prince." Crossing his legs, Mark regarded him with open admiration. "Your father knew exactly what he was doing, right up to the end. And he anticipated the family's opposition, even if he felt it was too important to let the issue slide. He trusted I'd explain his reasons, but just to be on the safe side . . ." He reached in his pocket and fished out a closed envelope. "He wrote this letter and asked me to give it to you prior to the reading of his will." He handed it to the prince, who did not open it. "Now the choice is yours. If you decide to honor the clause, this Ylianor woman will officially become a Caldwell, and you'll have a new addition to the family. If you don't, then no one will suffer except this Ylianor Meyer who, in any case, will never know of this provision."

"Cleverly put." Duncan chortled, though his mood was nothing amused. "I admire your logic, which gives me an easy way out." After toying with the envelope, he tossed it aside, as though severely tempted to burn it in the fireplace. "Too bad it doesn't also give me the easy conscience to carry out either decision."

"I can't answer for the conscience." He uncrossed his legs. "What I can say is that, if the will is really a passage into adulthood, then never has it been truer than in your case." Interpreting the prince's absorption with the closed envelope as a sign he wanted to be alone, he rose to leave. "I'll wait for confirmation of the exact date. In your message, you can simply write yes, if you want me to leave the clause, or no, if you don't want it. I'll understand and adjust the will to your instructions."

"All right." Nodding, the prince rose and extended a

hand. "Thank you, Mark, for your concern and your honesty." Then he sat back at his desk.

And he left with a lighter step than when he had entered the office, knowing his weight now rested on very broad and hopefully very capable shoulders.

CHAPTER THIRTY-SEVEN

Dear son, I know you're probably upset now. What the lawyer just told you is not easy to accept, I understand, nor is asking you to uphold what seems like a controversial clause in front of the rest of the family. That's why I want to take this time to explain my reasons and, in the process, tell you a little about myself.

Despite everything you might believe now, I have loved my family with all my heart – and you, my boy, in particular. You have made me very proud, and I know you have an important future ahead. My only regret in how I treated you is a certain coldness that has prevented me from displaying all the love, pride and affection I feel for you. I sincerely apologize if I hurt you in any way. For most of my life, I kept feelings bottled up inside, exercising an unnecessarily rigid control that, I know now, hurt my loved ones and me, at least until someone showed me how to express them without fear. And, if in the end I tried to make it up to you for my earlier shortcomings, I must confess that with your sister, Elizabeth, I could never quite achieve the same result. Still, you have to believe me when I say I loved and cared deeply for you both.

Then again, nothing is ever casual in life, not even when it comes to regrets. To have them means I had the misfortune . . . or the blessing of knowing someone who opened the door and freed my deepest feelings, which changed my life forever.

Are you in love, my son?

I hope you've found your special him or her already, so you will understand what I'm about to say. Love is such a complicated emotion. I had the privilege of feeling it at least twice in very different circumstances, and one thing I learned is that you cannot choose whom you love. Like a tempest, it hit me without warning or protection, leaving me no possibility of recovery. Not then. Not ever. And I lived it so intensely I didn't honestly care about the consequences.

By now, you must've guessed who I'm talking about, even if it probably offends your aristocratic taste. But this is not why I'm writing this letter. As you know, the woman I loved gave birth to a wonderful baby girl. Not my child, of course, since Mary Jane never pledged to me. But something about that little girl is mine. Something inside me screams every time I look at her that she's my own. That she belongs to me no matter how impossible it is.

Forgive me, son, if I sound so emphatic about something so uncertain. I know I can't explain what goes against nature itself, but she belongs to the Caldwells just as surely as you do. When death took her mother away from me in that sinister way, I clung to this child more than I should have in my right mind. But I guess it was inevitable, considering the uniqueness of our bond.

Thanks to her, I discovered a new form of communicating, not just through mere words, rather with an unexplainable touching of the minds. Unlike you or Elizabeth, she could hear my thoughts, read my mind and share my feelings. This, more than anything else, convinced me she belonged to me, or better yet that she was part of me.

Now I ask your support in helping someone surely mistreated since my death. Because of her power, people have probably accused her of witchcraft, like her mother before her, if not worse. And your mother was one who believed such lies, to the point I'm sure she did not want that little girl around after my death, which will make everything harder for you.

So I entreat you.

Ylianor may not be a blood relative but for sure, she used to be your friend during childhood. And even if she may have disappeared from Black Rose all together, searching in your heart today, I know you'll find traces of that friendship in the happy memories you must keep buried somewhere inside. Sometimes, love takes on unusual disguises, so if you chance to meet again, the two of you *could learn a lot from each other like when you were kids. Find her, wherever she may hide, and help her get what is hers by right and by love.*

Please understand this is not an order, merely a father's plea to his son. If you don't feel this is right, simply throw this letter into the fire and let the flames make ashes of it. At least this will silence it and my pained heart forever. As for the provision in my will, you can easily dismiss it for only the lawyer and now you know of it. Whatever your decision, I know you to be a fair man, and that's why I trust you'll honor my word, doing right by me and by her. And for that, I'll only love you more, because you are my beloved son, now and forever.

Your loving father, Charles.

Chapter Thirty-eight

Stunned!
And fucking mad!

If he had to give words to what he was feeling now, those would have been the first ones at the top of his head, along with all the questions that burned with the intensity of his enraged awareness. For how did she dare have such a special relationship with a man who was *not* her father? From a man who was *his* father, yet all he could think about was a stranger? A conniving thief of affections that would even get a reward out of it all?

And to think that him and Lizzy, his rightful children, had never gotten half of what his father had lavished so plentifully on her. Goddamn it! Why did he have to save it all for her, who meant nothing to the Caldwell family?

If his mother and sister heard of this, they would be so pissed off and with good reason. They had seen the witch's web from the start and had warned him. He had not listened and look where he was now — trapped in the same fucking enchantment his father was!

What galled him most was that, in a single sweep, Charles had confirmed everything she had claimed only the night before. Same things he could have easily dismissed as mere hallucinations or child's fantasies, had there not been written proof of them and in an official document no less! One his father had begged him to uphold and honor as a sign of respect. But why should he? Why should he bother with his father's feelings when his lay in a pitiful heap because of a woman he hardly knew yet could not stop thinking about?

Coursing the moment he had ever set eyes on the green-eyed witch that seemed to have a rare talent in upsetting his life in the most unexpected ways, he turned the letter around in his hands, imagining to feel his father's energy burning through the paper. Maybe he should take Prince Charles's advice and set the damn thing on fire until it was just a pile of ashes. Not that it would help silence those words. *Sorry, Father, just doesn't work like that, not since I've had the most incredible sex with her and with my angel only last night.*

Yep, things could not be more complicated. Rubbing his tired eyes, he could not stop the rush of sensations he had shared with her, from her first blowjob to the initially painful ass fuck that had become the greatest pleasure of all.

Maybe Chris was right all along.

Maybe she had manipulated him, using his newfound power against him to tie him hands and feet, just like she had his father before him. Conspiring and weaseling her way under their skins and into their family.

Ha! As if she could ever be one of them!

No, never, not in a million years, not even if she had plotted so carefully that his father believed it was his decision rather than her meddling. For there could be no doubt she had known all along what his father had planned. How could she not since she shared everything with him? And if he loved her as much as he claimed, could he have kept it a secret from her?

The surge of anger tasted bitter. So strong, it suffocated every attempt at reasoning. At breathing, too, for he had to take several gulps of air just to calm down. And staring at the rain still pouring heavily only worsened his already shitty mood.

Turning away from the window, his gaze fell on the letter again, and he nearly choked on the emotional intensity that had pervaded it, until a providential knock at his door answered his need to forget the entire matter, if not the woman herself.

"Yes?" Sitting at his desk, he fixed the door intently.

"Excuse me, sir." Popping his head around the threshold, David hesitated. "May I come in?"

"Sure." Duncan gestured him forward. "What is it?"

"I was wondering whether you'd be leaving tomorrow as planned with Lord Templeton." David advanced to his desk.

"Tomorrow?" He had completely forgotten about it. Not just about the trip, about how much he had looked forward to it just an hour ago.

For nothing beat being with Chris on the road, just the two of them, away from the rest of the world.

"Yes, I guess so." Then sensing that something was wrong, he narrowed his gaze on him. "Why do you ask?"

"Nothing . . ." The hazel eyes clouded at the evident lie.

"Come on, David." Irked, he scoffed impatiently, "What is it?"

"Well . . ." The man cleared his throat. "It's about your sister —"

"Lizzy?" Immediately concerned, he stretched out across his desk. "What's wrong?"

"Nothing's wrong with her," David was quick to reassure. "It's just that there's something troubling her, and she came to me for advice."

"Must be something important, then." His sister was a no-nonsense girl with a rational mind that was quite capable of analyzing things without giving in to their emotional side.

Except when it came to their mother, something she just could not help, and that he easily forgave.

"She thought it was." David took a deep breath. "Because she overheard your mother and Alicia Merryweather, and it seemed to her they were plotting something dreadful against . . ." He went silent as though he did not want to speak the name.

"Against Ylianor?" *Wasn't hard to guess.*

At David's nod, his heart sank. *Why am I not surprised? And why is everything only about her lately?*

"What are they plotting exactly?" Resigned to have the damn woman torment him until the end, he reclined on his seat.

"Lady Elizabeth didn't provide many details." From the way David looked at him, Duncan had the sensation he was trying to convey how serious the matter was. "But it's something bad for sure, which will happen as soon as you turn your back —"

"What sort of . . . thing?" He sat up straighter, his senses suddenly alert.

"She's not sure." David shook his head. "But I have the funny feeling it's related to what happened to Ylianor's mother."

"My mother had something to do with Mary Jane's death?" Incredulous, he leaned forward.

"Just rumors, sir." Quick to avert his gaze, David took a step back. "As you know, I was only nine years old when it happened, so it's just hearsay and speculations. What's true is that Mary Jane died during one of your father's absences from Black Rose."

It would serve her right!

Ready to dismiss the whole thing as one of David's fantasies, he was about to change topic when something apropos family patterns repeating themselves stopped him cold. Despite his fury, an icy hand gripped his stomach at the thought of losing her and suddenly, it did not seem like such a preposterous possibility anymore. Nor could it be a coincidence, not if he considered that bit about Mary Jane, taken away in a *sinister way* as his father had written, which seemed to fit into everything in the most menacing way. Like her master plans, which could snap a person's life before he had the chance to vent all his rage on her.

But by the gods, if she had to die, it would be his call — and his alone, in light of all the misery she was putting him through.

"I plan to be away for a while . . ." He frowned.

Maybe she deserved to live. If she had known about the will, why would she had been reluctant to return to Black Rose? And what about the fact that she was a mere nine-year-old when his father died?

"I know, Prince." David did not seem surprised. "That's why I brought it up."

"Naturally, you wouldn't have any ulterior motive for it." Remembering his angel's insight about David and Ylianor, his lips curved in a malicious snarl. "Right?"

David became crimson.

So my angel was right after all.

"I'm sorry," David blurted. "Please, believe me. I never meant to . . ." He swallowed hard. "I don't know what came over me . . . I . . . she shouldn't have told you —"

"Relax, David." He kept his tone even and reassuring on purpose, "She didn't breathe a word of it." He shifted his gaze to give David the privacy to recompose himself. "And she'll never have to 'cause she's not my property. I'm just glad there's someone looking out for her." And damn it! He meant every word of it, for the mere idea of losing her caused a fresh wave of icy desolation. "I guess it's best if I bring her along like you suggest."

"Yes, sir." Huffing in evident relief, David grinned broadly. "It wouldn't be a bad idea, not at all."

So she wins again. "All right, tell her to be ready tomorrow at dawn."

"Thank you, sir." David bowed slightly.

"Don't thank me. I'm not doing her any favors." *Particularly when the angel finds out.*

For Chris would take it as a second betrayal. And his angel's fury could be more than anyone could handle, also for a witch like her, no matter how powerful she had become.

CHAPTER THIRTY-NINE

"Prince Caldwell." A knock followed the call. "It's time to wake up."

"Yes . . ." He stirred on hearing the unfamiliar male voice behind the door. "Who is it?"

"It's Joe." The man hesitated briefly. "Lord Templeton is waiting for you."

Great! No, he had not told Chris about the news. And by the gods, would he be thrilled to know she would be intruding in their private time together on the road.

Smothering a yawn, he rose from the bed. After a quick stop in the bathroom, he dressed and grabbed the sack of clothes he had prepared the night before. Then leaving his bedroom, he caught sight of his angel on the lower level, looking quite satisfied with himself.

"Good morning, lover." As smug as a cat who had eaten the biggest mouse of all, Chris beamed in one of his most enchanting smiles.

"What's good about it?" Duncan growled tightly, his mood undoubtedly worse than he had anticipated.

"No one kept you company last night?" Chris taunted. "Serves you right for having abandoned me to your sister's mercy." He licked his lips. "Luckily, I found that pretty boy . . ." He gestured at the young man going down the stairs and almost to the ground floor. "Who was more than happy to comfort me."

Recognizing the man who had knocked on his door, he was not surprised. "You mean Joe?"

He was exactly Chris's type—not too tall, dark-haired, slim and with puppy-soft brown eyes.

"Can't remember the name." Definitely, names were not his angel's strongest suits. He had the bad habit of forgetting them as soon as he heard them, with very few exceptions. "But he's a new houseboy that your butler is training . . ." He smacked his lips. "Quite adequately, I might add." The defiant look he sent him was pure provocation. "He seems very eager to learn, even if it's not quite what poor Reginald is aiming for." A mischievous sparkle lit his blue-gray eyes.

"You're insatiable." Amused, he could not resist a half smile. "How old is he?"

"Didn't bother to ask." Chris shrugged. "But old enough, anyway."

After crossing the main hall and reaching Black Rose's entrance, he headed to the stables enveloped by a brisk morning air, made more pungent by the overcast sky. In the distance, he saw Ylianor, leaning intimately against David, and it only worsened his mood.

So he was the only one who had not entertained company, as Chris had so elegantly put it. And maybe he had been wrong, for his cold bed could not prevent the burst of fresh, hot rage at the mere sight of the very woman who was the cause of it all.

"Good morning, sirs." David's cheerful tone grated his nerves. "Here's your breakfast and lunch." The valet handed wrapped packages to both him and Chris. "And here are your horses." He gave them Fuzeon and Black's bridles. "Fit and ready to leave at your command."

"We're also ready." With a seductive slide, the angel mounted on his horse.

As he got on Fuzeon, he could not help overhearing David.

"I've packed your lunch." The man's soft tone was all for

her, "Together with a few of my pants, a jacket and a couple of shirts." He wrapped her hand around a knapsack. "It's colder where you're going, so at least you won't freeze to death. When you get back, we'll need to provide you with something to wear."

"Don't worry, David." She stroked his cheek. "I'll be fine with or without clothes." And the green eyes flashed mischievously as she took the knapsack.

I've been so busy taking off her clothes, I hardly noticed she had any. Then his gaze glued to her ass when she swung to climb on Starlet's saddle.

"Hey, lover, what the fuck is she doing?" Chris snarled. "I thought we were going alone. Arthur wants to see us, not her."

"It's a safety measure." Not giving time for the words to sink in, he kicked Fuzeon flanks and rode off without further delay.

"Hey, wait!" Racing to follow, Chris eventually caught up with him. "What safety measure?"

Not wanting to answer, he pretended he had not heard and pushed Fuzeon at a harder pace.

"You can't keep this up for the whole damn trip," Chris snapped, sounding less aggressive. "Talk to me, please. Something's terribly wrong, has been ever since she came back into your life, and you can't deny it. She's nothing but trouble, yet you can't keep away from her. Nothing but a servant, yet you treat her as a best friend, a longtime lover, when not a member of your family." Fueling up, his anger rose with the heat of his words. "And I forgive you for having forced her down my throat once, but why should I babysit her through our trip, which was ours alone if I recall? At least give me some sensible explanation before I decide to change road and get to Arthur on my own."

"Hey, I'm not happy about it either," he spat at last. "But I don't want to have her on my conscience." Taking a deep breath, he tried calming down. "Lizzy thought Mother was plotting to do something nasty to get rid of her once and for all, and David thinks it's the same something she may have done already when the girl's mother died. The ironic thing is that it happened during one of my father's trips, so he asked me to bring her along, to keep her safe from harm."

"Since when does David decide things at Black Rose?" Shocked, Chris's eyebrows rose.

"He doesn't," he retorted tartly. "And if you really want to know, it's partly your fault we're stuck with her."

"Mine?" Glaring at him, Chris tightened his knees around Black's belly. "How can I possibly be the reason we're on the road with someone I can't stand?"

"Not you, something you said." Averting his gaze, he kept it fixed on the road ahead. "Something about family patterns repeating themselves got me thinking so—"

"So now it's my fault?" Chris edged closer. "Then tell me why I get the distinct feeling you can't stand the sight of her, either. The other night you were in the sharing mood, even trying to convince me to accept a more permanent solution with that witch. Today you can't even look at her. Still, you insist on saving her worthless hide." He charged the words as though he would have loved to skin her alive himself. "Why? What happened?" At an obvious loss, he accelerated to flank him. "Not that I don't like this new twist," he was quick to add. "I can definitely relate to her better if you hate her," he snarled malevolently. "Only thing is—this change of heart is a bit . . . confusing, wouldn't you agree?"

This time, he chose not to reply. Not if he wanted to avoid drowning in the tide of his own fury that had been steadily mounting with each of his angel's objections.

"All right, you can also disagree, if you'd like." Chris grinned encouragingly.

What would be the point if not to choke on my own bile?

"All right, since you're not in the sharing mood today,

let's play a little guessing game." Chris creased his forehead in an obvious attempt to fit all the pieces together.

As his angel concentrated, he galloped harder, neither bothering nor caring to check if she was following at all.

"I got it!" He swung blue-gray eyes bright in understanding on him "Whatever's eating you must be connected to the lawyer's visit. In fact, now that I think of it, your mood changed dramatically after he left."

"He had nothing to say," he spat. "He wanted to arrange a date—"

"No, I'm not letting you off the hook that easily," Chris snickered. "Nor am I your mother who'll believe any bullshit just because it comes from your lips. No, your father must've disposed something in his will that you can't accept, right?"

If the angel hoped to get confirmation from him, he was dead wrong.

Which did not stop him, goddamn it!

"And considering how you're acting . . ." His voice trailed off as his eyes widened in disbelief. "Whatever it is, and nothing that goes by traditions I'm sure, must have to do with her." He angled his head behind a shoulder as though he wanted to look at her. "Did he dare mention a complete stranger in his will? In an official family document that—"

"Mention?" He collapsed as the truth, pressing on his chest and throat demanded a full release. "I wish he had only *mentioned* the damn witch, instead of being an egotistical fool thinking only of himself, even after dead."

"What does he say about her?" With a surprisingly gentle tone, the angel breathed the words slowly as if afraid they would revive painful memories.

"He publicly recognizes her as a Caldwell by . . ." The oppressively hot lump in his throat forced him to swallow twice before he could speak again. "Get this, adopting her!

Can you believe it?" He certainly still could not! "In an official document, my father adopts a complete stranger into the Caldwell family, even going as far as implying she might share his blood."

"Does he say she does?" Cool-headed now, Chris's tone was strangely even, probably to contain his soon to explode rage. "I mean, is she really his daughter?"

"No, she *is not!*" Duncan hissed, offended at the mere thought. "And he knows it, too, but an adoption is like telling the world she belongs to him, which is unacceptable however you look at it."

So what if the first time he had seen her, he had had the same sensation? At the moment, it was not only irrelevant. It was totally beside the point.

"And that's not all." The more he talked, the more enraged he became. "He also provides for her future as if she were a regular heir, leaving her a house I didn't even know existed." Taking a gulp of air, he threw back his shoulders. "Fuck! All he cares about is that bitch and not one word about Lizzy, his rightful daughter. And my mother . . ." He groaned inwardly, already picturing the inevitable fight. "She's going to be furious, to say the least."

"Is it legal?" Continuing his probing, Chris seemed to pursue a track of his own.

"Mark says it is." Distracted in spite of himself, his head swung to catch the blue-gray eyes. "Even if it's unusual."

"Who exactly knows of this clause?" The angel's lips twisted fiendishly. "Does she?"

"Apparently, only me, the lawyer and now you. As for her . . ." He shrugged. "I can't believe she knows nothing about it. She used the same trick on my father she used on me the other night—"

"The snooping around in your thoughts and feelings?" Chris sniggered. "To me, she's nothing but a damn spy."

He could not agree more, liking how he had called the sharing, which he refused to acknowledge as power.

"Yeah, a spy." Made perfect sense. "So how can you think that a spy like her, who could read my father's most buried thoughts, could ignore something so important?" Frustrated, he shook his head, his long hair flying around his shoulders. "I guess my mother was right all along. A conniving witch! That's what she is!"

"But there's more, isn't there?" Searching his drawn face, Chris seemed to know it for a fact.

"My father had the nerve to write me a letter." No, he had not planned to tell his angel about the letter! "And he begged for my help in recognizing that witch as a Caldwell." Everything just kind of rolled out with the force of an unstoppable avalanche. "Leaving me the choice to keep or remove his goddamn clause as I saw fit."

"So what's the problem?" Brightening all of a sudden, the blue-gray eyes flashed. "You could discreetly delete it from the will, and no one would know about it except perhaps the witch. But she doesn't count, right?"

"My father said I could, and so did the lawyer." So why was he making life so hard on himself? "Without the clause, there'd be no adoption, no inheritance, no nothing." In spite of himself, his sense of fairness rebelled against it regardless of all the consequences. "As if that would solve everything."

"If it's that simple to dismiss a dead man's claim, what's really pissing you off?" The blue-gray eyes blazed in complete understanding. "The fact that she gets a piece of the Caldwell pie? Or that she got your father's love?"

CHAPTER FORTY

She had watched them from afar, not daring to intrude in their conversation. She was already interfering enough as it was, trailing along uninvited in their private journey, shipped off by a David too worried to hear reasons.

For it was not her idea to leave Black Rose after it had taken her ten long years to get back to it.

Still, David had not listened to her and gone directly to the prince. And this was the result—two smoldering pyres of enraged powers that could lash out at any moment and burn her to a crisp faster than the bat of an eye. And for what reason she could only guess.

She had honestly thought her first sharing with him had been great. No, exceptional, since she had never expected it to take quite this form nor to lace the sex to the point of being mind-blowing. Well, for her at least since she was still reeling from it. For him, too, or so she had believed on perceiving his extreme satisfaction and feverish excitement. For the smug Lord Templeton, too, for his lights had shimmered in such a way there could be no doubt he had loved every minute of it. Then the blending together had taken everything to another level, one she was still trying to figure out, while the sensation that it had filled the huge void inside of her clung on.

But maybe it had not been that impressive, not to them given their considerably greater experience in sex. So there was no guarantee he would jump at the chance to continue, perhaps deepen this new exchange between them, not now that he was so close to exploding from the sheer force of the fury strangling him. She saw it as clearly as if she had been riding next to him, had seen his surprisingly red hue ever since catching sight of him walking to the stables. All directed against her, as if she had done something terribly wrong.

But what could it possibly be? What had she done to deserve this?

Now following Chris and Duncan several yards behind, she knew that the mass of rage and what felt like humiliation was coiling into a fiery ball that pushed out in a violent burst. He was about to strike her, destroy her to be precise, and he would have, had not Chris's energy restrained him in a rush of blue waves she had never seen from him before. Blinded by the utter intensity of the shiny blue energy curling around the darker one then mastering it, she watched them hurry to a shelter just off the main road, dismount and enter it in a dash.

As the door slammed behind them, she trembled from the close call as much as from the shock of Chris's unexpected protection. Whatever had gotten into him was as puzzling as what had happened to Duncan. And whatever had driven him, it was not to save her skin, for sure! Still, she would even have to be grateful to His Presumptuousness if and when he ever got out of there!

Taking the horses they had carelessly abandoned in front of the shelter, she thanked the stars that at least the weather had improved. After defeating the ominous clouds, Stella's rays now shone everywhere, their warmth giving her a measure of relief as she checked around for a place to settle the animals. The sound of waves licking the shore caught her attention and guided her down a narrow path. With Fuzeon, Black and Starlet at her heels, she reached a small river, the perfect spot to leave them tied to a tree and with plenty of grass to satisfy their needs.

It was pure beauty at its most essential, from the soft murmurs, to the golden sparks glistening on the water's surface at every wave, to the gentle breeze caressing her skin. Sitting on the low banks, she tried to relax and shake off the nasty sensations they had dumped on her, when a harsh tug yanked her and threw her right inside the cabin where Chris and Duncan were attacking one another, mouths and tongues violently clashing, muscles tense, cocks hard and ready for the explosive release. Duncan was so hungry, so insatiable in his craving that a surge of fiery lust melted her flesh to the bone. Oh, she would have loved to be part of their heated ritual, had he not realized he had unwittingly invited her. With a horrified snap, he severed the connection, brutally tossing her back to the river's edges, staring at the water with her body on fire and her mind in turmoil.

Serves me right for showing him what he's capable of and having agreed to David's insane plan!

As if they would ever want her along!

Well, she could certainly do without them, especially now that the water's coolness called to her boiling spirit or rather to the furiously throbbing ache between her legs. This prompted the shedding of her clothes and the dive into the cold stream. Arms and legs paddling vigorously to avoid freezing, she pumped blood and energy to glide through the dense liquid, thanking Prince Charles for having insisted she learn to swim alongside Duncan. Her senses completely taken, she let herself go, sinking in the element that she had never feared, in fact knew better than herself. It was just so blissful, she lost track of time all together, only vaguely aware of Stella's increased brightness and heat that stung her skin—

Where the fuck are you? Like thunder, Duncan's deep-throated voice crashed in her head and snapped her back to reality. *And where are the horses?* Not as mad as before, still his tone left no doubt he had not forgiven her for whatever it was she had done wrong. *Get your ass here! Now!* This last one was an order pure and simple. *We've wasted enough time already.*

I'm in the river. Not that he deserved an answer! *And the horses are here with me.* Still, she scrambled to get out of the water. *I'll be right there.*

Already to the shore, she climbed out and stood there, naked and wet. Seeing them coming down the path, she began dressing without any hurry, without rinsing either, her movements slow and deliberately seductive.

Of course, Chris ignored her.

Duncan, instead, could not tear his gaze away from her curves, however hard he tried.

Suppressing a giggle, she shivered in triumph at her ability to affect him despite his anger, or whatever else was eating him.

As a reaction, or more to spite her, Duncan reached out to kiss Chris. A hard, passionately wet affair that hit her with the force of his unquenchable craving for the striking blond man, still strong regardless of the sex they had just shared. Then he broke it off just as abruptly as he had started it and mounted on Fuzeon.

"Love you, too." Hardly fooled, the demon's lips curved in a sardonic snarl.

"Never as much as I do." This time, the prince was completely truthful.

When she reached for Starlet, she felt Duncan's gaze glued to her ass. Small wonder, since her drenched clothes clung like a second skin, exalting her shape like mere bare flesh could not. Nothing left to the imagination, just in case he needed a reminder, which he did not. Simply seeing her body had turned him on again, no matter how much sex he had in the meantime. The stir in his cock was too visible for her to be mistaken or to prevent the thrill of pleasure from coursing down her spine.

This was another aspect of power, one he best learn how to handle because she would do everything she could to use it against him, whatever the circumstances.

Satisfied by her little payback, she got on Starlet and followed them in resuming their journey.

CHAPTER FORTY-ONE

"You're going to kill her, if you keep up this pace." Sounding oddly concerned, the angel looked behind his shoulder at Ylianor riding a good way behind them.

He did not care.

Nor had he made it easy for her. Never stopping since he had resumed the trip, not even to eat. Never slowing down either, skirting villages to ensure faster travel and speeding through hills and valleys, where the vegetation was as green as springtime required. Deliberately heartless, he had pushed her resistance beyond what he thought she could withstand, amazed she had hung on without complaining or taking a break.

"She needs to earn her safety." Implacable, he shrugged coldly.

I hope she suffers through every single mile, and damn her and that fucking show of hers! However hard he tried, he could not forget his intense desire on seeing the wet clothes clinging to every one of her tantalizing curves. Sure, he knew she had done it on purpose, moving more seductively the moment she had felt his gaze on her. But it had not eased his arousal nor erased the satisfied smug on her lips, leaving him to wonder why she managed to manipulate him so effortlessly.

"I think she's earned enough for one day." There was a note of begrudged admiration in the angel's voice. "And so have we, considering night has fallen a while ago."

Too busy to drive her senseless, he had almost missed the moment Stella had set.

"You're right." Rubbing his tired eyes, he checked the area. "We've all deserved a shelter."

"And there's one." Chris pointed at a cabin just a short distance away.

"Yeah, I knew it wouldn't be a problem finding one." Guiding Fuzeon to it, he accelerated the pace. "Not on this traveled road."

"Just our luck we're going to the Hall." Chris grinned, following him. "And that we won't have to worry about our horses, 'cause you had the good sense to bring your stable keeper along," he mocked.

"It's probably all she's good for." If not exactly the truth, he did not bother lowering his voice, wanting her to feel all his scorn.

He had reached the shelter anyway, so left the horses to her care, disappearing inside with Chris.

"I'll take care of the fire." Too cold to be without it, he immediately set to work on the pile of wood next to the fireplace.

"And I'll see what's for dinner." Chris headed to the kitchen. "How about a bean soup, lover?"

"Fine for me, Angel." He angled his head in the direction of Chris's voice. Then shifting back to light the drier twigs, he caught sight of her. "Bring whatever you find over here." Turning his gaze, he ignored her completely. "We'll cook it on the fire."

"All right." When the blond angel emerged from the kitchen, he handed him a pail. "Here you go."

"Great." After placing it over the first timid flames, he reclined against the couch, with Chris curling around him.

"Apart from the company, this could turn out to be better than some of the nights I have to sit through at the Hall," his husky tone overlapped the loud crackle. "Where there are some real jerks who always think they're one-step ahead of

Arthur."

"Like that Trent fellow you like so much?" Chuckling, he gave Chris his full attention, well knowing the angel was deliberately cutting her off not just from the conversation.

From the entire evening.

"Trent's just the worst of them." Chortling, Chris seemed glad he was playing along and keeping a steady flow of gibberish about people she could know nothing about. "He's an envious bastard who can't stand me 'cause I took his place at Arthur's side." He settled in a more comfortable position. "So he's always trying to put me down, only he's too stupid to realize Arthur is getting tired of this jealous attitude of his. The last time Trent was his bitchy self, Arthur had him removed from the attic, forcibly I might add. Trent tried to talk some leniency into Arthur, but didn't get very far," he shrugged. "Hardly surprising, seeing what Arthur thinks of Trent anyway."

"Your opinion isn't any better." He grinned.

"Can you blame me?" Chris spat. "He's a nobody who'll always be a nobody, while I am all he'll never be." Spoken without false modesty rather with all the pride Chris could muster, for such was his angel's style. "Like the vice-leader's son, for one, and a lord for seconds. Plus, I've got something he'll never have, and for which he'd give his right arm."

"What?" He spun his head to lock his gaze on Chris's.

"You." Blue-gray eyes boring deep into his, Chris charged the words with all the erotic innuendo he alone could give.

And he realized his angel could not just cut her off from him. He could cut the universe off, and Duncan would never complain.

"Me?" He pushed back a few loose strands of hair. "How can he want me when he doesn't even know me? Probably only saw me that one-time Arthur invited me to the Hall."

"Trust me, lover." A hand on his chest, Chris prevented

his further objections. "That one was more than enough for him to wish you'd fuck him, rather than me."

"As I recall, he's not that bad looking." Truth was—for the life of him, he could not remember what Trent looked like. Not even close to something vaguely resembling the man. He just wanted to shake some of his angel's certainties, if only for fun. "So I just might take advantage of his—"

"Don't you dare," Chris hissed. "You're mine." His palm pressing on his crotch gave the measure of how possessively he meant it. "And Trent's never going to have you, like he'll never have anything else that's mine."

At the first serious fondling, his cock stirred to alertness, proving once and for all Chris's complete mastery over it.

"I'm sure that doesn't stop him from wanting what belongs to you anyway." The sensation was so good, he wished he could share it, but quickly suppressed the impulse.

No, he did not want a repetition of what had happened at the previous shelter, where the need to have her had caused him to call her save pulling back in horror the second he had realized what he was doing.

"Absolutely not." As though reading his mind, Chris's hand fell on a side, and he fixed the fire. "He's stupid, I told you, and envious of Arthur in particular." From the intent way he watched the leaping flames, the angel seemed hypnotized. "He always gets a weird look whenever Arthur and I are together, which reeks of jealousy from miles away."

"And Arthur tolerates it?" After stirring the pail on the fire, he sat back down.

"Arthur doesn't give a damn about Trent." Shaking his head, Chris's attention focused back on him. "Nor about any of the other boys, except for me." The self-satisfied smile was so enchanting Duncan just wanted to kiss him senseless. "And things would be just great between us, if he wasn't getting old." Very serious now, a twinge of sadness veiled his voice, "He's still himself, of course," he was quick to add. "But he gave me the impression he was losing it somehow."

"Do you think that's why he summoned us?" Knowing how deeply Chris cared for Arthur, he used his gentlest tone, leaning forward to cup his face and level their gazes.

"I wish I knew." Blue-gray eyes clouding, the angel shrugged. "But I don't." Furtively, he glanced at a side where she had remained standing. "What I do know is that we shouldn't take the witch along." The blue-gray eyes flashed annoyed. "Why didn't we leave her in the river?"

Yeah, why didn't we? Or rather, why didn't I?

Something inside had rebelled, even if the thought had crossed his mind. But that unexplainable instinct to keep her no matter what had sneaked up again despite his fury, and there had been no fighting it.

"I mean, if safety's the issue, she could've stayed over there until our return," Chris insisted aggressively. "I doubt your mother would've tracked her there. So why is she still here?" Merciless, his lips curled in a cruel snarl. "More importantly, do we have to share our food and bed with her? If her main task is to look after our horses, shouldn't she spend the night with them instead of us?"

"Oh, I'll sleep with them, no problem." Whirling around, she headed for the door. "They're certainly a much better company than either of you oafs."

"That's because they're the only company who'll accept the likes of you," Chris snapped.

"No, wait." Scrambling up, he went toward her.

"Why are you stopping her, lover?" Chris sneered.

Slowing down his rush, he hesitated, looking solely at his angel. "She should at least eat something."

"Don't worry about me, *Prince*." She smiled coldly. "I'm not hungry and if I were later, I still have today's lunch."

"Yes, which darling David prepared with his own loving

hands," Chris snickered. "Too bad he doesn't know how to use them in bed."

"So you've also tried him, haven't you?" Ylianor spat maliciously. "I suppose the master wasn't good enough that you had to go with the servant, too!"

"I don't care for lackeys when I got the best there is around." With a cold and furious flash brightening the blue-gray eyes, the angel jumped up to face her. "And unlike you, dearie, I can tell how a person is in bed just by looking at him," he scoffed haughtily, his tone rising along with the tension. "So it's only your fault he doesn't satisfy you like . . ." With heartless fiendishness, he pressed his palm on his shaft and rubbed it in a circular movement that was extremely arousing. "Like my lover does."

"You're wrong." The arresting green eyes blazed. "I'm quite satisfied with him, especially since he makes me forget a sorry ass like you."

Well, one thing he had to hand her—she had more spunk than he had given her credit for initially.

"You're so full of yourself you think everybody is jealous of you just because they want to share your bed!" She took a step back. "Well, sorry to disappoint you, *Lord Templeton*, but I neither want nor care to be with you in or out of bed."

"As if I'd ever want anyone as unskilled and as insignificant as you to touch me, let alone have sex with." An ugly snarl twisted his thin lips. "So you could've stayed in David's bed and saved us the trouble of having to protect you, though why would anyone bother with your worthless hide is beyond me."

"Anything that isn't about you is *beyond you*, Lord Templeton." Sarcastic and biting, she backed away. "Which is why I much prefer spending the night with the horses." She flung the door open. "And just for the record, I didn't ask to come along on this trip. Nor is it my intention to spoil your *precious time* together. So I'll be sure to cut short our forced closeness as soon as Stella is up again." Then she walked out of the shelter.

Stunned, he saw her ass swing seductively away and took his first step to detain her. *No, wait!*

The moment he screamed it in her head, Chris placed a restraining hand on his arm. "Let her go, lover, and good riddance." Turning to the open door, he raised his voice, "She's just a goddamn troublemaker and if she leaves now, she'll only do us a favor!" Then he slammed the door shut and attacked Duncan's throbbing equipment.

A couple of sharp intakes and the tension Chris had worked so hard to build shattered with his explosive climax. Pushing down the angel's throat, he let it all go in convulsive jets of thick fluid.

No, not all of it since his shaft remained as stiff as before the orgasm. So he pulled off Chris's pants, flipped him down on his belly and shoved his rigid cock through the tight ass ring, stretching it wide all together, all at once. His huge size fitting more snugly, he pumped faster hoping for another quick come.

What he really could not stand were the images of her intruding on his sex with Chris. Her body's voluptuous curves wrapped in those wet clothes of hers were driving him crazy. The need to touch and feel her was also insanely mounting, no matter how fiercely he rammed his way to the incandescent guts.

To block her, he intensified his furious hammering, blowing that enflamed rear to bits. Not that his angel would complain. It was exactly how he liked it, and the bigger his ass became the better. So he took no mercy on what he had now enlarged way beyond his convenience, which squeezed him just right on every side of the thick erection impaling his angel's fiery flesh.

If only he did not have her in his head and in the pit of his stomach, everything would be just perfect. Instead, he could not get rid of her. And if his erection strained under the heated fever that had turned it into a slab of marble, he was not sure if it was his angel's butt or her constant reminder.

Something about her just would not let him be, so defeated he surrendered. *Princess, please come back here and join us.*

She heard it.

He was sure of it, for their minds touched for a long moment. Not long enough, alas.

With the coldness she had used to snap at Chris, she slammed the connection shut, hurling him out of her awareness and leaving him unsatisfied despite his flooding the capacious behind with copious drops of angry juice.

CHAPTER FORTY-TWO

Something woke him up very early.

Something with a sense of urgency that made him scramble out of bed and run outside naked. And he was just in time to see her, all packed and ready to leave.

"Stop!" Duncan ordered.

"Goodbye, Prince Caldwell." Without even turning to acknowledge him, she strapped her knapsack to Starlet's saddle. "Thanks for saving my hide and have a nice life, you and that rat that keeps you company."

"I said stop." Firm in his intention to keep her by his side, he spelled out the words slowly. "And when your master commands, you have to comply." He took a step forward. "Because you are merely a slave."

"I'm not a slave!" Flashing angry green eyes at him, she spun around to confront him.

And damn her! She looked so beautiful, so enticing that his cock yelped in craving. "For all purposes, you gave up your freedom to me, remember?"

"Those were just words..." Hesitant, she lowered her gaze.

"No, they weren't." He was on her now. "And you know it." But pulling her away from the mare was a mistake.

Just touching her unleashed a fresh wave of a craving so deep he knew he could not resist it. Whatever happened, he had to have her, had to claim her sweet yielding flesh to quench his high-strung senses that had found no peace.

"You belong to me, however much I may resent it at the

moment." He worked hard to control the impulse to take her right there and then, flinging her down to the ground and drowning in her alluring body. "'Cause you are mine, and I will exercise my right to use you as I see fit." He raised her chin with a finger, gazing deeply in the green eyes. "So take Starlet back to her stall, then come inside."

Returning to the threshold, he watched her obeying his order. Then coming out of the stables, she walked toward him.

"Lover, what's going on?" A still sleepy Chris stepped behind him, yawning loudly until he became fully awake on catching sight of her. "Don't tell me you asked her to stay."

"I did." Spinning around, he returned inside the shelter.

"Why?" Chris chased him, the blue-gray eyes blazing in disaccord. "We could've gotten rid of her once and for all—"

"Actually, you had your chance to get rid of me, Lord Templeton," she retorted. "But didn't take it."

"What?" Clearly taken aback, the angel stared at her wide-eyed.

"And I also have to thank you." She lowered her head formally in a mock bow.

"You're thanking me?" Chris exchanged a questioning glance with him, obviously not expecting such answer. "For what?"

"For using your power to protect me against the prince's rage." She had such grave expression now that he had no doubt she was truly grateful.

Which meant he had really been on the verge of doing some serious harm.

"She may be right." He cleared his throat. "I was kind of . . . mad yesterday."

"Ha!" Chris sneered. "That doesn't even begin to describe it, lover."

"That's why you used your power to calm him." Relaxing

a bit, she took a step forward. "And shield me in the process."

"That wasn't power, dearie." An ugly smile crossed Chris's lips. "That was *fucking,* an art that still escapes you."

"But I'm obviously a fast learner since your lover keeps pulling me into the sex he has with you." She threw back her shoulders in defiance, green eyes aglow. "Whether I want it or not—"

"He's just the victim of your enchantment!" Chris spat angrily. "With you around, there isn't going to be any privacy from now on."

"I was invited." She looked at him earnestly. "Otherwise, I don't go barging into people's intimate moments, as Lord Templeton seems so good at doing."

"I don't believe he invited you," the blond angel challenged. "Not the way he feels about you lately."

"Sorry to disappoint you, but he did," she scoffed. "Not just once, twice."

"You're lying." Chris turned to him.

"I'm afraid I did." With two pair of eyes glaring at him, he had to admit his responsibilities. "But I shut her out as soon as I realized what I was doing."

"Not the second time, you didn't." Of course, she was quick to spot his inconsistency. "I threw you out of my consciousness. I was so fed up with you, with both of you, I slammed shut the connection right in your face."

"Lover, there's something seriously wrong with you." Chris's hurt look cut deep into his heart. "Perhaps you need to get your priorities straight. Then make a public announcement of what they are 'cause I'm really confused now." He furrowed his brow as though recapping them mentally. "First, you convince me to share this woman . . ." The pause was probably to give himself the courage to set the record straight. "With a passable result, I hate to admit."

However reluctant he sounded, there was no disguising he had liked it far more than he had anticipated or given her credit for so far. It was kind of obvious in fact, and not just to him.

Also to the self-satisfied spark lighting her beautiful green eyes.

"Then you're so pissed off at her you almost kill her, and I'm still wondering why I didn't let you do it," Chris scoffed. "Now you turn the tables again, and simply expect us to kiss and be friends as if nothing happened?" At a loss, he searched his face. "What is it you really want?"

"What I want, I don't think I can get." He stared back at Chris before clasping her arm and dragging her against him. "What I'd like is to wave my hand . . ." He gazed deep into her incredibly green eyes, his voice growing huskier as he tugged her closer, "And disintegrate her into a million pieces." He covered her face with his free hand, pretending to remove it from her neck. "But I also want to fuck her until she cries for mercy." He cupped one firm, round breast. "And rip her open with the blows from two cocks." His voice and breath got hoarse, "That crack her ass and cunt with one shove." His gaze caught hers and held it. "I'm still the master, remember?"

At her imperceptible nod, he claimed her mouth and forced her lips open, his tongue sweeping her wet cavity with avid strokes. Once again, she was his, and he could not believe he had to wait an entire day and night for this moment.

Then he stripped her naked.

It was the way he liked her best, with those shivers of hers creasing her flesh in rapid successions. And nothing gave him more the sense of being her master than having her skin rise to meet his touch, begging for more and rougher handling.

Ha! As if he was in any mood to satisfy her.

Pressing on her shoulder, he made her drop on her knees. *Now open wide and suck.* Grabbing his erection, he fed it to her.

Obediently, she tried gulping it down, which was an impossible task. Too long and too thick for her to suck something more than the engorged tip.

Or at least such was the case before Chris's intervention.

"Let me help you with that, lover." Striding seductively behind him, the blond man grabbed his cock with one hand. The other clamped her neck and held it glued on the massive meat piece now plunging beyond her comfort zone. Uncaring of her sputters, he forced her to swallow the giant shaft for real, swinging it back and forth in forceful slides that went way deeper than she could handle.

As deep as her stomach, or such was his perception.

Not that he lingered on her. He much rather relished the passionate kiss he had begun with Chris, an avid, wet exchange that had their tongues wrapping around one another, spinning his craving to a raging fire.

Feverish, he grasped Chris's monster and jerked it until it scorched his palm. Undoubtedly, his angel was getting high, too, if from the fondling or the strangling he was not sure, nor did he care. He only knew that every one of her coughs was an irresistible turn on that was pushing him over the edge, also thanks to the snug squeeze of her cheeks and tongue that attempted to block his descent. And failed every time, for his dastardly angel broke through her every defense, shoving his cock so far down she gagged on it.

"Lover, my ass is on fire with the need to have you." Leaning heavily on his back, Chris's breath tickled his ear. "I want you so bad I don't think I can resist one second longer."

No wonder Chris would want his cock all to himself. He

would do anything to prevent her from having it. And the way he still felt about her, he could not agree more.

"Happy to oblige, Angel." Grinning broadly, he tried to close the foreskin on top of the fat crown, an unattainable goal now that it had grown so hard and so big. "If you just let go of my slave, we can get down to it."

"I thought you first wanted to choke her." Driving his erection forward, he centered her throat again and would have sent her reeling back had he not held on to her.

"I think she'd be of better use if we keep her alive." Untangling her from Chris's clutch, he picked her up and carried her to the bed. "Or who else is going to suck you while I crack your delicious ass?"

"I suppose you're right." Settling on all fours over her, Chris pushed down to nail her head on the mattress. "Gotta hand it to you, lover." To be precise, he asphyxiated her.

Literally.

"You're always one-step ahead of anybody I know." Drawing slightly back was just a way to increase his swing and penetrate to his balls.

She gasped, which did not move Chris to pity. Instead, he seemed bent on punishing her for everything that had happened since her return to Black Rose.

Ha! As if he were the offended party! After his father's revelations, he had half a mind to strangle her himself and not with a cock!

Still and like he had told Chris, perhaps she could be more useful alive, so he ignored her repeated gags and went straight for Chris's narrow hole without bothering with any preparation. His beast was wet enough to beat any annoying friction standing in the way of his complete enjoyment of the tight space he enlarged with a single thrust.

Groaning loudly, Chris's butt opened up entirely and his hips moved forward, maybe as a reaction to his powerful blow, more likely his need to continue getting back at her in the most hurtful manner possible.

Duncan did not care. Steeling his heart against her and her evident need to share, he rammed the enflamed rear. The sensation of plunging into liquid fire was always the greatest turn on ever, so he would have focused on his and Chris's pleasure alone, had not the erotic dance stepped up and opened his mind in spite of himself.

In a flash, he let her have it all—his cock's triumphant rush to the guts, cramped and snug inside the fiery walls wanting to suck him dry. In return, he received the sensations of her mouth stuffed to her ears and wheezing for air, of her clit pounding in terrible ache, of his angel zeroing on her belly however far it was from her gaping cavity.

Not that she had meekly surrendered to him.

Not at all.

No matter how severely he gagged her, she fought back and antagonized his every attempt at smothering her, matching his ferocity with an equal fierceness that amazed him.

And he could just imagine what it was doing to his angel, who found provocations irresistible, particularly when in bed.

He was not faring any better. This giving and receiving of sensations was a powerful spell. There could be no other explanation, considering how fast he was losing it. Feeding off her blowjob and combining it with his ass fuck, he threw it back at her and amplified her awareness, which in turn fueled his pleasure to a new height every time he repeated the cycle. Like looking in several mirrors at once, his perceptions bounced on every shiny surface to reflect ad infinitum and with growing intensity at every rebound.

And what emerged most clearly out of all the refracted impressions was her extreme hunger.

Damn you for making me want you in spite of everything, he cursed in her head.

Not that he could give her the release she sought, not trapped as he was in that scorching ass. "Angel, what do you say if I asked you to stop fooling around and go for some serious punishment?" Breathing raspy in Chris's ear, he dangled the bait he knew his angel could not possibly refuse.

"Like in her ass?" The jolt in Chris's cock said it all. "Thought you'd never ask."

Brutally wrenching her hips, the angel capsized her and fitted her butt to his convenience. Then he pushed down and crashed in her behind.

Literally.

The pain so intense, he thought she would not stand it. *Princess, relax and stroke your cunt.* It was the only advice popping at the top of his head.

Which of course did not please Chris.

"No touching." Gripping her hand the moment it was about to slip between her legs, he pinned it to the mattress. "This is not for your pleasure." Bending to reach her ear, he snarled softly, "It's just for ours."

Too proud to beg, she clenched her teeth and fished the pleasure Chris was denying her from his end of the screwing, which moved him to pity.

"I think that splendid ass would be more enjoyable if you gave her the chance to relax and ease the friction." Despite what Chris aimed for, he could see it would be no easy conquest.

One thing he was beginning to learn about her magnificent ass was that it needed a great deal of coaxing to surrender. And taking it by force would only make it tense more and ruin the cock's chance to savor it to its fullest, also to an anal expert like Chris.

"Instead of trying to split it with that dry fit that won't get you anywhere." Even if Chris made it look like it was just perfect as it was, he had caught his impatience at being unable to impale her to the root, as was his intention.

"Maybe I could let her." Sounding dubious, the angel left her hand free. "But just until I'm in to my balls," he snapped.

So hurry, Princess, 'cause he'll be sure to make it extremely difficult for you to come.

I . . . I'll try.

Her soft voice booming in his head sent a surge of pure adrenaline up his cock and through his every fiber, much like her hand finally reaching her dripping cunt.

Boy! Was she drenched!

As her fingers flicked on her throbbing knot, he sank in the combination of everything that was happening. His ass burned from Chris's slams into what now had become yielding, submitting to the forceful ramming as if it had been born just for it. Stunning how quickly she shifted from pain to pleasure, not just adapting to the angel's ruthless treatment, mostly finding new pleasure out of it. Maybe her conviction she would beat him was what drove her to rub that clit of hers harder and more voraciously until she nailed it.

Caught in between of giving and receiving a hard cock up an ass, he did not slow down, not even when her scream sucked him to the hilt. And Chris, too, judging from the violent push in her ass. Which did not prevent her from coming again and again, or from kidnapping their minds the second he and his angel climaxed simultaneously.

Jumbled sensations whirled together. Fragments from Chris and from Ylianor collided and reversed on him in consecutive throes. Like a tide swallowing him up, the waves washed over him with renewed vigor at every new piece added to the mix. Impossible to discern who felt what, they rolled into a dark knot of pain that pressed on his chest. That suffocated him. The weight unbearable, he tried lifting it, but only her sudden burst of tears shattered the black mass into a million shards that pierced his heart. And when he looked again, it had vanished in a fitful cry that wrecked her body.

CHAPTER FORTY-THREE

"What is it, Princess?" Cock flopping out of the snug hole, he dragged her out from under the angel's body. "Please, don't cry." Burying her face to his chest and embracing her body trembling from the convulsive sobs, he cradled her, cooing soft nonsense in her ear.

"Lover, the more you humor her, the more she'll cry." Apparently insensitive, Chris scoffed, "The more you'll have to humor her." He snarled, "And there'll be no end to her crying. Or haven't you learned anything about women since you started fucking them?"

"Shut up, Angel." The twinge of guilt was impossible to suppress. "This is all my fault." *I'm sorry.*

Don't be sorry. Tear-stricken, her face was lovelier than ever as she tilted it up to stare into his eyes. *Tell me what I've done to deserve this.*

"He owes you no explanation." As though he had caught her unspoken question, Chris snapped at her, "He has every right to be mad at you, if he wants." Then raising his gaze, he fixed him alone. "Isn't that why you're the master, and she's just an insignificant slave?"

"For once, Lord Templeton is absolutely right." Getting a grip on herself, she stopped crying. "You owe me nothing." Straightening, she moved to get away. "And you and this insufferable lover of yours have every right to be alone, not dragging me along out of some misconstrued sense of protection—"

"No." Tightening his hold on her arm, he wrenched her

back. "You aren't going anywhere until I say so."

"To keep her will only mean more trouble." The blue-gray eyes flashed annoyed.

"To keep her only means we get to fuck her more, Angel." Pressuring her shoulders to the mattress, he sprawled her between him and Chris. "And that's all I'm interested in right now, seeing how much you like it, too."

"Me?" Chris spat. "I can barely tolerate her —"

"You can't wait to get in this splendid ass of hers again." Carelessly flipping her around to lie on her belly, he spread her buttocks wide and grinned.

For Chris's cock jerked. So hard, it went from limp to erection in a matter of seconds.

"Now tell me I'm wrong." At the obvious conclusion, he plunged a couple of fingers in her ass ring, still tight in spite of the earlier use and enlarged it all together.

Kind of hard to deny it, Chris averted his gaze. "We're still going to regret it, if she stays." Which did not prevent his shaft from trying to leap into the narrow entrance without bothering about its master's objections.

"Let me be the judge of that." Slipping one more finger inside, he rotated his hand to stretch it nice and large. Which was pure provocation, the best way to tempt Chris and overcome his jealousy.

And it never worked better than when the angel nearly licked his lips from the craving to possess her.

"You said it yourself after all." Feeling Chris about to give in, he locked his gaze on the blazing blue-gray one. "I'm the master, right?"

"Yeah, but why does she have to be your slave?" Reluctantly reaching out, Chris slid a couple of fingers inside, twisting them around his and increasing the force of both their penetrations. "There are so many of them out there, and you've never been interested in fucking them more than once or twice, even less if it came to share them with me."

"True, but then none of the others had such magnificent ass." Sliding up and down was another way to convince that hole of hers to surrender completely. "Which I'll gladly leave to your mercy."

"You will?" No need for special powers to know his angel was losing it fast. His shaft now as thick and as stiff as stone, he was dying for a taste of her.

"I sure will." Another couple of thrusts told him that Chris's resistance was breaking down. "Go on. Take it." Removing his fingers, he pushed the ass cheeks wide apart. "It's all yours."

Chris impaled it without a moment's hesitation. He literally went for her guts with his first thrust, covering her and shoving to the hilt.

Which of course would have been no thrill for her, had he not gone to her aid. Hand between her legs, he stroked the drenched folds of her moist cunt. The swell above the pussy pounded furiously. Not just in his fingers. In his cock, too, for she dumped the painful hammering on him, along with everything that Chris was doing to her.

With the ramming in his ass, he knew he would not last long before his body demanded its share of the action.

Since you're the master, you can join in at any time, she teased in his head, her senses liquefying from the need for release.

Hush, Princess. He intensified his brushing of her clit. *First, I want you to show my angel how totally I can command you.*

How so? Opening wide, her huge green eyes flew to his face.

I want you to come. Bending over, he nuzzled her neck, inhaling her scent deeply before he bit it. *Now!*

"No, lover, wait." Out of breath, Chris stepped up his pumping as though he was in a race. "Don't make her come." In and out, his beefy monster slammed inside her ring, almost carrying the balls with it, such was the force of his impact. "Considering what we have to put up for her sake, she shouldn't come at all—"

"Too late, Angel." The scream was only proof of what he had perceived before it even started.

Her muscles contracting and releasing all together unleashed the fiery mass from her cunt upward. Real pleasure this time, without any tears to follow, she convulsed in an apparently never-ending orgasm.

"But don't you dare come, Angel." Quick to grab his moment, he raised her shoulders, so Chris had to recline on his knees to give him room.

Not that he freed her rear. His beast embedded to the root, Chris simply waited for the prince to adjust his position under her. As soon as his cock centered her slit, he pushed her down, flattening her on his chest.

Claiming her dripping pussy was like an explosion of pleasure that took his breath away. Or perhaps his tongue ravaging her mouth was what did it. Either way, it was unbelievable.

She was deliciously tight. Real tight thanks to Chris's huge erection cracking her ass. And the result was her flesh clenching him on every side, crushing him every time Chris banged all the way to his balls. And the fact she was about to burst again accelerated everything to a spasm.

Then again, sweeping her slit and mouth kind of blurred the sensations into a heated ball of fire that would roll on its own. Like an avalanche, there was really nothing he could do except coordinate his beat with the angel. Knowing Chris the way he did, he could anticipate each move, to the point he sank to her belly the moment the angel drew slightly back.

His cock was most arousing, rubbing as it was against the thin barrier separating him from Chris, which felt more like he was stroking the angel himself.

With their synchronized pumping, it was just a matter of seconds before everything spun out of any control.

When she climaxed, there was no halting the tide. Like a deluge, it drowned him and dragged him along her ride, sucking his cock all inside and milking it until it was dry. Not just his. Chris was swamping her rear with convulsive jets of his own, gasping loudly and screwing her ass so hard his cock might as well have come out of her mouth.

Which was not what blew him away.

Unexpectedly, Chris grabbed his mind and hers, too. Relinquishing for once his tight emotional control, the angel flooded him with pieces of himself, a combination of light and darkness that hit him on all sides.

Shiny particles fused with black ones—this was Chris in his naked essence right down to the core. And he was truly unparalleled, bright and magnificent as he was now that he held nothing back from him and from her.

Not that he had time to linger. All it lasted was mere instants, still enough to glimpse what his angel's precious nature was all about. If he had seen Chris's most intimate self from time to time, such display was astounding, since he would have never thought it possible for his lover to open what he jealously guarded from the world to someone he claimed to detest.

Yet, there it was, and all for the woman who was shifting the balance between them somehow.

It was all so incredible, he could not suppress the surge of love shooting out and embracing his blond angel, in whatever form he was. And she was in it, too, tugged along by his gigantic leap toward the towering mass of flames and crushed by the sheer force of his feelings for the most amazing man he had ever known.

And it was so damn intoxicating he never wanted it to

end!

CHAPTER FORTY-FOUR

"Energy is everything, even if you've only been aware of it recently." Her gaze fixed on him.

On a break from the resumed journey, he nodded, admiring his angel's blond hair sparkling under Stella's blinding rays. Whatever the circumstances, Chris remained the most gorgeous sight of all, lying as he was on his back next to the shores of a lake where he had stopped for lunch. And he was just too tempting in those tight-fitting pants of his —

"And wishing you were on a bed with Lord Templeton isn't going to lessen its impact on you or on us." She giggled evidently amused by the images she had plucked out of his head.

Well, I'll be damned!

And no, he did not share this.

"You can read me that easily?" Vexed, he stared hard at her.

"Not you." She giggled mischievous. "Your aura, which is flashing like crazy with all your unspoken needs. So blinding, I really can't help reading everything you feel right now."

"That's not reading." Challenging on purpose, Chris's blue-gray eyes flashed menacing. "That's spying."

"Relax, both of you." She raised a hand. "Just because I read auras doesn't mean I *steal* thoughts or feelings, quite the contrary." Settling more comfortably, she crossed her legs.

"I didn't mean the aura stuff," Chris huffed annoyed. "But the mind reading."

"That's not how it works." She was quick to set the record straight. "I only have access to what you decide to let me know." She smiled ruefully at him.

A luminous affair that lit her beautiful face in a way that made him wish again he were on a bed with both of them, instead of in a field, listening to her fascinating explanation while his cock yearned for quite another situation.

"There are sharp barriers between us, which neither you nor I can cross without the others express permission." And he was sure she had no trouble picking up that particular wish of his. "So you choose if and when to let me in, sharing only what you feel like sharing, nothing more."

"That's comforting news." Distractedly, he glanced at Chris and noticed how attentive he was. "At least I can keep a secret if I want to." Or so he ardently hoped.

And yes, there are things I'm not in the mood of sharing.

"I wouldn't trust this witch if I were you, lover." Deliberately biting, Chris sat up straighter. "Not since one smile from her and you get in the sharing mood faster than you can say, *Stay out of my head!*"

Well, I'll be damned twice! Since when had his angel started reading minds, too?

"Only 'cause you've always used energy for your own gains," she was quick to snap.

"Damn right I have." There was no hiding the malicious undertone lacing Chris's voice. "And since childhood, I've had no qualms using it however I damn well pleased, 'cause I've always known I was different from the others."

"That's why you hated me from the start!" Her gaze widened as though she had suddenly understood something that had escaped her until now. "You sensed something similar in me, too!"

"I never expected to find someone like me." Chris exchanged a glance with him. "Never met anyone in all of my eight years who knew what power was, or who could qualify as a threat." His gaze shifted on her. "And the fact you were right next to what I wanted most, made you all the more dangerous," he snarled softly. "Because I believed only one of us could win the race to his heart." To emphasize his point, he reached over and pressed thin heated lips on his. "Even if I needn't worry." Spinning his head to her, he looked her up and down as though she was a worthless slave for real. "You haven't got what it takes for him."

If this was a bit extreme, he did not have the chance to set the record straight.

"Congratulations, then." Her bitter retort left no doubts to how she felt about it. "But don't think you've won just yet."

For the two of them seemed bent on going at each other's throats regardless of him.

"Hey, you two, aren't you taking all this too much for granted?" Irritated by their presumptuousness, he scoffed, "Since when do you get to decide what I want?" He looked first into the green eyes, then into the blue-gray ones. "Or can I have a choice in the matter?"

"Of course, you can and so far, you chose me." Leaning forward, the blond angel did not just press his lips this time.

He went for a full-fledge kiss, with the tongue sweep, the sucking and all the trimmings of a passionate exchange that stirred his cock to vigorous life.

"But you've proven I'm not as powerful as I thought." Breaking away reluctantly, Chris's gaze locked on her. "I believed I had gotten rid of you forever." A grim smile curved his thin lips. "Yet, here you are."

"No thanks to you," she sneered ironically. "It's just your bad luck your power didn't work that time." It was kind of obvious she relished the thought. "Not entirely anyway," she added as a sort of unwilling admission. "It's just a pity you should waste it like this, this power of yours that shines brighter and stronger than Stella itself." She shook her head sadly. "And that makes it all the more necessary for you to keep returning to the only source that can replenish what you exhaust so carelessly."

"What do you mean, Princess?" Extremely interested, he edged closer.

"You recharge Chris's power, even if you've never been aware of it." Her stunning green eyes blazed. "You alone have that kind of power. Nobody else in this world could ever supply him with the incredible amount of energy he needs to replace what he shares so freely."

"Is this a coded way to say he screws around a lot?" Duncan teased, ruffling the blond hair.

"Not so coded." She giggled. "Which only confirms how truly special your relationship is, beyond sex, love or friendship."

"The angel may need me, but what do I get out of it?" No, he did not like the idea of being just an energy refill.

Not one bit!

"In terms of energy, I mean." It simply grated his nerves, and also Chris's, judging from the expression crossing his face.

"You, my prince, may be even more powerful than both of us combined." She creased her forehead. "As for the two of you, I think, but it's just an assumption, that you're mirror images. If one burns too fast because he can't help spreading it around, the other saves too much because he can't release it that easily."

"Because his aristocratic taste gets in the way," Chris taunted.

"Exactly." She took a deep breath. "My prince, the problem with you is that you don't let just anyone in, even if you can't possibly hold all that energy inside. You need someone to tap into it and as far as I can tell, you've allowed only Chris this privilege."

"And you, Princess." *Or why else would I be able to head talk to you and you alone?*

I . . . I'm not sure. She blushed violently.

"Do I recharge you, too?" Like with Chris, the mere thought bugged the shit out of him.

"My power is different from either of yours 'cause it needs a specific channel in order to work properly." *Which is why I can head talk with you and your angel can't.*

And there was an undeniable sense of satisfaction in her sweet voice breathing huskily in his head.

"But your channel doesn't necessarily include sex, just someone receptive enough to let you snoop around his head." Chris threw back his shoulders as though he was getting ready to fight her. "Am I right?"

"How do you know, Angel?" So Duncan intervened to dampen his fiery essence.

"If your father shared stuff with her like you told me, the channel must've been already there without any sex involved." It sounded like a reasonable argument.

"Chris is right." Changing her position, she neared him as though in search of protection. "With Prince Charles, the connection came naturally from the start. Nothing prompted it, at least nothing I can remember."

"Then you had sex with *my lover*, and that opened a new channel." From the way Chris charged the words, it was evident he had not gotten over it. "Which didn't happen when you had sex with David."

"He was . . ." She furrowed her brow. "Impenetrable."

"Which doesn't stop you from thinking of pledging to him," the angel went on relentlessly.

"What choice do I have?" On the defensive, she bit back. "If I'm not safe in Black Rose, I can either leave or pledge." Her defiant gaze trained on him alone. "And David is as good a choice as any other, even if he's not fully open about himself, as if he has secrets to hide."

No, you can't pledge to David! The thought surged through him like it had the first time Chris had prospected such outcome. Everything in him rebelled to it, however irrational it was. For why should he care? Why was it that, the more she talked, the more he wanted to take her in his arms and reassure her everything would be fine?

From the funny spark lighting her dazzling green eyes, he feared she might have caught his intentions, however carefully he had shielded them. "The only good thing about it is that he doesn't love me—"

"At least you both love the same person," Chris snickered.

"What do you mean, Angel?" Reclining against a tree, he dragged Chris closer as a way to show her his were only random thoughts, nothing she should take seriously.

"That they both love you." The blue-gray eyes glittered in amusement.

If from his attempts to keep a distance from her or if from the notion of having the two in love with him, he could not tell.

"Did you think you had the exclusive right to it, Lord Templeton?" Ylianor mocked going on the offensive.

"I thought I did since I had gotten rid of the competition." A fiendish snarl twisted the thin lips.

"You didn't get rid of David," she retorted hotly.

"Why should I?" Chris glared at her. "He's no threat."

"Hey, hold it you two." This talking about him as though he were a bone contented between them was getting on his nerves. "I never noticed that David—"

"Come on, lover." The blue-gray eyes locked on him now. "That he loves you is as plain to see as with your girlfriend here." Turning to her, Chris's lips curled nastily. "But he'd settle for you, I'm sure." He gave her a hard stare. "You look enough like him to make a passable replacement."

Why is he so damn perceptive when it comes to sex and to peo-

ple's feelings?

It marveled him every time.

"And that's something you can't stand, Lord Templeton." Hardly intimidated by his aggressive manners, she stood her ground. "Can you?"

"Don't flatter yourself, dearie." Not falling for her bait, Chris drew back. "Yours is just a passable resemblance, and I mean *passable*," he hissed. "Your only luck is that you're both servants, which is the only reason David would agree to pledge to you."

True, David was a stickler about class and social levels, something he did not sanction.

"And you'd settle for that, Princess?" Despite his wildly beating heart, he tried to sound as if it were indifferent to him.

Which was the farthest thing from the truth.

"I could offer you a third option." As though he had the perfect solution in his hands, Chris smiled broadly. "I could check to see if my father needs someone at Fair Haven." Evidently pleased with himself, he glanced at her. "What do you say?"

"Are you sure you'd want me that close to you?" Ylianor provoked.

I have a fourth option, but I'll be damned if I share it with you. So he had to chase away the house his father had left her in Harbor Town, lest he became angry again.

"I'm hardly ever there." The blond angel shrugged. "And that far from Black Rose, you'd be out of harm's way and mostly out of my lover's reach." And his angel was not kidding.

Not at all!

"Sorry, Lord Templeton." Burying her head in his chest, she pressed her palm on his groin. "I intend to consume him before you get the chance to send me away again."

"Hey, he's mine." Wrenching her wrist, Chris removed

her hand from the stirring shaft. "Go find your own lover."

"Actually, I found two." Her free hand clasped Chris's, squeezing it tight to emphasize her point. "The most gorgeous ones of all, especially when they have sex." Sure enough, the images she sent him were extremely arousing. "You're beautiful together."

"You like watching us?" Genuinely surprised, Chris let go of her wrist.

"How could I not?" She swung her gaze from him to Chris. "Your sex is not just exciting. It's also playful, fun and full of connections."

"Yeah, something it can never be with a woman." Chris chortled cruelly. "So you can just eat your heart out."

"Well, some women have the bad tendency of mistaking sex for love." And a few of his experiences had more than confirmed this.

"All right, so we're not perfect," she rushed to defend her gender. "But only because we have to put up with the likes of you beasts."

Chris ducked to grab her, probably to teach her a lesson in good manners, but she was quicker. Scuttling away, she moved closer to the lake's banks, laughing excitedly. "Anyone cares for a swim?" Then without waiting for a reply, she stripped naked and dived into the blue water with a cry of joy.

CHAPTER FORTY-FIVE

"She does have a magnificent ass." Mesmerized, he could not tear his gaze away from her backside sliding into the lake, until those firm round buttocks of hers disappeared underwater. Then he shifted his focus on Chris. "Doesn't she?"

"It's nothing compared to yours," Chris snarled wryly.

"Don't give me that!" Pushing him on the shoulder, he pressed his weight on the angel's lithe body. "I know you too well to say you've never acted like this with a woman before."

"Only because I've never spent so much time with one." Defiant, Chris raised his chin as though daring him to prove otherwise.

"No, you don't fool me one bit." Playfully, he teased what was the beginning of an erection. "I can tell she does something to you, in spite of your sneering remarks and nasty attitude." Intensifying his sensual caress on Chris's crotch, the reward was a forceful jerk from the hungry cock. "What you did before, the . . ." He frowned in search of an apt term. "How can I describe it?" Which did not come readily to him. "That opening yourself completely is something you allowed me alone to glimpse and only a few times before, never a stranger, much less a woman." Catching the blue-gray gaze, he held it. "Despite all the *spreading around* she talked about, I know you keep your core well hidden from everyone, sometimes even from me. But she managed to bring it out in the open, and it was truly the most incredible thing I ever felt."

"Don't remind me." Averting his gaze, Chris shrugged nervously. "That was just her way of playing tricks on us."

"Somehow, I don't think so." Tilting his chin, Duncan forced him to raise his gaze again. "Are you sure she isn't opening a connection with you, too?"

"A woman?" This definitely got the angel's attention. "Never!"

"Being your usual cynical self isn't going to stop her." Laughing, he straightened to his feet. "'Cause I have the feeling she's set her mind on getting you, too."

"Over my dead body!" Chris spat.

"I wouldn't put it past her, regardless of the state of your body." He chuckled.

"Then it'll have to be over *her* dead body," Chris snapped.

"I kind of like both your bodies as they are—alive and ready for sex." Grinning broadly, he extended a hand. "Come on." Gripping Chris's wrist, he pulled him up without any efforts. "Maybe some cold water will do you good."

"Only if you tell me how long you're planning to drag her alongside us." Detaining him, Chris blocked his stride to the lake. "Given all her alternatives, she doesn't need us anymore." He tightened his grip on him. "Now that she's safe from your mother's clutches, she can look after herself wherever you decide to leave her."

"Yeah, she could." *Also if I left her at the Hall.* Which was a fifth option he had avoided listing before, not because he had not thought of it then, because he seemed strangely reluctant to let go of her. "But after all she said about energy and power, sticking together might strengthen us somehow."

"Just you and me, lover." The hint of a smile crossed Chris's thin lips. "In case you haven't been listening, you get nothing from her." Unlike his previous objections, this did not seem like pure provocation. "If that stuff about the ener-gy business, the recharging and all were true . . ." *Which they aren't.*

Even if Chris did not say it out loud, his thought about this matter was not hard to guess.

"We get something we both want from one another. But while she needs you only for the sake of a channel she can't have with just anyone, what do you get out of her?" The blue-gray eyes searched his face. "I never heard you com-plain about missing someone who talked inside your head."

"Only because I didn't know it was possible." And now that he did and had mixed feelings about it, he still could not deny how powerful it was to be so close to someone with whom you could actually share your thoughts and sensa-tions. "What I did tell you was that I wanted to find a wom-an, and she had to be a very particular kind." Angling his head behind his shoulder, he caught a glimpse of Ylianor splashing in the water. "And maybe, just maybe, I might have found her —"

"No, don't say it." Pressing his fingers on Duncan's mouth, the angel took a step forward. "What I don't under-stand is why I was enough for the better part of twenty years, yet now you need someone else all of a sudden."

"You forget that she was part of my life long before you came." He took a deep breath. "And even if I don't remem-ber her, something of those lost years must still be there."

"Yeah, but you survived without her for a good ten years," Chris challenged. "If I recall correctly."

"Perhaps it's just a question of growing up and needing something more." He removed a long strand from his face. "Whatever it may be, something tells me we'll find out soon enough." Crushing the angel against him, he tousled the thick blond hair. "Race you to the lake." Letting him go, he turned to the shore. "Last one in pays penalty."

"Oh, no, you don't." Running to the water, Chris entered

after him. "Only slaves pay penalties, and you've got the perfect one right here."

"Only if you catch me, Lord Templeton." Her voice shrill, she tempted him to get her as she swam fast to reach the center of the lake.

A provocation his angel could not resist, obviously. Just his luck the water was shallow enough he did not have to swim, so with a few strides, he reached her.

"Got her, lover." Wrenching her ankle, Chris tugged her back to the shore. "What would you like me to do with this very disobedient slave?"

"Let me go." Kicking and wriggling frantically, she tried to get free.

Impossible to say the least, considering how tightly Chris held on to her leg.

"I said let me go!" Ylianor shouted part playful, part serious. "I don't intend to submit to anything—"

"You'll do exactly as your master commands." Taking charge of the game, he clamped her other ankle and raised her so that her cunt gleamed under Stella's rays. "And that includes paying penalty for having entered the water without my express permission."

Her green eyes flew wide-open. "I didn't—"

"Shut up, slave." Dipping her backward, Chris sank her head below the water.

Duncan was quick to have her resurface.

"I know a fantastic way of keeping her mouth shut." His shaft already stiff in anticipation, he let go of her leg and clutched her arm. "And it doesn't imply drowning her."

"If you mean sucking our cocks, maybe you ought to consider giving this slave of yours some lessons." Dropping her ankle, Chris focused on him alone. "She isn't particularly skilled—"

"You're absolutely right." He settled her on her knees.

"So why don't you show her some of your finer tricks?"

"Me?" In mocking shock, Chris took a step back.

"Yes, you." Grasping his hand, Duncan dragged him back. "You're the only real expert of blowjobs I know, so it wouldn't hurt you to give her a lesson or two."

"Why should I let her steal my secrets?" Stubborn, the blue-gray eyes blazed in disagreement.

"Because I tell you to." With a tone that did not admit more stupid objections, he hurled Chris to his knees and crushed his face against the stirring erection. "So get moving and you, Princess . . ." Taking out his already huge beast, he rubbed the tip against Chris's nose. "You better learn fast 'cause I doubt my angel will be in the mood to teach you much else, once this is over."

"I know I'll regret this." Growling in dissatisfaction, Chris wrapped his palm around the thick gland. "But since it seems I got no choice in the matter —"

"You don't." Just to emphasize his point, he shoved forward, his senses already enflamed by the angel's mere touch.

"All right, then." Knowing perfectly well the tempest caused by the simplest of brushes, the bastard angel took infinite pleasure in stringing him along. "The first thing you got to remember about a blowjob is that it isn't just sucking and blowing." Tightening his grip on the taut organ, he jerked it a couple of times. "What you're actually doing is making love to a cock." His gaze switching on her, he stroked the skin up and down the enormous length. "A blowjob is all about adoring a cock. Whatever you think of the man attached to it is irrelevant. All that's relevant is the cock itself and your complete submission to its demands."

"Is that how you manage to suck Trent's cock?" To get back at his angel for his merciless tease, he mentioned the one man he knew Chris hated most out of all the ones at the

Hall.

"I never sucked Trent!" Chris scoffed haughtily. "Nor will I ever." Tossing back his head, he fixed Duncan. "Now if you want me to continue with my lesson—"

"By all means, Angel." Shoving the blond head forward, he made it plain he was dying for the hot taste of that fiery mouth of his.

"What cocks usually demand is for you to swallow them." To demonstrate, Chris's mouth slid all the way down to his balls in one quick intake that had him nearly spilling it all right there and then. "Which doesn't mean you should satisfy them all the times." Drawing away, the sneaky angel snarled, "You could just as easily start with a vigorous pampering of their sides." His tongue curled around the beefy rod, then brushed its every side hard. "Be sure to go from top to bottom." His tongue darting on the fat crown was pure ecstasy. "And don't forget the balls."

Not just a lap.

A voracious kiss cut off Duncan's breath.

"Then again, what you should never neglect is the sucking." Chris's brief swallow was just another appetizer. "And the more you gag on it, the better."

It was about as much as he could take. Clamping the angel's neck, he swung his hips forward, targeting the center of the wet cavity that was unable to close due to the giant shaft shoving down its throat.

Attentive and very interested, she followed as he face-fucked Chris.

Literally.

For there was no greater pleasure than sinking into that flaming cavity and losing all perspective.

No doubt about it—Chris was a master in the art of cock sucking. His tongue slid so deliciously over the stiff member, it practically drew the sperm out on its own. The very same he had pressing at the tip of his erection, burning from the need to burst and over flood the angel's mouth.

Which he did, because there was no point in holding back.

"There." Licking his lips like a satisfied feline, Chris got to his feet. "Now let's see what you've learned." Clutching her, he flattened her face to his engrossed groin. "And make it good this time."

I'll try. If she only whispered it in his head, it was because Chris had attacked her mouth, forcing her to open wide and swallow the gigantic beast that was avidly going for deep asphyxiation.

Linked to her sensations, he felt the cock's impatience as it slid frantically down to her throat, overriding her attempts to block it.

Going for total control, Chris yanked her hair back and pressed down in her cavity.

"Would you like some help, Angel?" However enviable the position, it could stand some improvement.

"I could sure use some." Evidently thinking along the same line, Chris grinned mischievous.

So he moved to stand behind her, his legs pressing on her back and trapping her between the two of them. Quick to take advantage of her captivity, the angel tossed her head against Duncan's knees, as far back as her neck would go without snapping. Now there was really no way for her to avoid suffocating on the monster plunging to her stomach.

If he thought it a bit extreme, he had to change his mind. She loved being at the mercy of Chris's cock. More than that, she was getting high on her constricted immobility that had transformed her in an object of Chris's pleasure. Dripping wet from her arousal, her pussy screamed her craving from a furiously pounding clit.

And of course, his angel went crazy simply smelling her

heightened excitement.

Yes, he had to hand it to her. She was just amazing, and the way she played to the angel's need for cruel domination was pure incredible to say the least, opening her mouth wider as though daring him to go further.

Which he did, nearly carrying the balls along until he exploded. With a loud gasp, fat drops of juice sprayed her all over, some falling inside her mouth, most staining her face and neck.

"Much better." Letting go of her, Chris glanced at him. "She might just get it right after all." Then he waved the still stone-like shaft in front of her nose. "Now be a good girl and lick it clean."

She scrambled to obey, lapping him thoroughly on every side, including the balls and the tip.

"So she deserves a prize?" Chuckling, he picked her up from her hips. Then circling her legs around his waist, it was no effort to slip his large erection inside her very wet, extremely drenched cunt.

"I wouldn't go quite that far." Snarling, Chris took the necessary steps forward that had her imprisoned between the two of them again. "She still gotta pay penance, remember, lover?"

"Impossible to forget." Since his angel rimmed her back ring seductively, it would be just a matter of time before she got the full load of the reminder. "Especially if you take her ass now."

"Well, what do you know?" Adjusting his position, Chris shoved. "Did you start reading my mind?" Another couple of thrusts and he was practically all inside.

She tensed as her front space suddenly shrank to fit the new thickness stuffing the rear. This was pure delight, having his shaft clenched by a flesh too tight for words. But to her, the angel's merciless slams were not as enjoyable. So he slowed down.

Relax, Princess. Bending on her ear, he nibbled it. *Do you want to stop?*

"Quit babying her, lover!" Chris sniggered, as though he had caught this thought.

"Jealous, Angel?" Latching on to the blue-gray gaze, he held it. "Or would you like me to baby you as much as I do her?"

"If she's really your slave, it's the last thing you should be doing." Annoyed, Chris impaled her to the guts. "What she needs is some good training."

"I agree." Penetrating to her belly was just as easy. "But not if you crack her ass every time."

"Oh, she can take it." Chris chortled.

The words hardly out of his angel's mouth, her body went from pain to pleasure in such rapid shift that stunned him. One moment she was suffering like she could not stand it one second longer. The moment after, she was about to come. That was how fast she adapted to the angel's rough handling.

"Oh, fuck!" Chris growled. "Why does she always end up liking it?"

How his angel managed to interpret the signs of her body was a mystery. He himself only knew it because he had linked to her.

"'Cause she enjoys defying you, Lord Templeton." Breath short, she wriggled her butt as though to provoke him further.

"Never as much as I'll enjoy cracking her." A vigorous back blow had her jump, and she would have fallen off, had he not tightened his grip on her.

"Never as much as I'll enjoy punishing both of you if you don't stop it this instant." Clutching her harder, he made sure she could not go anywhere except right where she was—between him and Chris, pumped front and back by two very greedy cocks wanting to split her apart.

The silky feel of her clean-shaven and moist pussy drove him to accelerate the tempo. She moved right along with him, adjusting her position to stroke her clit on his belly, which he found extremely erotic. Which also increased her hip rotation and drove Chris wild.

He could tell from the frantic rhythm that would soon drown them all. Ylianor first, for she seemed to command it all however much he and Chris pretended to play masters. And as soon as she buried her head in his chest and screamed her release, there was no stopping it.

It was simply useless to fight against the waves coiling from her body to his and to Chris's, too, for it was like she was connecting the three of them beyond their physical frames, weaving some kind of enchantment that tied them all to one another. So he did nothing to oppose it.

He just shoved one last time and unloaded it all in the tight-fitting squeeze of her dripping slit.

CHAPTER FORTY-SIX

"It's freezing around here." Huddling by the fire, she wrapped her arms around herself, thinking back over the distance she had traveled in just a couple of days.

To be honest, the images were kind of blurred. Too fast she had sped northward, sometimes without any time to spare on Silcamore's luxuriant farmland or on Rockyhorn's inhospitable mountains. The name said it all anyway, so small wonder the high peaks that surrounded the Hall spelled colder climates and tall trees that replaced the flat green fields. Still, she would have liked to enjoy it a bit more, not rush through it like someone was chasing after her.

Which maybe someone was, considering how hard Duncan pushed to reach the Hall sooner rather than later.

Which to her was just another sign that something was terribly wrong, something that started and ended with the very obnoxious Lord Christopher Templeton and his rapid mood swings that went from good to bad in the blink of an eye.

Now bad was all she perceived, despite Chris's apparent good humor.

Averting her gaze from the fireplace where she sat after having eaten a meager dinner, she focused on the striking blond creature half-sprawled on the couch. Not an open stare, the gods forbid, merely a peek from under her eyelashes to check on his lights.

Sure, on the surface, everything seemed fine, to the point he played it like he had accepted her and the tentative balance the prince had managed to establish. Deep down, though, it was a totally different thing, in spite of his opening up and allowing her to glimpse his core.

Or maybe because of it.

Either way, something was wrong. And if his erratic lights were not enough indication, she could tell from the unease gnawing at her stomach every time she sensed the demon's enthusiasm as not quite genuine.

Yes, something was eating him, something she could not fathom. All she knew was that his true nature could lash out at any time, and the consequences would be anything but pleasant for her.

She was the intruder after all, the woman who had upset his plans for total control over the prince's heart. She was the one who dared defy him and return to claim what had belonged to her long before he ever set foot in Black Rose. So only natural the hateful demon would direct his rage against her alone.

And somehow, Duncan knew it, too, which might explain his race to get to Rhapsen Hall before bad came to worse.

Shrugging away the ominous thoughts, she returned her gaze on the bright flames dancing in front of her. "I hope it doesn't get any colder than this, or I won't have anything appropriate to wear."

"You practically have no clothes at all, right?" Sitting on the couch behind her, Duncan circled her waist and tugged her backward in a tight hug. "Those you're wearing are David's."

"It's been a long time since anyone provided for my wardrobe." She shivered in his embrace. "I've mostly lived on cast offs from my father and the little that remained of my mother's dresses." She glanced at her worn pants. "If she were alive, I'd probably wear something more feminine." And better pleasing to her prince's aristocratic taste. "As it is . . ."

"That's all right, Princess." Bending, he buried his face in the nape of her neck, pressing his nose as if he wanted to inhale her scent to his lungs. "I rather prefer you without clothes anyway." Then raising his head, he bit her neck. "When we get back to Black Rose, I'll provide for your wardrobe."

"Lover, don't fall for that," Chris scoffed irritated.

The demon's icy tone made her sit up straighter.

"Fall for what?" Also on edge, she could tell how hard Duncan worked to keep his voice even and his tension at bay.

"In case you haven't noticed, women love to play victims of circumstances." The blue-gray eyes flashed in contempt.

"That's not fair, Angel." Lifting his shoulders, Duncan leveled his gaze to Chris's. "I only excuse this kind of talk 'cause you don't know women at all."

"Nor do I give a rat's ass about knowing them," Chris snapped, a look of intense dislike crossing his gaze as he lowered it on her.

"Don't worry, Lord Templeton." Angling her head behind a shoulder, she made sure to catch the impertinent blue-gray eyes. "The feeling is mutual!"

"Perhaps it's this . . ." A malicious snarl twisted his thin lips. "Gift of mine that makes me despise women." The cruel inflexion in his tone made her blood turn cold. "Can the expert confirm it?"

"Come on." Letting her go, Duncan edged closer to the demon. "Do you honestly believe power can influence your taste and make you resent an entire gender?"

"Why not?" Cool headed in spite of his lights becoming progressively redder, more similar to leaping flames about to burn her alive, he sounded as though nothing was wrong. "We don't know anything about it after all, except what this witch turned expert has told us, so mine is a legitimate doubt that—"

"It might." Nervously, she shifted away from him. *But better not find out,* she urged Duncan in the silent way only he could catch.

Or maybe not, for no answer cane, not even a clue that her message had gotten through to him.

"Then perhaps it's time I found out why the two are related." His eyes blazed with new vigor. "My gift and my hate for your kind."

Highly volatile, such was Chris and his power. Highly dangerous, too, particularly now that it sparked all his lights to an undefinable hue.

"Now?" Since Duncan was not taking sides, she deliberately raised the stakes to force a reaction from him. "In front of the prince?"

"My lover needs to know." He shrugged, his gaze never wavering from her. "So this is as good a time as any."

"Stop!" Duncan ordered thickly.

Yes, Prince, you tell him! Revived by his comeback, she tried head-talking to him once more. *And don't let him get his hands on me.*

Too late.

After one elegant jump, Chris wrenched her by the shoulders. "Why should I?"

Captive and immobilized, she tensed like a defenseless prey caught by the most vicious of predators, a ferocious beast that would first play with her then rip her apart.

And for sure the bastard loved the taste of her fear that, combined with Duncan's eerie silence, spelled certain doom for her!

"You want her to share our life." The blue-gray eyes fixed on the prince alone. "Well, to my point of view, she's done enough spying as it is." Raking a hand through her long hair, he avoided looking her way.

And damn him! His touch would have seduced her into blind compliance, had the irrationality of it all not paralyzed her.

"And damn her!" His touch deepened, trembling from repressed fury. "She's also managed to make me reveal what I'd rather not." To his way of seeing, this was unforgivable. "What I keep for you alone, lover."

The absence of a response from the man both she and Chris were working so hard to impress was puzzling to say the least. More like devastating, since he seemed to have slammed shut their connection, leaving a cold emptiness where his vibrant energy had been. And that made it down-right hurtful given how much it increased her sense of abandonment.

"So you can understand how that might piss me off just a tiny bit." Wrapping a hand around her neck, he squeezed.

And she wondered if he would snap it with one single blow.

"Still, I've been mighty patient with the likes of you." Shifting his gaze to her, he snorted, "You can't deny it." He seemed to take pride in his self-restraint. "Now it's time I show you what you and your snooping around are in for." He eased the pressure on her neck. "And who knows?" A dark, threatening grin curved his thin lips. "You might even learn something useful besides those blasted power theories of yours."

"I think I know enough as it is." She refused to be intimidated however hopeless the situation. "And no thanks to you." So she threw back her shoulders and glared at him.

"Wrong." The fiendish creature had no trouble calling her bluff. "It's all thanks to me."

Hardly surprising. This demon did not just love provocations. He thrived on them, to the point he would make sure his intoxication lasted as long as it could.

"So it's time you start admitting it." A pocketknife appeared in his hand. "But mostly, it's time I had some real fun with this worthless hide of yours." Clamping her arm so she could not budge, he leaned over the fireplace and heated up the blade over the flames.

Now why did she have the impression he would be using it on her?

No, it was simply *unthinkable*! The mere idea shocked and revolted her, for her people had no business with violence of any kind. No bloody murders, no serial killings, no fancy carnage, not even for the sake of a piece of meat to put on the table. That was why they were all vegetarians, and there could be no way around it. It was something so utterly estranged from their way of life, no one would ever even come close to fathom hurting an animal, much less a human being. Never an option! No matter how bad a situation could get, absolutely no one would ever resort to such extreme methods.

No one except Christopher Templeton that is.

That odious creature could be capable of the most horrendous deeds out of the blackness of his demon's heart. She was sure of it, since she alone had witnessed it with her own eyes. So anything was possible with him, even that he dared go against every principle her people stood for, and—

"Angel, what are you doing?" His voice oddly hesitant, Duncan appeared to be out of it.

Out of the shelter for certain, impenetrable to her attempts at reaching him.

"Nothing, lover." The demon shrugged nonchalantly. "Just want to teach a simple lesson to our nosy *Miss Know-It-All.*" After checking the knife, he placed it back on the fire. "Don't worry."

Then she felt it, and her heart sank to her feet.

Damn! She should have guessed it sooner that the despicable demon had cast a spell on the prince. Like a strong energy surge, it flowed from him to Duncan, trapping him in a fine web that prevented him from taking any action, powerful enough to isolate him from her.

Not entirely, though. If she managed somehow to touch him, he would snap back. So she stretched out her free arm, shifting her weight forward to reach him —

"Where do you think you're going?" Crushing her to the ground, he waved the scalding blade in front of her face. "I thought you were interested in learning about my gift." Deceptively sweet, he brushed the tip of the blade on her cheek.

"I already know all about it, Lord Templeton, so don't waste your time." She would probably regret it.

No doubt about it.

Still, she could not show weakness, or she would be truly finished.

"And let me go." With a decisive jerk, she tried pulling away from him.

"You aren't going anywhere, dearie, not until I'm done with you and with your miserable hide." He gripped her harder to block her. "Because my gift is to hurt people," his voice coldly detached as though it were another person speaking. "Because I get this urge to cause intolerable pain, and I can't even begin to tell you how much pleasure I get from carving a person bit by bit." Lowering the blade, he trailed it on her flesh. "Piece by piece." Hypnotically, he circled her breasts before going down to her belly. "Just like this." Without warning, he stabbed her thigh.

She gasped at the searing hot pain burning her leg. Then blood spilled on her pants. But at her squirms to get away, he pressed a knee on her chest and held her in place.

Completely disabled, she could offer no resistance while he removed all her clothes and stared in rapture at the cut. Then he made another incision next to it, tracing the blood mingling from the two wounds with a finger.

"Angel . . ." She heard Duncan's voice as if it came from another dimension, but at least he was trying to re-emerge from whatever black pit Chris had flung him. "I think we understand now, so you can stop —"

"No, you don't." Another merciless slash bit her arm. "'Cause I've tried telling you countless times before." His attention shifted all to the prince. "Only you wouldn't listen."

Gaze fixing on the black one, he seemed to be pleading for something she knew Duncan must have denied him in the past.

Then again, why should she care? And why did the blade keep knifing her soft flesh as though it were made of butter?

"You never wanted to know what I have to do in order to survive." Both her arms red from his gashes, he moved to strike her legs. "This is what I do, what I've been doing ever since you decided our phase was over." With precise hits, he littered her skin with deep lacerations that smeared it with reddish streaks. "And I have no choice or control over it."

"Liar!" If the pain was pure unbearable that everything throbbed violently, she would not allow it to silence her. "You decide who and when to strike —"

"Damn right I do!" With calculated cruelty, he ripped through her skin. "When I get this craving, I can't rest until I carve someone to pieces."

Suddenly aware of what the demon's power was all about, she raised her head to catch his gaze. "But then you heal them back."

This was the only way she could fight him — keep him talking and defy him at every turn. If she surrendered to the pain, it would be the end of her.

"Don't you?" She winced from his latest blow to her thigh.

"I do more than that, dearie." Contemptuously, he sliced another straight, bloody red line down her leg. "I erase their memory once I've healed them. That's how it works." Again, he focused on Prince Caldwell alone, interested only to have his complete attention, while the blade seemed to slide by itself on her battered flesh. "After I've selected a victim, I may or may not fuck him, which all depends on my mood."

So she perceived the erotic enticement that connected sex with blood for Christopher Templeton, and she might have climaxed on the sheer thrill of his pleasure every time he sank his knife in her, had he not been so determined to kill her first.

"But the sex is irrelevant." One well-delivered blow and she jolted.

Not that she got anywhere.

Like all the previous times and as hard as she tried, his iron hold had such a clamping effect, she could barely move.

"What I really need is to cut his delicious body to a bloody pulp." To emphasize his point, he stuck the tip of the blade in a fresh wound and tore it open.

Just like that.

Ripping through her skin as though it were some faulty seam of a worn-out fabric.

"Only when my bloodlust is sated, do I heal him and erase the memory of what happened." A bitter snarl curved his lips. "And the fool loves it!" He laughed at their idiocy. "And thinks it's been the best sex of his pitiful life."

As if anybody could ever love this kind of torture.

Then again, regardless of his claims, she had the feeling that what he was doing to her was quite unique—partly because this was no play, partly because he probably never did it to a woman, mostly because it was in front of Duncan.

And that changed everything!

"First, he's just a whimpering coward, begging for mercy

and crying over the slightest scratch." Probably wanting to prove his point on her, he dug deeper. "And I simply love to watch them bleed, squirm and beg for their miserable hides."

She did not give him the satisfaction of a single moan. Rather, she kept her ears wide open to catch the tiniest clue that she could use against him.

If she survived that is.

For, besides the sharp pain, he was unwittingly giving her a key to understand how this worked, a key to beat him at his own game.

"The best thing is seeing terror mounting in their eyes." Lowering his gaze, he peered in hers. "Almost like yours, honey, though do try to look a little more terrified."

"Otherwise it'll spoil your fun?" Ylianor sneered scornful.

"No, otherwise it'll spoil yours." The brutal stab was clear indication he planned to make it anything but. "And we wouldn't want that, would we?" A cold gleam lit up his beautiful blue-gray eyes.

And she had the weird sensation he had caught on to her arousal and to how it was feeding off his excitement.

"If it's so much fun, why have you never tried it on your lover?" Pulling herself together, she went all offensive.

"'Cause love held me back, or what I thought was love until a smart ass tells me he just recharges my energy, as if our love means nothing." He was getting angry now as he slit open another piece of flesh. "Silly me." He shook his head in forced amusement. "I thought I wanted him because I loved him. Turns out we don't love each other, just use our bodies for refills." Furious at the thought, he slashed randomly, without bothering to look where he struck. "Because I keep . . ." He frowned. "How did you put it?" Then creasing his forehead, he made a show of concentrating. "Spreading my energy around, so I have to return to my lover when supplies run low." He followed the blood covering her completely in an intricate network of small lacerations, all as evenly spaced as though part of a geometric pattern. "How about it, lover?" The knife stung her again and again. "Do you like this explanation to all we've shared since the first time we ever laid eyes on each other?"

By now, she was beyond feeling anything.

"Personally, it pisses me off." As though sensing she was slipping away from him somehow, he intensified his blows, aiming to hurt her worse than he had so far.

"She might be wrong," Duncan argued reasonably however garbled his words. "No one has enough knowledge in this matter, so why should we believe her?"

Prince make him stop. Since she had caught a more decisive note in his tone, she hoped he could hear her now. *I don't think I can stand this much longer.*

"No, the question is another." Apparently in need of more blood, the odious demon stuck the tip of the knife under her breast. "What gives her the fucking right to barge into our lives and take them apart?" The blue-gray eyes locked on the velvety black ones. "Like she did when your father was still alive, and she seduced him into privileging her over his rightful heir?" With cold, calculated fury, Chris did not detain the blade sliding underneath the soft mound, piercing the very delicate flesh until blood seeped in heavy drops.

If it was unbearable, it was still nothing if compared to the tidal wave of pain drowning her. Not hers, however sore she was all over. It all came from Prince Caldwell himself, a load so heavy it silenced his sense of justice.

And she became furious, for that abominable demon was using whatever had provoked Duncan's explosive rage against him, fueling it as part of his spell to keep him from regaining full control over himself. A spell that now looked awfully similar to a bridge of hate and fascination Chris had hooked on him to keep him paralyzed.

"You see, dearie, until you came along, he and I were very happy." Damn proud of his trick, Chris smiled smugly, cutting harder than before. "All he had to worry about was finding a suitable mate that would carry his beautiful children while still fucking with me." Pausing briefly, he made it a point to capture her gaze. "A perfect plan, wouldn't you agree, witch?" Another stab and the blade perforated deep inside her.

Just his bad luck she did not even whimper, everything hurting so much she found it difficult to concentrate on the single incision.

"Fuck you and your *perfect plans*, Lord Templeton." If she had to die, it would be on her own terms. "Or did you really think you could keep him all to yourself?"

"I fucking did!" This definitely irked the demon the wrong way, at least judging from the very new and very deep gash on her belly. "With his pledge mate tucked away in Black Rose and him at the Hall to fill his permanent council seat, I'd have had him all to myself."

"Then sorry to have spoiled your neat plans," she retorted hotly, ignoring the terror that lurked behind every one of his damn blows. "But I'm here now, and I intend to stay."

"Over your dead body!" He attacked her other breast, the only pink spot in a red-clotted pulp.

Minced meat! That was his final goal.

"I wouldn't cry victory just yet." Since this was sure to piss him off worse than he already was, she also shouted in Duncan's head, *Prince, you can't allow your angel to feed off your guilt!* If nothing else worked, maybe yelling might penetrate the honey-thick fog enveloping him.

"The lady still has spunk." In spite of himself, the demon sounded impressed.

Enough to halt his assault.

"Not that it's going to help you any." Quickly resuming

his carving, he added a more savage twist to his downward swings. "Not 'cause you are the only available victim at the moment." In a new escalation, he massacred the breast that had been whole only seconds before. "You're also the only one who looks like my lover . . . no, wait, I believe energy charger is more appropriate," he sniggered. "And has the further advantage of being a woman." He smacked his lips. "So how could I resist this mouthwatering combination, especially if she insists on sticking her nose where it doesn't belong?"

"You are just jealous he wants me back in his life." This goading of him was turning out to be the best antidote to the excruciating pain Chris seemed to be a master in inflicting.

"Jealous of a sorry ass like you?" Deeper and deeper he dug her flesh until he reached the bone.

Which did not quench his anger at all.

Not one bit!

"Ha! That'll be the day!" Not content in tearing her body apart, he moved his assault on a new level. "What I can't stand is the bloody irony of it all." Crushing her spirit while destroying her flesh—this seemed his new tactic. "It starts with a witch telling me love has nothing to do with my feelings." The bottomless well of emotions she had glimpsed when he had opened up now lashed back at her. "Imagine that!" Wide-eyed, he made a show of looking surprised. "I've been kidding myself all these years." The knife edged dangerously to her throat. "So if my love is a lie, what can I trust of my other feelings?" Luckily, the tip of the blade slipped away, targeting her arm instead.

"You are just a fool for taking my words the wrong way." Somehow, she had to resist his attempts at smothering her under the sheer weight of his hate pressing on her chest. "'Cause I never meant to say your love isn't real." At depleting her energy along with what remained of her air and blood. "I only mentioned the energy connection 'cause I thought it enhanced your love." And his ominous black cloud hovered over Duncan, too, which made it impossible for her to latch on to him. "Not because I wanted to demean it." Since his darkness shut off all light, her breath now came in rapid gulps. "And you're twice as foolish if you don't realize how much this can add to—"

"Add?" Chris spat. "Do you know what it comes down to?" He bent his head until his hot breath played on her face. "That I've lived a lie for nineteen fucking years."

"What you feel isn't a lie." She tried not to crumble under the pressure of having him so oppressive in every sense possible.

"Don't tell me what I feel, bitch!" Chris bit back. "I've always distrusted women and for good reasons it seems." Heaving, he calmed down a bit. "But perhaps I'm taking this out on the wrong person." Turning his head, he fixed the prince. "Since it's my phase mate who wants you in his bed and forces me to share my precious energy with the likes of you." He swung back on her. "But guess what?"

Since he had not stopped pounding her flesh, she lost all sense of her body, to the point she could not tell what part of her he was torturing.

"I can't harm him, 'cause they tell me I need his energy." He traced a finger over the jagged edges of her many wounds before licking the blood off it. "Which leaves you, dearie, to pay for all the consequences of his actions."

"Also for your inability to satisfy him?" Ylianor shuddered as he tore off more flesh. "In case you haven't noticed, your prince needs a woman in his bed, no matter how good you are, and killing me isn't going to change that."

This going at him was pure folly now, now that a part of her was so tired she wished he would let her curl on herself to die in peace.

He hissed, "But it'll be a good start—"

"All right," Duncan's firm tone blocked Chris's arm swinging down on her. "That's enough."

Hey, Prince Caldwell was back, and his escape from the black web proved how superior his newly acquired power was to the demon's.

"Now it's time to heal her," Duncan ordered quietly, expecting Chris's full cooperation.

"All right, lover." The enchantment gone, she knew the demon had no choice other than obeying. "But I comply only for your sake." After a thorough examination, he began cleaning the bloody blade. "If it were up to me, I'd leave her to bleed to death." Folding the knife, he pocketed it away.

Then he closed his eyes.

At first, nothing happened. Next thing she knew, a wave of freshness swept through her, the cool breeze quelling the scorching tissues that had inflamed her very spirit. Like a cold shower after a heated day, it calmed the pain and alleviated the burning sensation. More soothing than an ocean wind or an icy balm, it blew over each wound, closing the flesh magically and restoring it to its immaculate perfection.

Then an intense blue light blinded her and banished all darkness as it coursed through her every fiber. Within seconds, it erased all traces of blood and incisions, as if nothing had ever altered the skin.

When she dared breathe again, she was back in the shelter, free of any marks or scars, at least the visible ones. For everything else, her intact memory could playback the second by second agony she had just sustained.

This was the demon's final and cruelest revenge of all—awareness and the impossibility to forget this terrible ordeal.

Without another word, Chris got up and crawled into one of the beds, falling fast asleep. Too dazed to move, she turned to Duncan. And maybe he would have given her the comfort she sought, had he not vanished inside another bed.

Alone, she huddled in front of the dying fire, as close as possible to the heat, invoking sleep and oblivion. And for once, the gods listened.

CHAPTER FORTY-SEVEN

"There they are." Prince Caldwell pointed at bell-shaped red roofs gleaming under Stella's brilliant rays. "One more bend and we'll be at the Hall."

And not a moment too soon.

A thought she carefully shielded, she raised her gaze and pretended to be interested in the fabled Hall, the seat of the High Council and of its leader. One thing she had to admit—nestled between white snowy peaks and brown rocky slopes, the brilliant red roofs made a striking contrast that nearly took her breath away. Or maybe it was the Hall itself. Shaped like a series of crosses, the imposing structure consisted of a main body, a long and elegant building in sandstone, with three sets of arms outstretched at regular intervals. At the end of each arm, a square tower stood six stories tall, made in a darker stone, almost black and topped by the bell-like roof. At the very center, an eighth tower rose, the tallest and most ruined of all, different from the rest also because of its round shape and of the half-crumbled roof. Still, it took nothing away from the impressive sight.

Not just for its appearance.

For the sense of power pervading it, a form of energy that was new to her, but ancient to the world.

Not that she cared about it or the Hall for that matter. All she wanted was to forget what she could not during the half-day travel from the shelter Chris had chosen for his bloody show. If that was not an option, the real question was—why had she stayed?

She should have left them that night. Right after Chris had cut her to bits, not hung around like a blind fool hoping things would change. For they would not. The demon had made it abundantly clear, and Duncan had confirmed it when he had not even tried to reason out the folly that had taken place just the night before.

So why had she not split? Why was she trailing along to some unknown fate that could only get worse with every mile down the road?

She wished she had an answer. Mostly, she wished she did not have a sense of urgency that compelled her to stay beyond her will. As if something prevented her from leaving, which was ridiculous for the only true explanation was that she was a weak and spineless creature, as insignificant and worthless as Chris claimed.

Uncomfortable, she stirred. Hugging close the woolen sweater Duncan had lent her, she hoped to beat the incessant drizzle and freezing wind blowing from the mountains, if not to melt the ice layer that was freezing her heart.

"Hey, lover," the demon shouted from a distance, returning after having raced ahead to the Hall's front entrance. "It seems empty." He signaled Duncan to reach him. "Where's everybody?" Looking surprised, he made it sound like the Hall was usually full of people, coming and going at all times. "Spring is here, so council members should be gathering already." He glanced around perplexed. "The first session of the council should be in just a little while . . ." He frowned. "So why is no one here for it?"

Now that he mentioned it, she noticed the eerie silence hanging on the place as she rode into the Hall's front yard, right to the main door. Then an old man appeared from nowhere on the threshold, tall and proud in his white beard and candid hair, and the time for silly questions seemed over.

"Arthur, thank the gods you're still here!" Dismounting rapidly, Chris ran to him, his lights flashing like crazy.

The old man's were almost as blinding, so she had no trouble reading either one. Not the old man, who was in far worse shape, for he had fallen for Chris so hard and so beyond any hope of recovery that she felt sorry for him. Not the seductive demon, who recognized the deep bond of sex and feelings that tied him to the older man. Not exactly love, still close enough for Chris to deny it to himself and to Duncan, as though fearing the prince would get jealous of it.

Which was the last thing on Duncan's part, for all she picked up from his aura was a healthy respect and gladness for such bond and for all it meant to his angel.

"It's been a harrowing journey." Letting his guard down for a second, Chris smiled his most enchanting smile that flooded the old man with the full force of his emotions. "And Duncan messed it all up by bringing that woman along." The scornful glance he sent from above a shoulder was all for her. "We're sorry, but—"

"Sorry, dear boy?" Arthur embraced him fondly. "I summoned her, too, because she's essential for what I need from you." Letting him go, his gaze broadened to include Prince Caldwell. "That's why I told you to bring her."

"You did?" Puzzled, Chris exchanged glances with Duncan, coming up behind him. "Did Arthur tell you to bring her?"

"I didn't receive any instructions." Duncan appeared as baffled as Chris did.

"It wasn't an instruction, boys, rather a thought I sent you," Arthur retorted.

So she understood it had been a test, though nothing in either of their bewildered expression indicated they had passed it.

"Never mind." Shaking his head in resignation, he waved

a hand aimlessly in midair. "The important thing is that all three of you are here." Striding forward, he reached her as she dismounted from Starlet. "Welcome to the Hall, my dear. I'm Arthur Fairchild, Leader of the High Council." He extended a hand.

Blushing violently, she clasped it. "I'm Ylianor—"

"Meyer, I know." Squeezing her hand tightly, he held her at arm's length. "It's wonderful to have you here, after I've wanted to meet you for so long." He stared at her intently. "I must admit I was skeptical when Charles told me about you. I refused to believe him, and we even had a quarrel over it." He chuckled probably at the memory. "However, the things he later told me made me reconsider my point of view." He narrowed his gaze on her. "Now seeing you . . ." As he searched her face, he gave her the odd sensation he was looking for any recognizable traits. "Well, Charles may have been right in considering you his daughter." He angled his head as though a different perspective would confirm his theory. "There's a familiar air about you that reminds me of him and . . ." He shifted his gaze on Prince Caldwell. "Duncan, wouldn't you agree?"

"It's just a slight resemblance." At an evident loss, Chris swallowed hard, his lights saying how the leader's fuss over her irritated him. "But you're looking at her as if you've never seen a woman before." Recovering his wits, his tone became aggressive, "What's so special about her, anyway?" Chris's annoyance mounted. "How about a proper welcome to your friends, instead of giving attention to the stranger alone?" Sulking like a child, he shuffled his feet nervously. "And where's everyone? Why's the Hall so empty?"

"All in due time, my dear boy." Grinning broadly, Arthur gestured for him to be patient. "You're my only guests for now." His gaze swept the vast front yard as if to signal the place was all for them. "So all my time is for you alone."

Then folding her hand around his elbow, he walked slowly to the entrance. "Don't mind Chris's rash words, child." He sounded like a father trying to justify a much-loved son and his riotous behavior.

Which was all the proof she needed to confirm the fact the man was anything but impartial when it came to the demon, to the point he would forgive him just about anything.

"He needs you more than he realizes." He glanced up and following his gaze, she noticed both Chris and Duncan stepping through the threshold. "Only he's too foolish to know it yet." He patted her hand, probably asking for her sympathy. "And thank you for having awakened Prince Caldwell's power." So he knew about this, too. "I feel it coursing in him like a wild river in dire need of direction and training." He stopped to lock his gaze on hers. "Something I'm sure you'll teach him how to control thanks to the channel you've opened with him."

I wouldn't be so sure given how he feels about me. "We'll see."

"Of course, you will." He resumed walking, gently dragging her along. "And the best way to go about it is through sex, which remains the fastest way to awaken someone's power." He winked mischievously. "Not to mention the most pleasurable."

"That it was." *And the demon can just eat his heart out!* "But why did he have to wait for me? He has Chris who is so powerful—"

"Just because one has power doesn't mean he can awaken what's asleep in another." His watery eyes flashed as though he were glad Chris and Duncan had not affected each other in this, too.

Which made her wonder if perhaps there was something more he was not telling her, not with his words, not with his lights, either.

"So it's just a matter of having the right connections?" *And if so, what's the idea of the demon awakening my aura gift?*

"Not only. Let's say it's a combination of factors that sparks the energy flow, good or bad as it may be." Halting again, he peered inside her eyes. "And bad is mostly what you got from him, isn't it?" Evidently perceiving more than she intended to reveal, he pulled her into a tight embrace. "'Cause I can tell you tasted his darkness."

"I tasted it long before this godforsaken trip." *And I survived both times, so eat your heart out twice, Lord Templeton!* "We met as children, and I saw his transformation from a black demon to a shiny angel the moment he caught sight of Duncan." Drawing away, she shrugged. "But they don't seem to understand —"

"My dear girl, boys are such thickheads." He chortled amused. "They have trouble understanding even the obvious." Wrapping his hand over hers, he advanced to the front door. "You have no idea how difficult it was simply to get them back together."

"As if they could ever live separate." That was such a self-evident truth, it seemed superfluous even to say it.

"Of course, they can't." He nodded in agreement. "Their story is almost as old as time itself. They've traveled through many lifetimes together, changing genders and relations, yet being always as one. Their attraction is so strong it inevitably pulls them close, no matter who or where they are." He paused to take a deep breath.

And her imagination rushed to add details to this fascinating tale he was painting, some of which she had glimpsed herself when she was too small to comprehend, most of which she had observed during the journey over.

"Did they understand any of this?" His eyebrows rose in disappointment. "Absolutely not."

"So that's why their love is so frightening." So intense, so boundless on both sides she had no doubt it represented a power on its own. "And the connection is more potent than either has realized so far."

"Their love is one of a kind." He sighed wearily. "And you're right about the connection."

She saw his lights flicking in sad waves of longing. So he knew Chris would never feel for him what he felt for Prince Caldwell, and her heart went out to him and to his pain.

"That's why I did everything I could to re-establish it when that hothead of a prince decided he could do without Chris." From the firmness of his voice, she gathered he had been duty-bound to help them, regardless of his personal feelings in the matter. "As if anyone could do without that incredibly bright energy." This sounded like he was talking about himself and the hold Chris had on him. "You're in a privileged position, my dear." He hesitated, as if debating whether to go on. "They need you to explore their full potentials and to guide them through this new path."

"Me?" *Neither can stand me!* "I don't feel particularly wanted at the moment." She averted her gaze, uncomfortable under his scrutiny.

"Child, I know what I'm asking isn't easy," his voice soft and concerned. "Especially considering the energy you'll have to curb—"

"His darkness overwhelms me, Leader," she spat bitterly.

"But you'll find a way to tame it." Somehow, his vote of confidence frightened her more than Chris's black side. "I'm sure, 'cause they're your future much like you are theirs." Now almost at the door, he slowed down his pace. "You see, what I failed to mention before is that you're part of their connection." His aura waved, vaguely envious of her position. "In fact, you are the strongest link, since you've followed them for just as many lifetimes. Maybe this is your chance to prove to them your worth. Not just for the here and now. For all the past and possible futures you might share together."

"Then you'll first have to convince them." *And good luck*

with that! "I don't know if I can survive another hour with them, much less a whole bunch of lifetimes." Which sounded ridiculous to her since all she could think about was how to be gone from their lives now and forever.

And their common destiny be damned!

"Right now, there's no place for me between them." *Nor do I care for one.* "And since I don't know if there ever will be, I might as well get gone now."

"Don't rush into any hasty decisions." His wise eyes blazed. "Things are changing in such a way that it would be impossible for you to leave them." He heaved making it look like this decision would weigh more on him than on her.

Which was just pretense!

"Please trust me on this one." As though perceiving her diffidence, his tone went all convincing, "Staying with them to face the future together is your best option."

Ha! That's easy for you to say! "What if I don't care about them or whatever is to happen?" Ylianor challenged angrily. "The way you put it, I'm nothing but a slave who has no choice in the matter." *And I already got one master too many as it is!*

"Young lady, this is not about you!" His tone scolding, he scoffed, "This is about your world. And you have a responsibility to it, above and beyond your personal issues." His face became stern. "And I'm growing too old for your stupid games and silly quarreling."

At these words, she noticed he was not as old as she had taken him for initially. He just carried his years badly, the strain getting to him faster than he would have wanted.

"You do look very tired." Her voice almost a husky whisper, she brushed his face in a light caress that did not linger beyond a mere touch.

"Only a bout of incurable old age," he joked, making it sound like it were nothing. "That's all."

"Old is not a matter of age." She peered at his wavering

lights and at the odd shadow hanging over him. "You're weary inside." Letting her hand fall to a side, she averted her gaze to avoid delving deeper into his private matters.

"I am, my child." A faint smile crossed his lips. "But now that you're all here, I feel better already."

"I'm glad for this, Leader." *Not enough to stay, though.* "I just hope you're not counting on me for anything life-threatening 'cause I'm not planning on sticking around, no matter what you—"

"Hey, you two!" Chris's shiny head popped round the main entrance. "Will you hurry up?"

"Yes, we're coming." He picked up the pace. "Come on."

The way he tugged her along, she wondered whether he had heard her last words.

"The boys are getting impatient." Reaching the front door, he fixed Duncan. "What accommodations would you prefer?" He shifted his gaze on Chris for a quick peek before returning to look squarely at the prince. "A single bedroom or perhaps two or even three separate ones?"

"We'll take two adjoining bedrooms." Without the slightest hesitation, Duncan held the leader's gaze.

"Fine." Sidestepping them all, Arthur headed down the long hallway. "Then I'll put you on the second floor of the western tower."

She waited for Chris and Duncan to trail behind Arthur before following the small party, careful to keep a certain distance between her and the three men. This also gave her the chance to take her first serious look at the renowned seat of the High Council. As impressive a structure on the inside as she had seen it on the outside, the straight long corridor stretched up ahead without any apparent end to it or to the many doors lining both sides of the massive walls at regular intervals. If those were all bedrooms, the Hall would be able to fit more people than lived in her village for sure. The mere thought made her feel so out of place that she stopped gawking like people going around at their first big market fair. Instead, she trained her focus steadily on Chris and Duncan's backsides just as Arthur reached a crossway.

Left and right, the passage opened up, and Arthur made a left turn, walking briskly toward a massive stairwell she glimpsed at its far end. On reaching it, he clapped, and a servant came out of nowhere to stand next to him.

"Robert will take you to your rooms upstairs." Arthur gestured at the man now bowing to Chris and Duncan. "And when you're there, I expect you to resolve your issues, no matter how impossible they seem to be." His sharp gaze went right through the demon and the prince, probably leaping as far down as their cores. "Because the three of you have an important task ahead, one that will require you to work together as one in order to succeed. And I won't tolerate any failures." He eyed each of them slowly and in turn. "I'll give you however much time you need, but when I see you again I want to feel your connection, not your unbalance." His gaze went from Chris to Ylianor. "And there'll be no talks of leaving. I'm sorry if you don't like it, but the three of you must stay together for now. So get over your petty quarrels, resolve your issues and be ready to embrace your new responsibilities."

Sure, it was all very well for the leader to preach about duties and responsibilities. He did not have to play third wheel to a love that transcended time and space. He did not have to compete with a jealous demon capable of carving her to bits just because she dared seek a place in the prince's heart.

She was the only one who stood to lose everything yet again, including the little she had managed to retrieve before Chris's knife had shattered all her illusions. Not just about her adored prince, about his insufferable lover, too.

For Prince Duncan Caldwell and Lord Christopher Templeton were all she wanted. All she craved since leaving Black Rose. And she knew she could not take it anymore. Not from the prince, who kept her dangling on a leash, so close yet so far from his powerful body and brilliant mind.

Which was sheer torture, him and his ambivalent feelings for her turning everything into a wicked game that had spiraled her love and lust out of any decency.

Which was nothing if compared to her reactions to the cursed demon. Not because she understood his need to reveal the extent of his power to his lover, rather because he had chosen her to do it. And part of her had loved it, the part that had not been terrified that is. To her great shame, the feel of his razor-sharp blade had seemed like a loving caress at times, a thrilling game she could not wait to repeat, attracted to it and to the cunt-pounding creature by the very danger he exuded from every pore.

Truth was—this playing with fire made her feel as alive and as vibrant as merging into the prince's cool energy. Vulnerable, too, to the point she fantasized about being their special toy every time they trapped her between them and inflamed her senses. And if she had already fallen for one beyond any safety level, how could she possibly survive falling for the other one, too?

It would be all she needed to mess up her life good and proper!

Once the sex was over, and despite Arthur's claim that she belonged to them, she was just a nuisance for them. She saw it all too well, could not help seeing it, the difference between their love and their feelings for her. And the abyss between the two was enough to sink all her hopes and to strengthen her resolve to leave immediately, before she got the unwise idea of wanting more from both of them and set her heart up for another shattering disillusionment.

"Have I made myself clear?" After one final look, Arthur spun around and was gone.

CHAPTER FORTY-EIGHT

"What the fuck did you tell him?" Chris snarled as soon as Arthur was out of sight, grabbing Ylianor's arm as if to tug her upstairs.

"I believe Arthur told us to resolve our issues." Quick to wrap his hand on the angel's, he pressured until Chris released his hold. "Not worsen them."

"And I hardly said a word at all." Shaking her hand free, she edged closer to him as though asking for protection. "He did most of the talking." She glared at Chris malevolently.

And the angel was about to lash out again.

So he blocked him. "Why don't we continue this in our room?"

After everything that had happened, the last thing he wanted was for Chris to hurt her as badly as he had at the shelter.

Whirling on his heels, he climbed the stairs, dragging her alongside him while following Robert inside a giant room. An open side door led into the adjoining bedroom.

"If you need me, just call." After pointing at a bell hanging on the wall, the servant disappeared.

Striding into the second room, Chris slammed the door shut.

Ignoring both him and the angel, she locked herself in the bathroom. Which left him alone and very determined to overcome the terrible mood that he himself had contributed to bring about.

"Princess, get out of there!" He knocked loudly, prepared

to use extreme measures if necessary.

"Or else?" Ylianor snapped.

"I'll break down the damn door." And he meant it.

"Leave me alone!" Ylianor screamed. "I wish I had never known you."

Still, she opened the door and on stepping out, he noticed she had changed her pants and shirt.

"I'm leaving." Balancing the knapsack on her shoulder, she walked to get out of the room.

"Leaving where?" Clasping her arm, he detained her. "Arthur forbade any of us from—"

"I don't care, and Arthur doesn't know!" Angrier than he had ever seen her, she twisted on herself to wriggle free, without succeeding. "He can't even begin to imagine what it's like to be with two hideous beings like you and your haughty Lord Templeton."

She was right, of course.

Still, he preferred to address one problem at a time.

"But what will you do if you leave?" And just to avoid such possibility, he tightened his grip on her.

"Exactly what you wanted me to do," she spat.

"Me?" He wondered if he had sent her his stray thoughts about leaving her at the Hall in the hope he could forget all about her.

"Yes, you." She gave no sign she had actually plucked it out of his head. "We're in a new district, far away from Silcamore and your mother, so I think I can survive on my own." Tugging harder, she managed to retrieve her arm. "And the great leader's instructions be damned!" Spinning around, she headed for the door.

"No, wait." Reaching her from behind, he circled her waist and dragged her backward, crushing her against his frame. "Please don't go." Bending on her ear, he nibbled it. "Not until I've apologized for how wrong I've been." If he loved the way her ass cheeks had captured his cock, he had to suppress the surge of excitement lest it became too hard for him to think or talk straight. "About you, about everything actually."

"And I don't want to listen to any of it." Her frantic swings to get away from him stuck his shaft right smack inside the cleft between her buttocks. "Now let me go!" She raised her voice, "And I hope I never see you ever again!" She swayed more desperately. "Because I hate you —"

Her voice strangled, something broke inside, and he feared she would shatter within his arms. Linked as he was to her, he had felt the tight knot of pent-up emotions pressing at the back of her throat. Now it burst into uncontrollable crying that shook her body with its violent sobs and stained her lovely face with the flood of her tears.

I'm sorry, Princess. Turning her around, he buried her face on his chest. *I've been a damn fool, and I beg your forgiveness.* He kissed her cheeks, her neck, her hair. *I've allowed his dark side to get out of control, and that's unforgivable.* Worse still, he had unleashed such atrocity. The likes of which he could have never imagined could exist, not even if he lived to be a hundred. *I knew he could become dangerous, but I never thought he'd be so . . .*

Terrifying and revolting would have been the right terms, for he was still reeling from the unspeakable torture he had not been able to stop.

Hurtful in a way I never thought possible. He tightened his grip on her shaking body. *I just couldn't believe it.* The sheer incredulity that something like this could even be possible had prevented him from taking any action. *Which is why I didn't react.* It was the closest thing to describing the abyss Chris and his ferocious show had sunk him. *So I'm all the sorrier I couldn't do anything.* Too shocked by the cruelty of it all, he had failed her utterly, unable to offer the least comfort for what she had to endure. *Not even after I managed to stop his*

339

cursed spell. His lips all over her face, he tasted the salty edge of her tears. *But I promise I'll never let him get his hands on you –*

Just promise me you won't close me out, like you did after he was done. Somehow, she had been too quick to deflect his logical conclusion, which left him wondering how much he had missed of her ordeal.

For sure, she had fought back, refusing to give in to the fear she must have felt. Despite his thick fog, the one thing he had caught had been her biting retorts to every one of his angel's vicious blows. Which, knowing Chris the way he did, would have only spurred him to be fiercer than ever. Not to mention more aroused.

I don't know what hurt worse, if his callous knife-play or your cold indifference afterward. Sobbing less convulsively, she relaxed in his embrace.

You're right. I should've been there for you. Reaching her lips, he pressed them with his own. *And I wasn't. Too wrapped up in trying to figure out how someone like the angel could even exist in a world like ours.*

For such was the real question going through his mind during the half-day's ride to the Hall. And knowing that, in spite of everything, he still felt as strongly as before about the wicked creature only increased the acute awareness of all his princess had to suffer.

He's a demon. She seemed to have no doubts this was the only answer possible. *Nothing he did yesterday surprised me all that much.* She raised her gaze as though daring him to contradict her. *In fact, I kind of expected it.* Her crying now stopped, she twisted her lips in a snarl. *'Cause that's how black his heart is.*

And reading her brilliant green eyes, still shiny from all the tears, he realized she did not just understand Chris. She accepted him for who he was. Angel and demon, good and bad all rolled up in one. And this was almost as mind boggling as discovering his angel had such a morbid taste for blood and violence.

Could be, but it still doesn't justify him. He wiped off the glimmer of a tear from the corner of her eye. *Nor me and my cold indifference.* And being sorry about it only worsened his guilt over the awful way he had treated her. *Now I don't know how to make it up to you if not by trying to explain –*

"Am I interrupting?" Standing on the threshold, somber faced and beautiful, Chris was seeking an opening.

So he smiled encouragingly. "Ready to talk, Angel?"

"Absolutely." Stepping into the room, Chris closed the door behind him.

After carrying her to the bed, he gestured at Chris to sit beside her while he settled on the floor.

"What has happened so far is my fault, as the angel pointed out more than once." Still collecting his thoughts, he glanced at Chris with the hint of a smile curving his lips. "Which makes it imperative for me to explain and apologize." He paused to stare at the two rapt gazes completely transfixed on him. "But before I get any further, I want to make it clear this has got nothing to do with Arthur's request."

"It's easy for him to talk." Chris's expression was bitter. "He's not the one who'll have to put up with a forced relationship for the sake of duty and responsibility."

"I know, but let's just pretend he didn't say anything about it." He shifted on his knees. "Whatever our responsibilities, we first need to set our records straight, 'cause the choice to stay together has to be ours, not Arthur's."

"How do you propose we make that choice, lover?" In spite of the words, there was no trace of challenge in Chris's tone.

"By analyzing how we got to be here now." It was the most logical place to start after all. "And if you agree, I'll start at the beginning. At least what I feel is the beginning of everything." His focus turned to Chris. "Our incredible love." Reaching up, he stroked the angel's handsome face. "I love you like I've never loved anyone or anything before in my life." For nothing could dampen it, not even the monstrous viciousness of what had happened in the shelter. "And no energy business will ever make me mistake what I feel for you." He hoped his firm tone would erase all of Chris's doubts. "It's love, pure and simple. It's our own special magic, which keeps growing stronger with each passing day. All the time spent together just makes me want you more and more." His hand slipped to the angel's chest. "And I can't get over it. The way I crave you in and out of bed amazes me all the time 'cause it never lessened. Not once. Not even when I tried cutting you out of my life." And boy, those two years of separations still weighed on him. "Save to look for you in every woman I met, instead of accepting the simple fact that our link is unique and that in no other person will I find what you give me time after time."

"Lover . . ." Chris's voice broke. "I—"

"I love you, Christopher Templeton, third son of James Templeton." Cupping the angel's face, he kissed him fiercely. "You are the most beautiful man I've ever seen, the most vibrant and full of life, the brightest star ever, the undying flame of my heart and the only one who can understand me at a single glance." Another passionate kiss, then he released Chris. "Also the only one with a dark side so powerful it can eclipse your shiny bright angel side faster than the speed of lightening." He reclined on his heels. "And when you uncovered it last night, it was simply shocking." He searched the beautiful face for traces of the savagery Chris had unleashed so effortlessly. "How could you possibly—"

"I don't know how," Chris was quick to interrupt him. "I know no one else in this world would even harbor such sick fantasies, much less act them out." His tone softened, "I know there must be something terribly wrong with me. But I've had these impulses ever since I can remember." The blue-gray eyes veiled under the swirl of too many unmanageable emotions resurfacing all together, all at once.

So his heart bled for him.

"They just got worse after our breakup, to the point I can't control them." Chris clasped his hands. "But if I didn't act on them, I wouldn't be able to live."

That did it!

That broke down all of his qualms. For however outrageous and brutal Chris's survival was, he knew he would always forgive him in the end.

"So this is something you need to do." Hard as it was to grapple the sheer inhumanity of it all, he was really trying to understand. "And since you heal them back and there's no harm done in the end, I guess it's all right, though it doesn't excuse what you did to the princess."

And no, he did not want to see those fuzzy images that had plagued him the entire day long, or the sight of her body battered into a bloody pulp, lying there defenseless and asking for his help.

Something he had been unable to give, drowning as he had been in an ocean of anger and regret.

"Or how I reacted to it, for which I sincerely apologize and beg your forgiveness, Princess." Turning to her, he tilted up her face and locked his gaze on her mesmerizing green eyes, still full of tears. "I know there's no justification to my despicable behavior." He kissed her cheek softly. "All I know is that you belong to me. It's what I felt when I saw you the first time at the village, like I already told you. I had no idea who you were, not even a clue to your name, yet without a doubt, you were *mine*." He charged the term with all the erotic connotation he could muster. "Which doesn't give me the right to use you as an object, a sexual toy or worse a slave. And I'm sorry I deceived you, offering you a job and a home when all I wanted was to fuck you, alone and with my lover. And once that began, I took your compliance for granted, until I learned of David." He took a deep breath. "And it made me so goddamn jealous I couldn't stand it!"

Yes, now he could admit it openly.

"To make matters worse, this intimate channel between us has totally unbalanced my perception when it comes to you." Clamping her hands, he squeezed them tight. "I don't mean to sound ungrateful, but I'm not sure I want this gift of yours, much less having someone speaking in my head all the time, knowing exactly what's in my heart and mind —"

"It doesn't work that way," she rushed to defend her disturbing power. "You share only what you decide to share, like I already told you." She snatched her hands away from his grasp. "I can't steal anything you don't want me to have, not from your heart, not from your mind."

"Could be." Hardly convinced, he shook his head. "Still, this is all too new for me and so very confusing. To the point I'd rather not have it." He heaved. "That's another reason why I was treating you like a worthless slave." Same way his angel loved to treat her.

Only he had done it *for real.*

"Which you aren't at all," he hurried to add. "With you, I broke every rule in my book and went against every principle I used to hold dear, a true master of deceit, especially when it came to the other night."

He shifted uncomfortably. Would he ever be able to forgive himself?

"I cannot even begin to apologize, sweet princess." Repressing his useless self-pity, he gave her his full and undivided attention. "I let things slip to a point where your life was in danger, and I didn't even care. I wanted to stop him—"

"No, you wanted revenge," she retorted. "And this goes far deeper than the fact I opened a channel between us or that I had sex with David." Her eyes flashed. "No, this is something else entirely, something that happened before we left Black Rose. And I've been racking my head ever since to find some plausible explanation." Her expression became extremely sad. "What have I done to deserve your cruel indifference? What have I done besides being the willing slave you wanted me to be?"

"I wish the gods you were only a slave." Deciding to make a clean slate of it, he embraced her. "Truth is—you're so much more and not just to me." Drawing back, he stared deep inside her eyes. "And I couldn't accept it. Much less stand the thought of it." A finger under her chin, he tilted up her face to claim her lips, his tongue breaking inside her wet cavity and sweeping it whole. "When you described your relationship with my father, I only half believed you. For how could he possibly feel something more for a stranger than for his son and heir?" He could not tear his gaze away from her enchanting green eyes. "So I told myself that you were exaggerating and that in reality you meant nothing to him." Yes, it had been his most ardent whish. "Well, it turns out I was so fucking wrong." He breathed deeply to calm his wildly beating heart. "Not just because this accursed gift of ours made me realize how close two people could really be. So close, they become as one and this inevitably shifts the balance of a relationship, which is what must've happened to you and my father. As if that weren't enough, the damn lawyer informs me my father's will contains a clause written expressly for you."

"For me?" Her eyes flew wide-open.

"Yes, for you alone." He nodded. "If I decide to honor it, you won't need to worry about changing districts or pledging to someone you don't really like because Father wants to give you his name and adopt you as his legal daughter. In addition, he provides for a place all your own where you can stay for as long as you like."

"Really?" A stray tear rolled down her cheek. "He wants to adopt me?"

"You'd become a Caldwell." He worked hard to keep his tone light, for something inside him still needed to adjust to this whole thing. "My sister to all legal effects."

"Does he say I'm his daughter?" Ylianor's voice trembled as though she feared the answer.

"No, he doesn't." So his heart went out to her and his tone softened, "Since he didn't pledge to your mother, he says there's no blood relation between us. Still, you feel like his own, which is exactly how I feel about you. So he must be right, and you belong to the Caldwells, for whatever mysterious reason."

"Is it legal?" She frowned puzzled, her mind evidently working out all the possible angles.

"It's not a common practice, but it's perfectly legal." Briefly, his focus shifted on Chris who was listening with great interest. "As the official heir, I have the power to decide whether or not to honor this clause."

"Is there more?" As though expecting there was, she searched his face.

So he could not hide it.

"Yes, there is." And how much it still grated on his nerves! "What made me angry wasn't the clause in itself, but the letter my father wrote to convince me of your rights and to declare his love for you." He hesitated in order to silence the pain, throbbing in his stomach. "He loved you very much, Princess." The words were so thick in his throat that he had to swallow. "Much more than he ever loved Lizzy or me." The whole damn awareness stung like crazy. "This made me mad." Still did, despite his trying to convince himself otherwise.

"Furious, I'd say." Chris chuckled.

"That's an understatement." He grinned at his angel. "I wanted to erase you from the face of the world. I wished you'd never existed. How did you dare take my father's love away from me?" Merely saying this, he felt the same rage mounting again, which made him stop immediately. "As you already guessed, being the thickhead I am, I took it all out on you, even if none of it was your fault." He shook his head, his long strands flying all around his shoulders. "So I've got quite a few apologies to make." A bitter smile crossed his lips. "I'm just glad I can make them in person because the angels stopped me from committing a fatal mistake."

"I had to, lover." The blue-gray eyes blazed. "Otherwise you'd have never lived with yourself."

"True." He pursed his lips for this last part was the one he least liked. "But my rage was still there, and you used it the other night to prevent me from helping the princess."

Chris bent his head. "I admit I didn't particularly shine the other night —"

"I'd say it was one of your darkest moments," the prince intervened. "And I don't know what was more detestable — your bloody show or your merciless use of what I'd told you in confidence."

"So welcome to the world." Defiant, the blond angel raised his gaze. "We all use each other, one way or another, and our real motives don't always shine for their honesty."

"Perhaps not, but I want to be as honest and as straightforward as possible from now on." And he totally planned on keeping this particular promise. "Especially with the both of you." He broadened his gaze to include the two faces in front of him. "What happened the other night is as much my fault as the angel's, and I take full responsibility for it. I allowed it, blinded by prejudice and vengeance. No, no more of that. And no more of my taking decisions that affect others without their express consent."

Mostly, he needed to do some serious soul searching to get rid of all the lies and prejudices he had been feeding himself for the past twenty-one years, lies and prejudices that had messed with his balance and sense of justice in the most outrageous and unforgivable way possible.

"Which is why I have to apologize to you, too, Angel, for forcing you into this situation without offering you any alternative." He straightened. "No, no more of all that. I don't want to tie anyone to me or to some supposedly life-threatening situation. You're both free to go if you so choose. And I'll deal with Arthur. Or we all agree to stay together and strive to make it work between us, without jealousies, rage or all the terrible things that have driven us apart these past days on the road." He shifted position, his legs weary all of a sudden. "On my part, I want to be with you." He clasped Chris and Ylianor's hands. "Both of you." His gaze melted inside the fiery blue-gray eyes. "With you, Angel, because I cannot live without your love regardless of the energy business involved." Then he switched to her. "With you, Princess, because something inside me rebels at the idea of letting you go, even if I can't promise you anything right now." Freeing both their hands, he trained his focus on her lovely face. "I know this isn't what you want to hear, but I have to ask you for more time and for more space, so that I can find out what I feel for you and how to adjust to our special bond."

Sinking in her arresting green eyes, he read her disappointment. *Sorry, Princess, I can't offer more than this.* "This is the only reasonable proposal I can make right now. One I'll certainly stick to if you two are with me." He looked them squarely in the face. "So now it all depends on you. What do you want to do?"

CHAPTER FORTY-NINE

et rid of her!
GOr such had been his general intention, before that night at the shelter had spoiled everything!

Which was the last thing he wanted to think about right now.

"Hem . . ." He cleared his throat. "I think I owe some explanations of my own and not just for last night." Comforted by Duncan's encouraging gaze, he plunged into the murky waters of his black universe. "I'm sorry I didn't tell you sooner about the darkness that sometimes swallows me. Truth is—I didn't want to, 'cause I always considered you, lover, to be my clean self. I reserved the other self, the demon one, to the many victims of my uncontrollable need to carve them to pieces, unable to stop until they lie in a bloody pool, begging for mercy."

No question about it—he loved having that much power over another human being, craved the sensation of holding someone's life within the palms of his hands, playing it like it could go either way as terror mounted in their frightened eyes.

Which was not the point right now.

"Keeping those two sides separate has been my main concern for the past nineteen years." *Practically forever.* "And I thought I succeeded now." *Especially since I moved to the Hall.* "I had my victims, and then I had you, the only one I never thought of slicing up." *The only person I'd ever die for, literally.* "So much so that, during our phase, I never, ever got the urge to do it to anybody."

Sudden understanding brightened the prince's black eyes. "So when we broke up—"

"When *you* broke up with *me*, I couldn't have survived if I hadn't used my knife on all the pliable flesh you find day in and day out at the Hall." He made it deliberately sound as brutal as possible. "But that also started my fantasy about you. Not about cutting you. Mostly about leaving your memory intact once I was done." His gaze shifted to fix a point in space. "If it might seem evil, it would've been my way of showing you who I really was. And if it never came about, it was only because I feared losing your love."

But with her, everything changed.

"When you came along, it was like a dream come true." His focus now fixed on her. "I could act out my fantasy without harming my lover. And that's what I did last night." Hanging his head, he took a deep breath, knowing he had to say it, even if he did not really feel it. "I'm sorry, Ylianor—"

"No, you aren't," she retorted hotly.

Damn her!

He had forgotten she was a cursed witch who had no trouble reading his aura, or whatever the fuck it was that got her so deep under his skin that he could not stand it!

"You're right!" Chris snapped. "I'm not." Throwing back his shoulders, he raised his chin in defiance. "In fact, you deserved it for so many reasons I can't even begin to list them all." Still, he would try his damn best to give her the full load of his loathing. "Like resembling him too fucking much! And being so nosy, there's no privacy since you got here! And because it seems I have no choice but to share him with the likes of you! And last, but certainly not least, because you're a woman, a gender for which I've never had any sympathy." His gaze swung back to Duncan. "And now what you're suggesting is some kind of permanent solution with this same woman." Could anything be more ludicrous?

"A witch who can read your mind and the gods only know what else, when she isn't busy uncovering my core during sex."

"Hey, I had nothing to do with that!" On the defensive, she dared him to contradict her. "You did it all by yourself. It was your choice to show me your inner self."

"Choice? You pulled it right out of me, remember?" Chris spat angrily. "I couldn't care less about letting you know who I am." Although, if he had to be honest, it had been liberating, which was something he carefully avoided telling her. "Had it been up to me, I'd have never laid a finger on you, 'cause unlike you, dearie, I *choose* who I fuck and who I torture." His lips curved in a wry snarl. "And in neither case, I'd have gone for a sorry ass like you, had my lover not fallen prey to your sick enchantment."

Velvety black eyes concerned, Duncan stared at him. "Does this mean you don't want to have anything more to do with her, Angel?"

Unfortunately not, goddamn her! "Before I answer, lover, please tell me honestly what's so special about her." He tried to curb his aggressive tone. "Besides all this energy crap I mean."

"You mean besides the fact she feels as much a part of me as you do yourself?" Duncan taunted.

Ouch!

That hurt!

Goddamn him and his sense of balance and fairness.

"Yeah, besides that, too," he snorted, clenching his teeth.

"Strange as it sounds, her special meaning has to do with you." Searching her face, the prince's gaze slipped to her figure before returning on him. "No one understands us or our love like she does, to the point we can be our true selves." Still kneeling, he straightened until he leveled their gazes. "And no one, besides you, ever turned me on quite like her. Nothing is better than when she is in our bed, both of us screwing her at the same time and playing it like she's a slave completely subjected to our pleasures. And I know you feel the same way, too." Bending on his neck, he bit it before moving to his ear. "She can make us stronger. Even add something to who and what we are." Lips brushing his ear, he whispered, his hot breath tickling, "I know you object to women, but why don't you try to see her as a person for once?" He grinned broadly. "It could make a surprising difference, Angel. Trust me."

The only thing he trusted at the moment was his instinct about her taste for pain. Her surprising lack of fear and defiance during his heavy knife play had been unlike any of his other victims. Talk about having guts! And a twisted sense of excitement that was disturbingly similar to his sadistic one.

For the one thing he could not forget was her arousal. Astounding simply to think of it, she had fed off his excitement every time he had struck her or watched the thin red bloodlines mingling to form a pattern. And this told him she would be willing to try it again.

Fuck her and these tricks of hers!

Bottom line was—he could not honestly say he wanted her gone, though he would never admit it outright.

He took a deep breath. "There's just one last thing before I accept what you're proposing."

"I'm listening, Angel." Going down on the floor, the prince sat cross-legged.

"Promise me we'll have time just for the two of us." Leaning on his knees, he edged nearer to him. "Alone and away from her."

"Of course." Duncan embraced him. "Our present arrangement is temporary, for traveling sake alone." Pulling back, the prince regarded him intently. "When we'll get back to normal life, we'll have plenty of time to be together by ourselves."

His lover's earnest look was his capitulation.

"All right, then you convinced me, lover." *What the fuck? You only live once, right?*

"I'll be a part of this . . ." While frowning in search of the right comparison, the picture of a three-sided pyramid entered his mind.

Apparently made of solid stone on the outside, at a closer inspection he realized it had a hollow core that hid something far more important inside.

"Pyramid you're building," he added at last.

"I believe the word you were looking for was triangle." Duncan chuckled amused.

"No, lover, it wasn't." And as it flashed in his mind, he was sure of it. "Trust me." He smirked. "And it's much better than any old triangle," he joked. "In case you forgot, I prefer three-dimensional objects." The hint of a smile curved his lips. "And that pyramid seems the fitting image for our situation. Don't you think so?"

Both Ylianor and Duncan nodded as though they were seeing the same pyramid in their heads, too.

Which knowing them, they probably were.

"Then it's settled." And not a moment too soon, for tension was eating at him like never before.

CHAPTER FIFTY

W*hat's settled?*

One moment, Christopher Templeton was about to jump on her. The next, he was so deep in Duncan's mouth he might as well have been drowning, his fire literally smothered by Prince Caldwell's cooler and stronger energy. And maybe that odd bluestone pyramid had something to do with it.

Not that she could be sure. All she knew was that it had popped up in her mind probably at the same time it had in theirs. Strange how its apparent solid surface was in reality a clever disguise to hide the million lights flashing inside. Stranger still that Chris had caught it, as though plucking it right out of her mind.

Now this passionate kiss that was sinking the beastly creature into Duncan's essence seemed to seal his particular deal, not to mention fueling an insane desire that both found hard to restrain. Not just them.

To her, watching the play of lights and bodies from the outside, it was sheer agony. To the point she would have dropped on the floor and begged them to allow her to be the slave Duncan had just mentioned. And that had been when the pounding in her cunt had started and turned her antagonism for the odious demon into hungry craving. The same gnawing at the pit of her stomach and ordering her to let everything else slide for the sake of having one more taste of them.

If she had to stop and analyze this, the switch in her feelings would have struck her as plain absurd. One moment all she wanted to do was to run away from the both of them. The next, all she could dream about was to have their powerful bodies crushing her on every side. Which was not really the smartest way to go about this, since Prince Caldwell had not asked for her submission. He wanted her to make a choice.

Sure, a choice! As if she ever had one in her life!

She was not like Chris and Duncan who had *chosen* to be together the second they had met in Black Rose. She had no such privilege. She had grown up with the very same prince who had stolen her heart even before she had been old enough to realize it. And maybe, just maybe, he would have loved her, too, had not his forgetting all about her caused ten years of separation. So how could she possibly choose something after he had just told her he could not guarantee her anything?

Then again, no better time than the present to set her records straight, particularly now that he had managed to draw away from Chris and was looking at her with a questioning gaze.

"All right, since this is sharing time, I've got a few things of my own to take off my chest." She tried to keep still and stop rubbing her cunt on the mattress. "Like the fact you've been treating me like a worthless slave in *and* out of bed, like I didn't deserve any respect at all." She flared up just thinking about it. "Well, I got news for both of you." Her gaze swung from one to the other. "Nothing gives you the right to treat me like an inconsequential object, no matter how much I like playing slave in your bed." *To the point I lost myself in that cruelly twisted game of this lover of yours.*

Too disturbing a thought to share, she shook it out of her head. "And you took shameless advantage of it." Her gaze locked on the black one. "Not just because I agreed to become your slave way beyond the sex."

"Just for the record, Princess, it was exactly what I wanted," Duncan admitted candidly.

"I know you did." It was enough to recall how he had detained her near escape from that second shelter. "But you didn't stop there. You used whatever means you could to keep me dangling on a leash, like my love for you, my fear of losing you again and my hope you'd come to love me." If part of it had been her own doing, she did not pause to reassign blames. "Which is why I complied with your every whim however outrageous, also going as far as accepting your lover's bad manners—"

"Hey, I can be a gentleman when I want to," the demon scoffed annoyed.

"Not with me evidently, or I'd have never ended at the tip of your knife," she quipped. "Which is simply unforgivable. Not just because of your bloody show, which didn't impress me 'cause I expected that and worse from a black-hearted demon like you." If not exactly the truth, she made it sound as one. "Mostly because of that haughty contempt of yours, which is totally wasted 'cause I never, ever wanted to come between you and your lover." Her voice rose a notch, "In case you've forgotten like the prince did, I was there when your love first bloomed, so I'd be either dumb, blind or crazy to get in the way of something so unique and exclusive." The second her anger fueled up, her arousal worsened and for a moment, her mind went completely blank while lust clogged it.

Again, the connection between rage and sex seemed ludicrous and totally unnatural, if she was any judge of it.

"And since I'm neither, all I'm asking is a bit more consideration for who I am and for what we could accomplish together." Which was probably something exceptional, if Arthur's insistence they stick together was any indication. "That's my condition, if you want me to stay and still be your slave in bed alone." Searching both their faces, she noticed how intently they were following her. "Otherwise, I can simply pack up and leave like was my intention before the prince stopped me yet again—"

"No, no leaving." Clasping her hand, Duncan squeezed it possessively. "On my part, I promise I won't let things slide to the point they had last night, nor will I deceive you or play it like you're nothing but a slave." He kissed her hand. "'Cause you mean so much more to me, Princess." Pulling her into his powerful embrace, Duncan cooed softly in her ear, "Just gotta have more time to figure out what it is exactly."

"All right." If time was the only obstacle in the way to her prince's heart, she would give him as much as he needed. "I can accept that." Then her attention shifted on the demon, and the urge to provoke him was irresistible. "What about you, Lord Templeton?"

"I can't promise I'll stop treating you like a worthless slave out of bed." Chris did not just call her bluff.

He raised the stakes, goddamn him!

"But for sure, I'll have no pity for you in bed." This was more like him, particularly when his hot breath tickled her ear, his whisper low enough only she could hear it. "'Cause you're a slut worse than I'll ever be, and there's nothing you wouldn't do to get more cock and more pain."

A jolt of excitement coursed through her every fiber. Yes, it was exactly what she wanted, now more than ever, and how that intriguing demon had managed to sniff it out was beyond her.

"Is that acceptable?" Drawing back, he fixed her with open dare sparking his fiery blue-gray eyes.

What could she say?

"It has to be evidently." Playing it like his brashness neither intimidated nor fooled her, she threw back her shoulders. "Since all you think about is sex—"

"'Cause it's the only thing that has worked between us so far," Chris retorted.

"That's for sure." Amused, a twinkle brightened the striking black eyes, as Duncan's palm curled on the demon's engrossed crotch. "So I say we never lose sight of it." Stroking the shape stirring under Chris's pants, he made it grow to an impressive size. "And explore our pleasure in all its finer details as free and equal partners."

"Just pleasure, not pain?" Chris challenged.

"Well . . ." Duncan fixed her. *What do you think, Princess?*

And damn it if a part of her did not burn with the same craving she had read in the blue-gray eyes! Which maybe was not such a great idea—

"We'll decide when and if the time comes." Interpreting her hesitation, Prince Caldwell settled the matter for all of them. "In any case, Angel, you have to promise you won't try it again, unless she agrees to it. Is that clear?" His gaze never wavered from the demon's beautiful face.

"Crystal." Chris nodded, a gleam sparking his eyes at the door Duncan was leaving open on purpose.

Satisfied, Prince Caldwell shifted fiery black eyes on her. "And no more funny stuff from you either, about accepting things because you want to please me. From now on, being my slave begins and ends in bed." He peered at her closely. "Is that also clear?"

"Yes, Master." She giggled happily, throwing her arms around his neck and hugging him tight.

"I'll ensure you both keep your words, at least in bed." Still in her arms, he swung his head to confront Chris. "Agreed?"

"Yes." The demon clasped his hand and squeezed it.

"By agreeing to this . . ." Disentangling from him, she provoked on purpose, "Do I get Prince Charles's inheritance?"

However teasing she made it sound, this was important to her. If the news had stunned her, it had also confirmed that Prince Charles had truly loved her and wanted to do right by her. So not a figment of her imagination, his will would be the tangible proof of how much she meant to him. Which was something she had lost sight of, ever since he had died and precipitated her life in the abyss of her exile from Black Rose.

"What does that have to do with anything?" The prince looked vaguely hurt. "At the moment, it's not something I'm willing to negotiate. Just something I need to work out for myself."

"I believe this calls for a lesson," Chris snarled, exchanging a mischievous glance with Duncan. "She obviously needs a reminder on who's in charge here."

"Does that mean I'll always regret getting in a bed with you two fiends?" Ylianor joked.

"Probably." Flinging her back, Prince Caldwell pinned her down. "But I may just decide to give you what you want." He began stripping her. "If you're particularly good to both of us—"

"Oh I will," she groaned, her mind already floating away under Duncan's sensual touch that sent sparks of pleasure on her sensitive skin. "I'll do anything, if it makes you honor the will as Prince Charles intended."

Are you sure? Mocking softly, his fingers brushed her erect nipples, pinching and teasing to make them stand up and beg for more. *I might ask too much of you.*

Try me, Master. If nothing else worked, maybe flattery would. *I may surprise you.* Her breath short, it caught in her throat the moment he bent to flick his tongue on one throbbing tip.

Oh, this was divine if only she did not want so much

more —

"She talks way too much." Steadying her head, Chris's engorged rod went for her throat. "Don't you think?"

"I highly doubt that will keep her silent." Smiling broadly, the prince pushed her legs wide apart and sank into her drenched pussy. "At least in my head."

"Can't do much about that." Did she catch a trace of envy in the demon's tone?

She ardently hoped so, for he had to eat his heart out!

"But you can always punish her for the breach in etiquette." Slamming without the slightest mercy for the limited space in her mouth, he dug his cock as far as it could get. "Or didn't anybody tell her that it's bad taste to talk with her mouth full?"

I bet also when someone's strangling you, she quipped in Duncan's mind just to defy him.

If you don't shut up, I swear I'll help him. "Do we really need an excuse to punish her?" Penetrating to the hilt, he began a slow pump that was driving her crazy. "She's nothing but a slave after all."

Not just any slave.

She was Prince Duncan Caldwell's slave, at his complete service and that of his phase mate, Lord Christopher Templeton. And now she understood why Arthur had been so envious of it, why he had commented on her *privileged position* between them.

Hammered cunt and mouth, she was a helpless pawn of their exciting games and greedy cocks, both wanting to split her open. Chris, with his lurches to her stomach, suffocated her every time he shoved down. Duncan, with his fierce slams in her yielding slit, demanded more space every time his balls slapped her ass. Neither apparently giving a damn about her, they only used what most suited them, treating her like a mere object of their heated interplay.

And she loved it! Wanted more of it, like losing herself part in Duncan, part in Chris, leaving her body behind and melting their separate essences into one.

"I think she's having way too much fun." Stopping all of a sudden, the demon pulled out his giant beast. "Wasn't this supposed to be a punishment?"

"It was." Sliding out of her snug confinement, Duncan fixed Chris.

"Then we shouldn't touch her." Sniggering in his usual malevolent way, he wrenched her shoulders and rolled her over until her nose was in front of his erection. "Just have her service us while we have fun."

Great! That was all she needed! With her cunt on fire, Chris could not have thought of a worst form of punishment. But then, the dastardly demon knew it, at least judging from his extremely satisfied snarl as Duncan pulled him closer to the edge of the mattress.

"You won't last very long like this, Angel." Chuckling, the prince aimed for the narrow ring between his buttocks. "Not if I take your ass, and she sucks your cock."

"I'll take my chances." Splaying his legs far apart, Chris made her kneel by his side, gripping her neck to prevent her from going anywhere that was not on his stick. "Besides, this slave of yours isn't all that good anyway."

Sure, he was baiting her on purpose. Still, it grated on her nerves and prompted her to double her efforts to please him. Then Duncan stuffed his rear with his very slick monster, and both her ass and cunt pounded with the frantic need to have something filling them as well.

"Doesn't seem so." Up Chris's guts, Duncan's enormous equipment found no obstacles on its way. "From the way you're holding her neck, it seems you don't want to miss a second of her mouth."

"Not really." Gagging her good and proper, Chris forced

her to swallow his entire thick length. "Just putting up a good show for your sake alone."

And killing your slave in the process, she taunted, trying to fight off the giant tip wanting to choke her.

As I recall, he already tried that. Duncan seemed to have fun mocking her. *But he didn't quite succeed.*

Then a sense of deep caring flooded her, which told her he was just kidding.

"Don't waste your time on her, lover." At his next hip swing, she was ready for him and blocked his cock between her cheeks, rewarding it with a hard suck that had Chris groaning. "I'm sure she's complaining about how cruel I am to her."

"Her thought exactly." From Duncan's tone, she supposed he was wondering whether Chris had read her mind, or if it was just a lucky guess. "But the real waste is to leave that magnificent ass of hers unattended." His beefy shaft was so deep inside Chris that she could not see where one ended and the other began.

"Don't remind me." A definite twitch in Chris's erection signaled how interested he was about it.

Something Duncan had no trouble noticing, even if he played it like he had not.

So she continued to asphyxiate on the monster sliding down her throat, while the prince beat Chris's behind until it had stretched enough to accommodate ten more cocks the size of Duncan's. Eyes glued to the erection screwing in and out of the constricted opening, she became wetter and wetter just seeing what it was doing to Chris's rear. Amazing to say the least, the fierceness with which Prince Caldwell rammed was turning what once was a narrow channel into a bottomless pit. And it was exquisite. She just wished someone, anyone, would take pity on her and impale anyone of her holes with the same ruthlessness —

"Oh, fuck!" Sounding irritated with himself, Chris let go of her neck and grabbed her from the waist. "Why did you have to remind me?"

She caught Duncan suppressing a grin as the demon had her squatting on his flat belly.

"Need some help?" Without any effort, the prince raised her up in the air, holding onto her hips.

"Sure." He shifted his position, wrapping a palm around his piece to keep it straight. "Don't want her ass to get anywhere—"

"Except on your cock." Pressing her to his chest, Duncan clasped her waist and dropped her down over the tip of Chris's erection.

"Right." Then she nearly burst from the violence of Chris's rear stuffing.

To no avail, she tried breaking away. Prince Caldwell's iron hold did not allow her to budge. She could just sit tight while the odious demon cracked her open in his penetration to her throat. Or so it seemed, since he did not halt once, not even to give her time to adjust to the giant beast enlarging her all together, all at once.

"Better?" His hand slipping down between her legs, Duncan stroked her clit.

And everything became pure bliss, the pain in her backside replaced by the prince's velvety touch on the dripping knot that was closer to exploding than she had realized.

"For her certainly," Chris growled not too happy with the prince's initiative. "You're always too good to her, lover," he snorted.

"Actually, I'm just thinking of you." With an unexpected move, he pushed her forward and drove her head on Chris's.

With no choice in the matter, she had no way to avoid her lips from touching the demon's.

And things simply spun out of any control.

Not because he did not want her kiss. Because the harder he battled against her tongue, the deeper she sank into him, into his core it seemed. And his taste was so intoxicating she was getting lost in it, wondering how his mere kiss could make her tremble worse than his cock splitting her ass.

Too mind boggling to dwell on it, she continued darting her tongue simply to defy him, which made him all the more furious that he was actually kissing a woman and all the more inebriating. It was her small revenge for the bastardly way he pounded her behind like he wanted to destroy it and captured her tongue like it was the spoils of an undeclared war.

And she just could not stand the pressure. Thrown overboard by the jumble of sensations, she lost all perceptions of herself. Not at a physical level, for her body had never been closer to an orgasm. At a mental level mostly, since her mind was reaching out for both Duncan and Chris, coiling around them as though she wanted to connect them more than they already were.

The first contraction of her most shattering climax to date did just that. It opened a new channel between the prince and the demon. Using the cooler strength to shield herself from the blinding fire, she fused their raw energy together and made them touch for the very first time.

Completely stunned, both Chris and Duncan stopped moving, but it was already too late.

The tide swept them away just as she came for the second time, her scream trapped inside Chris's mouth exactly like the first one. This created a vortex that whirled everything together, especially the two male essences now flowing into one another as though all barriers between them had suddenly dissolved.

On the physical side of it all, her flesh clenching convulsively around Chris's equipment had squeezed it dry, much like the demon had done to the prince, both unable to contain the loads spurting in powerful jets from their stiff pieces. And only once it was over, did she release them.

Her energy depleted, body spent yet mind alert, she collapsed on Chris's chest. Duncan fell next to them, as breathless and as exhausted as she was.

Not enough, though, for his deep voice to ring out loud and clear, "Is this just sex?"

CHAPTER FIFTY-ONE

"No, it isn't *just sex*." Standing in front of a desk in the High Council's chamber, Arthur regarded his three guests, Chris and Duncan seated at opposite ends from each other with Ylianor dividing them. "It's a lot more, as you're just beginning to discover."

"Then it's true." Chris sat straighter. "I mean this energy business that she's been telling us about?"

"Power and energy are as much a reality as the chair you sit on or the food you eat." His heart tightened and he had to take a brief pause.

This always happened whenever he was around Christopher Templeton, the most beautiful and desirable man he had ever had the misfortune of laying eyes on. The most taken, too, since his heart belonged to another, had always belonged to another as far back as the farthest lifetime he could glimpse. So it was all the more stupid for an old fool like him to fall as hard and as deep as he had.

But there seemed to be no way around it. He loved Christopher Templeton like he had never loved anybody in his entire life. And no, all this business about energy and Virt had nothing to do with it, for Christopher Templeton was someone worth having even had he been without the slightest shred of power. Which was hardly the case, since he was the most powerful man around . . .

Well, almost.

Shifting his gaze away from the attentive blue-gray eyes, he trained it on the incredibly intelligent black ones. "Our ancestors called it Virt, a term sadly obsolete since there's no one left to train people in what is erroneously mistaken as magic or black arts." And maybe it was better this way. He could just imagine how difficult it would be to manage many Virts all at once. "No, there's nothing supernatural about it. Virt is just the ability to wield the same energy making up our lives, bending or using it according to the individual's very personal capabilities." He wanted to drive the concept into them.

Into Duncan mostly.

"Or so it was in the olden days. Now, thanks to superstition and unfounded beliefs, they have lost the ancient ways, so most of them don't know a thing about Virt, energy or power, not even if it's their own." *And that's both a blessing and a curse.* "The only sure thing is that people aren't aware of Virt until later in life." He braced himself for he had to glance at Chris again. "Except for the two of you that is." Quickly, he broadened his focus to include Ylianor. "Cases like yours have never happened to my knowledge." Which was not just his, rather the sum of all the leaders that had guided the High Council since the beginning of time. "Knowing and using your Virts from childhood is something so unique it defies explanations, for people never know of their power until they're fully grown."

That he was in the presence of three extraordinary people, he had no doubt. And if two seemed extraordinary for having managed such an incredible amount of Virt far longer than anyone who had ever walked the land, the third was equally exceptional, if not more. Not just because he was indeed the most powerful man around. Or would be once he trained his amazing Virt properly. Mostly because he had called to him the only two people who possessed an aware Virt at such an early age.

"You knew all about it?" Blue-gray eyes widening in surprise, Chris stared at him with a mix of fascination and pre-occupation crossing his face. "About my Virt, I mean?"

"Of course I knew, my dear boy." *Why else do you think the sex has been so extreme here at the Hall since you arrived?*

When the young adolescent had thrown himself in his arms, devastated by the loss of his phase mate, he had not just fallen in love. He had also seen how dangerous the break-up made a young and highly explosive, highly inflammable man, who was capable of blowing up the world just to soothe his shattered heart. And he lacked the power to control him. That belonged to one alone, same man who was sitting in front of him, his face so intent Arthur knew he did not want to miss a single word.

No, no one in this world had what it took to curb Chris's destructive side, save for Prince Duncan Caldwell. And since Duncan was the reason servants had left a very unstable Chris alone in one of the Hall's third-class waiting rooms, he could only count on his greater experience and on the sex to avoid sure tragedy.

So he had stepped up the sex in his boys, a harmless group who had fun sometimes but never as wild as since Chris joined them. He had fueled up everything, unavoidably he guessed for one made up only of fire, to the point that his boys now had a reputation they never had in the past. And that had kept Chris's energy sated and innocuous, at least for a time.

"It's my job to know." Not to mention another of the things he had inherited from his Fitting, the ceremony that had sealed his position as Leader of the High Council.

"But you never said anything about it." The lovely blue-gray eyes flashed in protest.

"What was the point?" His gaze caressed the beloved face. "A leader's main responsibility is to recognize people's Virts, whether asleep or fully awakened. Yours, my dear boy, was never hard to miss, not even when you were a toddler." He smiled ruefully at the memory of the child with the shiny hair, running around the Hall, cursing again the cruel destiny that had decreed to make them meet at such mismatched ages. "And even if today it attracts a lot of people, it has nothing to do with them or with me for that matter." He embraced the three-young people seated in front of him with a single glance. "You see, one thing to understand about energy is that it's a flow that usually requires two or more people in order to work. In fact, for many, the second person is essential to awaken it." Then he returned his focus on Chris. "Your fire, for instance, is never at its peak unless you're with Duncan." And that was as unfair as it could get. Regardless of all he knew about the handsome prince, he could not help feeling jealous of him, which proved what a foolish old man he had become. "The prince is the one who holds the key to your Virt—"

"And its control," was Ylianor's soft intervention.

"How perfectly right you are, my dear girl." A sad note veiled his voice.

He had stopped counting the times he had wished he could master his blond lover's fire. Not his call for sure, nor his privilege, just his duty to make sure that towering fire of his did not incinerate the world in a fit of rage.

"So we really have no choice in the matter." Annoyed, Duncan gestured nervously. "The way you make it sound, the angel and I are in it only for the energy, not for the relationship at all."

"Dear prince, you chose Chris long before you were born, before being aware of all this energy business as Chris called it." *And I do so wish things had gone differently in this lifetime.* "You two connected in a time long forgotten to share many lifetimes together, and it was always a free choice on both sides."

"If that's true, why couldn't I awaken his Virt?" Vexed,

Chris glanced at Ylianor.

"There are no rational explanations to energy and power, much as there are none for emotions like love." *Like my love for you, splendid angel-demon who has not just changed my life forever, but that of the entire Hall as well.* "Things happen because there are special bonds, most born before time or space. Most you ignore at a conscious level, only feel them at an instinctive one. So don't think you weren't good enough, rather that the Elspeth women alone have the power to awaken the Caldwell's gift." Trying to soothe Chris's disappointment was near impossible.

And his heart went out to him, wishing he had better explanations to offer.

"So don't worry about it, my dear boy." If anything, Chris always looked more beautiful than ever when a scowl crossed his face. "Just know you have a powerful bond of your own with Duncan, from which you benefit more now that she awakened him."

Prince Caldwell leaned forward. "So there are no set rules about when and how Virt can become active."

"Exactly." From the somber expression in the black eyes, he deducted that Duncan was analyzing all the latest information he was providing. "It's an entirely personal affair that depends on the Virt itself and the person carrying it." His attention trained on the prince for it was the priority of this meeting that he, above the others, understood. "As I said, a leader's responsibility is to monitor energy flows, making sure they never get out of control."

"Then I guess a leader uses the High Council to help him with this delicate task." Duncan fixed him intently. "Right?"

"In a way . . ." One thing about Duncan Caldwell—he was not just highly intelligent. He was also highly perceptive. "At least that's how it worked before Virt became neglected and untrained, something to be feared or to be ashamed of, a liability instead of an asset. Which doesn't mean we can't return to the old ways one day." Though frankly, seeing how the situation had degenerated, he was not sure it would improve matters at all. "Should that become possible, it would be very important to have members with Virts of their own to contribute to the leader's own supply, and the more powerful the easier the leader's task." This he added for Chris's sake. "Your father, Duncan, was an excellent energy reserve, just like you. In fact, his seat is waiting for you to fill it, so when are you planning on reading his will?"

Such was the customary practice for the permanent members' succession. When one died, the son or daughter could not take over until after reading the will that nominated him or her as the official heir. And he presumed Charles had nominated Duncan over Elizabeth.

"At the end of the summer." The prince shifted on his seat. "So I'll be sure to be here for next year's sessions."

If not sooner. "Yes, I understand." He nodded gravely. "Just remember that you have a greater responsibility, since your Virt is more powerful than your father's ever was."

"Why?" Puzzled, Prince Caldwell creased his forehead.

"Because, unlike Charles, you don't give it away to just anyone, only to carefully chosen people." And Christopher Templeton had always been his first and for a long time, his only choice. "So you keep a larger supply of it, which makes it more powerful. And you're extremely selective, Prince. I couldn't help noticing it while you were looking for a pledge mate, which you didn't find even if women are particularly attracted to you."

"With his looks, who wouldn't?" Chris teased, shaking his head in amusement, yet avoiding intercepting Duncan's gaze.

"Not just a question of looks." He pursed his lips. "His power has a lot to do with why women are attracted to him."

"Then they're in for a disappointment," Chris snickered. "'Cause his aristocratic taste keeps most of them away."

Of course, this pleased Chris way beyond what his satisfied tone implied.

"That's exactly the point, and that's what you have to change." He made it sound imperative. "My dear prince, I know you've given access to this abundant supply of yours to Chris alone so far." His tone became very serious, "But you have too much of it to channel it through a single person alone, no matter how powerful he may be." Glancing over to where Chris sat, he noticed Duncan immediately looking away.

So the woman had made them touch more intimately than they ever had. It was bound to happen given Ylianor's type of Virt. He was just surprised it had not happened sooner.

"I've been worried about you, Duncan, particularly when you broke up with the only one who had access to it at the time." He shook his head to emphasize how dangerous the situation could have become. "That's why I had to arrange for you two to get back together."

Actually, this was just one part of it. The main one was that he could not handle Chris anymore. No, after two years' worth of pushing sex to a level it had never reached before in the Hall, during Carl Strepton's pledge reception he had realized Chris was nearing another breaking point. And nothing could prevent him from lashing out this time except for Prince Duncan Caldwell, who again was the primary motivation for Chris's second near-loss of control.

"Arrange?" Duncan and Chris asked together surprised, exchanging glances in spite of their embarrassment.

"Yes, arrange." He chuckled. "The event I had Chris organize the night you reunited was for your sakes alone."

"You mean, all those people, the party . . ." Chris flared. "Everything was just for us?"

"Yes, for both your Virts are unique." His legs now tired, he leaned against the desk for support. "But can become dangerous if left alone —"

"Then why don't you train them, instead of relying on your intervention?" Prince Caldwell challenged annoyed.

"I should, shouldn't I?" He grinned. "If only that kind of knowledge wasn't buried with our ancestors." Somewhere so deep not even the Fitting had been able to retrieve it. "Besides, some Virts are so uncontrollable and dangerous I'm not sure any amount of training could curb them." His gaze swung to Chris. "Like yours, my dear boy."

"You mean . . ." Chris blushed violently. "You knew about . . . the dark side, too?"

"I've always known." *From the moment you stepped in here, I knew you'd be slicing people up just to silence that deep void and hurt your prince charming left behind when he broke up with you.*

Just another of the reason sex had to be so extreme in his boys, though he had known from the beginning it would appease Chris only so much.

"Then, since you seem to know all about it, please explain it properly." Chris raised his chin defiantly, the blue-gray eyes brimming with suppressed fire.

"You know, through the years we've been together, I've kept careful watch over you." Every day and every night of the two-year separation from Duncan, he had made it his priority to have Chris under his personal surveillance. Servants had to report on his every move during the day, while the nights he always managed to keep Chris in his bed the whole nightlong, to the point the entire Hall gossiped about his very obvious favoritism for the blond Templeton. He had not given a damn, not even when James Templeton had seemed concerned about his son's habits at the Hall. How could he tell James that his son would have blown up the entire world had he not seen to it that he did not?

So he had invented new rules for his boys to suit Chris's taste for pain, like the one about the man who could take the most abuse at the attic won the chance to sleep with him. *And what do you know?*

Chris won every time.

Hardly surprising! Whenever Christopher Templeton was around, there could be no competition in sex. As a giver or a taker, he was the best, no question about it.

"Not just for personal reasons." *Because I simply love you so damn much!* "Mostly because I wanted to study up close a Virt I've heard only from ancient traditions." This is where the Fitting proved invaluable. "Which is the rare ability to combine both positive and negative energy. And though you come from a very powerful family, no one else to my knowledge can blend these two opposite forces as easily and as effortlessly as you can." He paused to let the information sink in on their own. "That fiery core of yours is capable of the most opposite things. From healing to destroying, you can go either way faster than the bat of an eye. That's why you crave pain and pleasure in equal measures, and that's also why I never told anyone about it, not even your father—"

"He never cared for me anyway," Chris spat bitterly. "He only thinks of Steve—"

"Not true." He knew it for a fact, considering how many times James had come to him to inquire about his son's wellbeing.

For the one thing Chris had steadfastly refused to do was have a relationship with his father. And to think that for the past two years and a half they had lived under the Hall's same roof!

"Your father is a valued member of the council." Even though he knew he was wasting his breath, he had to set the record straight once again. "He is the vice-leader and a close friend of mine, as you already know."

Chris did not just *know it*. He had taken full advantage of his father's position, and with particular cunning and intelligence had used it to rise straight to the top of the Hall's hierarchy.

Which for one so young was no small feat, and he still wondered how his blond lover had learned to master so many tricks in such brief time.

"Your father is also very gifted and has pledged to someone equally powerful," he continued. "That's why he believed the firstborn would inherit all the family's Virt. Too bad that wasn't the case. Both your brothers are fine men but with no Virt at all." He folded his arms on his chest as he leaned back further against the desk. "Still, he insists that Steve should inherit the Templeton's High Council's seat —"

"He can have it!" Chris scoffed. "I don't particularly care for it, and you know it."

"That seat should be yours." *And not because I could fuck your brains out in an official capacity for once.* "Because you have the power and the responsibility."

"Tell that to my father," Chris sneered resentfully.

"James Templeton is a good man." Gaze locked on the blue-gray eyes, he tried pulling his young lover into their personal dimension. "I don't mean to justify him, but he's found it very difficult to deal with a son like you. You see, even if he has a similar Virt, he could never express it to its full potential because he lacked the proper connection, at least from a certain point on . . ."

The point when he, James and Charles had crossed paths and linked in ways that were impossible to predict, particularly now with John and Charles's sons picking up right where their fathers had left off so long ago.

With a sigh, he returned to the present. "Anyway, what he feels now, and perhaps fears, is how different you are from his other sons. And he has trouble accepting it."

"I'm bad, I know." Dejectedly, Chris lowered his gaze. "Only with my phase mate, I seem to redeem myself."

"No, don't blame yourself for using your Virt and causing suffering on others." He had to force himself to keep still while his every instinct screamed at him for not running to Chris's side and hugging him tight. "All your so-called victims are in search of a painful experience, even if they might not be aware of it. Their only perception is that you give them something unique and even if they forget the details, the general feeling remains long after the experience is over. That's why they keep wanting you."

"So my good looks have nothing to do with it?" Chris joked.

His heart plunged to his stomach, where he silenced its painful throbbing. "I'd be a liar if I said they didn't." He smiled ruefully. "As with Duncan, it's a combination of both looks and power that makes the two of you so appealing and dangerous at the same time."

"Not dangerous enough it seems." Mocking with a half-serious tone, Chris switched his focus on Ylianor. "To keep everyone out of our way."

"Ylianor is another matter entirely, my dear boy." He turned to Prince Caldwell. "When your father started talking about a Mary Jane Elspeth, I told him to leave her alone, thinking she'd steal his energy like most everyone else he felt attracted to. And Mary Jane seemed more dangerous than most for she had a Virt of her own, which is why I told him to keep away. When he didn't take heed, I didn't get overly concerned, not even when he couldn't tear himself away from her side." Straightening up, he took the few steps that separated him from where the woman sat. "Your mother was quite beautiful from what I remember."

"You knew her, Leader?" Wide-eyed, the startling green

gaze fixed on him.

"Not exactly. I only saw her once at Black Rose, but I could never forget her." He caressed her cheek. "That's why, when I became aware that he could head talk and share feelings, I knew it had to be Mary Jane's doing. And I was real happy that Charles had finally found the one to awaken his Virt, even if the thing in itself had nothing extraordinary. So I didn't take serious notice of the situation until he informed me that Mary Jane was pregnant. From the start, he told me he had the strange notion the child might be his, which was impossible under any circumstances. And since Mary Jane had pledged to John Meyer, Charles's claim seemed even more absurd, though never as much as his new link to the little girl, which to all extent, was stronger than the one he shared with her mother. At that point, I could no longer ignore the possibility of a relation. Certainly not a blood one, still something powerful and unexplainable connected you to Charles." With a finger under her chin, he tilted up her face. "Are you his child?" He studied her face for a while as if it could answer him. "I still don't know. The only certainty is that you have powerful gifts of your own and like Chris, you discovered them early in life, not surprisingly when growing up with Duncan."

"But I can't remember her in my early years," the prince snorted in frustration. "And we lost sight of each other for the better part of ten years." His black eyes flashed. "Did you also arrange for me to be lost, so I could connect with her again?" Sarcastic, his voice sounded edgy as if he felt deceived.

"Prince Caldwell, please." He let her face go. "Don't feel betrayed—"

"Point of fact, Leader, I feel manipulated by this energy business, by this Virt thing, by her, by you or whatever you represent!" Fuming, Duncan's tone was angrier than the occasion required.

"No, believe me." He raised his hand to calm him down. "It's part of my job—"

"It seems you haven't been doing it properly, Lord Fairchild," the prince retorted. "If someone like Ylianor escaped your notice for so long."

"Were it only that easy to determine what's important among the million lights and sounds flashing and booming in my head." He heaved. "You're quite right, Prince. It was my responsibility, and I failed in a way. I'm just relieved that it hasn't prevented her from awakening your Virt."

"Is that all she's good for?" However light Chris's tone, he did not think he was joking.

"No." *Unfortunately for you.*

He could totally relate to Chris's jealousy. He himself would have obliterated the gorgeous dark-haired man if it meant having Chris's love all for him, if it meant erasing the dark-haired prince from his young lover's heart and mind. Which was as impossible an illusion as hoping Christopher Templeton could ever stop loving Prince Duncan Caldwell.

"She's an integral part of you, Duncan." Resigned, he suppressed all those malevolent thoughts, incompatible with his role as a leader. "Like with Chris, I believe you forged the ties with Ylianor in another time and space, the same ones that pulled you together in this life as well, despite your . . . hem . . . loss of memory." He glanced at Chris briefly, who averted his gaze as if ashamed. "And I had nothing to do with your meeting Ylianor again. You found her on your own the moment you needed a new channel."

"But why use sex to awaken his gift?" No matter what his explanation, it was kind of obvious it grated on Chris's nerves, to the point he could not let it slide.

"Sex is a powerful exchange of energy, a deep sharing at all levels." He walked back to the desk. "Where physical intimacy often leads to mental connections faster than any other method."

"A training ground so to speak?" Duncan mused to no one in particular, while the black eyes glimmered in understanding.

"Exactly, Prince." He had to applaud him. "It can and should be that, too." The ghost of a smile curved his lips. "It's a pity very few people realize what they're really doing during sex."

"I think we're well aware of what we do in bed." Chris grinned ironic.

"Only since Ylianor came along." He chided. "Her gift is unique. Aura tracing isn't common among our people. And like you, Duncan, she's selective about her channels. Am I correct, child?"

"Yes, Leader." She bowed her head shyly. "Only with Duncan and his father have I been able to head talk and share things."

Extremely curious about a Virt he had heard from traditions alone, Lord Fairchild bent her way. "Tell me about aura perception."

"It can be very confusing at times . . ." She shook her head, her long hair falling around her shoulders. "Like when there are a lot of people . . ." Hesitant, she pushed out a heavy breath of air. "Because their lights flash like crazy and blind me." Then she raised her gaze. "Because to me, I see everyone surrounded by lights that wave according to their moods, and the impressions I get from it are sharper than just seeing their physical being."

"And these lights form a pattern, am I right?" At her nod, he went on, "So you could trace their passage through time and space."

"Perhaps . . ." Her eyes clouded as though she had never thought of using it for quite such purpose. "If I practiced."

"Yes, of course, practice is the key to true understanding." Lifting his gaze, he looked at the three assembled before him. "And you'll have plenty of time to train while you go about your task."

"Our task?" Duncan raised a skeptical brow.

"Someone has put our precious way of life in danger." *Someone who should've minded her own damn business instead of asking stupid questions all the time.* "Risking the natural flow of things by stealing something of value from the Nephis Valley."

"What's there to steal in the pledge's sacred valley?" Duncan stared at him.

Understandable the prince's bafflement, for their world blocked off all forms of adult violence. Except for Chris's that is, which was something so unreal and bewildering there was no explanation, not even by sifting through all the previous leaders' awareness.

"I suggest you three go there, find out exactly what is missing and who took it." This was as much as he was prepared to reveal at the moment. "Then retrieve it and return it to its assigned place." His commanding tone left no doubt he was giving a direct order. "It's a vital mission for our survival that will take all your combined skills and energy, which is why you have to stick together no matter what."

Speaking as Leader of the High Council, he knew they could not ignore his call, so he was satisfied when Duncan, Chris and Ylianor bowed their heads in acceptance.

"You'll need to work together as a team." And that was a task in itself. "And use your different yet complementary Virts, which will prove to be invaluable assets if you work as one. Only if truly united will you be able to face and defeat the dangers ahead. Duncan . . ." Striding to his side, he squeezed the young man's shoulder. "You'll be their leader, the mind of this threesome." Then he moved to the woman. "Ylianor is the spirit." And finally, he reached his beloved and clasped his hand. "And Chris . . ." His heart crushed painfully as he gazed at the stunning blond who would soon leave him alone again. "He's the body, the fiery energy directed by a sound mind and an aware spirit. Is everything clear?"

Duncan caught Chris's gaze first, then Ylianor's as though asking for their agreement. "It is, Leader," he announced gravely for all.

"Good!" Reluctantly unclasping Chris's hand, he returned to the desk. "Then get ready to leave immediately. Time is not your friend and the faster you move, the easier you'll accomplish your task." He watched the three rise from their seats. "And may the gods be with you."

For they would need all the help they could get!

CHAPTER FIFTY-TWO

" All right you two, it's time to talk." As bothersome as a pesky fly, Ylianor maneuvered Starlet between Fuzeon and Black.

"Arthur explained everything already," he retorted. "What's more to say?"

Besides the fact I'd have never wanted to be in this situation or in the one before this, kissing the damn witch and loving it, opening up like a phase first timer until she was so deep inside him she dragged his lover right in with her.

And they had fucking touched! Him and Duncan! Not their bodies. Their goddamn minds! And everything else, as all barriers had fallen away to pull them as close as no two bodies could ever be. And there was no describing the sensation or the embarrassment.

Now on the way to the Jeruashi Mountains, gateway to the Nephis Valley, he avoided direct eye contact and continued to keep his distance from Duncan, the same he had stuck to in the Hall's chamber where Arthur had piled so many information on him, he was still staggering from the weight of them all.

"I meant what happened before the lecture." Her mouth curved in amusement, as though he were a little boy who needed a reminder about what his father expected him to do. "The leader asked for our help as a team, but we can't work together if you two won't even look at each other."

No, she would not convince him, no matter how sound her argument. So he continued to fix the high snowy peaks in front of him, without even bothering to give a reply.

"All right, let's talk hierarchies." With a loud sigh, she pushed out a heavy breath of air. "Chris, if the prince is our leader as Lord Fairchild said, do you think it appropriate that you ignore him?"

He stole a peek in his lover's direction, quickly averting his gaze before Duncan caught him.

"Come on, Chris," she insisted. "Aren't you tired of playing games? Didn't we agree to be open and honest with each other?"

Fuck, no!

Still, he nodded.

"Then it's time we grow up and face our issues as adults, not act as children," her voice lowered a notch, sounding way too patronizing for his taste.

So why didn't she just shut the fuck up?

"If we are to accomplish anything of what the leader told us, we have to keep communication flowing among us." She glanced first at him, then at Duncan. "Which is exactly what you're not doing." Evidently irked by their persistent silence, she worked hard at staying calm. "Maybe, I'm going at it all wrong. Maybe you've never really known each other, in spite of all you've shared in and out of bed," she teased lightly. "So the first step is for you two to get a proper introduction."

"Ha! As if all the previous ones don't count!" Chris sneered ironically.

"They obviously don't," she quipped.

"Look, dearie, we've done things that would embarrass a beginner like yourself." A nasty snarl crossed his lips.

"You could've had sex standing upside down for all I care." Still, she blushed violently, as though she was actually seeing them at it. "But it hasn't taught you how to meet spirit to spirit. And even if you don't share thoughts, I know the two of you exchange some kind of coded signal, which is what I used to connect you on the inside."

Damn! The woman might just be right!

Reluctantly, he gave her his full attention. And what do you know?

"If we have this code between us, how can we recognize it?" These were the prince's first words since leaving the Hall! "Where do we begin?"

"Well . . ." She frowned as if unsure of how to go about it until a flash lit her green eyes. "Think back at the first time you laid eyes on each other, that summer day at Black Rose. Do you remember it?"

"Of course." How could he ever forget it?

If he lived to be a hundred, it would still be impressed in his memory, as clear and sharp as when it had happened.

And the same was true for Duncan, at least judging from his expression.

"Why did you know it was special right when it happened?" She tightened her hold on Starlet's reins. "I mean you were aware that it wasn't just a chance meeting. You were aware that it was the most important meeting of your lives right while it was taking place."

"We did?" The memories surfacing all at once were jumbling up things.

"Of course, you did." Her voice grew more hypnotic, "That's when you chose to travel life together. For you, Chris, it was a revelation, which is why your aura changed from dark to light at the blink of an eye. Remember?"

Again, how could he forget turning that bend in Black Rose and confronting the most handsome boy he had ever set eyes on? With the raven black hair fluttering in the ocean's gusty breeze, black liquid eyes catching his gaze as though expecting him, full lips curved in the hint of a smile and somber expression that read him right down to the core — Duncan Caldwell had not just heard him arrive over the sea's loud crashing waves. He had been ready to lift the load of fury he had carried all the way from Fair Haven to Black Rose and dissolve it in thin air, like smoke in the wind.

"You were waiting for me, lover!" Why had he never thought of it before? "Yet no one had told you I was coming, right?"

"If anyone knew, they didn't bother telling me," Duncan confirmed, his forehead creased in concentration. "Or maybe Father had known, but he was at the beginning of his illness and already confined to his room, so it might have slipped his mind."

"So how did you know I was coming?" Even more amazing, he could have sworn he had heard Duncan calling him *brother*, claiming him as his own, and it had made all the difference. "How do you always anticipate my every move?"

So that was the key!

When awareness hit him, he felt the dark prince inside him. No embarrassment this time as their energy touched, he accepted the new presence, surrendering completely to it.

"Because I claimed you that summer day, exactly like you remember." Wrapping around his fiery essence, Duncan squeezed him tight.

"Then it's true." To give it words seemed useless, but he needed to say it anyway. "I am *yours*."

"You are." There was all the possessiveness and erotic undertone to make him want to jump off Black and kiss him right there and then. "And I can track you down 'cause you send me a ..." Duncan paused as though in search of the right word, one that would make sense in the real world anyway. "Wave, I suppose, and I've learned to decode it somehow."

"Your Virts must've allowed you to recognize the kindred spirit in one another the first time you met," she added in a soft tone.

After all the mean things he had told her about being an

expert, her voice had lost that teacher-like inflexion he had found so terrible.

"Now concentrate on the wave." She beamed at him as though she had read his unspoken compliment. "Do you see it?"

Closing his eyes, he focused on it. Boy, did it look incredible and more resembling a bridge than a beam. Sharply designed, it connected his self to Duncan's and shone whenever one of the two sent a signal. And since it never dimmed, he guessed it was a permanent signal, something neither him nor his phase mate ever turned off, not even once.

Which made perfect sense and explained the tight bond that not even a two-year separation had succeeded in severing. And that was the most awesome part of it all. The part that proved, beyond a doubt, his love for Duncan was real.

And the incredible rush of emotions caused by such an awareness overwhelmed him. Surging to the top, it drowned his senses. Pumping through his blood, it shot straight to his heart and head, until it flooded the bridge with the violence of it all. It was too much.

The joy, the sheer happiness, the love, the attraction and all the other stuff that had just blown him apart—it was simply too much to stand.

So he broke down.

With a gasp, he burst into tears. And as he sank deeper into the bottomless well of his feelings, he glimpsed the angry child he had once been, the same whose bitterness he had carried since that far away summer day. To think of all those years that had passed, and he was still not free of him, not free of all the anger and rage it had built up ever since his father had cast him off, like he needed punishment for some unknown crime. Which perhaps he did, seen how evil he could become. Or perhaps it had all been a false perception of his eight-year-old self, quick to judge his father at surface level alone, without considering all the proper variables first.

Either way, holding on to that fury made no sense now. He had to let it go.

So he did.

Crying his heart out, he slumped on Black just as Duncan's quiet strength curled tightly around him like a comforting blanket and held him in his embrace. Not just his energy, his body, too, for his strong arms were around his waist now.

"Come on, Angel." The prince pulled him to let go of Black. "I'll carry you." From atop the saddles, he made Chris slide on Fuzeon, settling him in the front. "Please, Princess, would you mind—"

"Not at all." Quick to grab Black's reins, she tied them to her saddle, before checking the area. "And I'll take you to the nearest shelter straight away."

Uncaring about anything else, he snuggled inside Duncan and lost track of time, which was irrelevant anyway. As the angry child's rage evaporated, his essence fused into the prince's, and he was inside the safest place he had ever known. And that was all that mattered.

CHAPTER FIFTY-THREE

"These mountains are going to kill me, lover." Riding single file on the edge of a narrow passageway skirting a massive rocky wall on one side, Chris glanced down at the steep drop into oblivion, had Black chanced to misplace his footing. "Literally."

She could totally relate.

Only consolation, this was a good day. On a bad day, she had to walk Starlet for the path was so restricted both rider and horse could easily slip to their death at the bottom of a sharp fall.

It had been like that ever since leaving the Hall about a week before. Rough going as she followed Duncan and Chris southward through the high white peaks, forced to go up and down like in an endless rollercoaster—first climbing the almost perpendicular rises to the top only to descend precipitously into green valleys. And their rich pine wood forests coiling up the slopes until low clouds hid them from view were no reward for all the effort it took just to get there, though maybe the shelters were. Not for the places themselves, rather for the opportunity to crash exhausted and assuage the fatigue with a deep, dreamless sleep.

Which left not just her, mostly Chris and Duncan, little or no time for sex, having to rely on fire alone to heat up their icy bodies at the end of a long day spent without the comfort of Stella's warm rays and with temperatures near freezing.

"If they won't do it, this forced sex deprivation will." The demon steered Black closer to Fuzeon given how the path had suddenly widened to plunge into a valley. "It's not fair that it's been so long since I've had your fabulous cock up my ass or down my throat." Grinning broadly, he flanked Fuzeon. "Too many fucking days that I've been too tired even to give you a proper goodnight kiss." Sounding like a disappointed child, Chris bit his lower lip, probably to stop it from trembling.

Well, one thing she had to hand him—the demon without sex was as unthinkable as his being without air.

"And what about our training?" His gaze broadened to Ylianor who had just moved next to Fuzeon's free side. "I was just beginning to get the hang of it and looking forward to finding new channels between us."

In spite of his jocular tone, she knew how deeply that liberating flood of tears had affected him. And the prince knew it as well, because he had crushed the demon against his impressive frame while carrying him on Fuzeon's back to the nearest shelter, wrapping that incandescent energy mass within his cooler one. Then he had linked to her and allowed her to feel what he felt about the most powerful connection of all. Like the amazement of touching the very fire he had always perceived whenever having sex with the tantalizing creature, and that now made it a reality over which he would need to keep watch. As Arthur had said, with power came responsibility, and she had no doubts he would take his seriously when it came to Christopher Templeton.

"You'd just love to find them, wouldn't you?" Duncan chuckled. "Imagine what you and I could do if we head talked."

"Oh, I've got quite a few ideas about that, which I haven't been able to test because of this damn traveling." Chris licking his lips like a satisfied cat that had caught the biggest mouse of all left her no doubt about what he meant. "Just give me the chance—"

"I was just getting to it, Angel." Duncan suppressed a cackle as though his impatient lover jumped ahead too fast, too soon.

A trait she was sure Duncan loved above all his others and hoped would never change.

"What would you want us to do?" Uneasy, she sat up straighter on her saddle.

"I would like to see if you can reach the angel." It sounded like a dare to her.

Which made it all the harder to resist, even if she knew better.

"Directly?" The fiendish demon would just love to strike her with that scalding fire of his! "I don't know . . ." She glanced at Chris. "Will he let me?"

"Why shouldn't he?" Duncan turned to the demon.

'Cause he hates me. And that was just for starters.

"Hey, I'm not going to bite." The way his lips curved in a vaguely threatening snarl, she wondered whether he had read her mind.

"It's not your bite I fear, rather . . ." *Your flames.*

"Princess, if you don't share information, we won't get anywhere. Remember what you told us?" Great, all she needed was for the prince to use her words against her. "Ours is a three-sided team, but so far only two sides are connected."

Tell that to your insufferable lover. "Well . . ." Not that she would give the odious demon any satisfaction by admitting how truly on edge she was. "To begin with, he doesn't want me to come close to him."

Chris's eyebrows shot upward. "I don't—"

"That's what you told us at the Hall," she retorted. "Remember?"

"I was angry then," Chris scoffed.

"But your feelings haven't really changed." Nor would

they ever as long as there was space for only one inside his heart. "And your lights are blinding enough as it is. Even if you were to want me, I don't think I could stand it."

"All right, Angel, promise you won't hurt her." From Duncan's brisk tone, it was kind of obvious he wanted to speed up matters. "Not intentionally anyway."

"I promise." Chris frowned, a funny look crossing his face.

"Now you can try reaching him while I'll monitor you." The black eyes swung in her direction. "If anything should go wrong, I'll pull you out."

Sure, and will you do it before or after I'm a pile of cinders?

No use sharing this thought with the prince, just like she had not all the previous ones. If he was right about insisting to tighten their link on every side, she could not forget that impenetrable wall of fire that was Christopher Templeton on the inside.

"All right, here I go." Closing her eyes, she had to calm her wildly beating heart.

It was one thing to talk about it, quite another to take the actual plunge. And his goading her was not helping any, his bright flames fluttering in the distance. Irresistible like an erotic dance, he taunted her to try it, to prove she was not afraid of him.

I'm not, Christopher Templeton! She would be damned if she backed down now. She would jump into that tantalizing fire if it were the last thing she would do. And if it killed her . . . well, it would serve them right!

Already, her cooler energy was cringing and scorching despite the distance. Which was nothing she needed to focus on. Her target was right in front of her, and she need not think of anything except to get to his core.

So she emptied her mind, fortified her heart and leapt straight into the flames.

CHAPTER FIFTY-FOUR

Princess, no! Seeing her take the first rushed step toward the giant enflamed pyre towering in the distance, he knew she was going for sure danger. *Wait!*

Ignoring the warning he yelled in her head, she ran forward to vault straight into the flames. Like she was responding to some unspoken dare and wanted to show him just what she was capable of achieving.

Only natural she could not sustain the extreme heat.

As the scream of pain reached his mind before it did his ears, he maneuvered Fuzeon to stop Starlet and catch her as she slumped on the horse's back.

"Let me help, lover." Quick to come to the rescue, Chris grabbed her on the other side, and together they laid her on the ground. "And before you start accusing me of anything, I swear I didn't touch her." The blond angel let go of the limp body. "Believe me. I didn't do anything."

"I know." His energy was already fast at work to awaken her and cool her burning spirit. "I was there, too." On his knees, he caressed her pale face concerned. "But you burned her all the same. As she feared, your aura is too blinding for her."

"Must be *her* problem." Staring on the opposite side of her, Chris frowned. "'Cause you seem all right with it."

"Don't play dumb, Angel." Wearily, he shook his head. "It really doesn't suit you, especially since you know she doesn't have my kind of Virt." He raised his gaze to lock it on the blue-gray one. "As she guessed, and Arthur confirmed, I alone can handle that irresistible fire of yours."

"Then why did she jump like she didn't know better?" Chris's argument sounded reasonable. "And before you get overly worried, she's not dying or anything. She just lost a lot of energy pulling that stupid stunt of hers."

Was it his impression or was there a note of admiration in Chris's tone?

"That's all." The hint of a smile curved his thin lips.

"All right." Glancing upward, he could swear this *stupid stunt of hers* had impressed Chris far beyond what he was willing to admit. "Now pass me the water." His attention focusing back on her, his energy coiled more tightly around her and replenished what she had drained during her confrontation. "And let's get her back on her feet." As soon as Chris complied, he sprinkled some drops of water on her face until she regained consciousness. "Princess, welcome back!" Raising her head gently and pushing away her long strands of hair, he cradled her to his chest. "How do you feel?"

"Dizzy, thank you." Slurred voice, she coughed as if her body was having trouble setting back in motion. "I must've fainted."

"You sure did." Chris grinned smugly.

"Come on." He hauled her up slowly. "Let's see if you can at least sit up." With great care, he raised her to an upright position. "And maybe drinking will help." Handing her the water, he watched as she gulped it down. "Good." Pressing her head to him, he stroked her long hair. "And now you have to rest." Not trusting her strength, he held her tightly. "We must be close to a shelter anyway . . ." Though he was at a loss to say just where it might have been.

"It's right up our path," she whispered huskily. "About five miles down the road, to the left."

"Wow, talk about a snappy comeback." Amazed and

amused at the same time, Chris smiled warmly.

"I'd rather talk about Virt." Evidently, and as Arthur had observed, her aura reading had far-reaching potentials, some of which she was just learning to recognize now. "And since it's just a few miles away, I'll carry you, Princess."

"No, thanks." She shook her head defiantly. "I think I can manage."

"That wasn't a suggestion." Straightening, he clasped her hand to pull her upright. "It was an order."

"He's right." Taking her other hand, the angel helped set her on her feet again. "You're too weak to ride."

"No, I . . ." Stubbornly, she held on to her claim.

But when both he and Chris let her go, her bluff crumbled miserably, and she had to grab them back just to keep from falling.

I said — you ride with me, and that's final. After mounting on Fuzeon, he pulled her up behind him.

And she was so relieved she leaned on his back for support.

I'm sorry, Princess. He squeezed the arms she had circled around his waist. *I didn't realize he could be so dangerous for you.*

I told you he doesn't want me. And she would have sounded a lot angrier had she not been so weary.

But maybe, just maybe, Chris was not the object of this anger of hers.

He has to accept me before he gives me access to his inner self, her soft voice boomed in his head.

Then why did you jump without taking any heed? The angel's question seemed all the more justified. *Not even mine.*

Still, he did not have the heart to ask her outright. Partly because it would take too long to get a precise answer out of her, and she was too tired for that. Mostly because there was something about the dynamics he was noticing between Chris and Ylianor that he needed to analyze and comprehend, before he made any sort of reasonable guess on what was going on between them.

And even if he does, I don't know. She shrugged helplessly. *Maybe the only way we can establish a link is through you since his light doesn't affect you.*

You're wrong. The shiver running down his back on touching the fiery power at his side was proof enough. *I'm as much a victim of his attraction as is everyone else, if not more.* A rush of excitement coursed through his blood as images of his angel's naked body flashed through his mind.

You know what I mean! She slapped his back affectionately. *And you're just lucky he hasn't played his scary game with you.*

Something about the lightheartedness of her tone reminded him that *his scary game* had not turned her off entirely, which was not just surprising. It was plain odd.

Anyway, we could devise a way of being together through you. He could tell she was getting excited at the mere idea.

Yes, but we'll think of it tomorrow. Given her condition, there would be no more training at least for the rest of the day. *Now you need to rest, and that's another order.*

His energy slowly spread through Ylianor, and she drowned and surrendered her residual strength, to the point that when they reached the shelter, she was fast asleep.

CHAPTER FIFTY-FIVE

"I hope she feels better in the morning." Glancing at her limp form in Duncan's arms, he followed inside the shelter. *And good riddance for tonight!*

It was just about as much as he could have taken.

For the damn witch had done it again! Jumping on him like she had the first time he had ever set foot at Black Rose and in both cases without his slightest provocation. Yet Duncan seemed to blame him anyway, as though it were his fault!

Which it was *not*!

"Do you really care?" Sarcastic, the prince sounded deliberately offensive.

So he lost it.

"You're right," he spat. "I don't!" Nor would he ever! "Why should I?" Barely keeping his voice down, he watched Duncan lay his precious princess in bed. "In case you haven't noticed, I had nothing to do with it. She did it all by herself, and I never even got the chance to stop the fool before she jumped straight at me." Then stormed out of the bedroom, unable to stand the tenderness with which Duncan slipped her under the covers, tucked her in and hovered over her like she was dying or something.

To calm down, he set to work on lighting a fire. The shelter was freezing, and some heat would do them all lots of good. And since he was a master at it, after just a few minutes of the first twigs crackling, the flames enveloped the bigger logs and leapt to the top of the fireplace in a bright blaze.

"So all right, she was a little rash." His tone vaguely apologetic, Duncan appeared behind him. "But even if she had taken all the necessary precautions, you wouldn't have allowed her through, would you?" Sprawling on the carpet in front of the fireplace, rather than on the couch behind him, he kept his gaze fixed on him.

"Well . . ." *No, I'd have burnt her to cinders!*

Which had been his instinct the first time around, and he was just sorry he had not acted on it when he had the chance.

"Let's say I still have my reservations." Noncommittal, he stirred the fire one more time before moving to Duncan's side. "And I know I promised to be more tolerant or something to that effect, but I can't stand having her around every goddamn day of this cursed trip! Nor do I particularly relish having to share you and everything about you with the likes of her! Sorry, lover, I just can't." Locking his gaze on the black velvety one, he tried to convey how impossible the whole thing was turning out for him. "It doesn't work that way with me, and that little charade of asking for my consent while Arthur breathed down our necks only made me feel more trapped in a no-win situation." If things were not quite as he was making them out to be, he still could not stop the avalanche bursting out of him.

Still, he might just have kept his trap shut, had the prolonged abstinence from sex not messed with his mind like it was doing right now.

"With Arthur short of ordering it and you wanting to assuage your guilty conscience, there was not much of a choice for me except to agree to your terms. So you can understand how my *commitment* seems kind of forced out of me." All right, maybe he was being a tad bit unjust and taking it out on the one man who had made of balance his way of life.

"Now all I want is to have our alone time back and don't tell me the traveling prevents it."

"Listen, Angel, I understand how hard this is on you." Cupping his face, Duncan held it between his palms. "I do." Then his piercing gaze penetrated straight to his core. "And I'd turn back right now if we didn't have a mission to accomplish." Not letting go, the black gaze caressed his face. "Or would you rather we disobeyed Arthur outright and returned home just for the sake of some privacy?"

Goddamn him and his always so sensible arguments!

With Duncan, it was always like that. He liked people to reason things out, and Chris for one often failed to do it all together.

"This has nothing to do with Arthur's mission," he tried arguing. "This has to do with us—"

"My point exactly." Duncan grinned as though he had him precisely where he wanted. "Can't you see it's the chance for us to grow and learn something that will truly make us special? Can't you see that the leader is offering us the unique opportunity to prove ourselves, if only we can manage to get beyond our petty selves?"

"I wouldn't have any problems with that if she weren't trying her damnest best to get under my skin," he huffed. "Which is the one place that's always belonged to you alone."

"Just for the record, 'cause I really don't understand." Letting go of his face, the prince distended his long legs toward the fire. "Do you object to her because she's a woman or because she's Ylianor Meyer?"

Because it's her! Yes, definitely. "You know I can't stand women under any circumstances—"

"You're lying." Spinning to his side, Duncan pinned him against the couch, pressing his massive frame to keep him from moving. "It's her, isn't it?" Hot breath on his face, he had no room to budge. "The fact she's a woman is only incidental, isn't it?"

"Fuck you!" His attempts at pushing Duncan back failed miserably. "And her for having always meddled between the two of us!" Letting his arms fall, he had no choice besides scrunching up against the couch. "She's always been a goddamn witch like no other woman I've ever known, and that's what makes her intolerable." Yet also exciting, so very arousing that he could only wonder whether his body had a totally different opinion than his mind did. "So you can understand if I can't wait to get rid of her—"

"Like it or not, she's becoming a part of us." Prince Caldwell made it sound so matter of fact he feared it would be a forever type of deal. "And that's what's really eating you, isn't it?" To make everything worse, he bit his neck causing a spark of pain that was more similar to a jolt of pleasure. "Sure, you never wanted anyone, man or woman, to come even remotely close to where I am, but what you didn't expect was that you might actually like it. Not just because you like her, because the extra competition turns you on like crazy."

"Fuck, no!" His temper flared, because the man had centered the heart of the matter.

"Don't you now?" Duncan snarled, his voice becoming hoarse, "I know you far too well to mistake certain signs. Like looking at her when you think no one's watching or like daring her to take more of me when we're in bed, which heats you up so bad you could burn not just her, me, too."

"She pisses me off the way she looks so fucking much like you!" At least that was one of the things that most bugged him out of the many he had to ignore every day. "And I can't stand it that I might have ever wanted her over you."

Since this was as far as he would go in admitting stuff he had no business bringing up, he attacked the full lips with an angry growl that threatened to swallow him whole.

Duncan's reaction was swift. Breaking inside the warm cavity, his tongue counterattacked for control, battling silently in a fierce fight Chris for sure had no intention of losing. But when the man overcame his resistance and swept the hot mouth like a conqueror, his hands flew to the bulging crotch pressing on his belly.

Mouthwatering erection already straining within the pants, he freed it in a second and gobbled it down to his throat. By the gods, how much he had missed it! Missed everything about it, from the silky feel of the soft skin to the hardness sliding to his stomach. Now still incredulous he was squeezing it between his cheeks, he gagged on it, glad to suffocate for such an unparalleled delicacy. No other cock was even remotely comparable to Duncan's perfection.

And he had seen so many of them he could qualify as an expert in the matter.

So no other cock deserved all of his efforts and his utter adoration. It was exactly what he was doing. Licking its every stiff side, he bobbed up and down the long stick while pressing all the way to the lap, at least until the prince flipped him down on the ground.

Back pinned to the carpet, Duncan straddled him and fed him the beefy beast, shoving so far down he wondered whether he was trying to reach his ass. Not that it would have been a problem. It belonged to him anyway, so however he chose to claim it would be fine with him. Just as long as he rammed it to bits that is.

Groaning, the prince intensified his hip swing and slammed more of his rigid rod down his throat. With a couple of well-aimed thrusts, he let him have it all, balls included it seemed. Or if not quite, still close enough for his capacious mouth to try swallowing them along with the rest.

Then Duncan had the bad idea of opening his fly and clasping what was itching for a fast come. And having him puff hot whiffs of air over the tip was sure trouble.

"No, lover, don't." Oh, he would never be able to hold it together if the skin of his piece kept sliding to the hilt. "I can't—"

"I know you can't." Husky and seductive, Duncan's breath pushed out in between gulps of his fiery shaft. "So just come for me now, Angel."

The mere words sent the juice speeding to the exit. But what made it burst out in copious jets was his lover sucking him to the root while stuffing his own cock, the whole fantastic length of it, all the way to his stomach.

This was simply too much.

Not just for him raising his hips to dig inside his phase mate and strangle him with all the fluid spraying everywhere.

For Duncan, too, whose heavy load was shooting down his throat in a fast rush of pungent drops.

"Now that our basic needs are sated, what do you say we have some serious fun?" Chuckling, Duncan wrenched his hips and capsized him.

After a few brusque pulls, he discarded his pants on a side. "On one count, I gotta admit you're right." Spreading his buttocks far apart, he rubbed his not so limp cock on the cleft. "Since we started this journey, we've had less time to ourselves." Which only made it grow to a gigantic size and firmness. "And I've missed it, too."

"I told you, lover." The sensual stroking was driving him insane again. Already his piece was a slab of stone just from the anticipation of the slam into his narrow hole.

And the harder, the better, all that enlarging and stretching all at once always pushed him over the edge in no time.

"Though I also have to admit she's kind of fun in bed." In the state he was in, it took no effort to allow this to slip. "Only it's not the same when it's just the two of us."

"Yeah, she changes the balance between us somehow." As though having read his mind, Duncan stopped sliding and aimed. "Then again, it's just a matter of adjusting to the different way we have to play with her as opposed to our usual way of doing things."

The ferocious blow cracking his ass wide open was exactly his usual way of doing things.

"I kind of like these games more than the ones we play with her." This was a lie for sure. Still, he was floating away too fast to care.

He just wanted his ass pumped until time stood still. That harsh beat was making his body rock back and forth, while rubbing his cock on the carpet. Another sure come, if he was any judge of it—

"I said we'd have fun." Catching his near explosion, Duncan pulled out in the nick of time. "And I meant fun." Dragging him up, he flattened him to the closest wall.

Then he flayed his legs apart, bent his back, raised his ass to his convenience and shoved in the not-so-narrow back ring. If anything, this hurt more than the first time, perhaps given the position, perhaps given the extreme heat scorching his butt.

Either way, he loved it and melted in the sensation of his ass, now turned into a fiery sheath, clenching the biggest equipment of all. And this fiercer pounding was an attempt at finding the path that led to his throat.

His cock twitching from the need to come, he went to wrap his hand around the long length.

"No touching, Angel." Beating him to it, Duncan clasped it firmly. "This belongs to me now, and I'll be the only one allowed to play with it." He jerked it a couple of times.

So he gasped, for the load had all risen to the tip, and he was about to lose it again.

"One last rule." Whispering his throaty voice, Duncan's

breath tickled his ear. "There'll be no coming for you unless I say so."

And goddamn it!

He was in no position to comply. "Lover, I don't think I can hold it—"

"You'll have to." To make it easier for him or because close to a come himself, Duncan popped out of the snug confinement one more time, dragged him to the couch and sprawled him on his back. Then he just had to get the legs out of the way to claim the inflamed rear again.

Which would have been ecstatic had the torture of not having the freedom to climax not put him more on edge. Already, his body screamed for the release his lover was denying it, and the strain was getting to him.

"Can't resist, Angel?" With a ruthless blow that split his ass in half, Prince Caldwell snapped his attention back on the pleasure mounting in rapid waves.

"You know I can't," he protested. "You're just too good, and you're making my ass dance so fast I just have to—"

"All in due time." The black eyes mocked him as the prince changed position once more.

This time, it was on the table, where he lay sprawled, back down, legs to the floor. For Duncan, it was less strenuous since he did not have to cradle his legs. So it became sheer agony, for his lover's monster had no impediments in nailing the cramped back channel.

Which was not so tiny anymore.

Which left him to wonder just how large the screwing had made it become, probably enough for two cocks to fit in it easily. And the repeated hammering was only enlarging it further, increasing also the delicious friction against the fleshy walls clenching around the massive erection stretching everything beyond any reasonable size.

Then finally, Duncan grasped his cock. "I must say I'm

impressed." Smirking amused, he flicked the soft skin up and down. "I never thought you'd resist this much."

"But not a second more." Arching his back, he managed to slip more cock inside his ass and inside the man's palm. "So please, lover, I beg you—"

"Yes, Angel." Intensifying both the pumping and the jerking, Duncan licked his lips. "Come now."

The effort of holding back blended with the heat and passion coursing through his every fiber. Together, they coalesced in a single point right beneath the tip of his erection. Then it burst in convulsive throws that shattered him, more so when Duncan reclined on his belly and filled his rear until not one drop remained.

CHAPTER FIFTY-SIX

"Now that's what I call fucking." Grinning widely, the angel slid down the table into his arms. "And I'm sorry I lashed out at you," his tone sincere and remorseful. "I didn't mean half the things I said. It's just that I get so mad sometimes—"

"My fault, Angel." Stroking the shiny blond head, he cuddled him closer. "I should've known better than to deprive you of sex for so long."

That Christopher Templeton could not function without sex had become obvious since their reunion. If for everyone else sex was essential, for Chris it was as vital as the very air he breathed.

"Yeah." Raising his gaze, Chris chortled. "That always kind of messes with my mind." Then burying his face on Duncan's chest, he inhaled his scent deeply. "And it has nothing to do with her."

"I know." Prince Caldwell tightened his embrace around the warm body. "It's all this damn traveling in the mountains."

"And being stuck together doesn't help, either," Chris pointed out.

"We can't very well send her off to sleep in the stables," he joked for the mere idea seemed preposterous to him.

"Why not?" Not to his angel, though. "I'm sure she wouldn't mind, seeing how much she loves horses." Despite the more teasing note to it, he had the sneaky suspicion Chris meant it for real.

"Come on." He bit his neck. "Be serious." Latching on to the blue-gray gaze fixed on him, he held it. "You can't possibly think of leaving her out in the cold just so you can have your space with me."

"Sounds like a perfect arrangement to me." Stubbornly, Chris's eyes flashed with a malicious gleam.

"Not to me, Angel, sorry." Letting his arms fall, he took a step back. "I couldn't do it." He went to sit on the couch, comforted by the fire's warmth. "I just couldn't."

No, the mere notion of leaving his princess out in the cold was simply heartbreaking, just like imagining her curling on herself to make the most of the little heat a stable could provide.

"Your heart bleeds just at the thought, doesn't it?" Getting nearer, Chris fell on the seat next to him, his tone concerned and worried.

Suddenly, he realized it had been only a provocation on the angel's part to see how far he would be willing to go for this particular woman.

So besides applauding his cunning, he had to admit that she was worth more to him than any of the others he had sex with, like she was special or something.

"Let's say I don't think it's fair." Even if his devious angel had guessed it before him, it was no reason to give him the satisfaction of blurting it out loud. "And I don't mean just about the sleeping arrangement." Which was why he kept his tone as even as possible, as though the issue was not all that important.

As though she was not that important to him, which was the farthest thing from the truth.

"Also about the selfish way we've been acting around her." Reclining against the headstand, he tugged Chris until his head rested on his chest. "Not just 'cause we don't bother hiding anything of our love or sex. Most times, we don't even ask her to participate in our games, simply play it like she isn't even there in the bed with us." Straying a hand on the blond head, he raked his fingers through the thick strands. "We're always kissing . . ." Bending, he brushed his lips on Chris's thin ones. "Touching . . ." His fingers deepened the caress, sliding down to Chris's groin. "Making love in front of her, even if we're not on a bed." Hardly surprised to find his angel's cock ready for another round. "Yet, she says nothing of it." And he did not like it at all. "Not a complaint. Not a single request for a kiss. Not even a cry for attention. I'm so concentrated on you that I hardly notice her during the day. And only when we reach a shelter, do I remember she exists at all."

Not entirely the truth, still close enough for his conscience to rebuke him.

"This isn't what we agreed to do when we talked at the Hall." Drawing back, he regarded Chris coldly. "And you're not doing yourself a favor by shutting her out at every turn." He rolled on a side, pressing his weight on an elbow. "Have you considered that, if something happened to me, you and the princess would be the only ones who could help me?"

"I may not have thought of it." Chris shifted nervously. "But you know how hard it is for me."

"I know, and I don't want to force your hand." After his angel's blunt sharing, his heart went out to him. "Just tell me there's hope for change."

"The fact that I could've burned the living daylights out of her but didn't should be enough hope for you." Tentatively, the hint of a smile curved the thin lips. "Seriously, though, I did try to accept her. That's why I did nothing when she flew at me—*absolutely nothing*—and even went against my better instinct to strike back."

"Which you didn't . . ." Just to be on the safe side, he had to ask. "Right?"

"She's alive, isn't she?" Chris sneered. "But I wouldn't count it as a victory if I were you. There are just too many variables at work between me and her that I can't say for sure how much my attempts at changing will affect the outcome." He paused as if in deep meditation. "What I can say for sure is that I didn't want it to end this way."

He searched his beautiful face for a long moment. "I believe you." Leaning to kiss away his doubts, he claimed the entire cavity opening up for his inspection. Hard tongue tip sweeping the interior, he filled his senses with the taste of his angel, gulping it down in between raspy breaths.

"And while we're at it, I'm tired of hearing all sorts of nonsense about something no one really understands." Looking sorry the kiss was over, Chris sat up straighter. "I don't believe in energy. I believe in emotions." Staring at the flames leaping high, he seemed lost for a moment. "I love you." And the blue-gray eyes shifting squarely on him shone with such intensity it drained his lungs of all their air. "I don't know if it's the right word, but I can't think of anything more appropriate to tell you how deeply you affect me, have always affected me." Chris edged closer. "And that's all I'm prepared to believe in, lover."

After this heartfelt declaration, what could he do if not show how concretely he believed his angel's words?

Embracing Chris and capturing the thin lips, he toppled him until they both stretched out on the couch. Full weight pressing on the angel, he devoured him with the hungry intakes of his tongue ravaging the heated cavity yielding to him. Then a small adjustment and his stone-like cock nudged at Chris's butt hole. One shove was all it took to get him to the guts, the back ring still so dilated it took no effort at all.

Once firmly inside, all he wanted was to melt in the fiery core that beckoned him, had always beckoned him though he had not been aware of it. Now with the new understanding flowing through him like fresh blood, he could respond more appropriately and bring their connection to a far superior level, one that would bond the two of them tighter than ever before.

A level where they could be as one.

Strengthened by Ylianor's teaching, his barriers fell away as his energy wrapped around Chris's. Amazing how snugly the blond angel fit inside his invisible embrace, and how right this combination seemed from whatever angle he analyzed it. So right, he wished he would never have to let Chris go.

Body sinking into his angel's taste and feel, mind drowning in the awareness of how much more went on between them, he began to lose it. Everything was so incredible that his orgasm spun out of any control. So potent, he almost missed the moment his spirit fused inside the angel's shiny core.

Almost . . . but not quite.

Not since the giant pyre that had become Chris wavered in anticipation of his touch. So he claimed it all, instantly becoming one with it, hardly surprised that the flames neither burned nor blinded him despite the intense heat. He—and he alone—was Chris's master, the only one who could control the angel with a simple squeeze that cooled down his extreme temperature and his unpredictable temper. Which was another potent awareness that had him coming again, just like Chris, and slipping away from reality to reach a different dimension where time and space had no meaning.

Alas, it did not last forever.

Both he and a very bewildered Chris returned to the here and now, and to the question burning on the tip of his tongue. "Still having doubts about the energy business, Angel?"

CHAPTER FIFTY-SEVEN

"We should try repeating the experiment." Duncan's black gaze searched her face.

After a whole day's worth of traveling, she was not so eager to confront the insufferable demon again. She would just rather ride in silence, enjoying the changing scenery now that the mountains seemed a memory of the past.

And not a moment too soon. Checking around the hot plateau filled with short green plants, relief ran down her back.

The green expanse of vegetation was simply incredible. Maybe because it looked much like the sea of her native home, which she missed far more than she dared admit. Or perhaps it was because she had no idea what the majority of these new plants were, so scrutinized them attentively every time she had the chance. Either way, she was glad they had replaced the pinewood that had cut off light and warmth, forcing her to dreary and freezing rides. The hotter temperatures were also a welcome change, particularly since they would make travel easier . . . if only His Haughtiness Lord Christopher Templeton allowed it.

"I'd like to repeat the night part of it." The blue-gray eyes lit with a mischievous gleam.

Yeah, sure, he would! They had not needed to tell her anything about that. She had picked up on their new connection, their new awareness and just about everything else they had been through, sex included, from their bright and very talkative lights.

"As much as I'd like it, too, I don't think we have time to stop." Duncan grinned regretfully. "I was thinking more along the line of our connections. If you and the princess can't establish a link on your own, I could act as the go-between like she suggested." His dark head swung elegantly to face her. "Right?"

"If your energy comes between us . . ." She shrugged, pretending indifference. "I could jump in without going up in smoke."

"All right, let's try it then." Duncan turned to the demon. "Now relax and reach out for me while I do the same."

"Yes, sir." Happy as a boy who had finally gotten his favorite candy, Chris smiled, an infectious affair that had her stomach churning.

Not out of the sheer beauty of him. Out of bitterness, because he probably would never smile at her in that enchanting way he reserved to Duncan alone.

"You are the master." Straightening on his saddle, Chris's gaze expressed all the love and passion he felt for the prince, which reflected in his aura and made it shine.

Feeling suddenly sorry for herself, she followed their energy as it joined then drifted away. Oh, damn it! She was just being a silly fool, and the pangs tightening her stomach were only a waste of her precious energy. Useless even to feel slighted, since it was kind of obvious by now that there was no place for her between them. Nor for anyone else either, true, which was no consolation at all.

Bottom line was—they would never be hers and looking at the beautiful empty shells riding by her side, she realized that accepting this truth would be her real test.

Not because it still hurt every time Chris accused her of intruding in his space. No, worse of *spying*, even if she played it like it was just another excuse to get back at him. She could have probably lived with that, were she not moved beyond words every time she watched their erotic dances, even if the hateful demon did not always invite her to join them. So what?

They were so stunning, she would have gladly just watched had she only managed to turn off their auras, at least the part of it that spoke of the depth and exclusivity of their love and bond. So she was an even bigger fool to delude herself that either could ever accept her as a part of —

Princess, join us.

If Duncan's voice startled her, it was nothing compared to the instant shift reuniting her with them.

Come on, his voice urged huskily. *Don't be afraid.* There was no risk of that.

With Prince Caldwell shielding the demon's fire, only a few isolated sparks escaped his dark hug.

He's not going to hurt you, not this time. Then he broadened his soothing embrace to enfold her, too.

By the gods!

She could hardly believe it!

They were actually allowing her into their sacred circle!

And she could not stand it, the great surge of emotions swelling the tears she had not cried for days into a painful knot pressing at the back of her throat.

No. No tears. Tightening his grip, Duncan squeezed her. *Snuggle closer instead. Be with us.*

But she could not.

You are so beautiful together. She hesitated holding back. *You couldn't possibly want me.*

Why not? He sounded vaguely amused. *You taught us about connections and the way to use them, but they're meaningless without you.* A series of random sparks told her that Chris did not just agree with Duncan.

He was also beckoning her to become part of them.

So her resistance faded.

Next thing she knew, cool energy coiled around her,

crushing her between him and Chris, stuck between them in the same exact position as when they pumped her front and back.

No, this is much more. His energy flared. *None of my wild sex with the angel prepared me to feel my lovers as close as they are right now.* Had she possessed ears, he would have whispered this in one of them. As it was, the words seemed to float by themselves carried only by the energy flowing between them like the air they would normally breathe. *Now come. You know there's one last thing left to do.*

Yes, and it was the most important one of all. Without fears or prejudices, she had to surrender to them, both of them. Which she had every intention of doing, because maybe she had been wrong. Maybe they did belong to her. She just had to be patient and let them come round to it on their own time. Like the prince had asked at the Hall, time would be the key to true connection. But if she did not take that first step, if she did not prove she was ready to let them claim the whole of her, she would get nowhere.

For how could she possibly ask them to accept her if she did not accept them first?

So she clasped the darkness with its fiery core and plunged straight into their dimension, one made of scalding passion rippling from the surface all the way to the bottom. And like she had wished when she had first connected them, she became part Duncan, part Chris, as though their different halves could coalesce only inside her. Like during sex, when her body was the only means they had to join their three separate fleshes into a single one.

So she opened up entirely to her two men and became one with them.

CHAPTER FIFTY-EIGHT

"Wow!" That touching and becoming one had blown away his mind. "That was simply amazing!" Nighttime inside the first free shelter Ylianor and her aura Virt had found. Sitting on the floor in front of a blazing fire, he looked at Duncan. "What now? How are you going to top this one off, since it's such a tough act to follow?"

"We stay here until we understand what happened exactly, how we managed that incredible merge of minds and spirits. And how we could repeat it." Crouching on the carpet next to him, Prince Caldwell seemed determined to get to the bottom of it. "And I don't care how long it takes us, but we're not leaving until we figure out what has prevented us to be as close as we were in that energy dimension."

For him, the answer was simple, and he had to thank her if he saw it with such clarity. Because, like it or not, she had just taught him the only lesson worth a damn out of all the things she had been preaching.

"If you mean what has kept us apart so far, then I know exactly who and what to blame." For it all had to do with the load of anger he had been carrying around forever, which prevented him from opening up to her and accepting the fact that circumstances required them to be more intimate than he would have normally consented with anyone who was not his lover.

This pushing her away all the time had also stood in the way of that balance Duncan had sought from the start, only he had been too thickheaded to understand it. And now that he did, he could only wonder what else he had missed while busy in his blind opposition to her.

"And it has all to do with my father." Only natural he would begin right where it had all started—his neglected childhood and the man he considered responsible for it all. "'Cause he never loved me and always preferred my brothers, Steve in particular." *And he still does.* Nothing in his Hall experience had convinced him of the contrary. "Whatever he and Bran did was great, while nothing I did ever pleased him."

"Come on, Angel." The prince tousled his hair. "I doubt your father did things to hurt you deliberately. Like Arthur said, he probably didn't know how to deal with your . . ." He creased his forehead. "Uniqueness, which is why he might've been overly protective and strict in his ways, but only for your own good."

Ha! As if he ever gave a damn about that!

"You'll never get over your bad habit of justifying people, will you?" Chris snapped.

"Why should I?" A wide grin lit Duncan's beautiful face and stopped his heart from beating. "They say it's my most endearing trait."

"Not true." He stretched out to clasp his lover's hand. "Your big fat juicy cock is." Slipping to Duncan's crotch, he fondled his favorite piece for a brief second.

Which was just a temporary respite from the pain surging simply by talking about it.

"It's just too bad it can't solve everything, can it?" Smiling crookedly, he squeezed what was now growing under his palm.

"No, sex can't solve everything." Gently, the prince removed his paw from the delectable prize. "Sometimes, we just have to reach deep in ourselves simply to know what the problem is."

"My problem is my father." Resigned, he let go of Duncan's shaft. "And I'm not saying you're wrong about your analysis." In fact, he was probably right. "But I was too young to think that through. All I knew back then was that my father's love and support went to Steve and Bran. While all I got was his anger and disappointment on the rare occasions he noticed I existed. And I couldn't stand it!"

"You're exaggerating," Duncan's soft tone held no trace of scolding, which made him all the more grateful his lover was being so matter-of-fact about it. "Your father noticed what you did. Didn't he take you to the Hall when you were just a little kid?" He had shared this one bit of information on one of the breaks from sex during their torrid phase. "But he never brought neither Steve nor Bran, right?" And he obviously recalled all the details about it.

"Yeah, right." Not that he remembered any of it. He had been too small for that. Just Arthur and a few other people at the Hall had taken pains to describe that particular incident to him. "A coincidence for sure. I like to think he wanted to teach me the ropes from early on," he joked making it sound like this would not be relevant to the case he was building against his father.

"No, I think it was because he wanted to show you off, which means he didn't just notice you. He must've been proud of you, even if he hid it from you." He wondered why Duncan always managed to set things into a new perspective. "Another thing that tells me your father did take notice of you is the fact he sent you to me."

"That was just a lucky move." A fresh wave of rage washed over him. "Or he'd have packed off his precious Steve or Bran long before he ever sent me away and without any hesitations."

"Still, I can't blame him." Circling him from behind, Duncan cradled him against his chest. "If it wasn't for him, we might've never met."

"That's beside the point." Not that he had any complaints about the way things had turned out in the end.

Seen in retrospective, his father's decision had been the best he ever made about him, for his life had literally changed the moment he had met the dark-haired handsome prince.

"And you're looking at this all wrong." For his father could not have possibly known what would have happened, which was the reason it still grated on his nerves so much. "It wasn't 'cause he loved me or took notice of me. It was 'cause he hated me, or he'd have never sent me as far away from him as he did. You do know how much distance there is between Fair Haven and Black Rose, right?" He angled his head to stare into the velvety black eyes.

"Yeah, I do." The two were at opposite ends from one another after all.

"And I was only eight years old at the time, so do you get it now?" Shifting position, he leaned against the powerful frame, extremely glad for all the cool energy that embraced him. "That's how I see it." So glad, he wanted to sink in it and forget about everything else. "The fact I met you is no consolation, not for his behavior anyway, 'cause he acted as if he didn't give a damn about me." He contemplated the high flames lighting and warming the room, the red licks spreading a soft glow that seemed perfectly attuned to his mood. "That's probably why, when I started cutting up people, I fantasized of doing it in front of him." This was another painful admission, one that required he paused to catch his breath. "Just to get his attention," his tone grew husky. "Or whatever reaction that would make him feel bad about how I had turned out. Mostly, I liked to imagine the look of horror slowly spreading on his face the second he realized I was carving a live human being to pieces." He shook his head to clear it of the sick fantasy. "Other times, I wished he were under my knife."

Swinging his gaze on the opposite side, he caught sight of her, huddling on the floor, and he suddenly realized it did not bother him at all to let it all out in front of her.

"Does this mean I'm cruel?" He returned his gaze on the fire. "Or maybe the question should be — why do I get these impulses when no one else does?"

Because no one else in his world practiced any sort of violence, at least not to his knowledge.

"I think it might just be a reaction to all the negative feelings you've cultivated through the years." Duncan's deep strokes on his chest cooled his burning flesh. "You feel slighted, in need of revenge and punishment, so that's the best way you know of dealing with it." The cool touch slipped to his belly. "And it's true no one else in their right mind would ever think of hurting people the way you do, but then no one could heal them back like you can. And more importantly, no one else lives emotions the way you do, which is so passionate I'm not surprised they become uncontrollable as often as they do."

"Yeah." That made perfect sense. "Like the sheer hatred for my father."

"I think you never hated your father, Angel." Grave and persuasive, Duncan's voice became huskier, "Quite the contrary, you love him a lot."

No, not possible!

He could not have mistaken years of hate that foolishly! Could not have taken it for granted, feeding off it his entire life. He simply could not have!

Yet, the pain cutting through his heart told a different story. One of a little boy so desperate for his father's love he would have done anything, including lying about his real intentions.

As the awareness ripped him apart like a knife that tore

his insides out, he had to curl on himself simply to control the fiery surge shooting to the surface. And there was no defense against it. The heat and pressure already too intense to bear, he was ready to burst and lash out at the cause of his pain.

But Duncan was there to prevent just that. And the way his tight embrace and soothing energy coiled around the fire of his raging spirit and snuffed it out was simply amazing.

"Oh, lover." Clinging to him like he was hanging on for dear life, he buried his head inside his arms. "Maybe you're right." And it hurt simply to acknowledge it. "After this assignment is over, I'll have a talk with my father, a man-to-man talk such as we've never had." Which was mostly his fault and his persistent hiding from James at the Hall, adamantly refusing to have anything to do with him in spite of Arthur's entreaties. "I need to tell him who I am, if I find out in the meantime, and ask for his . . ." *Forgiveness? Love? Respect?*

He was not sure any of these would satisfy him. Still, they would have to do for now, at least to get started.

"He's my father after all." He tried a confident smile, but it came out wrong, his lips twisting in a bitter snarl instead. "So he should accept me for what I am, shouldn't he?"

"I'm sure he will." The prince squeezed his shoulder. "I've been telling you to do it for years."

"I wasn't ready." *Not at all.* "Now thanks to both of you, I feel a different energy, which can help me deal with him, too."

"What about your mother?" Her voice was so low he had to prick up his ears.

"Interesting you should ask." He sent her a penetrating look.

If she wanted to get into a debate about his dislike of women stemming from his relationship with his mother, he was ready for her.

"I'd have gladly cut her up more than a few times, even if she adores me." More than Steve or Bran, he knew he was her favorite. "And I suppose that's the real problem, 'cause she's always been too protective of me, always wanted more of my love than I was willing to give her."

"So you didn't welcome her love." Her eyes glittered in understanding.

And his heart skipped a beat.

Surprised, he glanced one more time at her silhouette lit by the red flames. Long lustrous dark hair glowing, the heavy strands partly hid her face as it pressed on her legs, chin digging on her knees and gaze averted to the fire. The more he watched her, the more he wanted to take her in his arms and just hold her.

Which was plain absurd!

"Not at all." He shrugged indifferently. "I used to think that my father would've loved me if she hadn't interfered between the two of us." *And boy, didn't that resemble his current situation with the witch?* "Not that it was all her fault." His mother's face floated to the top of his head, something he quickly suppressed. "I allowed her to defend me on more than one occasion in front of him." Cowering behind his mother's skirts was more like it. "And I still regret it. Now that I think about it . . ." Creasing his forehead, he retrieved the old scenes of his parents arguing over him. "The more she protected me, the more Father picked on me. What she could not understand was that her protection ended up harming me in that very competitive family of mine." *And driving me away from my father.* "I can't say I hate her. She's my mother after all. I just wish she'd acted differently when I was a kid."

"Could this explain your feelings for women?" She kept a neutral gaze on the fire.

He knew it! He knew she would jump at the chance to

blame his mother for the awful way he had treated her.

"I don't think so," he retorted trying to keep his glee at bay. "Ever since I can recall, I've liked men alone." Even if it sounded more challenging than he intended, he did not change tone, "I love everything about them—their bodies, their sex, their elegant straight lines that are so much more exciting than any woman's treacherous curves will ever be. And that's just for starters." He stared intently into her mesmerizing green eyes. "Men are straightforward, rational, logical and to the point where women . . ." He hesitated a fraction of a second, before deciding to let her have it all without discounts, comforting lies or anything else besides his uncensored opinion. "They're petty, jealous and devious, without an original thought of their own, yet capable of talking for hours on end about nothing. Hard as I try, there's not a single thing I like about them. They're unappealing in and out of bed, despite my lover's attempts to convince me of the contrary. They lack in passion, cold and calculating creatures that they are, always trying to turn everything to their advantage, sex and love included."

There! He had said it. And he was not sorry, not one single bit. Nor was he concerned about her feelings, not one single bit.

"If you hate them this much . . ." Duncan cleared his throat as though he could not believe his ears. "Why haven't you ever thought of cutting one up?"

"Well, the thought crossed my mind once, as we all recall," he joked. But when his humor resulted in stunned silence, he knew he had to change tactic. "I'm sorry, Ylianor." And make real amends this time, not the fake ones he had offered at the Hall. "It was a bad joke—"

"Terrible." She averted icy cold eyes from him.

"You're right, it was." Angling his head, he tried to catch her gaze anyway.

Somehow, this was too important to have it slide any further than it already had.

"I know I haven't apologized for my conduct, so please forgive me." To emphasize his point, he edged closer to her. "I didn't know what I was doing."

"You knew exactly what you were doing." Bitter, she turned her head away to avoid intercepting his gaze. "Only now I know why." Then she changed her mind, and angry green eyes flashed in his face. "I was just another woman standing in the way of a man's love for you, whether it was your father or the prince's makes no difference. Since you couldn't hurt either them or your mother, I was the perfect replacement, the same hateful creature you had already driven away from your lover's side ten years before." Clogged by the rush of her words, she had to gulp for air. "Which also explains why you didn't even feel guilty about it, not just about your knife scene, about everything you did to me since you first set foot in Black Rose."

"Need I remind you, dearie, that you attacked first?" A nasty smile crossed his lips.

"What choice did I have?" She blushed violently. "You were dangerous, so full of black rage I thought you'd destroy us all, Black Rose included." As though realizing her voice had risen, she toned it down a notch, "But I could've never hurt you, and you knew it." She spat, "You were too sure of your Virt to fear mine."

Well, she was right about that, for he had never considered her a serious threat.

"No, what happened at Black Rose was worse in a way," she scoffed. "The prince had you so enthralled that you blinded me out of carelessness, not because I was a threat."

"Yes, but if your prince was so important to you, why did you let me win so easily?" Still puzzled at her reaction after all those years, he sat up straighter. "Why didn't you fight back?"

"What would've been the point?" Raising her gaze defiantly, the green eyes blazed hotly. "I could never beat your fire, no matter how much energy I'd have thrown at you." She took a deep breath, obviously in an effort to calm down. "Besides, fighting never got me anywhere," she added in a sadder tone. "I fought to keep my place next to Prince Charles, but death took him away. I fought to keep Duncan, but you took him away. I fought to keep Black Rose, but Lady Caldwell took it away." She shifted her gaze back to the fire as though ashamed he and Duncan could read the pain that was slicing her apart.

"Maybe you just didn't fight hard enough," he offered.

"Maybe that explains why I punished myself for so long." A light spread on her lovely face. "Blaming myself for having lost everything as if it were my fault."

"What do you mean, Princess?" Only because Duncan had not spoken for a while did not mean he had not followed their discussion attentively.

Chris had caught him more than once studying now him, now her to understand better what had made them tick.

"Nothing, my prince, nothing of importance." She lifted a shoulder nonchalantly.

Not that either her words or her gesture fooled him into believing her.

"Like a silly girl, I thought I deserved to suffer 'cause I was wicked." Her lips curved in a wry smile. "The witch's daughter they called me, so why should I have been entitled to anything? Truth was—I just felt sorry for myself and unworthy of love, not even the one I gave for granted. For your mother made me feel like I stole your father's affection and she had no qualms in saying it to my face. How can you possibly think that a great and wonderful prince like my mate could ever love a lowlife like you?" As she repeated Sophia

Caldwell's words, he had no doubt they were the exact ones the stern woman had uttered more than ten years ago.

And it tightened his heart just perceiving all that load of pain she must have carried for the same amount of time, to the point his healer sense went crazy with the need to do something about it.

"She was so convincing that, at one point, I believed I had imagined everything and that our mind sharing was just an illusion of mine." Slowly, her gaze swung to Duncan. "And it was so devastating that, losing you seemed almost irrelevant. And having to put up with my father's scorn didn't help things, only again I couldn't blame him, just myself. He hadn't wanted me after all, not a witch's daughter to complicate a life that my mother had already messed up good and proper, since she never loved him, only Prince Charles." A sad smile crossed her lips. "Well, you may both think me mad, but it was the only way to survive until you, Lord Templeton, made me open my eyes to what I had allowed myself to become."

Fire crackled and the smoky whiffs blurred her pale features as Duncan dragged her over and crushed her against him, burying his head in the nape of her neck, their heavy strands mixing. And it was strange to see how similar their hair was, so much that the abundant mass seemed to come from one head alone.

Reclining against the couch, he waited for the prince to pour his cooing nonsense in her mind. Though he had no clue about it, he was sure it was the reason his lover was holding on to her so tightly. Then finally, he disentangled from her.

"That night at the shelter, I wanted you to hurt me." Still flattened against Prince Caldwell's broad chest, she adjusted her position to fix him. "To show him what I was really like, to expose the mess I was inside. So I have to thank you." She bowed in his direction as though in mocking respect. "You opened my eyes, showed me what a fool I've been all these years. A pitiful, whimpering child, I never took charge of my life. I always delegated to others and subjected to their every whim, in the hope I could finally deserve their love." Her voice grew harsh, "If I'm good, he'll love me back." She snorted, "That was my best line out of the many I made up to justify my lack of self-esteem." She swallowed hard. "Well, I'm through with that!" She paused to raise her chin in defiance. "And I am extremely grateful to you, Lord Templeton, for helping me start on a different path."

Duncan caressed her long hair, raking his fingers through her thick strands. "So we're on a self-awareness journey, are we?"

His teasing tone was unable to hide his deep concern.

"Mostly, yes." She nodded. "I know now I can't ask of others what I can't give myself. How can someone love and respect me, if I'm the first to hate and mistreat myself?" This seemed reasonable. "Now I'll have to learn to accept who I am, so the rest of the world can finally do the same."

"Wow, you've got quite a task ahead of you." He mockingly wiped his brow from invisible sweat.

"And not an easy one either." Prince Caldwell reached in his breast pocket. "However, I want to give you the support of someone who loved you very much, in spite of what others told you or of what you yourself might've imagined." Hand in the pocket, he hesitated, his dark eyes searching her face. "I wasn't sure I'd ever let you read this letter. Now, though, I think you deserve it, if only to strengthen your faith in yourself."

"What is it?" She took the envelope from his hand.

"It's what Father wrote to me . . ." In his slight pause, Chris noticed how difficult this was for him, and how far he had come from the furious man who had left Black Rose just a couple of weeks before. "To us, actually, before dying."

She unfolded it carefully as if afraid to tear the fragile paper and began reading aloud.

CHAPTER FIFTY-NINE

At first, the words sounded slurred as though they were crowding her eyes. Then she was not reading anymore, and Prince Charles's voice filled the room.

Not just his impression.

The inflexions, the way she pronounced certain expressions was Charles's all right. There could be no doubt about it.

Amazed, he listened to his father telling how much he loved her. Head bowed, he could almost see him, sitting in a corner by the fire, the familiar tone asking him to honor the will in its entirety.

When the voice went silent, a lonely tear rolled down her cheek. "Thank you," she whispered huskily, handing him back the letter. "I hadn't realized—"

"No, thank you, Princess." Clasping her hand tightly, he refused to let it go. "I hadn't heard his voice for so long."

"Your father's voice?" Chris looked confused. "What do you mean?"

"The princess read the letter as if she were my father, using the same voice and tone I remember from childhood." He pocketed the letter before squeezing Chris's shoulder affectionately.

"I suppressed all memories of him because it hurt too much." She sighed. "But the emotions in that letter brought them all back."

"I'm sorry you had to go through all that." Enfolding her within his arms, he made her smaller frame disappear inside him.

He had already said it all in her head, right after hearing her sad tale, moved beyond words in a way that hurt his heart just thinking of all she had suffered.

"Sorrier still that my family should be responsible for much of it." No, he did not mind repeating the same words out loud, for the one thing he was struggling to accept was the unimaginable abyss of his mother's cruelty.

Which was darker than anything Chris had said or done so far.

"Believe me." Lifting up her chin, he claimed her sweet lips for a long kiss that had his tongue ravaging her wet cavity.

"I . . ." There were just too many emotions swelling inside her that for a moment, he feared she would burst out crying. "I do." Somehow managing to hold it all together, she rewarded him with a crooked smile.

"Good and this just proves there are a whole lot of things I still need to learn about my family, which until now I thought was as average and as normal as any other." Far from it, since his father's unconventional connections and his mother's black heartedness had made sure of it. "And even if my father, as you heard, was not too outspoken in his affections, he has always been there for me, ready to give precious advice or a word of consolation whenever I needed it." Too bad he had not been around when the phase had started.

It was his only regret. That Prince Charles's death had deprived him of the guidance he needed when the confusing time that preceded the phase had begun.

"So, unlike either of you and everything considered . . ." Shifting position, he focused on the bright flames. "Mine was a happy childhood —"

"You can't say that for sure since you don't remember

pieces of it." She glanced at Chris.

Following her gaze, he spotted a funny look on the hand-some face. Well, it would probably remain a mystery, which was not that important anymore. "Even so, I know I had lov-ing parents, adoring sisters . . ." *Both of them.* He grinned at the princess who stuck her tongue out in mock disagree-ment. "At least from what they tell me." *And I have a much better place where you can stick that tantalizing tongue of yours.* Playfully, he licked his lips. "Plus, I had a special friend and a fantastic phase mate all in one." Grabbing Chris, he made sure to kiss him as long and as hard as he had her before. "Though nothing beats my life today, with two exciting lov-ers." Broadening his clutch, he pulled her in the same em-brace that had already flattened Chris to him. "Even if they just tried justifying their terrible tempers with pitiful tales of sorrow and rejection," he joked over their heads, bending to kiss first one, then the other.

Still, their stories had struck him profoundly. Not just be-cause of the unhappiness that still throbbed inside both, mostly because their experiences seemed oddly similar, as though Chris and Ylianor were in fact mirror images of one another.

Laughing out loud, the blond angel snuggled closer. "All this talk has given me a certain appetite for . . ."

"Not food, I hope." He chuckled while fondling both seductively.

"I guess not, if it's the same appetite we're all feeling." She wriggled under his touch as she reached for his lips.

"Which means that isn't the direction your lips should be going." Quick to wrench her neck, Chris pushed it down un-til her face pressed on Duncan's groin. "Now be a good girl and show your master how much you appreciate his cock." Then the arresting blue-gray eyes were all on him. "I'm just sorry we don't have a better slave available," he joked, get-ting caught up in the game and excited by his control over her.

"I'm sure this will do." Taking out what was fast stiffening, he fed it to her. "It's not like we can find another anywhere around here, can we?"

Getting in the game and treating her as an object was half the fun. His angel's acute arousal at enslaving her to his rough handling was another part of it. The rest was her delicious mouth curling around his thick shaft and drawing it to her throat. Hard intakes and exquisite tongue laps were just a few of her improved skills in the art of blowjobs. No question about it—she was a fast learner who was acquiring the most adept techniques to please the most demanding master of all, Christopher Templeton.

Yes, his angel.

For most of her efforts were all for him in the hope of earning his acceptance.

Which made her surrender such a sharp contrast to the merciless way he enjoyed playing with her.

Yet, they both loved it beyond anything either would admit, at least to him, so he had no objection about their games becoming rougher and rougher.

"Not on such short notice, I'm afraid." Pinning her head down, Chris forced her to swallow his entire beast in one gulp alone.

In one outrageous gag seemed more like it, given how loud she sputtered and gasped.

"Which is why we should avoid suffocating her before we're done with her." Making Chris ease the pressure on her neck, he was relieved to hear her breathe normally.

"As usual, you're no fun," Chris scoffed in mock annoyance.

Just for the show of it, the angel let her go as though the game had lost interest for him. Which was the farthest thing from the truth, given the considerable shape swelling his pants.

"As usual, I'm the master around here." Reluctantly shifting her head to Chris's side, he scrunched it to his crotch. "And now I'm ordering you to come in her mouth."

"Really?" The twitch in the angel's erection was so impressive it practically jumped into her mouth with all the pants on. "Then I'll obey immediately." Unlatching his fly, the giant shaft popped out, soon disappearing inside her wide-open cavity.

She gobbled it up, literally, and sucked it to the balls, uncaring if his hip swings strangled her more times than not. Like he had already observed, she seemed perfectly willing to go that extra mile for the sake of pleasing Chris, and this time was no different.

The best part was that he had full control over every one of her intakes. He set the rhythm for her head bobs over the monster targeting her stomach every time it dug deeper. And she liked it so much she was dripping all over the long length sticking down her throat, running her lips down to the root and using her hands to increase the sliding effect.

For sure, the angel would not last long. She was getting so much better at this that he would lose it within the next five seconds or so.

"Fuck, lover!" If not less.

Clamping her head, Chris choked her with a seemingly unstoppable gush of semen.

"I didn't expect to come so soon." He did not release her until she had licked clean every side of his still rigid piece.

"I did." And now he could have his share. "'Cause in spite of what you think, this slave is getting to be pretty good at this."

"Just passable." Of course, his angel would disagree. "Nothing more."

"Sure, tell that to her ass." Picking her up, he carried her to the bed. *Which is just as delicious as your mouth, Princess.* Knowing how Chris would want to play it now, he sprawled her back down across the mattress.

"That's exactly what I'm planning on doing." Entering the room, Chris took place at her feet.

"And I suppose it won't take you much longer than it did before." No, there was something about her that got to Chris in a way few other people did. And for him watching from the outside, it was one of the most erotic things of late.

"Only if she's particularly tight." Lifting up her legs, he spread them in the air and adjusted the narrow entrance right in front of the tip of his erection. "Which she probably isn't, 'cause she's too wet."

Glancing upward, he noticed the heavy honeydew lining her slit. Talk about drenched! She was dripping and hammering with such hunger she would probably come the second Chris stuck his equipment inside.

No, Master. Her sweet voice in his head thickened his cock into a marble slab. *Less than that for sure.*

Shut up, Princes. Suppressing a laugh, he straddled her face. *No one gave you permission to talk. Your only task at the moment is to suck my cock.* Shoving, he impaled his twitching shaft deep to her throat.

Pure delight, her velvety moistness drove him crazy. Her mouth yielded at each of his thrusts, opening wider as though she wanted him to reach her rear from the top.

Immediately, Master. This time, it was not only her voice. *I just want to serve you best I can.* Her sensations mingled with his, and he was suddenly aware of them.

What about my phase mate? Pure provocation on his part, he knew it as he sank so deep in her mouth she choked.

Oh, he has no need of my compliance to do what he does best. At her coughs, he eased his penetration to allow her to breathe. *Hurt me.*

And though this was an undeniable truth, she charged it

with such a thrill of anticipation that he had to wonder why he had brought together the only two people in the whole world with such an aware and cultivated taste for pain in bed.

In front of him, Chris closed her legs then shoved between her round buns, fierce and ruthless as only his angel could be.

Ouch!

No, she did not say it. Not even thought it, to be fair. Only the pain hitting him was a clear indication his angel had been particularly brutal in his possession.

"Still no reason to crack her ass open with one blow." Even if her waves of pain were already retreating, he needed to slow down Chris's ride, if he wanted this to last any longer.

"Sorry, lover," the angel snickered. "Just thought it would improve its usually worthless performance."

"If it did, you'd come the second you stuck your cock inside it." Already, his angel was losing it, trapped as he was in that erotic hip rotation of hers.

Exactly what she did he was not sure. All he knew was that, just when he thought he had given her all the cock he had, she managed to screw more of it inside, then clenched it so hard it had no choice except unload as fast as it could.

"And open her legs," he ordered, stuffing her mouth with a couple of well-aimed plunges.

As Chris complied, he leaned over and flicked his tongue on her swollen clit.

It was her undoing.

Already, she quivered under Chris's merciless beat ramming her behind and stretching it to an unbelievable size. So strong her need to come, he had the sensation of a ball of fire lodged in his stomach that was about to explode. With his deep, luscious strokes that also reached the puffed lips of her starving slit, everything accelerated.

Arching her back, she slammed her butt against Chris's crotch and gagged on his huge equipment, all the while sucking more cock in both her ass and mouth. But what pushed her overboard was when he shoved three fingers inside her drenched pussy.

At first, she froze. Then the scream started in his head just as the convulsive swells shattered her body. So he and Chris intensified the pounding to a frenzy, which made her come more times than he cared to count. He was slipping anyway, the pressure on the tip of his erection requiring a fast come. So he did, same as Chris spraying her rear with his repeated jets.

Next thing he knew, his plane of existence shifted, and he was beyond time and space, beyond physical reality itself. For how else to explain what he was looking at right about now?

Like empty shells, the many lifetimes he had shared with both Chris and Ylianor stared back at him. Similar yet different, with repeating patterns sometimes, all had a common thread, though he could not quite determine what it was. All he perceived was that this particular life was a new beginning. Not a repetition, not the end of a long journey either, this one had the express purpose of breaking his chains and setting him free forever.

Not just him.

Chris and Ylianor, too, since they were inextricably linked to him.

Then the awareness faded, and he collapsed exhausted on his two lovers.

CHAPTER SIXTY

How do you like the desert, Princess? Black eyes twinkling mischievously, he glanced around the flat expanse that had erased the abundance of plants and animals of the plateau.

Actually, the Wadirum Desert, the gateway to the Nephis Valley, was proving to be harder than she had imagined. Steeply rising temperatures during the day and equally abrupt falls at night for one, then blinding light and intense heat made travel impossible during Stella's peak hours. Before the fourteenth and after the twenty-second hour was the only safe time to ride, so Duncan pushed until only her aura reading skills managed to guide them. It was harrowing simply to spend the mid-days cooped up in a shelter, too exhausted to do anything except pass out, wore down by sweltering heat and fatigue. But to take it a little slower was not an option, not after he had allowed them to stopover for days to talk, reconnect and have glorious sex.

Fascinating. But also disturbing and unsettling.

Brownish sand everywhere, only the rocky cliffs eroded by time and wind broke the monotonous desert stretching out as far as the eye could see. Also beyond, since the horizon had no perceivable boundary between land and sky.

Which gave the illusion the two were one.

And that merely intensified the sense of desolation coming from the lifeless place. As if she were the only living spirit in the world!

At least the scenery was not bad. It had a wild beauty all

its own, what with those tall, odd-looking stone columns, made more beautiful by their colors shifting at every slant of Stella's rays.

It seemed almost as though their shapes, not just their shades, varied as well. A trick of the light no doubt, like when looking at clouds that first seem to be one thing, then another. Same as the intriguing pillars, to the point she could swear she could detect more shapes beneath the consolidated ones, perhaps dating before the erosions. So her fascination was never-ending.

The best part, though, were the rare patches of changing sand. From brown, they became pinkish rose salmon, bright yellow and every shade in between, intense hues that matched the texture perfectly, whether grainy or floury. Oh, she wished she could take just one stroll barefoot, which was not in his agenda.

And thank the gods he had slowed down to a more leisurely pace now that they were crossing this particular stretch.

But I wouldn't trade it with Black Rose. The more she looked around the vast emptiness, the more she missed it. Like a dull pain in her stomach, she yearned for the sharp cliffs and the thundering sea that alone had always infused her with surges of energy.

You miss our home and the sea, don't you? Small wonder he understood perfectly.

He was just like her in this respect.

She merely nodded.

We'll return home soon, Princess. He sounded confident they would. *Don't worry.*

I'm not. She threw back her shoulders to prove it to him. *The longer the journey, the sweeter the return.* She smiled bravely to emphasize her point.

Is that what you thought when I asked you to come back to Black Rose? Straightening on the saddle, he swung his head to catch her gaze.

I had to. After all the sharing she had done at the shelter, those bad memories had lost some of the power to hurt her.

And she had to thank both Chris and Duncan for having brought it all to the fore and released it somehow.

To all effects and purposes, your mother had exiled me. Her tone remained lighthearted, *Not that I let her stop me.* She giggled. *Black Rose was still my home, so in defiance to her orders, I'd sneak back every once in a while, just to steal a glance at the house, at the cliffs and at the sea.*

You cheat! He grinned broadly.

She stuck her tongue out. *It was a matter of survival.*

I bet it was. His grin spread to his black eyes, now twinkling amused. *You're just lucky you know Black Rose much better than my mother ever will, so she never caught you.*

My luck would've run out eventually. Like it had when her eleven-year-old self had gone back to see why he had abandoned her and, on meeting him by accident, he had not recognized her at all. *My real luck was when you happened to knock at my house in the village.*

Luck or destiny? Only natural he should wonder.

First Arthur's words about their past lives and connections had instilled a reasonable doubt that there might be something more to this particular reality. Then the experience at the shelter had confirmed everything, at least to her, for she had seen the many lives and patterns linking them to one another and to a very definite path.

Considering all we've seen and heard. She cocked her head, studying him for a second. *And that, without me you'd have never discovered your Virt, I'd say it was a matter of destiny.*

Then we better hurry to get our task done. Tightening his knees around Fuzeon, he spurred the horse forward. *'Cause I can't wait to see where this destiny of ours is going to take us.*

The brief pause over, the race to the Nephis Valley was on again, with the landscape changing imperceptibly during the five days that followed. Limestone replaced sand and the first plants appeared timidly over the horizon until one day, they were out of the desert.

Just like that!

Fuzeon came closer, and Duncan pointed at a mountain chain looming not too far ahead. "See over there, Princess?"

Not really knowing what she was supposed to look at, she nodded.

"That's the entrance to the Nephis Valley." He gestured in front of her.

"Where? I can't see anything except for . . ." She squinted until she saw a narrow split between the apparently impenetrable rocky walls. "What looks like a crack in the rocks."

"Exactly." Duncan smiled at her. "Nature has hidden the entrance, and no one imagines a tight slit in the mountain walls would lead to it."

Itching to see the fabled place, she urged Starlet forward. "Have either of you ever been there?" She turned to the gorgeous men riding by her side.

And boy, were they simply too attractive for her own good!

"A typical female question," Chris sneered. "Do we look like pledged men?"

"Yes, you do," she retorted playfully. "You've pledged to each other."

"I wish." And Chris sent a wistful glance in Duncan's direction.

Too much longing for her not to avert her gaze and try hard, very hard, to forget all about it. "Even so, maybe you witnessed one."

After all, it was customary for the pledge mates to bring a person who was either a phase mate, a friend or a relative.

"Nah, no one ever asked us." Firmly gripping the reins, Duncan looked at her.

"We probably didn't give the impression of believing in it." The demon grinned widely.

"What happens there exactly?" She had just heard a vague recounting of it, so curiosity made her blurt out the words before she caught Chris's contemptuous gaze on her.

"Again, another dumb question." An annoyed scowl distorted his beautiful clear features. "How should we know?"

"Come on, Angel," his throaty voice scolded gently.

So Chris still had his good and bad days, also now that the three of them had cleared the air and were trying to change their old patterns. It was just too bad, because she might really get used to the different Chris she perceived underneath the varnish of the old one.

In his right mood, he felt like a new man, an exceptional companion brimming with the pure joy of being alive and using every excuse to have fun in whatever dashing fantasy took his fancy. And in bed, he was utterly fantastic, his sex always laced with that veneer of cruelty she was appreciating, if not downright craving, every day more.

Damn him!

She almost loved him then, his sardonic yet playful attitude capturing her heart and crushing it in spite of his million shortcomings. So damn him twice, for at those times she believed he might even like her in his own very personal way.

She should have known better, of course. Those moments were always too short lived to keep feeding that deluded imagination of hers.

A bad night's sex, a wrong word, a snappy remark or any such futile excuse and old Chris resurfaced, with his sarcastic and biting comebacks, all designed to hurt her. And the fact his patience was thinner than usual because of the stressful journey through the desert was no consolation.

"We're all tired." The black velvety eyes flashed in under-

440

standing. "Still, it's no excuse to be nasty." He spun to her. "About the pledge, I know that, when the couples and their group get here, men and women split up in two different shelters, since it's tradition they be separated the night before a pledge. Then the leader holds the ceremony the following day in front of the two witnesses, during which the mates choose a family name, either his or hers. Once it's over, the pledged couple spend the night and the next day in one of the shelters, while the rest of the group waits in the other." He creased his forehead as if trying to remember more details, then shrugged. "That's basically it."

"I see." She maneuvered Starlet to flank Fuzeon. "So how are we going to go about our task, my prince?"

"I wouldn't make any plans yet, since I've never been here." *And I have no idea how to determine what could be missing from this valley,* he added in her head. "Let's see how we feel when we get there."

"I think we should honor traditions." The hint of a smile crossed the demon's lips. "For tonight, Ylianor should stay in one shelter, while we take the other. If we follow the ritual, we might have a better chance to discover what's missing here."

"I totally agree!" Exasperated by his nagging attitude, she spat, "I don't think I could stand spending one more night with you!" And she hoped to have hurt him at least a fraction of what he usually did to her. "Or with you, either." Her gaze blazed on the prince, even if it was not entirely true.

"Hey, what did I do?" Half teasing, half-serious, the concerned black gaze searched her face.

Nothing, my love, this isn't about you, she reassured him. "It's just that some rest from you two will only do me a whole lot of good."

"Tired of us already?" Duncan mocked. "I thought you adored us."

"In case you didn't know it, there are limits to adoration." A sweetly ironic smile curved her lips. "Besides, I'm sure you'll survive the night without me."

"We'll keep so busy there won't be any time to worry about survival." And Chris's malicious gleam told her exactly how he planned to spend the night alone with Duncan. "Or about you."

You can have him all to yourself for all I care. He's yours anyway, isn't he?

She averted her eyes on the off chance he might read this thought as well and answer. She withheld it also from Duncan, for what was the use in sharing? And while she was at it, what was the use of letting the dastardly demon affect her so much?

Whatever she said or did, it would not stop him from turning her slightest comment into another weapon against her.

"You won't need to, Lord Templeton." Raising her gaze, she noticed she had practically reached the low rocky opening that up close resembled a woman's pussy.

"Can't wait for that to happen," Chris hissed back.

"Hey, you two, we're almost at the shelters." Duncan indicated what looked like a tunnel that was barely visible through the stony entrance. "So will you please cut it out?"

In silence, she got off Starlet and led her through the bedrock incision, down the passageway that widened into a clearing with two shelters built on either side of another fracture in the mountain walls. Which she guessed was the real entry point to the Nephis Valley, narrower than the one she had just passed through and not meant for horses, only humans.

"We'll spend the night here." Prince Caldwell glanced at the two shelters. "And tomorrow we'll go to the valley."

"I'll take care of the horses." Reaching out, she caught both Fuzeon and Black's bridles. *And I'll take the left one.*

Stepping forward, she steered the three horses toward the stable, which was common for both shelters.

Are you sure you want to be alone? Duncan's deep voice echoed huskily and a little concerned in her head.

Yes, just as you need your space with your insufferable lover. Not allowing him to slow her down, she walked away faster. *He's giving off too much steam, lately, 'cause he's not used to being with a woman for so long.*

So you noticed? The prince chuckled.

Kind of hard to miss. His ironic tone nearly made her smile.

I'm sorry about his nasty moods. He took a deep breath. *Sorrier still that he takes them out on you.*

The caring note in his raspy tone made her turn.

Which was a mistake.

Just tell me this isn't another punishment. Long hair fluttering in the soft breeze, black eyes flashing, lips curved in a challenging smile, her heart skipped a beat.

No, make that several beats all at once.

It isn't. I just need my own space, too. Feeling her resolve weaken, she breathed the words before she had time to change her mind. *Don't worry. I'll be fine, or I'll send a voice if I need anything.*

"Haven't you finished saying goodbye to your witch?" Deliberately mocking, the demon tugged the prince's arm. "Night is falling fast, and the gods know she needs her beauty sleep." He smirked. "And badly, too."

"Without you around, I'm sure I'll get plenty tonight." She just could not resist snapping back at him.

"Coming, Angel." With a resigned look, he spun to follow him. *Goodnight, Princess, you know where to find me.* Then he strode to the right-hand shelter. *And sweet dreams,* he whispered sensually after he had already disappeared inside the shelter.

CHAPTER SIXTY-ONE

A lone at last!

Slamming the shelter door shut, he could hardly believe it.

Days of having to share his lover with her, and now he could have him all to himself once again. It was absolutely worth a celebration, which was exactly his intent on cornering Duncan, taking out his cock and swallowing it to the hilt. After all, what better way to tell him how glad he was to have this night to themselves?

And the shaft now as stiff as stone seemed to agree with him, shoving down to his throat to get more of his wet pampering. Which he had no trouble providing despite the gurgles and gags standing in the way.

What this magnificent cock wanted, this magnificent cock would get.

So he opened wider and deepened his intakes until his tongue hit just the right spot. That one bit of flesh that drove his lover crazy and made him spill his guts in no time at all.

Wrenching his hair, the man tried to yank back his head. "No, wait—"

Too late!

The juice was already pouring all inside his mouth, gobbled up faster than the fat drops bursting out until none remained.

"Delicious." Licking his lips, he rose and pressed them to Duncan's, then forced his tongue inside to share the pungent flavor.

Which of course got his prince hard again, the new erection rubbing against his equally swollen stick and making his resolve to take things a little slower fly out the window.

So he pushed Prince Caldwell backward until they reached the bed. From there to having him lay down, it took just a few seconds, lesser still to strip off both their pants and straddle him. Then spreading his buttocks far apart, he centered the tip of that fat thick unparalleled monster right into his asshole, sliding down to the hilt despite the burning until he sat on his crotch.

With the fabulous piece all up his ass, he could not sit still. Already, the forceful hip swings were impaling also the balls along with the rest, so only natural he wanted to join in the dance. Nothing beat the furious pumping anyway, the friction scorching his cramped fleshy walls and the repeated slams stretching that narrow back channel into something unbelievable. And all at once, for this awesome beast was so big that after the first drills, he felt his rear become the bottomless pit that magnificent cock needed to suit its aristocratic taste and unload its precious fluid.

But what accelerated everything was his bending down and capturing his lips. Now kissing and fucking at the same time—this was unbeatable! The combination was just too good to last, with the added bonus of having his cock trapped between them.

So as his tongue battled the prince's and his rear clenched around the beefy rod cracking it in two, he lost it. All together and without the benefit of a single gasp, his load shot out all over their chests.

Best thing, his lover's come was stuffing his butt, dripping down his thighs from the sheer mass and force of the liquid aimed at his guts.

"Much better." First round of sex over, he fell on the mattress next to Prince Caldwell. "I didn't think this journey would be so difficult, lover."

"It's not the journey." Duncan pursed his lips. "It's the company."

"Come on, not fair!" *Fuck! Can't you see how hard I'm trying?* "Give me a little credit for my efforts. I've behaved well enough so far, all things considered."

"And you have to give her credit for opening a new channel between us." Why the man insisted on defending her, it was beyond him.

Or rather, he was beginning to suspect why, and he did not like where his guess was going. Not one bit!

"Yes, I'm grateful," he granted annoyed. "Really, I am, but after years of keeping my distance from women, you cannot expect me to see one every single day for the past month or so and be happy about it." No, definitely, this was not his style, and the sooner she got it, the better for him. "So please, don't spoil tonight by talking about her." Which he himself could not stop doing.

Somehow and against his will, she had crawled inside his awareness and refused to leave.

"Besides, she needs her alone space just as bad as we do." Stretching, he reached for Duncan's cock, playfully teasing it to prep it up for the next round. "If not more."

"How do you know?" The expression on his lover's handsome face told him she must have said something to that effect inside his head.

"That's easy," he sniggered maliciously. "If I hadn't read it in her body language, it would've been enough to analyze her history." His touch deepened to raise the prince's interest faster. "Which as it turns out, she spent alone and unwanted except for the first nine years." *And guess whom she has to thank for that?* "She didn't just live it. She had to learn to accept and even like being alone, or she wouldn't have survived."

The one thing that had struck him about her pitiful tale was how resilient she was in spite of all her pretenses to the contrary. And that had earned her a sort of grudging respect from him.

Not that he would tell her, of course.

"So she must be as fed up with our presence as I am with hers," he concluded.

"Do I detect a note of sympathy?" The dark head angled toward his sprawled form, mouth dangerously close to his shaft that constant fondling was turning to marble.

"In case you haven't noticed, I'm not an uncaring monster." *How could I ever be?* "I'm a healer for gods' sake, and that healer sense always gets in the way, whether I like it or not."

The last thing he had wanted was for it to kick off at her tearful story, which was exactly what it did. For damn it, he had no way of avoiding it.

"Plus who, better than me, could relate to those feelings?" Now that he thought about it and considering all he had gone through, it seemed eerily similar to his own bad experiences. "And I can tell you that, however terrible they might've been, she was getting used to them." He clasped the beefy erection more firmly. "Even happy I dare add, until you spoiled it all by knocking on her door."

"Are you saying I did her no favor by bringing her along?" Evidently more interested in the conversation, the prince blocked his sensual jerking.

"You did her no favor the moment you got back into her life." Resigned, he let his hand fall and raised his gaze. "She was ready to embrace a fairly uncomplicated existence, when there you go, upsetting all her neat plans." Shifting upward, he reached over for a brief, tender kiss. "And you're such a dashingly gorgeous prince, how could anybody in their right mind ever resist you? And from all I've seen, she's got less resistance than most people I know when it comes to you. So she had no choice except to yield to your commands and forget all about what she wanted to do." Deepening the kiss was just another means to arouse his lover's cock even against his objections.

"I thought I was giving her an alternative." Having understood he was fighting a losing battle, Duncan gripped his hand. "A way out." And pressed it on what had become a veritable beast.

"That's a laugh!" Now that it was once again in his grasp, all he craved was to suck it again. "You were just being selfish, and that's by your own admission." Still, sliding the soft skin up and down the extensive length was better than nothing. "You saw her, you wanted her, and you took her. End of story."

Prince Caldwell averted his gaze. "If only she wasn't so damn attractive in and out of bed, all this might've never happened."

You mean if you weren't getting hooked on her big time, right, lover?

But since he did not care to find out for sure, he kept his trap shut.

"And with her around there can be no . . ." *Privacy.*

If he did not say it, it was not because he did not think it. Rather, he did not want to scorn what was a gift of sorts. For what good could Virts accomplish if people considered them as liabilities rather than assets?

Yet, to Duncan's heavy heart, his resembled more the former than the latter.

"Ironic, isn't it?" Duncan chuckled in fake amusement. "That I should find her after I've looked so long for a woman like her."

"How can you be sure she's the one?" 'Cause the gods forbid if I'll have to put up with her any more than I have to! "You had no idea what you wanted then. And you still don't now. She just . . ." *Stuck her nose where it didn't belong.* "Happened along—"

"Her Virt didn't just *happen along*," Duncan retorted sarcastically. "Nor did mine."

"Makes no difference, since you didn't even know Virt existed," he snapped back. Then seeing the prince getting uptight, he opted for a gentler tone, "I'm not saying she isn't the one." *Just praying she isn't.* "Simply that it's too early to tell. The only certainty is that the way we are now is a bit too tight for me." Lying back down, he placed his head on his chest. "I'm just glad to be alone with you tonight, your last night as a free man."

"What are you talking about?" Duncan tensed.

"Just getting in the spirit, lover." A wide grin curved his lips as he pressed on his stomach, his mouth straying to the hungry shaft demanding attention.

"Then I suggest you make it extra good this time." A hand on his neck, Duncan forced his head over the tip of the gigantic erection.

"Already on it, lover." Since this was the beginning of round two, nothing better than a radical change of pace. "And on your exquisite ass."

"Is that how you plan to make it better?" Amused, he opposed no resistance when rolled over on his stomach.

"Absolutely." Straddling him, he stuck a couple of wet fingers inside the tight ring, which opened up and swallowed them whole. "'Cause in all the excitement of fucking her, you've forgotten how badly you need it, too."

And damn it! If he could get through one blasted fuck without thinking of her, he would be the happiest man alive.

To wipe her off his mind, he sunk more fingers inside the cramped hole that had no trouble sucking them as it had the other ones. Then he twisted them to enlarge the space and get it ready for something much bigger.

Prince Caldwell groaned. "All right." He raised his butt, "You convinced me."

"I knew it wouldn't be hard." Shifting his weight on his arms, he nudged the tip of his beast on the tight opening. "And that you'd see it my way."

Then he shoved with all the fierceness of his desire to possess what his phase mate rarely gave away. Or to be precise, to no one except him, which made his claim all the more exciting, particularly now that he had broken through the narrow constriction and was hammering to the guts.

All it took was a few more blows to split his lover's rear. Then once his cock was firmly inside, he rammed to increase the speed and the heat of his equipment sliding against what had become a fiery sheath.

He liked it best this way, and he knew Duncan did as well. Too often they had done it during the phase to misunderstand the signs. Plus, the frenzied back swings that matched his forward thrusts were clear indication the prince wanted to accelerate the dance.

Spin it out of any control was more like it.

For this rough pounding of that delectable asshole was pushing him overboard faster than he had anticipated. Everything burned so hot that it was like his fire had just erupted and left his body behind. Or maybe all this playing around with energy during sex was changing his pleasure somehow.

Either way, his cock scorched every time it rubbed against the stretched rear channel, the friction setting it ablaze also when he slammed to go beyond the available space. To come out of the throat would have been his aim, even if he already knew he could not make it.

Not because his shaft was not long enough, only because he could not last that long. He had to spill it all and soon, 'cause the pressure was strangling him.

At that moment, his phase mate came with a loud gasp. And everything blurred when the throw back of his orgasm was a tide of cool energy that shot through his blood. The sharp contrast with his own heat blew away his mind, and he burst.

The end of round two marked the beginning of round three. Without any time for recovery, he barely finished pumping out the last drop that Duncan was already toppling him.

His cock as rigid as if he had not just sprayed the bed sheets, he went for the mouth first. A short-lived affair that lasted just enough to stuff the huge piece down his stomach and have it suffocate him good and proper.

Then on to his next target, Duncan splayed his legs far apart and nailed the back ring with one thrust.

Small wonder!

His ass was still as large as it had been at the end of round one.

And given the ruthlessness ramming, he began losing it immediately. There was no point in resisting anyway. This night would be all about fast and furious sex, cramming it inside an ass or a mouth until it exploded and got ready for the next round.

And he was totally on board with this schedule. So he facilitated the prince's penetration to his guts, jerked his cock and let it go, already relishing the start of round four.

CHAPTER SIXTY-TWO

"Ready to go?" Duncan checked on both her and Chris assembled near him in a small circle, his back toward the narrow slit between the stones that marked the beginning of the path to the Nephis Valley.

"Yes, my prince." She nodded, eager to get going.

Seventy-two hours, two full days, had passed since her arrival, and they had been barely enough. First, exhaustion had taken its toll, so one day had flown simply sleeping off all the excitement of the past month or so. Then on the second day, her plans for some regenerating alone time had gone kind of awry, on the account that she could not stop thinking about them. Or missing them, to the point her heart crushed painfully now that she saw the dark and blond heads almost touching.

Still, it had not been a total loss. For one thing, she had not given in to the urge to call Duncan. One thought from her, and she was sure he would have ended their separation. This in itself made her feel stronger and more of a survivor than she had given herself credit while cooped up in that lonely shelter.

And it had worked wonders on them, with the demon even going as far as embracing her tightly the moment they had met again.

Imagine that!

"Then let's go." As the leader of their small group, Duncan was the first to crawl through the rocky incision.

Chris followed him. Then it was her turn, and she had to

squeeze through the narrow entrance with the cold stone pressing her back and front.

Now studying the long, seemingly endless canyon cut through high mountains, she could hardly contain her excitement. Maybe not all Chris's fault, for something in the air around her was definitely getting to her, starting from the intriguing rift stretching out like a tortuous river, maybe the same that had eroded it through thick bedrock eons before. Now with tall stonewalls flanking this tight uphill path, the winding twists and turns seemed to her like the spiraling coils that in her mind connected the spirit to the body.

"I think this is a spiritual journey." She reached them.

"Why do you think so, Princess?" The black velvety gaze searched her face.

"Because this place is so . . ." Glancing around at the overly confined space, there was no way she could miss it. "It's full of auras from the many people who must've gone through here." Only it did not feel right, because they clung to stonewall as though they did not want to leave.

"Small wonder." Glancing upward, Chris's gaze fixed on the impenetrable mountains that cut off practically all of Stella's rays. "This place looks like a trap."

"Yes, you're right." Now she noticed it. "The auras are like trapped in here." That explained why it affected her so much. "And they shouldn't be. They should be free and . . ."

Oh, darn! She was making no sense, yet Duncan needed to know.

So she shared it all, from her vague sensations to the stronger perceptions she had picked up so far—all without uttering a single word.

Thanks, Princess. She loved his deep voice vibrating in her head. *I think I get it now.*

"I'm guessing these auras stay here 'cause they represent the past lives that you have to discard, in order to begin anew with your pledge mate." If she continued to talk, it was only for the demon's benefit. "Like shedding your old clothes and wearing new ones sort of thing, so that you're clean and ready to face your new future together with a special person by your side."

"Then no one's better qualified than we are," the demon teased. "It seems we haven't done anything besides interpret our past to decide what our future will be."

"So let's go and meet it." Spinning around, Prince Caldwell strode forward on the route that was barely wide enough to go single file.

She fell in step right behind him, the demon at the rear.

With Stella's rays fading, the place seemed even more mysterious and out of the ordinary, also given its bad habit of trapping everything that entered in contact with it. Like light—if it managed to filter through the high peaks, it had no way out. And it was no use for the imprisoned rays to reflect on the rocky ground then bounce off to the walls before dropping back to the ground. Like a fish taken out of the water, they thrashed like crazy until they went suddenly still. Same thing with the heat—without any means of escape, it stagnated to the point the air was so dense it was almost unbreathable. And the smell was no different, though she liked it well enough. Musty, hot and spiced with nothing resembling either plant or animal, the acrid odor was as heavy as the air carrying it, and it burned her nostrils and throat.

But what fascinated her most was the running water crashing in her ears. Not that she actually saw any. Hard as she peered around, nothing revealed the slightest trace of any liquid anywhere. Still, the sound was so deafening it broke the silence, so she stopped looking with her eyes and started searching with her perception.

Soon enough, she felt it coursing through two parallel canyons that bordered her path at a higher height. Hidden inside the stone itself, it was as though water had created an alternative route, after having retreated from the main road.

At the third or fourth curve, the passage widened enough for her to walk on one side of Duncan, Chris on the other. And now that she was getting further inside, the mountains seemed to swallow her up and cut her off from reality itself. They were too tall and impending to ignore. Not entirely straight but bending on the upper edge, it made them more foreboding and reduced the passage to a dark tunnel where anything could be possible. So, yes, maybe she was heading for a whole new dimension, one without any visible sky, with little or no light and with high bedrock walls closing in on every side.

Suddenly, the rift tightened again, and they had to proceed single file once more. So they divided again. As she retreated to the central position between the two men, she wondered whether she would reach her destination before night fell. Not that it mattered much. As long as she was on this enchanted trek, there was no significant difference between day and night. Then all such thoughts fled her mind when the path came to an abrupt halt in front of an apparently impenetrable stony wall.

"Now what?" Pressing against Duncan's back, Chris scrutinized the seemingly unbroken surface.

"Now we look for a way out." Duncan's philosophical reply was a clear sign he was already examining the surface. "Which could be this." Shifting to the farthest left side, he indicated an extremely small crevice in between the solid rocks. "It'll take a bit of an effort, but I'm sure we can make it through."

"A bit?" Chris ran a hand on the uneven edges that would require several contortions in order to squeeze through them. "That's an understatement." He chuckled. "And if everything else hadn't been enough, this definitely puts a damper on my pledging to anyone, had I ever the insane notion of asking a woman for it." Of course, the blue-gray eyes were all on her.

"Don't worry, Lord Templeton." She giggled. "With your bad temper, no woman in her right mind would ever take you as a pledge mate."

"Their loss." Shrugging, the demon bent on her ear. "And my gain," he whispered seductively.

What if he was right?

She refused even to think it.

"I suggest you leave all these fascinating questions if the time ever comes for you to pledge," Duncan joked, bending to fit inside the cramped opening. "And concentrate on the task we have at hand."

"Right, lover." As soon as the prince disappeared through the hole, Chris also scrunched through the cleft.

Then it was her turn, and the moment she re-emerged on the other side, she knew she had stepped into another world, one where mountains enclosed an exquisite green valley, guarding it like a precious gem with their snowy peaks and rigid walls.

Breathtaking and magnificent, she now saw the water flowing inside stone channels that circled the enclave's perimeter, before falling like a smooth cascade into a pond at the eastern edge. And the contrast between the white snows above and the glittering green below would have kept her gaze glued, had something else not imperiously demanded her attention.

Responding to the pull, she glanced in the cascade's direction until she caught the brilliant light flashing relentlessly. And how odd, these many lights flickered just like a million auras all rolled up in one, blazing like crazy under the unbalance of the innumerable and contrasting moods forced together.

CHAPTER SIXTY-THREE

Do you hear that, Princess? On stepping into the valley, he had not even been able to look much around, too loud the noise deafening him.

Hear what? An adorable puzzled expression made her lovely face more beautiful as she glanced around disoriented.

All right, so he had missed her. More than he had dared admit to himself, sometimes even during the scorching two-day sex marathon with his angel. And if she had just sent his way the slightest whiff of a thought, he would have carried her to his shelter himself and never let her go, regardless of Chris's objections.

The humming. Now that he was getting used to it, he could focus on the strange structure behind the cascade. *It seems to come from that . . .*

What was it, exactly?

It was hard to tell, since he had never seen anything like it. If he had to take a wild guess, he would have said a pyramid, though a very weird one.

No, but I see the lights. She squinted as though they hurt her eyes.

What lights? He could see none. The structure was completely in the dark now that Stella had definitely set.

Here. Advancing, she came closer. *I'll show you.*

Suddenly, a million colors exploded in his mind.

Ah, those lights! Blinded, he had to breathe deeply a couple of times to adjust to their intensity. *By the gods, they're amazing.*

Aye, they are. Evidently having adapted as well, her voice sounded more adamant and out of the daze from the too many lights blazing all together, all at once. *And they probably mean something –*

Whatever it is, must be related to the structure. He pointed at it.

What structure? She fixed her gaze on the general direction he indicated and blinked once or twice. *I can't see anything with all these lights turned on.* In frustration, she shook her head, the long black hair flying all around her.

Then it's my turn to help you. He grinned amused.

He was getting to like this sharing thing. When he had entered the tunnel and she had drowned him with a whole bunch of different sensations in the matter of a second, he had understood her perfectly as though he had felt them himself. Then that trick of the lights going off in his head made him realize there was so much more to this Virt than he had given it credit before. The potentials were enormous, and if only he had not been acting like a spoiled brat, he might have seen them sooner and taken advantage of them, rather than chastising the one person who had made it all possible.

Like what he was doing now, picturing the structure in its wholeness then transferring it to her.

Now I see it. Breathing heavily, her voice sounded faint amidst the acute humming. *But don't you find it odd that you and I should see and hear different things coming from the same place?*

Exactly my thought. And he did not like it one bit. *The way this thing is playing with our perceptions makes me think that it knows about our different Virts.* Which left him only one logical question. *So what does the angel see?*

I doubt we can ask him right now. Vaguely ironic, she glanced behind her shoulder.

Following her gaze, he had to admit she was right. His beautiful angel had turned into his energy self, the blazing fire that was his trademark.

And there he is. Nose up in the air, she was obviously tracking his flight.

So he raised his gaze, and damn if that seductive creature was not an impressive sight, whatever shape or form he took, also now that he hovered next to the structure.

He's beautiful, she whispered huskily, her admired tone saying so much more than the words just had.

At least to him.

Couldn't agree more, Princess. He just wished he had time to probe her feelings. *But let's concentrate on the structure, shall we?*

Yes, of course. She blushed purple.

Not because of his scold.

Probably because she knew she had given herself away, which she had already when the angel had embraced her earlier. Priceless her expression then, not to mention that slight embarrassment of hers that had told him just how much she had missed him and Chris.

If only these lights weren't in the way. Hesitating, she analyzed them more intently. *I think they are some sort of energy field guarding the structure, a protection against intruders.*

I guess it considers only you an intruder. He could not explain it any other way.

Not true. Her lips curved in an enchanting smile. *The demon sees them, too.*

And how appropriate that nickname of hers, for Chris had always struck him as being both an angel and a demon.

Here, take a look. The image of Chris melting with the shiny lights and becoming one with them popped to the fore. *So, if you want my help, you must tell him to shut them off,* she pointed out, her tone more serious.

He's already working on it. And his senses mixed with the

angel's.

Blended as Chris was with the lights, it was not hard for him to find their source inside a vibrating metallic container hidden at the bottom of the pond. Drawing on Duncan's own Virt, he dived underwater and struck the unfamiliar object with fiery darts, until he managed to shut it down somehow.

Better, Princess? He spun to confront her.

Much. Her green eyes sparkled in gratefulness. *He made the entire valley plunge into darkness.* She sounded extremely impressed. *Please thank him on my behalf.*

You can thank him yourself once we're done. This could really be a lot of fun, if he did not have a mission to accomplish and no idea on how to go about it.

Whatever it was, it had to involve the bizarre pyramid. The more he studied it, the more it seemed out of his world, the more it resembled the image the three of them had shared at the Hall. Built on a large triangular base, it was a giant tower composed of many small three-sided pyramids fastened together or better yet, framed one inside the other. The peak high up in the sky, each little pyramid was unique, made of varied materials and colors. Like some were of stone, impenetrable to light. While others were transparent, almost glass-like.

Single pieces notwithstanding, this structure was alive and powerful. And it wanted him. Had been calling him ever since he had stepped in the enclave, for whatever mysterious purpose it would serve it.

It's incredible. Her admiration for the elegant form reverberated through the confusion of the humming. *And those small three-sided pyramids remind me of the one Chris thought about, remember?*

How could he forget? *The one he used to describe our relationship and that we all saw.* He nodded in agreement.

Yes, the triangular pyramid. The image filled his mind.

Maybe this place was already calling us. He was sure she was already thinking along the lines that this could not be a coincidence. *How many pyramids does it contain?*

A lot. Too many to count for sure. *Come.* He took a step forward. *Let's get closer.*

It did not take long for them to reach the base of the multi-pyramids tower, with the extra bonus that his angel had returned to his very attractive human form.

"All right, let's make a circle," he commanded aloud for Chris's benefit. "And try to discover what secrets lie buried here."

Seating in front of the pyramid tower, he directed his lovers on either side of him. Then opening his arms, he clasped their hands, nodding at them to do the same. As soon as Chris and Ylianor completed the circle, their minds joined.

And the pyramids suddenly flared up again.

Not like before, rather each pyramid came alive with a light of its own. Colors ranging from intense white to dark blues and greens, yellows, reds, oranges, all mixed in a kaleidoscope of shades, without the ominous flashes or the blinding effects they had previously.

"And concentrate on the pyramids." Too tall the tower for him to look up at every single one, he used his perception more than his eyes to absorb what was happening. "That's where we have to start looking for whatever is missing."

Quick and curious, Chris's dazzling energy ran up and down the entire structure, not lingering on any one piece, rather taking in the whole.

"Something is out of place." Chris squeezed his hand once he was back to human.

"Something like what, Angel?" Tightening his grip, he made them close ranks.

"Wish I knew." Shrugging, Chris raised his gaze to check on all the pyramids at once.

Following his direction, he expanded his awareness to every piece singularly, sifting through each and sinking into its particular uniqueness until all he felt were the shifting colors, all he heard was the humming. And it was so loud now that it clogged his head. The different sounds coming from each pyramid flowing together to create a melody of its own. High-pitched and harmonious, it would have been beautiful had he not caught that discordant note. Almost imperceptible at first, it grew more fastidious as soon as he focused his entire attention on it. Off-key — that was how the whole tune played in his mind now, spoiling the perfection of it all. Something was definitely missing, something like a note that should have been there, yet it was not. "But where does it come from?"

"Probably the same place where the hole is," she was quick to provide, having followed his reasoning.

"What hole?" For the life of him, he could not perceive a break in the surface anywhere on the tower.

"The one where its heart should be." Her arresting green eyes locked on his. "Which is at the very center of it."

"Angel, do you think that missing something you noticed could be at the center of this tower?" Spinning his head, he fixed his gaze on the shiny blue-gray eyes.

"Let me check." Under his watchful gaze, the angel's fiery sparks narrowed on a precise spot of the structure, positioned near the top.

Now he saw it, too, the almost invisible space that was void. And it coincided with the source of the offbeat in his head.

The demon has found it, my prince. Excitedly, she gestured at it.

And that's also where the missing note comes from. The more he listened to the pyramids' song, the more he was sure of it.

Another pyramid must've been there. She took their reasoning to the next logical level.

Yes, and it must've been a special one, Princess. Or why else would she have perceived it as the heart of the whole thing? *Why don't you see if you can find the traces of what it was exactly?*

I'm right on it. And she was indeed, isolating the open space and reading the faint signs still available.

Then a sharp and clear picture formed in his head.

Do you see it? She sounded proud of herself.

I do. Though it did not make much sense. *A pyramid with a sphere inside? Is there a similar one in the structure?*

Together, the three of them went through each single piece to determine whether a duplicate existed, which it did not. From the transparent to the solid-looking ones, no pyramid hid a core or a sphere for that matter.

That's probably why someone took it, but who would go to all the trouble of removing it? Perplexed, he checked around the valley as though expecting that someone to pop out from behind a rock or something. *And how did they do it?*

Let me see if I can focus on the aura traces of the very recent past. This was proving to be a great training ground for her Virt, better than anything they had devised among themselves.

Watching his angel's acrobatics on the structure, Prince Caldwell wondered how the many pyramids had survived the loss of their heart.

They couldn't have. She was evidently on his same wavelength. *Besides, the pattern of the missing pyramid is still fresh, a clear sign it has not been gone long.* She was already exploring the broader area of the Nephis Valley.

First lingering on a couple of spots nearby, probably where the couples and the leader stood for the pledge, she moved further back until her heart raced with the awareness of recognition.

I can't believe it! Then she flashed him the person whose

aura she had just picked up now.

What? And he could not believe it, either. *What was David doing here?*

I don't know, but he wasn't alone. At the words, a dark-haired woman with high cheekbones and hard sculptured features popped in his head.

Cecilia Hurst. Now what was she doing here? *That's Cecilia Hurst.*

She took the object with David's help. He had to give her credit for making a splendid job of suppressing her curiosity and not asking who Cecilia was.

How could they? Seen how far up the missing piece had been, he guessed that either Cecilia or David, if not both, had some kind of Virt that had helped them to bring it down.

One or both of them must have the Virt to move objects. Only natural she would confirm his suppositions. *Now I understand what I detected in David but couldn't quite put my finger on.*

So he has a gift, too. And how strange that, like his angel, David had been so close, yet he had never suspected any Virt in him, either.

He must, otherwise this Cecilia wouldn't have brought him along, would she? Her logic seemed inescapable. *I mean I don't think it was David's idea . . .*

We'll ask them soon enough. Because the next item on his agenda had just become to confront them. *For now, I think our task here is over.* Not just because he was suddenly exhausted. Because his princess was about to collapse from the depletion in her energy, something he immediately set to rectify however low his own supply. *We found out all we could tonight, so I suggest we leave.* Before he had to carry her back to the shelter.

If you can tear your lover away from his new toy. She giggled amused at Chris's blazing flights around the structure.

He grinned. Could he be prouder of his fiery angel than

he already was? Or more in love with him for that matter?

Still, it was time to go, so he squeezed the bright energy he had kept wrapped inside his, as a way to command his angel's return.

He's coming. He pressed the hands he had kept holding on to, just as Chris repossessed his body. "He's as tired as we are." Latching on the alert blue-gray gaze was all he needed to know he was right.

"And he can't wait to get to a bed," Chris added with a mischievous twist in the thin lips.

"Hardly surprising," she quipped. "He'd never leave a bed, were it up to him."

"Hey, I heard that." Chris was quick to flare up, even if only for play.

Laughing, he cocked his head. "How right you are, Princess." Then his dark energy overflowed her to strengthen her dwindling reserves for the trip back to the shelter.

A grateful smile lit her beautiful face, and his heart skipped a beat.

Which he ignored while he released his control, before getting to his feet. As if by magic, the humming went silent, and he would have moved away, had not his stiff muscles made it hard to take the first step. His sore limbs were literally screaming for mercy. Without even noticing it, he had stayed fixed in the same position for hours. And night had come and gone, replaced by a crisp, clear dawn.

In a daze, he retraced his steps back, too tired to notice anything, hurrying instead along the downhill path. Soon, he arrived at the wide clearing with the two shelters, and it was like he had been gone for an entire lifetime. And now that he was back, there was no way he would allow her to be alone.

Wrenching her elbow, he dragged her toward the shelter she had occupied, with Chris at his heels saying nothing.

Barely managing to reach the bed, he saw to it that both his lovers crawled under the sheets, before collapsing fast asleep next to them.

CHAPTER SIXTY-FOUR

H*ungry!*

He was so damn hungry, with a voracious emptiness that was about to devour him from the inside. But food had nothing to do with it, and his huge cock throbbing painfully was all the proof he needed.

Clasping it firmly, he opened his eyes. What he craved — had always craved it seemed — was sex, sex and more sex. Even more than his usual abundant share of it, as if an uncontrollable urge had taken his body hostage. Imagine that!

He, Christopher Templeton, who had made of sex the driving force of his life, wanted more of it! And not just from men. The way he was feeling this morning, he would have gone for whatever holes he could find, women included.

Which was pure heresy.

Blasphemy, if he considered that she was right in front of him, curled on a side and with her magnificent ass staring him in the face. One shove and he would probably get to her guts before she even woke up —

Nah, this was definitely not right. He could not possibly want her this much. Not her. Not a woman.

Better to roll on a side and check out the window to determine how long he had passed out. Last thing he remembered was dropping exhausted on the bed and now, judging from the light out, he guessed he had slept an entire day and night, if not longer. So only natural he wondered if anybody else was as awake and as famished as —

"I'm starving." The stiffness pressing on his back could be

only Duncan's. "And it has nothing to do with food." Sliding the tip of the giant erection between his buttocks, he seemed ready to dig his beast inside the first hole he found. "All to do with this scrumptious ass of yours."

"Hey, not fair." Jerking his shaft harder, he shifted to facilitate Duncan's penetration. "My cock wants a piece of ass, too."

"Lucky for you, we've got an obedient slave just waiting to satisfy our needs." Reaching out and grabbing the body that he had ignored on purpose, Duncan dragged it in front of his cock. "So take advantage of it before I take it myself." The tip of his erection broke through the tiny ass ring.

And his stomach caved in with the pleasure scorching him everywhere.

Another thrust and half of that fabulous piece lodged inside, which melted his senses and fired up his cock in such a way that he had to act fast. He absolutely had to impale a tight hole for himself, if he did not want to burst from the craving of it. And at this point, it really did not matter whose hole it would be.

Wrenching her hips, he aimed for the tiny ring in between those deliciously round buns of hers. That was when he realized she was wide-awake, even if she had said nothing. Too bad, because he would have much rather preferred to wake her with the pain of his possession, but it could not be helped. Circling her waist to pull her backward, his hand slipped down, and his fingers became instantly drenched.

Fuck! "There isn't much to take advantage of." Annoyed, he removed his hand. "Not with her being as wet as she is."

"Your problem." Drilling his ass like it were butter, Duncan had reached his guts and was now going for the throat. "Not mine."

Oh, he would have just loved to push her away, were his intense need to have her not so overwhelming. Like a fever, he just had to have her or die from the sheer wanting. So he swung his hips back to swallow more of his lover's unparalleled cock and tugged her against him. Fierce and rough, he wanted to stick it in her with one shove alone, hoping she would jump from the pain.

Which goddamn it she did not.

Instead, she opened wide, evidently wanting it more than he cared to know. And since this did not dampen his enthusiasm, his inability to crack her ass at the first thrust strengthened his resolve to do it sooner rather than later. When his second try did not get him to her guts, he became irritated. The position's fault for sure. Being on a side and with a cock stuck up his ass, he did not have too many margins for maneuver.

"She's too dry, Angel." Chuckling softly in his ear, Duncan seemed to make fun of his predicament. "If you want to make it easier on yourself, you should try her cunt first." To make it more obvious the prince was taunting him, he stuck a couple of fingers in her asshole, which she sucked to the hilt without any problems. "That ought to get your cock slick enough for her ass."

"You're really getting a kick out of this, aren't you?" Not that he had much choice in the matter.

He was going up in smoke from his own lust. He had to have her *now*!

"Is it that obvious?" Beaming, his lover slammed so hard the balls got through his rear hole.

Well, almost, for the burning he felt all together could have no other explanation.

"Just be fast about it, Angel, 'cause I don't think I'll last much longer." Another vicious shove and the balls just about slipped to his throat.

"That's easy for you to say." Changing his shaft's destination, he aimed for her pussy. "You're inside the best place there is around, while I got . . ." *A fucking woman!* "Her."

Just to think it was sacrilege.

Still, he stuffed her extremely wet slit, and boy! Did it melt his cock to the core with all that intense heat and moistness enveloping it, clenching it so tight it could have severed it from his crotch. Amazing this sensation and so very different from anything he knew, he could not quite leave the spot. Not just yet, since his beast's eagerness to pump her was in sharp contrast with his mind's shocked disbelief.

"Seems like the lady has something more to offer besides her ass and mouth," Duncan mocked softly.

"Yeah, and damn her I can't seem to be able to leave it." His breathing short, he knew he would not manage to stick to his original plan.

What he had begun as a mere excuse to slick up his cock was turning out the best thing of his life. Plunging to the hilt, her wetness clung to every side of him, sucking him up in a velvety honeydew no ass could ever provide. And he adored it, to the point he never wanted to leave. No, not even if it meant ramming her ass.

So he lost it.

Already, his ass was about to explode from the effort of containing an equipment so big it was splitting him in half. This extra bit about how unexpectedly pleasurable her cunt was, really blew him away.

Not fast enough that she did not beat him to a most shattering come. If her pussy convulsing on his cock had not been sufficient proof, her scream proclaimed to the whole world what an astounding orgasm she was having. Which swelled his monster to such a size it had to burst, unable to sustain the pressure pushing at its tip.

That was also the same time Duncan drowned his ass with his own uncontainable juice.

Hardly sated, as soon as the cock quit dripping inside his behind, he jumped up and arranged her on all fours. Time for revenge, he blew her rear to bits with just his first hit, having to prove to himself that nothing had changed. That he was still the same old Chris who hated women and only considered their butts and mouths as passable sexual targets. And that his lifetime convictions were still intact in spite of what had just happened.

Unfortunately, he could not procure her the pain he had hoped to inflict. The more brutal his pounding, the more she loved it. Had been loving it from the moment he had first impaled her yielding flesh, as though she had been drowning in pleasure ever since awakening.

Like she was under a spell or something.

Which to him was another sign that this place was doing something not just to him, to all of them.

Her pleasure became a near orgasm the instant Duncan sank his gigantic equipment in her slit. Then he had to claim her mouth in the fiercest and most arousing kiss he had ever seen.

And damn him! It set off a craving to ravage her lips that he found utterly intolerable.

If he managed to suppress that urge, he could not tear his gaze away from their bodies dancing seductively in front of him. Partly his fault, for his hammering her sweet behind forced her hips to swing in a certain way. Mostly Duncan's fault and the way he was devouring her. Like a man literally starving, he had her mouth trapped in his, probably her tongue stuck to his throat. And the mere thought of it was what made him lose it a second time.

Well, again she beat him to it, her body swelling under his eyes and sucking his cock to the root. No scream this time, but then how could she possibly manage it?

She was too deep in the prince's mouth to be able to emit

the slightest sound. And the load both he and Duncan were shooting inside her was a further hindrance.

Dropping to the mattress, he carried her along with him, strangely reluctant to let her go. Without unscrewing his still quite rigid piece, he fell on his back and had her sitting on top of him.

"I'd try something different, seeing how much you're liking playing with her." Quick to rise with an equally swollen equipment, Prince Caldwell detached her from his cock and lifted her up in the air. "It's something I could never try given my angel's taste." Chortling, he turned her around and screwed her cunt on Chris's erection.

With that unbelievable heat, his core began melting once more.

"She's too wet to feel anything." Only this time, he put up a semblance of resisting her allure.

"Not for long." Taking position behind her, he aimed for her slit, too. "Trust me."

Before he could protest again, Duncan shoved, and everything went all-cramped all of a sudden.

Boy, if this was not a terrific way to stuff her pussy and make it feel as crammed as an ass, he did not know what else was.

"Thought you might like it." Smiling in evident satisfaction, Prince Caldwell thrust forward.

So Chris retreated to give him the extra space, slamming back the moment he withdrew.

"And she's nice and tight, just as you like it." Nice and exploding would have been the exact words, seeing how two monstrous sizes like theirs were stuffing her to her ears.

Not that she complained any. Adjusting her position, she actually made it easier for both of them to plunge to her stomach without any effort at all. And she was so loving it all it was indecent.

At least to him and to his lips, which were now so close to hers that his craving to kiss her spun out of any control. Like with her pussy before, he just had to claim her inebriating lips to himself, had to savor that mouth of hers fully, not hurriedly like Duncan had forced him to do the other time.

Same time he had realized he might actually like kissing her.

So this time, he went for them himself, clamping her neck and bringing it down on him.

Shocked, she flung her eyes open, her questioning green gaze staring at him.

Of course, he ignored it. Too busy taking her mouth forcefully, like a conqueror on an expedition. And she tasted so damn hot he could not get enough of her. His tongue ravishing the whole of her sweet opening, he drank her down to his balls, relishing her surrender and his teeth bruising her soft lips. Then it was her tongue as he sucked it to his stomach, holding it prisoner so he could sweep her at ease.

More!

This was turning out to be so much more than a mere kiss. He wanted to swallow her, to eat her up and keep her inside him forever. Because drowning in her flavor was not enough.

Not even close to sufficient.

He never wanted to wash her taste away.

Good thing that, the more he sank in her, the wider she opened as if sensing he would accept nothing but total compliance with his demands, whatever they would turn out to be.

Well, he had several in mind, all beginning and ending with Ylianor herself and his really bad craving to possess her all. So splitting that cunt of hers was just skimming the surface as far as he was concerned, considering also what an irresistible addition was brushing his cock against Duncan's.

Not even in his wildest dreams had he ever imagined it could unleash such a tempest in his senses. And matching their tempo did not help matters any, not while his control slipped faster than ever. Which marked another end of the game. Not just for him, for all of them at the same time.

Surprisingly still full of energy and excitement, he waited for Duncan's next move, which was to sprawl her on the mattress, place her legs around his waist and go for her cunt again. So open and defenseless, mouth slightly ajar, she was a perfect take for his still very hungry cock. Pressing his knees around her head, he nailed her mouth with a vicious blow that had her gasping for air and jolting for an impossible escape. Trapped as she was between him and the prince, she had no way to dodge either of the beasts stuffing her good and proper.

So he insisted, wanting her to gag on him, until that urge to taste her did not hit him again.

Fuck! He had thought to quell it once and for all with that incredible kiss. Instead, he wanted to savor her cunt, something he had refused to do, not just with her, with any woman. Never, not even by mistake, had he stooped as low as stroking that wetness women hid between their legs, his interest always focusing on the only two holes worth a dam— mouth and ass. *Remember?*

Evidently, he did not, since he stretched out, ready to nibble her to death if that was what it took to get the extra feel of the same flesh he had wanted to carve only weeks before. As irrational as it sounded, he bent on her breasts, usually the trait he most despised about women, and fell on the soft mounds like they were the most enticing cock in the world. Those very tempting, very erect tips merited the repeated flick of his avid tongue and the hard intakes with which he tried milking them. When that did not work, he went ahead and bit them, his shaft stiffening all together from grazing the taut buds so mercilessly.

Oh, sure, she jumped. He would have been disappointed had she not. Still, he did not allow her to end his torture, only satisfied once she submitted completely and arched her back as though asking for more.

He had no problem delivering, nipping a fiery trail down her flat stomach, until he came right above her pussy. There he stopped fascinated.

For one thing, hers was clean-shaven, not hairy like most other women he had seen, which made a whole lot of difference. For seconds, his lover's slippery monster was making mincemeat of it, and that frantic disappearing inside the wettest hole ever was a show he did not want to miss.

"Feel the need to explore more of her, Angel?" Raising his gaze, he met the black sardonic stare, an ironic snarl curving the full lips.

"The gods help me." He could hardly recognize his voice in the hoarse whisper bursting out on its own, "I want nothing but to taste her all over."

"No problem." The prince's rigid piece pulled out of the sticky trap. "I'll find another warm hole to stuff."

"Let me help you." Curving his lips in a wide smile, he gripped her hips and raised them for Duncan's convenience. "Someone once told me this particular lady has a magnificent ass." He spread her buttocks apart until the not-so-tight back ring was at his lover's complete disposal. "But maybe you ought to verify it yourself."

"You really make it impossible to refuse." Chortling, Prince Caldwell nudged the tip of his erection on what Chris was offering.

And it looked so scrumptious he was kind of sorry she would get it instead of him.

"Wait, lover." Well, he could still make her sweat for it. "Let me check if you're wet enough." Lowering on the enormous piece, he engulfed it whole in one gulp.

And her taste exploded in his mouth, as pungent as the smell teasing his nostrils. For the very first time ever, he savored a woman and nothing but. And it did not disgust him, did not turn him off either.

Not at all.

On the contrary, her flavor seeping to his lungs was the most erotic thing of his life while he cleaned his lover's shaft with luscious laps. Up and down, he washed away all traces of her, sucking the cock voraciously to make sure he had missed nothing.

"I think that ought to do." Evidently burning for her ass, Duncan lifted his stone-like equipment and jerked it a couple of times. "Feels wet enough to take both your asses at the same time," he joked.

"I wish." Making a show of how disappointed he was that such a thing was a physical impossibility, he straightened and clasped the stem firmly.

After guiding it between her buns, he would have slammed it inside without pity when the unexplainable urge overtook him once more. What was it about her today that he just had to shift his aim and lick her asshole instead of letting Duncan ram it to bits?

Whatever it was, it was enslaving him to the point he could not tear his tongue away from her butt, rimming it lavishly as though it were not drenched already. Then again, he was about to lose it simply digging into her as he was — mouth, nose and chin buried between her widespread legs, and cock sliding to her stomach.

"All right, enough for you." Yanking his hair, Duncan tossed his head far back and impaled his throbbing beast deep inside her behind. "This ass is mine now."

Everything was getting so much hotter that he nearly came the second Prince Caldwell's engorged size stretched her puckered opening out of any proportion. She wriggled instead, if out of pain or pleasure he had no way of knowing. Still, just hoping it was the former caused another near climax.

Which was nothing when Duncan crushed his head on the wide-open cunt.

"Taste her here," he ordered, clamping him so he could not refuse. "'Cause this is what women are all about."

And damn him if it was not the most fantastic thing of all!

So many tender folds to ravage he did not know where to begin. Without annoying hair, brushing the tip of his tongue over every single one was pure delight. Her velvety feel and thick honeydew clung to his face and fingers, extra arousing as he lingered on the puffy edges of those swollen lips that demanded immediate stuffing.

Ha! As if he would let her have her way!

She was already having too much fun as it was, practically on the verge of another explosive come if he knew anything about her reactions. So he steered clear of that greedy trap of hers and went for the interesting knot right above it.

Incredible women could be so exciting, and if anyone had told him he would have actually liked to fondle a drenched cunt, he would have scoffed incredulous at such madness. Or maybe what was getting to him was her blind surrender to his petting, which left him free to go either way, pain or pleasure if he so wished.

When he zeroed in on her swollen clit, it was his undoing.

Hers as well, for at his first serious rub, she accelerated both ass and mouth fuck, with both sets of balls almost swallowed along with the rest of the cocks. At his second stroke, she quivered, her muscles tightening in anticipation, as Duncan slammed more ruthless than ever into her rear. At his third go at that delicious morsel, she shattered.

Literally.

While she thrashed like she was prey to the sea's angry waves, the prince pulled out his cock from her ass, stuck it inside his mouth and came with powerful and very choking jets. At this point, resistance was futile.

Intoxicated by the combined tastes of cock and ass, he let it all go down her mouth with a violent outburst that blew his mind away, not just his cock.

As though ready for him, the witch drank down his every last drop, then did not release him until he was slab of marble again and ready for round four.

Which was as insufficient to satisfy his raging fever as rounds five, six, seven, eight and so on during the longest sex spree of his life.

CHAPTER SIXTY-FIVE

Impossible to determine how long he stayed in that shelter, on that bed, unable to eat, sleep or do much of anything except sex, sex and more sex.

Not just him.

Duncan and Ylianor were as much prey to this cock-wrenching spell as he was, both powerless to leave the bed in the frenzy of one more heated fuck, one more luscious screw, one more explosive come.

Strangest thing of all — he craved her with a fierceness he had only felt for one alone — his lover.

For Duncan alone, had he ever foregone the rest of life itself for so long and with such passion. Never for a woman, which made it all the more enchanting and bewitching.

Gone all prejudices, his desires ran wild, unsettling his usual self-assuredness until he doubted his lifetime convictions. As his craving for her spiraled to an all-time high, he wanted her with a fiery intensity that would have shocked him had he not been under this odd sexual magic. A true witchcraft if he was any judge of it, for the damned woman alone could quench his unbearable ache. Then again, what else could he expect from a witch?

In the endless days and nights that followed, he burned from the sheer need to have her over and over. Whenever his tongue touched hers, fire erupted, forcing him to jump on her, clawing and rolling on top of her, incapable of tearing away from her kiss. Devour her — that was his goal most of the times. Whether he stuck a tongue or a cock inside her made no difference. She had to be *his*, with a ferocity he never believed he would ever feel for a woman. It also pushed him to a totally new edge, one where his fire played on her skin, stirring such exquisite lust, the likes of which she had never known in her entire life. And on directing the darts of energy on her most sensitive spots, she would go up in smoke.

Well, almost.

For sure, it sparked her excitement, and consequently his and Duncan's, to a fever pitch.

Not that either of them needed it.

His appetite, combined with her heated response, amazed even Duncan. Only natural, since he had made her tremble in pain alone, never in pleasure, which was the new twist that ushered his sex, and theirs, into a whole different and superior level.

Safe to say, this was what kept the three of them trapped in the shelter. As his skin grew hotter with each passing day, time and space lost meaning. So he melted in Duncan and Ylianor's essences, and nothing else mattered except sex morning, mid-day and night. His body and mind linked to theirs became his only reality, with the sole interruption of food or sleep when exhaustion overtook him.

How long did it last?

He could never tell later, but it was enough to wake up one day without the hunger gnawing at his stomach to turn to Duncan and realize he was not the only one free of it.

"If we don't leave now, we never will." Up and about the shelter, Duncan was packing in such a hurry he threw everything in a jumbled heap of clothes and stuff inside the same sac.

Since he could not agree more, he rushed through the motions of cleaning up, with Ylianor at his side speeding through every task as though the ground burned under her feet. Then he bolted out the door and mounted on Black before the impulse caught up with him again.

And good riddance Nephis Valley!

Disoriented, he kicked Black's flanks to make him run away from the blasted place as fast as possible, hoping no side effects would linger. Following Duncan's lead, he set out on a new journey, wanting to forget all about this dastardly experience. Which was the reason he began sifting through all the unanswered questions about what they had uncovered before the folly had struck, the only way he could think of to keep from staring at her and wondering if maybe, deep down, he really did like her so much more than he had admitted to himself so far. And what if it had not been a spell at all?

The gods help me!

"So our new mission is to retrieve that . . ." He still did not know what to call it exactly. "Missing thing from the valley."

"A pyramid," Duncan rectified. "And it isn't missing. It's been stolen." He glanced at both him and Ylianor. "But why would anyone go to all the trouble of taking an innocuous piece from a much larger structure?"

"A structure that is responsible for pledging people," she reminded. "And the pyramid we're looking for is the heart of it all."

Good thing the three of them were on the same wavelength, all wanting to tear their minds from what had just been the most gloriously sex-filled days of their lives.

"Plus, it wasn't just anyone who took it." Her voice softened, "It was David."

"David?" Now that was news to him. "How do you know it was him?"

"I picked up his aura while you were busy flying around the pyramid," she was quick to inform.

"Well, I'll be damned!" Not to mention impressed, for he

would have never thought that little twerp would have the guts to pull off a stunt like that. "But if he's involved, he must've used some sort of Virt." This was the only sensible explanation.

"Or it could've been the woman who was with him." Her brow furrowed as though in an effort to remember. "What was her name, my prince?"

"Cecilia Hurst," Duncan supplied.

His dry tone told him that, in spite of everything that had happened between them, his lover felt no great love for Cecilia.

Then again, how to blame him?

Chris himself could not stand the woman, so he could totally relate!

"Nah!" He waved a hand aimlessly in midair. "That can't be right. What kind of Virt could Cecilia possibly have?" None, as far as he was concerned. "It's more likely that David has a Virt of his own." Because he refused to believe the other one had anything to do with it.

"Yeah, and I'm real curious to find out what it is." Given the wry note, he guessed Duncan was also sad that David had not told him about it. "'Cause like the princess observed, it's doubtful he was there only for the ride."

"So you think he did the dirty work himself, eh?" Cocking his head in her direction, he tried catching her arresting green gaze.

"Hem . . ." Thrown off balance, she swallowed hard.

No, she definitely was not used to receiving any kind of attention from him, which explained her hesitation and that adorable blush spreading on her cheeks.

"Yeah, probably." Fighting to keep control over her emotions, she flashed an enchanting smile.

"And where do you suppose they've hidden this so very important missing heart?" So he provoked her on purpose.

"And do you think they'll return it to its rightful place once we show up?"

"I suppose that all depends on the woman who was with David, Lord Templeton." Calling his bluff, she recovered all her smugness. "So the real question is—who is Cecilia Hurst?"

ABOUT THE VIRTUS SAGA

Erotic Dark Fantasy Paranormal Romance Series that Explores the Dark and Light Sides of Power and Love between Three People

The Making of a Trio: The Virtus Saga shows how power and love can be equally shared!

Now completed, Laura Tolomei's erotic dark fantasy series is continuing to receive critical acclaims, which has prompted a new completely revised edition of the first book of the saga. This was necessary to explain with more detail the concept of a world free of violence and to include many brand-new scenes that will surely attract more readers. The fiery MM and MMF sex keeps them hooked to every page. The titles say it all. Book 1 The Sex, book 2 The Game, book 3 The Festival, book 4 The Leader, book 5 The Pledge, book 6 The Heat, book 7 The Princess, Book 8 The Lord, a special Not In The Game, Deleted Scenes from The Game, and the new Book 1 Virtus Sex, The Sex: Author's Cut—they all drip passion and lust woven inside an imaginary frame ruled by magical powers, divided between good and evil and struggling to survive.

The way it all starts and progresses, nothing is as it seems. Soul-mates Prince Duncan Caldwell and Lord Christopher Templeton share a love that is unrivaled until Duncan takes shelter in Ylianor Meyer's dilapidated shack. Ylianor has always loved Duncan, and while Duncan is attracted to her, she remains a servant—okay to bed, but not acceptable consort material. Unwilling to accept it, Ylianor vows she will do anything, even come head to head with his insufferable lover, to stay at his side.

But there is more going on than either of the three realize. Lord Arthur Fairchild, Leader of the High Council, knows his planet Sendar is doomed unless the predestined Hero steps in and blocks the darkness threatening to take over. And even if one person alone fits the bill, Arthur does the unthinkable—not only does he summon the Hero, but the Hero's consorts as well. Sendar needs these three special people to become fully aware of their powers and learn how to use them together. Sendar needs these three special people to work together above and beyond their personal issues. Sendar needs these three special people to become one whilst being three to make it through the difficult times ahead. If they do not, the Virtus that hold all of Sendar's secrets could destroy them all.

The Virtus Saga Books:
Virtus Sex, The Sex: Author's Cut, Book 1
Completely revised, this edition of the original publication Virts, The Sex, is doubled in size and has many newly added scenes.
Novel—LGBT, ménage, M/M gay, dark fantasy, paranormal, romance, series—April 5 2019, eXtasy Books, http://lallagatta.com/eng/_virtus_thesex.html

The Sex, Book 1
Novel LGBT, ménage, M/M gay, dark fantasy, paranormal, romance, series—March 15 2010, eXtasy Books, http://lallagatta.com/eng/_virtus_thesex.html

The Game, Book 2
Novel—LGBT, ménage, M/M gay, multiple partners, dark fantasy, paranormal, romance, series—May 15 2010, eXtasy Books, http://lallagatta.com/eng/_virtus_

thegame.html

Not In The Game, Deleted Scenes from The Game Book 2
Novel—LGBT, ménage, M/M gay, multiple partners, dark fantasy, paranormal, series—April 6 2018, eXtasy Books, http://lallagatta.com/eng/_virtus_notgame.html

The Festival, Book 3
Novel—BDSM, LGBT, LGBT, ménage, M/M gay, dark fantasy, horror paranormal, romance, series—July 15 2010, eXtasy Books, http://lallagatta.com/eng/_virtus_thefestival.html

The Leader, Book 4
Novel—LGBT, LGBT, ménage, M/M gay, dark fantasy, paranormal, romance, series—February 1 2012, eXtasy Books, http://lallagatta.com/eng/_virtus_theleader.html

The Pledge, Book 5
Novel—LGBT, ménage, M/M gay, multi partner, dark fantasy, paranormal, romance, series—September 1 2012, eXtasy Books, http://lallagatta.com/eng/_virtus_thepledge.html

The Heat, Book 6
Novel—LGBT, ménage, M/M gay, dark fantasy, paranormal, romance, series—November 15 2012, eXtasy Books, http://lallagatta.com/eng/_virtus_theheat.html

The Princess, Book 7
Novel—BDSM, LGBT, ménage, M/M gay, dark fantasy, paranormal, romance, series—September 15 2014, eXtasy Books, http://lallagatta.com/eng/_virtus_theprincess.html

The Lord, Book 8
Novel—BDSM, LGBT, ménage, M/M gay, multiple part-

ners, dark fantasy, paranormal, romance, series—October 1 2014, eXtasy Books, http://lallagatta.com/eng/_virtus_ thelord.html

Coming soon:
Virtus Game, The Game: Author's Cut, Book 2
Completely revised, this edition of the original publication Virts, The Sex, is doubled in size and has many newly added scenes. Read the unedited version of the first chapter now.

Novel—LGBT, ménage, M/M gay, multiple partners, dark fantasy, paranormal, romance, series

For more info, check out the Virtus Saga official pages: www.lallagatta.com/eng/virtus-the-saga.html

ABOUT VIRTUS GAME

This book was previously published as Virtus, The Game but has been completely revised and doubled in size, with many newly added scenes.

When Prince Duncan Caldwell has to enter Cecilia Hurst's Game of Masters and Slaves, he already knows he'll have to play Master if he intends to retrieve the pyramid Cecilia stole from the sacred Nephis Valley. And his choice for a slave can only be Ylianor Meyer, however fiercely Lord Christopher Templeton resents her and her overpowering erotic intrusion in a trip that should've been his and Duncan's alone. No, make that in a love that should've been his and Duncan's alone! Then things precipitate into chaos and Duncan's new responsibilities will inevitably change everything forever, their personal balance included.

Such is the new setting of the Virtus Saga, where nothing is as it seems. Not the world, since its all-pervading sex drive hides a scary lack of violence. Not the people, since soul mates Prince Duncan Caldwell and Lord Christopher Templeton share a love that is unrivaled until that fateful knock on Ylianor Meyer's dilapidated shack.

This book picks up right where Virtus Sex, Book 1, leaves off and explodes the lust and the leadership that brings estrangement and chaos into this intricate three-way relationship. It's a unique connection, laced with jealousy and violence that are unknown to their world. This is not just another erotic dark fantasy series. This is the making of a trio. Of three remarkable characters that must overcome their uncontrollable lust to face the truth about themselves and their planet if they want to defeat the darkness about to devour them. To be as one whilst three! To share power and love in equal measures. This is their real challenge, the lesson they must learn. Otherwise, how will their world survive?

"Who is Cecilia Hurst?" *And why don't I give a damn about her, only about Prince Duncan Caldwell and his phase mate, Lord Christopher Templeton?*

Oh, fuck!

If she could just concentrate on piecing together the sketchy information gathered at the Nephis Valley and find the stolen heart, she would be the happiest woman alive. Instead, Ylianor Meyer's attention kept shifting on the two gorgeous men riding by her side, which made it unproductive to focus on anything besides the scorching memories of their stay in the pledge's sacred valley and their consequent hurried escape from it.

If it had been a spell, which she hoped it had not, it could not have happened with two more breathtaking creatures than the one she had loved all her life, and the one she was coming to appreciate after weeks spent traveling together.

Under her eyelashes, she stole a peak at *her prince*. Slightly older than his shiny blond phase mate, the very masculine Duncan Caldwell had raven black hair, falling to his shoulders, dancing black eyes, a chiseled face with a square jaw over a tall, powerful, well-built frame with muscles rippling at every movement. Yes, he was impossibly gorgeous and impossibly taken, given how much he loved the very striking and very smug Lord Christopher Templeton.

Who was a real demon, no question about it, had been ever since he had walked into Black Rose with a load of rage and fury so great it would have annihilated anyone. Though not him, the eight-year-old boy that looked like an angel and had the core of a demon.

Goddamn him and his regular features with that aristo-cratic nose, the short thick hair flashing brighter than Stella's rays and those intriguing blue-gray eyes she found hard to read at times. As if it were not enough, he was also tall, and his less muscular build spoke of a natural grace, elegance and sensuality that were impossible to resist. And goddamn him twice for having her fall all over him, as if she did not know he had despised her from the moment he had set eyes on her.

There was no way around it.

Not just around his arresting appearance. Mostly around his preferences, since he was even more unreachable than the man whom he loved above and beyond his own life— Duncan Caldwell.

And to think that, however different they were, both had the same erotic charge, the undeniable allure to beguile men and women alike. Which made it all the stranger they would ever end up in the Nephis Valley, the place where couples tied their knot to have children. *Hardly the place for two such attractive men and me in the middle to look for clues and end up in heated, passionate sex that still burns me all over simply remembering about it.*

Then again, she would have never been there, had David Smith, Duncan's supposedly faithful valet, not insisted that the prince take her along on his trip. He and his concern that Lady Sophia Caldwell might harm her had been her undo-ing. Or perhaps, it was all Duncan's fault for believing David and his insinuations about how evil his mother could become.

Which was no fabrication, considering how much she had already suffered from the dreadful woman ever since she was born. And that there was no end to her cruelty had be-come kind of plain when she had thrown out little nine-year-old Ylianor from Black Rose, her native home, banning her from ever returning. Just her bad luck that, despite all the impediments blocking the way, her son had found her again and brought her back to stay as Black Rose's new stable keeper.

Or so she had hoped until David had got it into his head Sophia Caldwell might put her in serious danger and packed her off to follow the two stunning men, one of which would have gladly reduced her to cinders, rather than have her intrude in his alone time with his adored prince. And the fact they had an agenda to keep had not improved matters any.

Thing was that the High Council Leader, Lord Arthur Fairchild, had summoned them to find the missing piece of the sacred valley's symbolic structure. Not just Chris and Duncan. Ylianor, too, as it turned out for the Leader of the High Council had made it very clear the three of them were to work as one. Duncan as the leader and mind of this small group, Chris as the body and she was the spirit of it all. *Hey, who would have ever imagined that?*

Now she had a long sitting in front of the mysterious tower of three-sided pyramids to prove she belonged with them. Their bond sealed by the unexpected after-effects that had kept all of them chained to a bed for days on end, prey to unforeseeable sexual cravings that refused to let her go also now that she was miles away from the wretched place.

"The real question is what was that all about?" Chris blurted.

No, the real question was why could she not suppress the torrid images that had already started a furious throbbing between her legs?

"Wasn't it clear enough, Angel?" Duncan grinned.

However mocking the tone, she could not help feeling stung by the prince's sheer love for the blond, beautiful demon, knotted in the throaty endearment.

"At least now we know why pledges take place there." The prince chuckled. "The way it influences people . . ." His grin widened as he gazed at Chris. "It would make it easy to commit to a woman, even for someone like you."

"That was just madness," the demon spat hotly. "A trick

of the damn pyramid! Something that would never happen under regular circumstances."

Yeah, sure, as if he could dismiss his odd reactions that easily, him, Christopher Templeton, who had never stooped as low as to touch a woman before in his life, except to stick his cock in her ass or mouth. Well, guess what?

He had not just sampled her all over using the most seductive stroking ever. He had also played with his fiery energy all over her body as if she were his beloved. Unreal to say the least, yet never in her life had she felt warmer and safer than inside the same flames that had tried to burn her alive just days before. One mere touch from him and her blood had raced. Her heart had thumped so loudly she was still giddy from his passionate kisses and fierce sex. Uh, how she had begged for more, yielding to his demands the way she had with her prince alone. And how she would do it again in a heartbeat, regardless of how much he hated her guts.

"Whatever the reason, I never thought I'd see my angel kiss a woman so passionately," Prince Caldwell sniggered, his black eyes sparkling in amusement.

"Not funny, lover." Chris turned red. "I was under a spell, remember?"

"Yes, I'll be sure to mention that when I spoil your immaculate reputation at the Hall." Duncan laughed out loud.

The Hall being the seat of the High Council, the highest ruling body of their lands, it was also where Chris had chosen to live after Duncan had ended their phase. Or to hide, depending on the point of view.

"You wouldn't dare!" Chris hissed, his blue-gray eyes sending blazing darts in Duncan's direction. "I'll deny everything."

"If you can." Tightening his knees around Fuzeon, his black horse, the prince flanked Chris. "I'm not sure about what we did with that pyramid, but pledges are notorious at reproducing their own living side effects."

Meaning that no pledge, no children, for no amount of sex between men and women ever produced any life.

"It couldn't . . ." This time, Chris paled all together, his face draining of all blood as the implication of what his phase mate said sank in with a loud thud. "We didn't . . ." With an enquiring gaze, he spun to her, quickly imitated by Duncan.

"Hem . . ." Now it was her turn to redden under their scrutiny." If the structure's main purpose is to help couples have babies, it's unlikely it works since it's missing the heart." Then catching their looks of relief, she was quick to add in a naughty tone, "Or so I think."

"That's what we hope, Princess." Duncan's tone confirmed he also was not looking for heirs, not at the moment anyway. "But if things should work out the more traditional way, you'll have to do the honorable thing, Angel, since I can't possibly pledge to her."

"What?" Chris's face turned even paler. "That's ridiculous!" Licking his lips nervously, he narrowed an icy cold stare on her. "Are you pregnant?"

Now funny he should ask.

Among other things, Christopher Templeton was a healer, and that was just for starters. Like the rest of them, he had powers, or Virts as Arthur Fairchild had told them the ancients called it. And like her, Chris had discovered the ability to wield nature's forces to his bidding from the earliest years possible. As far back as childhood, for he and Ylianor alone had been aware of what most adults knew nothing about or would learn only later in life.

That was why she was an aura tracer. Seeing people's ethereal bodies in their million combinations of colored lights that shifted according to their moods was one of her specialties. And best of all, she had managed to awaken Prince Caldwell's sleeping potential. Something not even his phase mate had been able to do, however overpowering he was.

So, eat your heart out, Lord Templeton!

Now Duncan's incredibly strong Virt coursed through his every fiber, more formidable than anything her world had seen, as confirmed by Arthur's own words, a seemingly boundless pool of cool, deep and potent energy that had apparently laid dormant for the better part of his twenty-one years.

Then there was nineteen-year-old Chris. So very powerful, he was fire through and through, a pyre so strong it could disintegrate just as easily as heal, erasing the memory of it if necessary. Not that he was always so merciful. Not so cruel, either, as when he had decided to show his rare talents in front of the prince, no less.

While carving her to bits in the process.

Appalling, if not downright monstrous! Her people did not kill animals, not even to eat them. You could just imagine how utterly shocking the sight of someone slashing live flesh could be. And getting a kick out of it, too!

No, had it come from any other person, she would not have thought it possible for the way of her people had never included any form of adult violence as far back as time itself, at least until Christopher Templeton had the bad idea to show his face around. Being the black hearted demon he was, she had not allowed the utter shock of it all get to her.

No, she had fought back, refusing to give in to his sadistic knife play, when not going as far as feeling a twisted sense of pleasure at some very particular incisions of his.

"It's too early to tell." An amused snarl curved Duncan's lips.

"Not necessarily." She shifted position on Starlet's saddle. "Whoever is the father . . ." And she deliberately spun her gaze from one to the other to make sure they understood she included both. "Any offspring of yours would have so much Virt it couldn't possibly hide its presence, even at an early stage."

"Great." Chris took a deep breath of relief. "This means

there's no foreseeable danger of —"

"But the first stages are always tricky," she cut him off, pressing a palm over her flat belly. "And I've been feeling kind of queasy since we left the valley."

"Hey, they might be the warning signs." A dazzling smile split the prince's handsome face.

And her heart stopped dead.

Literally.

Yes, she knew it. She was a fool simply to hold on to her love for him, given how his lights went crazy whenever around the horrible demon. For there was no way he could hide his deep feelings for his angel, not to her, not to her aura reading Virt. But to be fair, she had been there first. At a time when Duncan had not even known Chris existed, she had fallen in love with him beyond any hope of recovery. Just three years younger and barely old enough to stand, she had allowed her dark handsome hero to chase her on Black Rose's many hills, relishing the feel of being with him in the place that was his home, too. And he had always been there for her until something had gone terribly wrong and caused a ten-year separation.

All the demon's fault for sure, what with the prince unexplainable forgetting all about her during the ten-year-estrangement. Too bad for him, his plan to become Prince Caldwell's sole claimant had backfired in the most delicious way, and she had returned to be at Duncan's side, stronger than ever.

More in love than ever, too, particularly now that sex had complicated everything, to the point she had not bothered hiding it from him. What would have been the point anyway?

Prince Caldwell would have sensed it eventually. Better to come clean about it, even if she had no guarantees things would change any time soon. He had told her as much at the Hall, admitting straight up he could not return her feelings. Still, he had not cut her out entirely, asking for more time instead. So, if time was the only obstacle in the way to her prince's heart, she would give him as much as he needed. And Lord Christopher Templeton be damned.

"Who knows?" Duncan's gaze dropped to her belly. "We might have to—"

"Will you two cut it out?" Irritated, Chris pursed his lips. "Don't you think I suffered enough as it is in that damn valley with its fucking side effects?"

What do you say, Princess? The amused glance he exchanged with her was nothing if compared to his deep voice booming in her head. *Shall we let him off the hook?*

That Duncan Caldwell owned his father's gift to share thoughts and emotions had been the most exciting twist of all. For too long she had missed Prince Charles talking in her head, something that had started as far back as her memory would go. Words and feelings alike, she had drowned in his sensations and been as close to him as no daughter could ever be to a father.

Which he was not, since he had never pledged to her mother, Mary Jane Elspeth. So, she shared no single drop of blood with the Caldwells, however similar her appearance was to Duncan's. She looked so much like him she could have easily passed for a twin, which infuriated Chris every time his blue-gray gaze chanced to glance her way. Still, it made no difference as far as family ties went.

Charles's only children were Duncan and his sister Elizabeth, no matter how hard little Ylianor had tried convincing him of the contrary during the nine wonderful years she had spent with him. Only natural she would mistake Virt for a non-existent family connection and call Prince Charles, Father, while Duncan had nearly lost it when learning about it. About the will, too, and his father's intention to adopt her into the Caldwell fold, giving her a name and a position that was an outright acknowledgment of all she had meant to him. Now, she could not wait to know if he would honor it in spite of all the obstacles standing in the way, like his own reservations and mostly his mother's fierce objections.

But if it never came about, she would not complain. Not since she had managed to re-establish a link that Prince Charles's death had severed in the most atrocious way. She still reeled from the agonizing silence and the unbearable emptiness suffocating her when he had closed his eyes forever, unable to stand either.

Then his son had knocked at her shack, and she had known she could have it all back again.

You decide, my love. All sweet and yielding, she pretended to go along with him. Were it up to her, Christopher Templeton would be dangling from that hook for the rest of the day and possibly the night, too.

"Oh, come on." Not for Duncan, though. "We were just talking—"

"No, you were being a pain in the ass." Chris glared at her, as if he had picked up her intention.

So, all right, nothing in their long ride over had changed the demon to the point he had become the angel Duncan claimed he was. The gods forbid! Christopher Templeton's nature continued to swing from one extreme to another. But then, what else could you expect from someone made of fire?

Unpredictable and uncontrollable, such was his essence, and no amount of incredibly sweet sex or heart-to-heart talk could alter it in the least.

Yet against her better judgment, she was coming around to the idea of liking him more than she had claimed so far. It was probably the reason for her slip in front of the multi-pyramids structure, which had not failed to catch the prince's attention. Not that it surprised him any. So, all right, maybe he had guessed her change of heart before she did herself, and now she wished she could ask for his support or for some sensible advice.

Ha! If only she was not falling for him harder than she had originally assessed. So hard, she could never quell her heart from jumping to her throat every time his arresting black eyes traveled in blatant appraisal all over her body. For nothing had prepared her for the tempest of the senses he unleashed so effortlessly.

So, she was back to square one, unable to think things through because both men blinded her to the point all she wanted was to be their special toy and nothing else.

"When we should turn our attention to serious matters," Chris reminded.

"As you wish, but I'll never forget how you and the princess looked on that bed." Prince Caldwell cocked his head. "Kissing and fucking like you had no tomorrow—"

"Cut it out, lover." His tense tone revealed just how upset the demon was at the memory. "I can't forget it either, if that's any consolation."

"Hey, there's no need to get uptight about it." Duncan seemed bent to make Chris relive the experience, whether he wanted to or not. "You were damn arousing." The images running through his head made her flush. "Not just 'cause you did it with a woman for a change. 'Cause you even went as far as using your fire without hurting her." His black gaze brimmed with glee, as it fixed on Chris with a love so powerful she felt embarrassed merely to see it. "I'm very proud of you, Angel." Then he changed register, "If I were you, I'd never forget this experience 'cause pledges need happy memories."

"My dear prince, let me remind you that you're in dire need of an heir worse than I'll ever be." Shoulders thrown back, Chris flashed blue gray eyes in challenge. "If worse comes to worst, perhaps you'd be the one to profit more from all this."

"Yeah, right." The velvety black eyes twinkled maliciously. "I can just imagine my mother's reactions if she thought the princess carried my child," he retorted sarcastically. "She'd be so thrilled she'd probably get a heart attack."

"Only after she killed Ylianor." Chris burst out laughing,

obviously imagining Sophia Caldwell's hate for what she considered an unwanted meddler in her family's affairs. "And maybe you, too."

She worked hard at keeping a straight face. If they could joke about something that had caused her insufferable pain for the past eighteen years of her life, it was only thanks to Duncan and his resolve to break down the barriers that stood in the way of their true unity. And she for sure had some pretty heavy load of her own to get rid of, all beginning and ending with Duncan's own mother, at least until her sharing it with the demon and the prince had not lightened it somehow.

"Would you two get over yourselves?" Ylianor snapped in mock exasperation. "What makes you so sure I'd pledge to either of you?"

"Why wouldn't you?" Offended, Chris's head swung to the prince. "Can you believe it? She wouldn't even want us."

"Aren't we good enough for you, Princess?" Half teasing, half-serious, Duncan searched her face.

"I might have other plans for my life." She giggled mischievously. "Which may include someone else entirely like David," she taunted until the prince's scowl made her quickly change subject. "But this is beside the point." She had almost forgotten Duncan telling her how jealous he had felt of the man. "We should concentrate on finding who stole the pyramid from the tower in the Nephis Valley, and Cecilia Hurst seems the most likely candidate." David, too, for she had picked up his aura together with Cecilia's during the long night in front of the multi-pyramids tower. Only, and out of respect to Duncan, she preferred to concentrate on the former.

The man was no ordinary one, after all. Not just Prince Caldwell's personal valet since forever, he was also a close and trusted friend of Duncan's, something she hoped would not change given this recent discovery.

"So, who is Cecilia Hurst?" Her gaze swung from Chris to

Duncan.

"She was one of the prince's flames." The blue-gray eyes blazed, probably under the influence of a memory.

"That's hardly significant," she scoffed. "From what I can tell, there's a long list of them." Which had all been part of Duncan Caldwell's search for a suitable pledge mate after he had ended his phase with Chris.

An unsuccessful attempt, she was glad to report.

"The girl is bright, not to mention highly perceptive." Ignoring her, Chris's focus trained on Duncan alone. "Too bad she doesn't want to pledge, or I might just have proposed."

"It happened some time ago, Princess," he was quick to block Chris's sarcasm. "Right after I broke off with the angel."

"A wise choice you should've stuck to." Oh, boy! Was she glad for the chance to get back at the demon. "But you can still reconsider it."

"No way can he live without me, dearie." Spitting fire from every pore, Chris raised himself on the saddle. "I'd have gotten him back no matter what."

"I wouldn't be so sure," she bit back. "Had Arthur himself not interfered to get the two of you just to meet again, you'd be history by now." And the fact that the Leader of the High Council loved the demon in such a desperate way made his gesture all the nobler.

Chris growled, "Why you presumptuous witch—"

"Cecilia has nothing to do with what happened between the angel and me." Duncan's tone was firm as though to dispel any doubts.

One thing she was noticing about him was that he was getting a kick out of her quarrels with Chris, which she was not sure was such a good thing.

"She was one of my first experiences with women and an odd one at that." The prince paused as if to recapture some of the old memories. "Sex obsesses her." Given her people's propensity to do it as much and as often as they could, she was not sure how Duncan meant this. "I've never seen any-one do it with so much effort yet get so little out of it." He frowned in puzzlement. "It's like her mind works overtime to undermine what her body should know by instinct."

"Hey, since you're such an expert, tell us what sex is," Chris provoked in mock dare.

"Well, my dear angel, sex is your beautiful body lan-guage." The prince's attention was all on his blond lover. "The way you react to my every touch is what tells me how much you want me to claim you, possess you in all ways possible." His voice lowered, "Then you swing your ass, and I can't take it anymore. I just gotta have you, gotta melt in that irresistible fire of yours until nothing matters except my cock stuck up your ass or down your throat, until we both shatter in pleasure."

There was a comprehensible momentary suspension as she felt the vibrations travel from one to the other.

"All right, you convinced me." Eyes glowing with lust, Chris seemed ready to jump off his horse. "Let's stop and do it here."

"I was merely answering your question." Duncan smiled regretfully. "It's a shame Cecilia can't even come close to understanding any of this. Her mind always prevents her body from joining in the fun, 'cause she uses a cold and ra-tional approach to what's hot and fiery by default."

"Cecilia is just a bitch out to make any man pay for her lack of sexual satisfaction," Chris snickered. "At the Hall, she always goes around with that stern expression of hers, like she wants to chastise everyone for taking pleasure in sex. Which is something so beyond her that she's got no hope of ever getting it." Kind of obvious the demon knew her well enough and couldn't stand her.

"I bet she doesn't approve of the Arthur boys either," Duncan offered.

Now who were the Arthur boys, she had no idea.

If she had to take a wild guess, it would have to involve

Chris and Lord Fairchild's need to find a way to control what no one could except for the dark-haired prince. And knowing Chris, this way would have had to do with sex.

"That's an understatement," Chris snarled. "As a high and mighty council member, she abhors our innocent orgies and harmless parties, to the point she'd erase them from the Hall's life if she could." He gripped his reins harder. "And if it wasn't enough, she's a permanent member, too, which means I'll have to put up with her forever."

Right. Had Cecilia only been a temporary member, she would have had to leave the Hall after three years. How long they stayed in office, such was the difference between the twelve permanent members and their twelve temporary counterparts.

"And I bet she already can't stand you." Ironic yet to the point, she had no doubt Duncan was right.

"Hates my guts is more like it." Never one to let the chance to demean people he did not like, Chris was only too happy to tear the poor woman apart. "She's a jealous bitch who hasn't taken it kindly that I rose higher than she ever will in the Hall's hierarchy."

Had she mentioned how vain Christopher Templeton was?

"'Cause I got the looks she never will." The demon licked his lips like a satisfied feline. "And a position she can just reach in her dreams."

"At least she's an official council member." Just for the heck of it, she loved to ruffle his feathers the wrong way. "While your title is what exactly? Besides being the leader's sex toy, I mean."

"That's a whole lot more than Cecilia will ever be." Scornful, Chris threw back his shoulders as though getting ready for a fight. "And being the leader's lover and the son of the vice-leader is really all you need to get to the top of that place."

Yes, definitely Christopher Templeton had such a high

sense of self nothing could bring it down.

"All in all, she's one of the worst women at the Hall." Smirking, he glanced at Duncan. "I'm not surprised that, in the end, you dropped her for her phase mate."

"Her phase mate?" *Uh, do tell, Prince.*

Not that she shared this thought. Just tried to keep her extreme curiosity in check knowing how little he cared for her unwanted invasion of privacy.

Yes, 'cause the sad thing was that Prince Duncan Caldwell had not accepted his Virt of head talking all that readily. To put it mildly, he still had a world of reservations about it, most stemming from her and her constant presence in his mind.

"Rowena Sentry." At the name, Duncan flooded her with the woman's face.

Quite different from Cecilia's hard cut features, Rowena had a lovely warm smile, dazzling blue eyes, blond hair falling softly around her perfect oval face with a straight nose and tempting lips.

"She's beautiful." She took a deep breath.

"At least she's feminine." Chris grinned. "While the other one . . ." Meaning Cecilia. "Looks like an ugly man."

"They were phase mates until Rowena decided she wanted men in her bed." Duncan intercepted her gaze. "And Cecilia never got over the break-up."

Nothing strange there. Phases often ended abruptly. It was an adolescent thing after all, her people's special way to discover and explore sex with a friend of the same age and gender. Just her bad luck not everybody had one. And not having had it herself, simply watching Chris and Duncan's easygoing relationship had made her realize how much she had missed out in her life.

"What you have to understand is that Cecilia was an orphan." The prince sat up straighter to tighten his hold on Fuzeon. "She lost both her parents when she was very little. An aunt took care of her, but then she died when Cecilia was only ten. It's hardly surprising she fell in love with Rowena and believed her phase would last forever."

"Didn't Lord Templeton have the same insane notion?" Oh, she was asking for it.

She knew it!

Only could not resist provoking the detestable demon to his face.

"We lasted, dearie." Of course, Chris would strike back. "They didn't."

"That's because Rowena was very interested in men." Prince Caldwell lifted a shoulder. "She thinks they're more fun in and out of bed, at least until she got the urge to pledge."

"Don't tell me she had the nerve to ask you!" That this was new information for Chris was evident from his shocked expression.

"She did." Duncan made it sound like he was sorry he had not accepted her offer.

Just to make fun of his blond lover.

"I refuse to believe you regret it!" Which got Chris flying off his horses.

"She wasn't a bad lay," the prince kept taunting. "I could've lived with her, had I been ready to commit to a woman."

For her, it was not a question of being ready, rather of being too choosy. Duncan Caldwell had such an impossible aristocratic taste people seldom met his extremely high standards. Which was why he had few friends, no mate and no stable keeper, as Anne Peacock, Black Rose's cook, had so aptly put it.

"What's happened to her now?" She pushed some loose strands off her face.

"She's happily pledged to an older man who stays at home and looks after their son while she goes around, screwing any available male." The demon beamed. "In other words, she's got the perfect pledge."

Small wonder Chris should know. His love for gossip had become clear from her first day on the road with him. And something told her he had used it abundantly in his rise to the top of the Hall, taking advantage of all his influence and information to become the number one.

"Theirs works perfectly." The prince nodded in agreement. "Also 'cause Oliver prefers to dedicate his time to farming. He has such a gift for it and uses such innovative techniques no one else dares put into practice, to the point that he has managed to turn parts of Cecilia's desert lands into green and fertile areas."

"The man is nothing short of a genius." There was a note of healthy respect in Chris's tone she had never heard before, if not connected to the prince. "My brother, Steve, says so, and he should know 'cause he was Oliver's phase mate."

"I've no doubt he is." There was no hiding Duncan's admiration, either. "Anyone who could make plants sprout from a wasteland is."

"But Rowena cares nothing for this," Chris pointed out. "Even if he's a good man, he's too boring for her taste. That's why she's always after every pair of pants passing her way."

"Completely unlike her phase mate, who cares little for men and has way too many responsibilities as it is." Amused, the black eyes sparked. "Besides her council duties, Cecilia is also the heir of the Blandry District, a desert land west of the Nephis Valley."

"Yeah, and unfortunately a neighbor of ours." Chris hung his head in mock despair. "Our district, Dartmouth, is just south of the Nephis Valley and borders with Blandry."

"Please, don't tell me we have to cross another desert." After how stressful travel through the Wadirum Desert had been, the last thing she wanted was another go at those steeply rising temperatures and Stella's rays blazing all day on her head.

"I'm afraid so." Duncan shrugged apologetically. "And it's right there." He indicated the vast emptiness just a few miles away. "She probably keeps the missing pyramid at Blue Oasis, her home, which is where we're going right now."

"I see." Now she understood why Duncan had seemed to follow a definite direction, despite his rush to leave that enchanted shelter in the Nephis Valley. "But how do you suppose we look for it without arousing suspicions?"

"That's easy." Prince Caldwell seemed certain of it. "By entering her Game, which starts in just a few days."

"You received her invitation?" Chris sounded surprised.

"I most certainly did." A flash and the image of a red carton slip with an emblem engraved on it filled her mind. "In fact, I think she invited me to all the editions, all four of them."

"Then she must really like you." Chris seemed impressed. "I know for a fact she has never asked the same person twice and only after a very rigid selection."

"Then I guess she must think I'd be particularly good at playing her Game." Duncan chuckled.

"Her Game?" Now why did she have the sneaky suspicion she would not like this new twist? "What game?"

"Well . . ." Duncan exchanged a knowing glance with Chris.

"Oh no, lover, I'm not going to help you." The demon held up a hand as though to block the prince's unspoken request. "It's your idea, so you tell her."

"All right, then." Prince Caldwell cleared his throat. "As I said, Cecilia is obsessed with sex. After I met her, she devised a game for it, with strict rules about how to play. Like the one about participants having to be at least two but no more than three together, 'cause there are only three roles available — master, guest or slave."

"Slave?" She knew she would not like where this was going.

Even more, she knew she should have stayed at Black Rose instead of following them around like a lovesick puppy.

"Yes." Duncan spurred Fuzeon to get closer to Starlet, her beautiful gray mare and a gift from Prince Caldwell himself. "On entering the Game, you have to choose who plays what. Then you've got to follow every rule for that particular role." His piercing black eyes bore into hers as though wanting her to have no misunderstandings about what would happen. "Take the slaves, for instance. They have no rights, to the point they're forbidden to do anything, including speak or eat, without express permission. Their only purpose is to serve, and they can't refuse to have sex. Or to obey their masters' every order however outrageous it might be. They can starve to death, 'cause they're not allowed to ask for food or drinks. Only their masters can provide these things, and sometimes masters aren't so merciful."

"So, masters have total control over their slaves' bodies and minds, right?" This was not too difficult to get.

"Right." He rewarded her with a luminous smile splitting his handsome face. "They dominate their slaves completely and will accept nothing but total surrender."

And that's where you got your idea of turning me into your slave. Dots connected fast. *Isn't it?*

It was practically what she had been doing with Duncan ever since leaving Black Rose, enslaved to him body and mind at least as far as the bed went. Only difference, she had no one to blame except herself for having surrendered everything to him. True, he had asked her to do it. And she had to spoil it all by accepting.

Partly, he confirmed. *Though Cecilia is still a dilettante at this.*

"And what's the guest supposed to do?" Whatever it was, she suspected it would fit Chris's needs perfectly.

"Guests are a step up from slaves, so a master cannot order them around." *And yes, my angel would have no problems playing guest.* "They're free to do pretty much what they want, but only if their masters' consent to it."

"Sounds a lot like our present arrangement." Which was a relief in a way. At least it would prove no hardship to enter this game of Cecilia's. "There's no need to guess what role I'll be playing."

"Actually, Princess, there's also an age limit for each role." It was kind of obvious Duncan was ill at ease.

Not because she would play slave.

Because she seemed to have no choice in the matter, yet choice was all her dark handsome prince believed in strenuously.

"Masters must be twenty-one or older, guests nineteen and slaves at least eighteen." Duncan took a deep breath. "I've played guest once, but for obvious reasons, I've never played with the angel—"

"'Cause I could never play slave." The demon threw back his head defiantly.

"While I have a natural talent for it, right, Lord Templeton?" Ylianor challenged.

All right, whom was she kidding?

Truth was she loved being Prince Duncan Caldwell's slave. Not just because she got to service him, because she got the other one in the bargain. And there could be no greater pleasure than being at their complete mercy. If the prince seduced her every time he got his hands on her, the demon laced his sex with that extra veneer of cruelty she was coming to appreciate every day more. No, crave was the right word, particularly after he had revealed the extent of his fiendishness. As though that knife of his had awakened something buried inside her, to the point she sometimes fantasized they could repeat it . . . just to see how far this intriguing game might get.

So, yes, she was a slave through and through and would have gladly dropped to the ground to obey their every whim, had they only ordered it right there and then.

"You said it, dearie, not I." From his noncommittal tone, there could be no doubt he thought her nothing better than a slave.

And that sent a thrilling shiver down her spine.

Because no matter what he said, she would get him in the end. And nothing would work better or faster than playing it like she had no will of her own.

"No one is born slave," Duncan was quick to rectify. "It's simply a question of balances. And like you said, Princess, this seems to fit our present arrangement, at least when we're in bed." No surprise he would underline this particular detail.

Things had slid so far down when he had been angry with her and had treated her like she was a slave *for real*, which was the farthest thing from the man he was and the principles he had upheld ever since his childhood.

"Our age doesn't help us, either, 'cause it determines our roles." Again, he seemed sad she would get the short end of the stick. "Neither you nor the angel could play master, nor can you be a guest, so . . ." He hesitated. "But we'll do it only if you agree to it." This definitely improved his mood. "I don't want to force you into anything, Princess." The caring gaze he sent her way melted her heart. "Like we agreed at the Hall, you are no slave. You are an equal partner of this arrangement of ours, so I'll understand if you'd rather not play this game."

Oh, could she love him more than she already did?

"Should such be the case, all we've got to worry about is finding another way into Blue Oasis." He flooded her with a most enchanting smile, as though to reassure he did not consider this as a setback at all.

"Sure, losing a whole lot of time in the process." The blue-gray eyes blazed in annoyance.

"Oh, I'm sure we can be inventive enough." The long, black hair fluttered as Duncan spun to confront Chris. "Even if this game is the best opportunity for us." Then his gaze locked on her. *Not to mention the most exciting.*

She swallowed hard, her face growing hot with the images he was sending her.

"What's important in this Game is the interplay between a master and his slave." His voice became husky, "'Cause it tests their limits and determines how far they can both go. The master in submitting his slave, the slave in obeying her master's every order." The picture he painted was so arousing her clit throbbed furiously, "Most people don't understand this. They think that any slave would do, so they bring someone who's inconsequential. They are such fools." He snorted contemptuously. "They don't realize that, without a connection between the two, the Game becomes a sterile repetition of heated fucks." Glancing fondly at the demon, he beamed. *And I know you understand why the angel could never be a suitable candidate for playing slave.*

Yeah, she totally got that. The difference in how Duncan related to her as opposed to how he related to the demon was the key that would spin this particular game out of its rigid structure.

Yeah, you get it. Duncan's broad smile splitting his beautiful face was her unique reward for being on his same wavelength. "The fact slaves can't talk will be an extra turn-on for us." *'Cause we don't need limited words, right, Princess?*

"That would be cheating!" The demon flared.

Sometimes Chris was too perceptive for her taste. Like right at the moment, when he seemed to have heard his lover's silent musing.

"Since when have you followed rules, Angel?" Duncan raised the stakes. "And just for the record, don't think I'll make it easy for her only 'cause I know what she likes —"

"You'd choose the exact opposite." She could practically count on it. "Wouldn't you?"

"Sure, just to spite you," Duncan joked.

"As if I didn't know it already," she scoffed. "That you'll use our connection to . . ." *Get a real kick out of what they'll do to me.*

Exactly. His full lips curved in a most attractive grin. *The angel was right. You are a bright girl after all.*

How devious. She stuck her tongue out at him.

How delicious! "But, we'll do it only if you agree to it." His voice now serious, it was obvious her assent was very important to him.

What you're proposing is a game within the Game. She still could not believe he was cutting the demon out of this, wanting her to be his playmate in a way Chris could never be. *Right?*

Right again, Princess. The liquid black eyes shone with barely suppressed arousal. *And it'll be loads of fun. You'll see.*

And damn him!

She could not wait for that to happen, though she acted like she had not heard. "Has Cecilia set up a special place in Blue Oasis to play this Game of hers?"

"Yes." The prince nodded. "She has devoted an entire hall to it."

Unbidden, the images came to her of a large rectangular chamber. Lit by torches hanging on the walls, it was full of alcoves with comfortable leather couches around low black tables. Everywhere she looked, people had sex with just about anything that moved. Smoke, sweat and sex oozed from the stonewalls, hazing the naked people sitting on the tables and the more dressed ones hovering over them.

"What an odd setting." She sifted through Duncan's pictures. "The dress code is strange as well."

"Masters wear robes." The projection he sent her was of a man dressed in a dark blue tunic that fell to his ankles. "Guests have bare chests and wear either pants or skirts. Slaves are naked."

So only natural she wondered how she would look on one such low table.

"Oh, you'd make a most erotic addition to that chamber." Duncan smacked his lips in evident anticipation.

"If I decide to participate." No, she would not give him the satisfaction of an easy surrender, no matter how fiercely her body stung. Why should she?

He had taken too much for granted already, using also her foolish love against her. If she were to accept anything, it would have to be on her own time!

No point in sharing this, she straightened her shoulders. "I'll think about it while we get there." Then fixing her gaze on the long road ahead, she pretended nothing else mattered.

ABOUT THE AUTHOR

Laura Tolomei lives in Rome, Italy, and is the author of 28+ books in her very particular and unique genre—Erotic Romance with an Edge. Novels that are on the edge of accepted conventions, such is her trademark, and she guarantees an erotic earthquake with each book! Among others, they include the critically acclaimed scorching dark fantasy Virtus Saga, all ten books of it, along with the kindred spirits of both the ReScue and the Soulmate Series, not to mention her horror novels as well as a few historical ones.

On a more personal note, she has been traveling the globe since age five and has no intention of quitting. Then, having been an avid reader her entire life, she decided at age forty to write her own stories and has not looked back since.

For more info, check out Laura's website:
www.lallagatta.com
www.lauratolomei.com

www.ingramcontent.com/pod-product-compliance
Lightning Source LLC
Chambersburg PA
CBHW071628260626

47170CB00001B/11